A Corner of White

THE COLORS OF MADELEINE

BOOK ONE

JACLYN MORIARTY

ARTHUR A. LEVINE BOOKS
An Imprint of Scholastic Inc.

TO CHARLIE WITH LOVE

Text copyright © 2013 by Jaclyn Moriarty

Library of Congress Cataloging-in-Publication Data

Moriarty, Jaclyn.
A corner of white / Jaclyn Moriarty. — 1st ed.
p. cm. — (The colors of Madeleine ; bk. 1)
Summary: Fourteen-year-old Madeleine of Cambridge, England, struggling to cope with
poverty and her mother's illness, and fifteen-year-old Elliot of the Kingdom of Cello in a
parallel world where colors are villainous and his father is missing, begin exchanging notes
through a crack between their worlds and find they can be of great help to each other.
ISBN 978-0-545-39736-0 (hardcover : alk. paper) [1. Interpersonal relations — Fiction.
2. Magic — Fiction. 3. Missing persons — Fiction. 4. Color — Fiction. 5. Princesses —
Fiction. 6. Cambridge (England) — Fiction. 7. England — Fiction.] I. Title.
PZ7.M826727Cor 2013
[Fic] — dc23
2012016582

10 9 8 7 6 5 4 3 2 1   13 14 15 16 17

Printed in the U.S.A.   23

First edition, April 2013

Book design by Elizabeth B. Parisi

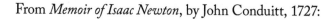

From *Memoir of Isaac Newton*, by John Conduitt, 1727:

[Isaac Newton] received the famous problem which was intended to puzzle all the Mathematicians in Europe at four o'clock in the afternoon when he was very much tired with the business of the Mint where he had been employed all day, and yet he solved it before he went to bed that night.

From *The Kingdom of Cello: An Illustrated Travel Guide*, by T. I. Candle, 7th edition, © 2012, reprinted with kind permission, Brellidge University Press, T. I. Candle.

Introduction

The Kingdom of Cello (pronounced "Chello") needs no introduction.

When to Visit

Look, in all honesty, visit Cello when you have the time. It's a popular tourist destination all year round, so there's no "peak" or "shoulder" or "off" season. (No seasons at all, as a matter of fact, at least not in the traditional sense.)

I suppose there are various festivals you might like to see, but I can't think why. These invariably take place in the villages and towns of the Farms, and if there's one province in Cello that you'll want to skip, it's the Farms.

The Farms

Hold on a moment, what can I be thinking? The Farms! Why, you'll love them! The golden wheat fields, the cherry orchards, the laconic grins and ambling gaits of the Farmers! As the provincial motto promises: "Sure as hokey-pokey, the Farms'll charm the heart right out of your belly."

Not too great with anatomy in the Farms, but those Farmers are the most endearing bunch of muffin-baking, pastry-making, fiddle-playing folk you'll ever meet.

(Blahdy, blahdy, hooray for Farmers! Blah, blah, pumpkin pie! etc.)
(Seriously, though, if you're short on time, give the Farms a miss.)

Why Visit Cello?

The question is wrong. Correct question: Why would you *not* visit Cello? Keeping in mind that you can always skip the Farms, *why on earth would you not visit Cello?*

A Corner of White

PART 1

Cambridge, England, The World

$\mathcal{M}$ adeleine Tully turned fourteen yesterday, but today she did not turn anything.

Oh, wait. She turned a page.

She was sitting on the sloping roof of her attic flat and she was reading a book. Only, she was not concentrating on the book. She was listening to her mother, who was just inside.

Madeleine's mother was sewing and watching the quiz show. And she was answering every single question. Snap, snap, snap! She was shooting out the answers like a popcorn machine. She was answering before the host even finished asking.

"What is the capital of Ecuador?"

"Maputo!"

"From the French, what six-letter word —"

"Frisson!"

Each time Madeleine's mother answered, a contestant on the television also answered, but a moment later. The contestants' voices sounded calm and quiet.

An ad break came on. The sewing machine stopped. Madeleine's mother climbed out through the window and sat on the roof beside Madeleine. The spires of Cambridge University traced themselves against the sky behind them.

"Tonight," said Madeleine's mother, "we'll have supper out here on the roof."

Madeleine closed her book.

"We'll be cold," her mother continued. "I'll bring blankets."

Madeleine nodded.

"We'll eat your leftover birthday cake. It doesn't always have to be beans for supper, you know."

"No," Madeleine agreed.

"And we'll stay out here and watch the stars until we fall asleep amongst the blankets."

Madeleine and her mother sat side by side, and sighed.

They were thinking the same thing.

They would not eat supper on the roof tonight.

Madeleine's mother would keep sewing until midnight and would only stop to flex her aching fingers.

They sighed again.

They were remembering the same thing.

Supper tonight would be beans. They had eaten the whole birthday cake yesterday.

If only they had saved some.

"Right, then," said Madeleine's mother. She climbed back through the window. The sewing machine started up.

The sewing machine was a Harlsbury Deluxe Model 37B. Madeleine's mother had won it in London many years before.

She had won it on the quiz show.

One day, soon, she planned to compete on that show again.

Only this time she would not just win the sewing machine. This time she would also win the plasma TV, the luxury towel set, the holiday, the barbecue, *and the car!!!* (That was how the quiz-show host — and Madeleine's mother — referred to the car: italics and three exclamation marks.)

So, each morning, Madeleine's mother phoned the TV station to "register her interest" in competing on the show.

Once a fortnight, she mailed in an application to compete.

Every month or so, she took a bus to London, walked to the TV station's offices, and had a friendly chat with the receptionist. (You never knew who might be influential.)

And every night, she watched the show and answered every question.

Bang, bang, bang! She shouted out the answers like a fireworks display.

And every night, she got every single question wrong.

(The capital of Ecuador is Quito. *Frisson* doesn't even have six letters.)

PART 2

Bonfire, The Farms,
Kingdom of Cello

*T*en feet of snow had fallen overnight.

It was enough to bury the Dudleys' cows.

It was enough to crack the branches of the silver maple tree that had stood for more than a thousand years in the grounds of the Bonfire Grade School.

It toppled the pyramid of pumpkins. And the Bonfire Pumpkin Committee had been building that for over a month.

Now in the bright mid-morning, the Town Square was overrun with pumpkins. Townsfolk were kicking pumpkins around like soccer balls. Or lining them up around the fountain's edge, to take potshots at them with air rifles.

(Or quietly gathering them into their coats to take home to their kitchens for soup.)

Elliot Baranski was sitting at a table outside the Bakery Café.

A pumpkin thudded up against his boot. Without looking down, he shifted his foot, and the pumpkin rolled slowly away.

Elliot was holding up a library book. His mother, Petra, sat opposite him. She leaned in to read the book's title:

Spell Fishing: Tips and Techniques for Netting the Spell You Desire.

"Can't be done," said Petra, and sipped her coffee.

"If I leave today I can be at the Lake of Spells by Thursday," Elliot said. "I'll catch a Locator Spell."

"Can't be done," Petra repeated. "You can't choose what Spell you get at the Lake. Can't even guarantee you'll *catch* a Spell. You know that."

"This book says I can. It's got science and statistics and — see . . ." Elliot flicked through. He pointed. "Footnotes. It's got footnotes."

"Uh-huh," said his mother, but she gazed at him.

There was a fading bruise on Elliot's left cheek. His right eye was swollen shut. A scar the shape of a closed umbrella ran down the side of his neck.

"Elliot," she said. "Take a break."

He shook his head dismissively.

"Every time you come home you've got more injuries," Petra said. "It's like you're out collecting scars. You just got back last night and already you're heading off again? You need time to recover."

"This trip to the Lake of Spells will be a break. It'll take a few days to get there for a start. There won't be any danger up north, and by the time I catch the Locator Spell I'll be ready to go where it takes me."

His mother laughed. "Oh, yeah, no danger at *all* in the Magical North. Just that colony of werewolves. Just dragons out of control, gangs of Wandering Hostiles, and a serious risk of frostbite. It'll be a regular holiday. A right cup of tea."

"Ah." Elliot shrugged. "I'll be fine."

"You're fifteen years old. You've missed too much school already. Your buddies miss you. Your *town* misses you!"

Elliot looked around. He breathed in the square's smells of snow, wet dirt, fresh bread, beer, and crushed pumpkin. Across the way, Clover Mackie (town seamstress) caught his eye and grinned, waving from the porch of her spearmint green house. Closer by, Isabella Tamborlaine (high-school physics teacher) climbed onto a small stack of pumpkins and performed an arabesque. Jimmy Hawthorn (Deputy Sheriff) applauded the arabesque, then shouted to a waiter at Le Petit Restaurant to fetch him out a knife so he could carve a jack-o'-lantern.

"Town seems fine," Elliot said. "Although —" he paused. "What's with the pumpkins?"

"Ah, you've been away too long. You know at least that the Princess Sisters are touring the Kingdom at the moment?"

"Heard something about that."

"Well, the Sheriff applied for our town to be included in the tour. He got a bunch of people to help him build a pyramid of pumpkins. It's supposed to be like a drawcard. A reason for the Princesses to visit. The Selectors are coming through today, though, so not much chance of getting chosen now."

Elliot raised his eyebrows. "Can't they rebuild it?"

"Not by this afternoon." Petra rubbed her nose. "You're getting me off the topic. All right, Elliot, if the town doesn't need you, your ball team does. Even with all the games you've missed, you're still their best player. You're the reason they've made it this far. Why not stay a couple of weeks until the finals?"

Elliot put the library book into his backpack.

"Gotta get going," he said. He tightened the straps and looked at his mother hard. "I'm not staying here for a ball game."

"Well, what about the farm? I was going to get you to fix the wiring in the greenhouse before you went. And there's all sorts of other things."

He laughed a little, and stood, backpack over his shoulder. "You could rewire this entire town faster than —" He clicked his thumb and finger with a crack. "Don't start telling me you can't run the farm without me."

Petra shrugged. Then she studied him.

"Elliot," she said. "I've rented out Dad's shop."

The slam of a car door shot through the commotion in the square.

They both turned. Across the square, Hector Samuels (County Sheriff) was standing by his car. He gazed at the chaos of pumpkins, and a sigh lifted his shoulders.

Elliot and Petra turned back and faced each other again.

"Did you hear me?" Petra said. "I've rented out the shop."

Elliot gripped the straps of his backpack.

"But when I find Dad," he said, "and bring him back —"

His mother nodded firmly. "When you find Dad," she said, "and bring him back, we'll deal with the new tenants then. For now we need the cash. Shop's been empty a year."

Elliot let go of the straps. His palms were indented with parallel white lines. He watched these fade.

"A family called the Twicklehams are taking it," Petra continued. "They're from Olde Quainte. Not exactly the province for electronics repair, I guess, but they swear to me they're on top of it. They'll be here in a month."

Elliot looked up at the clock tower. "I'll head home now and do my laundry," he said. "Get some provisions. Take the 3:30 northbound train —"

He stopped. His mother was twisting her mouth in that way that always clicked her jaw.

Her jaw clicked. As usual, this surprised her.

Then she spoke again, only now her voice had changed. It had gentled and softened. He had to bend to hear her.

"Elliot," she said. "The fact is, it's tough starting my days without your blueberry muffins." She closed her eyes. "You make the best muffins in the province."

"Ah, nonsense," he said, but then she opened her eyes and she let him see, for just a moment, how things really were for her.

How they'd been since his dad went missing, since he himself had gone off searching for much of this last year. The broken pieces of her.

He turned away.

Frowns ran across his face. They settled, fled, returned. Little *v*'s of frowns, like birds in children's drawings.

His bruises seemed to darken.

He stood and watched the square.

Now a different expression, impatient, caught his forehead. Abruptly, he dropped his backpack onto the chair and strode away.

His mother watched him.

Elliot stopped in the center of the square and scratched the back of his neck. He traced a line in the snow with his boot. The line turned a corner, then another, until it formed a square. A square in the square. Children rolled pumpkins past him.

He looked up. His gaze found a pickup truck parked across the way. It was loaded with empty crates.

He walked to the truck, grabbed a few crates, returned, and lined the crates along his snow tracing.

The playing children stopped and stared. He picked up a couple of pumpkins and put them in a crate.

Now adults watched too. He ignored them and kept working, heading back to the truck for more crates.

One or two people figured out what he was doing and joined him.

Within moments, several more were helping. The pace picked up. Crates ran toward the center of the square, and armfuls of pumpkins ran toward the crates. They were taken and positioned, two pumpkins to a crate. Crates lined up on top of crates, pumpkins neat inside them. Slowly, the base of a pyramid formed.

The Sheriff watched, bewildered. Eventually, he threw off his coat and ran to help too.

Assembly lines passed pumpkins hand to hand like a high-speed dance. Someone dragged a ladder from the back of the Pennybank Store.

Elliot took a step back.

At least twenty people were working on the pyramid now.

He swiveled on his heel, left them to it, and returned to the Bakery Café.

His mother squinted up at him, proud.

"That was a sweet thing to do," she said.

"Half the pumpkins must be gone or smashed," he shrugged. "So I used crates. It'll make a smaller pyramid, I guess, but it should look okay."

"It's going to be really elegant," his mother agreed.

Elliot grabbed his backpack again.

"Okay," he said.

Petra tilted her head, questioning.

"Okay," he repeated. "I'll stay another couple of weeks."

She reached out to touch his sleeve. It seemed like she might cry.

"I'll stay until the finals. But the day after the game," he warned, "I'm gone again. To the Lake of Spells. I'll use the book. I'll catch a Locator Spell. I'll find Dad."

She nodded.

"I'll go see about the wiring in the greenhouse now," he said.

He didn't look back until he reached the clock tower, then he stopped and watched a moment while they finished off the pyramid. A girl nearly fell from a ladder, her hands slick with sweat. A crate began to teeter near the top, and somebody shouted and caught it. There was applause and hollering, cursing and cheering.

The Sheriff glanced back, saw Elliot, and gave a mighty salute of gratitude.

Elliot relented, raised a hand and a half smile.

Then, with the faintest tremble of a shrug, he turned around and headed toward home.

PART 3

Cambridge, England, The World

1.

*H*e was watching through the window for Madeleine.

His hands were on his head.

His name was Giacomo Cagnetti, but he went by Jack. He was an Aries, and fifteen years old, and the hair under his hands felt bristly. This was even though, when he turned to the side to catch his reflection in the glass, well, his hair appeared to him soft and smooth.

Behind him, also watching through the window, but in a distant, transfixed way, was Annabelle Pettifields (but she went by Belle). She was a Libra, and the same age as Jack. For as long as he'd known her, and they'd met when they were five or six, the first thing that came into Jack's head when he saw her was *daft*.

The word *daft*.

Imagine if Belle knew that. Sometimes a fingertip of fear would press a spot just behind Jack's ear, at the idea that he might accidentally tell her. He could be drunk or high. Or the sun could be shining on the Cam, and they could be sitting side by side on its banks, watching ducks and punters and tourists, and he could just come out and say it: "Whenever I see you, I think *daft*."

You couldn't forgive that, could you.

Especially as they were best friends.

Right now, though, what was bothering Jack was his hair. He kept touching it, hoping to find it soft after all, or at least to find a region of softness. It used to be as silky as a BBC announcer or a violin concerto, didn't it, his hair, was the thing. Back when he was a kid? But it must have turned coarse when he was thinking something else, the roughness slipping in strand by strand, and today was the first time he had noticed this.

He took his hands down from his head and examined them instead. The new wart was still there. He'd been hoping it might have cured itself, but no, there it was, on the side of the middle finger. He was prone to warts.

Now, how could you have a nice simple fantasy about reaching for a girl's hand if you always had to be adjusting the fantasy to make sure you were reaching with your non-warty hand?

Also: How could you imagine a girl running her fingers through your hair if you kept hitting the point where the girl pulled away and said, "Whoa, coarse hair, eh?"

These were very basic fantasies — holding a girl's hand, letting her gently touch your hair — and not so much to ask.

Belle murmured, "There she is," and Jack looked, and there she was, turning the corner from Sidney Street onto St. John's.

Madeleine Tully, fourteen years old and a Pisces — her birthday had been just the other day.

She was wearing her red wellingtons and black leggings, her green skirt and her powder blue coat, that wide black-and-white chequered headband she liked — it was pulling her (soft, soft) dark hair away from her forehead — and she was carrying a tangerine umbrella.

She was walking through crowds of scowling people dressed in grey.

Here come the colours of Madeleine, thought Jack, and the colours went right through his bloodstream now, sailing on tiny boats — spinnakers fixed with little toothpicks.

My hair is like wolf's fur, he thought suddenly. *It appears to be soft — wolf's fur — but it's probably quite rough to the touch.*

That made him feel better. Thinking of himself as a wolf.

*   *   *

Jack, Belle, and Madeleine were home schooled together, although not always at home.

On Mondays, it was Federico Cagnetti. He was Jack's grandfather, and he taught them History.

On Tuesdays, it was Darshana Charan. She was a former micro-biologist, currently a bedder (which is what they call a cleaner at Cambridge), and she taught them Science and Mathematics in exchange for free babysitting of her two little girls.

On Wednesdays, it was Olivia Pettifields — Belle's mother — and her role was French and Citizenship.

On Thursdays, it was the computer guy who lived downstairs from Madeleine. He did ICT (Information and Communication Technology) and Geography, and he didn't get anything in return. It was just, he'd been at the party when they agreed to do home school-ing, and was halfway through his fourth pint.

And on Fridays, it was Holly Tully — Madeleine's mother — and she did English Language, English Literature, and Art. (She also did general knowledge in the sense that she got them to help her practise questions for her quiz show.)

Today was Monday, so it was Federico's day.

Federico Cagnetti was tufty.

There were tufty white eyebrows, tufts of hair on both sides of his otherwise bald head, and more tufts growing out of his ears and on his knuckles. He was tall but he was angled at about seventy-five degrees — his body stood up at a slope. Most of the time he scowled, even when his words were mild or friendly.

"The daffodils are tasting of the sun," he might say in his Italian accent, "and I will tell you only this, that they are supreme above all others in their beauty!" and as he spoke, ferocious lines would deepen on his forehead. He only smiled when he was angry, nervous, or sad.

He was a porter at Trinity College — one of Cambridge's more famous colleges — and on Mondays, they met him in the small office directly above the porter's lodge. Nobody was sure if he had permission to use this office, and actually he smiled slightly whenever footsteps passed the door — or even at the faintest rustling from the hallway — so maybe he did not.

Now, however, they were sitting in the office, and Federico was blowing his nose into a large white handkerchief.

He folded the handkerchief and pressed it into his trouser pocket, frowning deeply as he did so, as if the handkerchief had failed him in some way. Then he bent forward so that his chin was pressed against his chest. He always started off this way: without looking at them.

"So many people," he said to his chest. "So many extraordinary people have come to this university! They might not be here *now*, but does that matter? Does it matter? Because are they not still here in their own way?" His voice, which had begun as a mumble, rose into a roar and he lifted his chin with his words and looked around at them furiously: "And what are we doing? Are we sitting here? Are we sitting here?!"

"Yes," agreed Belle complacently.

Jack and Madeleine nodded too, and then Federico's ferocity relaxed into a pleased sort of frown, and he reached back and poured himself a coffee.

There was comfortable quiet for a while. The rain fell outside and students' voices rose up from the Great Court. "It's not *today*, is it?" a girl's voice was saying, and two boys were laughing and not answering her. "It's not *today*?" she said again.

"Here we sit in Trinity College, which is an honour and a privilege, and why is that?" Federico's chin was back on his chest. "Why is it an honour to be here?"

"Because you're letting us," said Belle. "And teaching us and that."

"Why else?" said Federico irritably.

"It's so old and that, and so historic, and they've got, like, so much money."

"How old?"

"King Henry VIII started it, didn't he?" said Belle. "And that was around about 1546, and what he did was, he got together two other colleges that were even older, from the time of the medievals, wasn't it?"

"Everything very good," Federico told her, "except for the bits where you say 'didn't he?' and 'around about,' and all your other uncertainties. Who taught you this? I did. These uncertainties, they are an affront to my knowledge!"

"All right, then," agreed Belle.

Jack was watching Belle's face as she chatted with his grandfather, and he was thinking that she was actually quite bright. She just had a slow way about her at times.

When Belle gave aura readings she was whip-crack fast. But if you asked her a general question, even a basic one like, "All right?" she thought about the answer for too long. Sometimes it was because she was trying to make up her mind — she could be indecisive, being a Libra — but often she just forgot the question altogether.

More than that, though, were Belle's features. Her eyes were big and wide, and she forgot about blinking for long periods of time. Other people blinked at regular intervals, but not Belle. Now and then her eyes would go into a flying panic where she'd blink and blink to catch up.

She had one of those sweet faces, the kind that people call soft, or baby-faced, with the top lip raised slightly, as if she was meant to have buck teeth but didn't get them.

Finally, she actually believed in auras.

Whereas she mocked Jack for his interest in horoscopes.

With all that, it wasn't surprising that Jack had got into the habit of seeing his friend Belle and thinking: *daft*.

"Here, then," Federico was saying, and Jack looked away from Belle and saw that his grandfather was gesturing towards a black bowler hat. It was sitting face-up on the table, next to his coffee pot. "Here then, inside my hat, I have hidden the names of famous people who were once here at Cambridge! You will pick a name from the hat, and then what will you do? You will read about them! And then, do you know what you have to do?"

"What?" asked Belle.

"*Become* them. You will become them! Because that is why you are honoured! You can walk the streets they walked, see the sky they saw, climb the trees they climbed, read the books they read, eat the food they ate, and so it carries on."

"Not the same sky," Jack said thoughtfully. "It's always shifting. Stars die and you've got yourselves black dwarves or neutron stars or black holes instead."

"A lot of trees are dead too," said Madeleine. "From bleeding canker disease."

"I wouldn't mind getting that," said Belle. "It'd sound good, wouldn't it? *Oh, sorry, I can't do my homework, I've got the bleeding canker disease. Oh, no, sorry, I can't spare any change, I've got a wicked case of bleeding canker disease.*" She touched her cheeks. "But not on my face."

"Why do you need a disease to explain that you don't have any change?" wondered Jack. "If someone asks for money, just say you haven't got any."

"I hope we're not eating the same food the famous people did," Belle said. "It'd be mouldy."

"Or digested," said Madeleine. "'Cause they ate it."

Federico ignored them.

"Now, can anyone name a famous person who was at Trinity?"

"That girl from the Matrix movies," said Jack. "Hang about, no, she *was* Trinity. That was her name."

"You are all so funny!" Federico grinned furiously, and then he grumbled, "Ah, the names are in my hat," and held the hat out towards Belle.

Papers crackled beneath Belle's fingers. At first she was concentrating, but then her head tilted slightly and she was lost, her hand gently moving around while she thought about something else.

They waited.

She remembered at last, pulled out a paper, and read it.

"Charles Babbage," she said.

Federico gave one of his grimaces of pleasure. "Ah, now, Charles *Babbage*! Do you know who that is, Belle?"

"He's the dad from *Mary Poppins*," Belle said at once.

The others looked at her doubtfully.

Federico frowned. "This does sound like the name of a character from a children's book, Belle, you are right. But it is not. Well, it is a never-mind. You will look it up! And you will tell us next week! And then you will *become* him! All right?"

"All right." Belle folded the paper and refolded it again, until it was smaller than her smallest fingernail.

"You'll lose that," said Jack, but she ignored him.

Jack was next to pick from the hat, and he got Lord Byron.

"That's the poet," he said.

"Mad, bad, and dangerous to know," Federico said. "The ladies, they liked this man."

"That's all right, then," said Jack.

"You've got to walk around being *him*?" Belle said. "Ah, well, lucky you're such a good actor." She laughed so hard at her own joke they had to hit her on the back.

The hat was passed to Madeleine.

She reached in, then opened her palm, and there were two folded papers on it.

"Don't unfold those papers!" said Federico at once, panic etching his cheeks. "Choose. Choose first! And you must only unfold the one you choose!"

Madeleine stared at her hand.

One folded paper was close to her wrist, the other was near her fingers.

A shaft of sunlight swung through the window and landed on her palm, splitting the papers.

They all looked at the window.

The rain had stopped. There was blue between the clouds. Outside, everything was very quiet, as if people felt unsure of the sunshine — even a single word might risk the return of the rain — then suddenly, somewhere, somebody coughed.

"Which one will you choose?" whispered Belle.

Madeleine chose the one closest to her wrist.

"It's Isaac Newton," she said, and then uncertainly: "Didn't he discover gravity?"

2.

Imagine that, Jack was thinking.

Sunlight glinted on wet cobblestones, and Madeleine was moving away from Jack and Belle. Her mother was approaching.

Madeleine's mother, Holly Tully, had come to Cambridge eight months ago now, along with her daughter and her sewing machine. At first, Madeleine had enrolled at Netherhall's, the school on Queen Edith's Way, which is how Jack and Belle had met her. Within weeks, however, Holly had held a party at which she somehow persuaded Jack's grandfather and Belle's parents, along with Holly's own new friends, Darshana and the computer-guy-downstairs, to start their home-schooling arrangement.

Both Holly Tully and her daughter were oddly compelling when they spoke. Their voices seemed pitched in a way you had to bend your head to catch; in a way that hit Jack in his stomach, then rose pleasantly to the centre of the back of his neck.

Madeleine used her voice to talk about unexpected things like vanilla beans, taxes on cigarettes, the wingspan of a butterfly, and product placement on TV shows. Holly used it to go on about education, freedom, the quiz show she planned to win, and chocolate.

Here was Holly now, walking through the shadows and the sunlight. The heels of her boots were tap-echoing. She was wearing black jeans, her hair in a high ponytail that fell past her neck — a long neck, but more swan than giraffe, Jack thought. A pile of clothes, wrapped in plastic, was up over Holly's shoulder, her thumb looped through the coat hanger hooks.

Madeleine reached her mother and turned to wave goodbye to Jack and Belle.

Imagine that, Jack thought again, and this was the phrase that came into his head whenever he saw them together.

Madeleine and her mother — their bright eyes, their clothes from Oxfam, their attic flat —

And they used to be wealthy.

They used to live all over the world. In Paris, New York, Amsterdam, Copenhagen, and farther north in places he half thought were imaginary. There used to be yachts, hotels, champagne on terraces; they used to float on moonlight-laced rivers.

When Jack cast his gaze over Madeleine's former life he caught glimpses of sails swelling in gusts of wind, reindeer stamping and breathing mist, diamonds woven through plaits and spilling like raindrops down a window.

Some of these images Jack had invented himself, but still.

There'd been a father too, who was something high up in a multinational corporation. The family had moved around the world with a set of wealthy friends. The friends were of different shapes and sizes, but all had bewildering names.

Jack had gathered these names together by the stems; he'd arranged them in a vase that he kept to the right of his mind. At night, before he fell asleep, he'd breathe in the fragrance of each, the details that Madeleine had shared.

But she didn't know half their star signs.

She hardly even knew her own.

Early on, when they'd just started home schooling together, he'd written a note on the margin of her page: *What's your star sign?*

She'd turned to him, "What does my star sigh?" and he'd seen how much she liked the idea that she owned a star, and that it sighed; he'd seen in her eyes that her mind was rushing through the possible words that it could sigh.

It's true that his handwriting was bad: The *n* looked a lot like an *h*.

But when he'd crossed it out and written *sign*, underlining the *n* three times, a vagueness had wandered onto her face, and she'd thought for a moment, then said, "Pisces," and smiled.

Madeleine's family had been so wealthy, almost everything they'd done had been for fun or charity. One or the other.

Holly Tully had competed on that London quiz show once as a joke — or a stunt, or for charity — Jack was not sure which, he thought maybe all three. But now the sewing machine that she'd won was all they had left.

"So what happened?" Jack asked.

"It went like this," Madeleine replied at once, her face breaking into a grin, as if he'd asked her to share her favourite joke. "We were in Paris for a charity gala, so I decided to take the Eurostar to London. Just, you know, for fun. For the weekend. I used to run away some-times, see? But before this, I always came back. Anyway, I got on the train and guess what?"

"What?"

"Mum was there! Turned out she'd been thinking of leaving Dad, and when she realised I'd run away again, she thought: Why not come along?"

"Why not?" Jack agreed faintly. "All right, so you came to London on the Eurostar together, but how did you end up here in Cambridge?"

"We decided to let a random stranger decide our fate. When we got off in London, we saw a woman with a green umbrella standing on the platform. We followed her and this is where she came."

Jack, who was never speechless, stared.

"You know the funny thing?" said Madeleine. Her smile faded, and Jack leaned in, expecting a tremble, maybe tears — that she missed her father, or her wealthy life, that she wanted to go home.

"In the entire seventeen and a half times that I'd run away from home before, my mother had never come once?" Abruptly, the shine and joke were back in her eyes, and before he could ask another question she was asking him instead.

She wanted to know where his parents were. Why he lived with his grandfather. Why he wore those high-top shoes. Whether he'd ever shaved his eyebrows. What he thought of economic liberalism.

Jack found himself telling her about the accident that had killed his parents when he was two, about the malfunctioning fountain in his grandfather's hometown in Italy, his own alligator phobia, the time he'd tried to climb across a drainpipe five storeys off the ground to impress a girl, the fact that he had no clue what economic liberalism was — and she listened fiercely, her hand over her mouth, her laughter spilling over and over.

She often made Jack feel as if his future was in stand-up.

Her mother was like that too: You could get them both to fall into hysterical laughter with a flicker of your accent. A saunter in your speech. A dumb quip about a broken teacup.

Madeleine and her mother.

There they went now.

Turning to wave and grin once again, and then walking away. Trouser legs and pleated skirts streaming behind them; plastic that rippled with sun dapples.

Jack turned to Belle, and she turned to him.

"We're meeting her later to ride to Grantchester?" Belle said.

Jack nodded. "Bit hungry now, though."

"Chicken souvlaki?"

"You read my mind."

"Your aura's looking a bit off," said Belle.

"You and your auras," said Jack.

"Sort of flecks of grass on it. You getting the sniffles or something?"

Jack held up his middle finger. "Got a new wart," he said.

"Ah. That'll explain it, then."

He flicked the side of her cheek, quite hard, and she said, "Ow," and then they set off.

3.

They were riding their bikes out to Grantchester — Madeleine, Jack, and Belle — along the path through the meadows by the river.

The wheels of Madeleine's bike flew over dried mud, and she herself flew into a memory.

A cow sniffed and looked her way, and she was out of it again.

She told them the memory while they ate scones under the apple trees, deckchairs slung low to the ground.

"I was riding a skateboard — we were all on skateboards — going down a hill."

"Where was this?" said Belle, eyes closed.

"Genoa. In Italy. We were there for a summer. I was going fast — I was ahead of the others and the hill was steep. The road swerved and suddenly there was an intersection with cars flying by in both directions. So I jumped off the skateboard. And that was when I realised how fast I was going. I did that thing where your feet go —"

She stopped and drummed her fists on the table.

"No. Wait. It was faster than that, more like —"

This time she drummed her fingers instead, fingernails clicking like a typist, fingers tangling and tripping one another.

"You know, when your feet are in a panic, trying to catch up with your body."

She paused.

"I came so close to falling," she said. "But I didn't. I saved myself."

She broke a scone in half, spread it with jam, and took a bite.

"That's it? That's the memory?" Belle sat up, and nearly lost control of her deckchair.

"No. There was a six-car pile-up. While I was saving myself my skateboard rolled onto the highway."

"Oh, all right, then." Belle regained her chair's composure, and closed her eyes again.

Jack hit the side of Belle's head. "*Oh, all right, then?* A six-car bloody pile-up. *Oh, all right, then?*"

Madeleine laughed, then looked thoughtful.

"Nobody was hurt," she said. "Except the cars, I guess."

They all reflected on this.

Eventually, Belle said: "Did you cry?"

"I never cry," said Madeleine. "I'm not a crying kind of girl."

"Who were you skateboarding with?" Jack asked. "Was it Tinsels and Corrigan and Warlock and that lot?"

"Your friends had the daftest names," murmured Belle.

"My father was there too," said Madeleine. "He was farther up the hill, on the side of the road. I remember, when I picked up my skate-board — it got thrown into an embankment along with pieces of broken windscreen, but it was okay — anyway, when I picked it up and started heading back, I saw my dad. That was the year he had a beard. He held his hands in front of his face, clenched them into fists, and swung them down through the air. I remember it looked like he was demonstrating how much longer he planned to grow the beard. Then he turned suddenly and walked away."

They were quiet in their chairs.

Jack licked the cream from his fingers. He tried to think of a joke.

PART 4

Bonfire, The Farms, Kingdom of Cello

*A*lanna Baranski, owner-manager of the Watermelon Inn, wore a knitted orange hat with a pom-pom the size of a tennis ball.

When she was pleased about something, Alanna shook her head from side to side, like disbelief. Now she sat on the front steps of her inn and watched as her nephew, Elliot, approached. He wove between guests and their children playing in snow, stopping once to raise an eyebrow when a snowball hit his cheek.

The pom-pom on Alanna's hat set to swinging. She leapt up to give him a hug.

Elliot felt her shoulder blades right through her parka. He stepped back and studied the lines of her cheekbones, while she herself studied the bruises on his face.

They sat down on the steps. The sky was high with blue. Sunlight glared at the snow, and glanced off the side mirrors of cars in the parking lot. Beyond the parking lot, the river flashed and glinted.

"How are things?" Elliot said.

"Well." She tapped her fingers in turn. "Corrie-Lynn's nightmares have just about stopped. We're halfway full, which is better than we've done in a while, what with nobody getting any contractors in, crops being how they are. And the pipes didn't freeze overnight. So, I think it's safe to say, Elliot, that things are looking up."

Elliot reached a gloved hand behind him, and knocked on the wood of the door.

"Thank you," said Alanna. "You're always thinking, Elliot."

He smiled. "Where is she?" he said, and squinted out at the jumble of kids in snowsuits.

Alanna pointed through snowball fights and snowmen to Elliot's little cousin, Corrie-Lynn. She was digging in the snow with a spade.

"She's trying to find the new sprinkler system," Alanna explained. "I got it installed just yesterday for the gardens, and now she's furious with the snowstorm for burying it."

They both watched Corrie-Lynn. She was crouching low, hacking at the snow, ferocious with concentration.

"Anything I can do?" Elliot tilted his head back toward the Inn.

Alanna shook her head again. "You're such a sweetheart. One day you might put up some coat hooks for me by the front desk, but there's no rush for that. I hear you're staying in town for two weeks this time, until after the finals, and you've *already* fixed the wiring in your greenhouse!"

Elliot raised his eyebrows. "What are you, psychic? I finished that wiring ten minutes ago."

"I was talking to your mother on the phone just now. She also said you rebuilt the pyramid of pumpkins this morning."

"Not me. The town."

"The Sheriff must be over the moon." Alanna sighed. "He wants that royal tour here so badly! Can't think why. I mean, those Princess Sisters . . ."

They both chuckled.

In the distance, a train whistle sounded.

"The Selectors will be on that train, I think," Alanna said. "Let's hope they like your pyramid."

Elliot laughed. "It's not mine," he said.

The train whistle sounded once again.

At the Bonfire Railway Station, Hector Samuels, County Sheriff, was running from his car to the platform.

The train approached fast. The station guard was waving a flag and picking something out of his teeth.

The Sheriff stood tall. In his head, he was practicing a dignified, "Welcome to Bonfire," and holding up a hand to help the Selectors down.

Tears formed in his eyes. Somehow they had built a new pyramid. His town had built a better, smarter pyramid. Like a phoenix rising from the ashes of the snowstorm, like a surprise party just for Hector.

That Elliot Baranski, he made your heart hurt. The things he'd been through this last year, yet he'd rolled into town last night, and rebuilt the pyramid this morning.

They'd get selected, it was certain. Those Princess Sisters would roll into Bonfire themselves soon, and flags would unfurl, the high-school band would play, trumpets —

Hector realized he was wearing his old duffle coat, and wondered if he had time to get his good jacket from the backseat.

But no, the train was here: a sudden shock of clatter and roar into the station.

And then, through the roar, cutting through the engine and the shrieking of the brakes, cutting through the station guard's whistle — cutting through it all came the low, deep throb of the warning bells.

The warning bells were also ringing through the town.

At the Watermelon Inn, it seemed for a moment like the sky was joining in with the clamor and laughter of the children playing in snow.

Then the place flew apart like hands tearing at a jigsaw puzzle.

The doors of the Inn were thrown open, and people pushed, shoved, and poured inside. Voices screamed the names of children, or shouted, "What is it? What's the code?" Then, as the bells carried on, "It's a Gray, it's a fifth-level Gray!"

Within moments, the doors, security gates, and shutters had all slid, rattled, and slammed shut.

Scarves and bags were left scattered on the snow, alongside upturned snowmen.

At the station, the train almost stopped.

Then, as its engine hushed, the warning bells filled the air instead.

The Sheriff's hand was already raised in greeting. He could see their faces — the Selectors' faces — just behind the window of the first-class carriage doorway, ready to disembark.

That was the point when the train's security shutters clanged down — *bang, bang, bang,* all along the carriages — and the train itself picked up its pace, resumed its rattling roar, and sped away down the line.

The station guard was bolting the door to his guardhouse when he realized that the Sheriff was still outside. Standing frozen at the edge of the platform, one hand in the air, his old coat flying outward in the wind.

The guard had to fumble for his own safety jacket, unbolt the door, run across to him.

By the time he got there, the fifth-level Gray had torn bloody stripes into the Sheriff's bare hands and right across the flesh of his face. It had ripped through the cartilage in his knee.

Long after the warning bells had stopped, the front room of the Watermelon Inn retained its hushed, excited jitter.

The guests wanted to stay and talk, repeating the same stories. Phone calls were made and word passed around that Hector, the Sheriff, was in the emergency room but would most likely recover. Everyone else in town, it seemed, was safe.

Talk changed to other things. Three different seasons were expected for tomorrow. Somebody thought that the Butterfly Child had been found by the Chokeberry River, but others thought that that had been a hoax. Le Petit Restaurant did the best roast duck with a maple glaze in the province, and their vanilla-pear brûlée was to die for.

Behind the talk came the *clink, drip,* and *splat* of snow melting outside. Alanna and Elliot handed out coffees and slices of pecan pie.

Across the room, Corrie-Lynn was curled on a couch by the fireplace, reading a book.

"That's the owner's daughter," somebody murmured. "Poor little thing."

Elliot paused at the coffee urn.

"I know," replied another guest. "Her father was killed in an attack a year ago."

"I heard that two other locals disappeared the same night," chimed in a third voice. "The little girl's uncle, I think — used to run an electronics repair shop downtown. And a local teacher too. Vanished. Both of them."

"Not a trace?"

Elliot scratched his neck. He set down the cup he'd been about to fill.

He moved through the murmurs and stopped at Corrie-Lynn.

She did not look at him. She was staring at a page in her book.

Elliot turned his head, to read the title of the book.

The Kingdom of Cello: An Illustrated Travel Guide.

He'd seen it here before. They kept it on the mantelpiece, along with tourist brochures and pamphlets on local attractions.

He lifted the book out of her hands, but still Corrie-Lynn did not look at him. Her gaze transferred itself to her empty palms.

He watched her a moment, then read the open page:

A Note on Colors

While Cello is a wonderfully "colorful" place, in the traditional sense of that word, it is also home to a large population of "Colors." These are living organisms: a kind of rogue subclass of the colors that we see when we look at a red apple or blue sky.

Now I happen to know a man (Wilbur) who has had nothing but luck as far as Colors are concerned. He's only *ever* encountered the sweeter Colors — fourth-level Pinks (cast a whole new light on things for you), second-level Greens (coax out the beauty of your smile), and so on.

However, let me be honest. Wilbur's experience is rare (and I do sometimes wonder if he might be having me on). The fact is, there are dangerous Colors in our Kingdom. I myself have a very fine scar across my left wrist — the result of an encounter with the tail end of an Amaranth Cerise (mistook it for a Crimson), and during your visit to Cello, you are likely to meet locals who have lost family members to attacks of Gray or splashes of Violet. The risk should not be underestimated: A major attack of first-level Yellow (also known as Lemon Yellow) *can* kill off (or, at the very least, blind) an entire city.

However, do not be alarmed! Major attacks are rare, and you simply need to be equipped with the appropriate protective clothing. You should probably also get to know the system of warning bells.

By no means should you let the remote possibility of a Color attack deter you from a visit to Cello.

Elliot closed the book. He felt a gathering inside him. He was going to throw the book across the room. It would hit the wall, its pages would fan out, it would crumple to the floor with a thud. He felt the throw inside him, his shoulders tensed, ready.

Then he curled it back down.

He put the book back on the mantelpiece. He straightened its edges.

He sat down next to Corrie-Lynn, gathered her onto his lap, and held her tight.

PART 5

Cambridge, England, The World

1.

*I*t was Monday again.

In Federico's office, Belle stood to tell them who Charles Babbage was.

She began by unfolding the name from the hat and holding it out for them to see.

"Charles Babbage," she said. "His name rhymes with *cabbage*."

Federico nodded firmly. "It does."

"And it sounds a lot like *baggage*," she offered next.

There was a long pause. Belle leaned the backs of her thighs against a chair and turned to gaze through the window. The silence continued.

"Got any more than that?" wondered Jack.

"I'm not really fond of cabbage," said Madeleine.

Belle turned abruptly, her eyes astonished. "Aren't you?" she said. "But what's not to like?" Then she burst out laughing.

Jack and Madeleine laughed too.

There was a sound like someone trying to start a pull-string lawn mower. It cut into their laughter.

It was Federico sighing. Sometimes he sighed in a deliberately noisy, guttural way, repeating the sigh, escalating the sigh, until they noticed.

"All right," said Belle easily. "Well, as far as I can see, Charles Babbage was the guy that invented the computer. Only this was in the days before computers, so he didn't really invent it after all."

She sat down.

Federico's face furrowed. "I see what you are saying," he said —
then in a mildly thunderous voice: "Say more!"

"Ah." Belle stood up again. "Charles Babbage was all right," she
said. "He invented a couple of machines cause he was sick of adding
things up in his head. But he couldn't build them, see? What with no
money and no technology in those days. So, like I said, he didn't actually invent the computer. But the half-arse machines he *did* build,
those kind of, like, *were* early computers." ·

She stretched her arms into the air, as if pointing out the mould-
ings on the ceiling. Her phone made the squeaking noise that meant
she had a text message (Jack said it sounded like a dying rat), and she
raised her eyebrows thoughtfully and took the phone from her pocket.

Then she remembered where she was and put it back.

"All right," she continued irritably. "What I actually liked in the
story of Charles Babbage was — see, there was this girl who was his
friend, and she was wicked. So, I want to do her instead. Can I?"

"You want to do a different person?" Federico demanded. "A *wicked*
person?"

Belle nodded.

"This wicked person, she was at Cambridge?"

"What's that got to do with anything?"

Federico sighed flamboyantly. A gasp of a sigh this time, with a
suspenseful break before exhaling.

Belle raised her eyebrows at the others.

"He means cause this is supposed to be about people who were here
at Cambridge," Jack explained.

"That's daft, then," said Belle, "cause this was, like, in the olden
days, when they didn't let women in. They only let them in, like, yesterday. So that makes no sense, Federico. This is history, right? Well,
my woman is from history. So. Therefore, and that."

Federico lifted his eyes and his hands. Voices sounded from the
corridor, and he dropped his hands and scratched his nose rapidly,
until the voices passed.

"All right," he said. "All right, switch your project. I am intrigued by your woman out of history who is wicked."

"Wicked doesn't mean *wicked* —" Jack began, but Belle was talking.

"Okay, yeah, so her name was Ada Lovelace and she got to be friends with Charles Babbage. She *really* liked his computer machines. So she invented programming."

"Seriously?" said Jack.

Belle nodded, then shrugged. "I think so."

Federico was gazing at Belle. "Tell me now," he said, "this, what you have said, this is *all* that you know about Charles Babbage?"

"That's all there is *to* know," said Belle, sounding hostile. "And Ada's the wicked one, cause this was in the old days when women, kind of, like, didn't know stuff. But she knew programming. So . . ." She was trying to look at her phone surreptitiously.

Here, Federico seemed ready to engage in another theatrical exhalation, but a toilet flushed somewhere down the corridor and he blew the sigh away and moved to a new topic.

2.

*W*ednesday night, they were sharing chips from the chip wagon in Market Square. Madeleine had just had a bleeding nose — she'd been getting them a lot since she came to Cambridge, something to do with allergies — and, as usual, Jack and Belle had argued about the solution. Belle wanted Madeleine to tip her head back, but Jack said she had to tip it forward. They batted her head back and forth between them until the bleeding stopped.

Now they were sitting on steps. It was late, and the vinegar was sharp, but the streetlights and moonlight were soft.

Jack said to Madeleine: "Does he ever call you? Your dad, I mean. Or write or, like, email or send you stuff?"

Madeleine shrugged.

"It's one thing," persisted Jack, "for your mother to split up with him. But that doesn't mean he has to split with you. You should Skype. And he could be your Facebook friend. Open the lines of communication and that. He could LOL at your status updates."

"If they were funny," Belle put in.

Quiet circled the three of them.

Belle's fingers scrabbled for the crunchier chips. "It's lucky you've got Jack and me for friends now," she said to Madeleine. "Friends with regular names is what I mean. No disrespect to Tinsels and Warlock and whatever, but they're not even names."

"They're good names," said Jack with an edge. Belle raised her eyebrows.

"Besides which," Jack continued, his words lining up along the edge, "besides which, it's not that Madeleine's lucky to have *us*, it's the other way around. Belle and Jack. We're just single syllables. Like a couple of cow turds. Her name's a whole bubbling brook sort of a name. Three syllables. That's a lot."

Belle's eyes began a rapid blinking, then stopped.

"My name," she said, "is actually Annabelle."

Jack swivelled and looked at Belle. His mood transformed, the edges sliding right off him.

"It *is*," he said, proud of her. "You've got all those syllables too! You're not a cow turd at all."

"And yours," she continued, "is Giacomo."

That made the three of them laugh loudly.

*O*n Friday morning, Madeleine's mother took them for English and Art.

Sometimes they met at the café in Waterstones, which is a bookshop, since every half hour spent in the mere physical presence of books (claimed Holly Tully — she had heard this on the radio, she said) enabled your subconscious to absorb up to 1.5 percent of the contents of those books. Belle and Jack were keen on this idea, but Madeleine laughed about it all the time.

Today, however, they were at the flat. Madeleine and her mother were side by side on the couch, and Jack and Belle were on kitchen chairs facing them.

Holly Tully leaned forward, joining her hands finger by finger. Now her hands were steepled and she gazed over the spires at her three students in turn.

"You're trying to look like a teacher," said Madeleine.

"Before we begin," said Holly, ignoring her daughter, "Jack, can you get that book on the sewing table? That big blue one there — no, that's a pattern book and not in any way big or blue — yes, that's the one. No, don't give it to me, just hold it a moment."

Jack read the title aloud: "*One Thousand Random Facts.*"

Belle leaned over. "*One Thousand Random Facts,*" she repeated, placing the emphasis on the word *facts* whereas Jack had emphasised *random*. Jack turned to her with an insulted expression, at which she shrugged.

"That's why you're trying to look like a teacher," Madeleine said. "Cause you're planning not to be one today."

Holly continued to ignore her. "If you could just open the book at any page, Jack, and ask a question."

"All right." He flicked through the pages, whistling to himself, then said, "Here's a good one. What is philematology?"

Now Holly turned to her daughter. "The only way this home-schooling thing is going to work," she said sternly, "is if you forget that I'm your mother and respect me as a teacher."

"You're funny," said Madeleine. "It's like you keep surprising me that way."

Belle took the book from Jack's hands and flipped it to a different page.

"Who is Samuel Langhorne Clemens?" she said. "I mean, who's he better known as? Not, like, who *is* he? Cause you could just say Samuel Langhorne Clemens."

"You see." Holly turned again to Madeleine. "It's true that this brief interlude of question-asking — it's true that it might *incidentally* help me prepare for my quiz show, but its *primary* purpose is to enliven your young minds."

Jack took the book back.

"Should I run out and get coffees?" he said as he flicked pages. "On account of, the moon is in Aries, which means I have a greater need for cappuccino than usual. All right, this is a good one. Where does gold come from, Holly? Originally, I mean."

"And then we'll move straight on to poetry or art," said Holly, "with freshly enlivened minds."

"A win-win," Jack agreed, and then, "Hang about," because Belle had taken the book from him again. She was concentrating, shaking her head, turning a page, shaking her head again.

"Just ask anything," Jack instructed her.

"She's not answered the first ones yet," Belle argued, and Jack said, "You're taking too long, I could be back with the coffees by now," reaching for the book, and somehow it slipped from their hands and hit the floor with a slap.

At that point, Holly Tully changed.

The light on her face shifted.

"I'll tell you what," she said, speaking through the new shade of light. "How about you three go and do some sketches of King's College Chapel. For Art, I mean. As an Art lesson."

The others gathered their things, chatting, but Madeleine was looking sideways. Her mother was weaving her hands together, but this time the weave wouldn't work. The hands would not intertwine.

Something startled in Holly Tully's eyes, and she pressed her fingers hard against her forehead.

4.

$\mathcal{L}$ ater that day, Madeleine was riding home alone.

There was a sketch, half a sketch anyway, in her backpack: a faint outline of the King's College Chapel with a detailed foreground study of the wrapping from a Twix bar.

Her mother would like that.

She was riding the dusk-grey spring-cold streets of Cambridge.

She turned in to a quiet street. One or two parked cars and a roller door spray-painted with words — those strange crushed words that graffiti artists use.

Her foot hit the pavement and she used it to scoot herself along a moment. Something odd caught at her and she stopped.

A thin white line, the very edge of a folded piece of paper, was stuck in a crack in a parking meter.

She stood astride her bike.

The meter itself was out of service.

It was tilted too, like a tree almost uprooted, the concrete at its base slightly split.

Madeleine looked away again and, as she did, everything she knew began to settle on her shoulders.

She knew this.

That philematology is the science of kissing.

That Samuel Langhorne Clemens is better known as Mark Twain.

That, originally, gold comes from the stars.

And that her mother knew none of these facts.

Madeleine gripped the handles of her bike: A big, bold statement was unfurling itself across her mind, and she didn't want to see it. She turned away from it, reaching for more facts. She told herself: *I also know this.*

That Charles Babbage was born in 1791; that he was bad-tempered and brilliant; that he wrote letters to the editor complaining of the noises of the night: organ-grinders, hoop-rollers, and street musicians just outside his window. That he closed his eyes and dreamed machines that could solve mathematical puzzles without making mistakes. That he filled every room of his house with *almost*-computers. Each time he got halfway through a machine, he'd think of a better way, then move to the next room and start again.

She knew that Charles Babbage clambered through life, leaping from foothold to handhold. But he couldn't help noticing that everybody else was climbing wrong. They were missing the obvious routes, they were slipping and grazing their knees. He had to keep pausing to tug at his ear and call: *Can you not see that you are doing that wrong? Ah, let me try to explain.*

He wrote a letter to the poet Tennyson once, to complain about a line in a poem.

"Every moment dies a man,
Every moment one is born," was the line.

If this were true, wrote Babbage, sighing, *the population of the world would be at a standstill. In truth, the rate of birth is slightly in excess of that of death.*

He suggested that Tennyson say instead:

"Every moment dies a man,
Every moment 1 1/16 is born."

Although, *strictly speaking*, he added, *the actual figure is so long I cannot get it into a line.*

His train stopped once — cows on the track — and instead of reading his newspaper, he invented a scoop. A metal scoop called a cowcatcher. Soon, all over England, they were hooking them onto their steam locomotives, sweeping the cattle away.

He saw things that needed to be fixed or unlocked — the postal system, lighthouse signals, life assurance — and fixed or unlocked them. He invented codes, untangled clues, made skeleton keys. He found ways to clear paths, get through and get across.

Madeleine knew all this because she had been reading.

When they'd first got here to Cambridge, she'd started collecting facts, half joking, to help her mother practise for the quiz show.

But then she had realised, first, that Holly was serious about the quiz show and, second, that she forgot every fact Madeleine offered.

So Madeleine stopped sharing.

But she kept collecting. In her previous life, she had only ever read fantasy novels, but now she read facts and more facts: books, scientific journals, newspapers, travel magazines. It was a strange new addiction, but the *fact* was, facts took her sideways so she didn't have to think.

Now she stood on the side of the street, astride her bike.

The statement was back, and though she scrambled for more facts, it blazed at her, and it was this: *I want to go home.*

That was wrong. They never had a home, more a lifestyle. What she meant was, she wanted her dad. She wanted to fly from this place, to fly into his arms. She and her mother had fun together, sure, but the true colour — the dazzle of colour, the firecracker sky in their life — that was her dad.

Her mother disagreed. "We don't need him," she said. "This is our new life." She swooped and swerved around Madeleine's arguments and questions. "Trust me," she said. "It's better like this. We hardly ever saw Dad before! He was always so busy."

"Whereas now we get to see him all the time. Ingenious."

At which, her mother would turn on the sewing machine.

It was up to Madeleine.

She couldn't convince her mother to go back, so she had to make her dad come here and fetch them.

Only, how could she get through to him? She could phone or email, sure, but that would achieve nothing. His assistants would answer. He was always doing something important or distracting. When he got the message, he'd be too angry to return her calls. Even if she found a way to speak directly to him, she'd have to get through layers of his anger.

And even if she *did* calm his temper, there'd be something else. Another layer that she couldn't figure out but knew was there. Something that always seemed to block the pathway to her father, lately — to his heart.

It was impossible.

She could never unlock, untangle, decipher, get through. She could never fly back into her father's arms. She was trapped and they would never get home.

As soon as she let herself think this, she knew it was true, and the truth draped itself onto her shoulders, like a child who leaps at you from behind, clambers onto your back, clings to your throat —

Madeleine got off her bike.

The funny thing was, she thought now, if she'd reached into Federico's hat that day, and drawn out Charles Babbage's name, well, she would have held a name that could clear pathways.

But she had chosen Isaac Newton.

The gravity man.

She wanted to fly, and she had chosen the man who would bind her to the ground.

She leaned her bike against a wall and saw it again — that fine line of white along the seam of the parking meter.

She tried to pull it out with her fingertips but it was too deeply embedded. By holding two fingernails, one above and one below, she managed to grasp the edge and slowly draw it out.

It was a thin piece of paper, folded in half.

She unfolded it and read:

Help me!
I am being held against my will!

She laughed aloud, looking at the base of the parking meter: the split concrete.

"You're trying to escape," she said, then glanced around to check that nobody had seen her talking to a parking meter. The street was empty.

It was growing dark, everything turning shades of grey.

The paper in the palm of her hand made her shudder suddenly.

I am being held against my will!

What if it was real? A message from a stranger who was trapped?

Strange place to put it, though, she thought, and smiled again.

I am being held against my will.

On the darkening path, she took paper from her backpack, and she wrote a reply to the note.

She folded it and slid it into the parking meter until it too was nothing but a fine white line.

Then she rode away.

Bonfire, The Farms, Kingdom of Cello

5.

*R*ain was falling fast and sharp: streetlights and parked cars cowering out there in the dusk.

Jimmy Hawthorn, Deputy Sheriff, stood at the window with a whiskey. Across the road, in the high-school grounds, Elliot Baranski was throwing a ball against a wall. Each time Elliot threw, the ball disappeared into an arc of half-light, then reappeared with a splash.

"You got a fax there?" Jimmy said, still watching through the window.

The Sheriff was at his desk; he eased back in his leather chair and reached behind him to the fax machine.

"Ah, shoot," he said.

Jimmy watched as Hector pressed at the bandage on his right hand. Wide white bandages diagonaled across his cheeks; a smaller square was centered on his forehead.

"They keep lifting off," Hector explained. "Taking the skin and blood with them. They all seem to be at the wrong angle — kind of angle where a bandage doesn't stick. Worst one's the back of the neck. Hurts like blazes when I reach around like so —"

He tried to demonstrate, and winced.

"Don't do that on my account." Jimmy smiled. Then his smile changed to a mild frown, and he went to speak, hesitated, and spoke: "Hector," he said, "you read their column in today's *Herald*? The Princess Sisters' column?"

"It's out already?" Hector looked around the station eagerly, and Jimmy reached for the paper and slapped it onto Hector's desk.

The Sheriff turned to page 7, and read the column:

Dearest, Sweetest, Most Arduously Marvelous Subjects of this! our Fine and Salutary Kingdom of Cello! Hello!

And Welcome to this! the Third Week of our Tour, and I think this must be our Fifth Column for that sweet pea of a newspaper, the *Cellian Herald* [*Editor's note: It's their sixth column, in fact*].

As a feather tickles a toe, so! how thrilling it is to you all! — as you line the streets and carriageways, as you swarm into the concert halls, as you gather at openings of hospital wings and throng to the christenings of ships, as you raise your hands, as you toss bouquets — as you do all this, sweet Subjects, in the sparkling course of this! our first official Tour of the Kingdom.

It is scarce to believe that we have lived in our Kingdom a mere fourteen and fifteen years respectfully [*Editor's note: respectively? Jupiter is 14 and Ko, 15*], and in those years, we *had*

believed we'd seen it all. Yet, in this! our first official Tour of the Kingdom, we realize it is not so!

Why, everywhere we turn there's something new! We turn once and look! it's a painting we'd never even *heard* of, let alone seen! (but which, we are assured, is famous throughout Cello). We turn again and look! it's a vibrant town named Lightning, whence forks of lightning shower from the sky — and we watch in awe from our carriage as the good people of Lightning gather those forks, to sew into the bindings of their factories. (I'd give away my last peach-nettle candy for a chance to visit Lightning again.) We turn again — and find we have to pause for dizziness (ha-ha). (Or we turn again, and guess what, we have come full circle and are back in front of that obscure painting!) (ha-ha once more).

We are writing now from our Emerald Carriage, which is quickening apace through the northern, somewhat industrial region of the Farms — hence, the mighty chaos of the handwriting. Apologies for the scrawl, especially for the wayward line that just sprang from that word!! [*Editor's note: As we have set the column in type, the scrawl of the Princess Sisters' handwriting is not apparent here.*]

What have we done today? We visited the town of Applecart in the Farms! We were *delighted* by their giant moose made out of pinecones, their museum of cross-stitching, and a recital by Applecart's youngest pianist, Dorian Jo (aged eight).

The Farms are, of course, famous for baking, and Applecart did not disappoint. Princess Ko (that is to say, me, for I take the pen for this column) had morning tea with Applecart's dignitaries (the mayor, hospital administrator, and post-office clerk). A chat was had by all. We partook of raspberry muffins and sweet-potato pie (only slightly scorched on the underside — Applecart! Stop apologizing!). I enjoyed these baked goods (the coffee, however, was a *little* strong for my taste) while Princess Jupiter slept in the carriage. (Tonight, Jupiter will attend the functions in Turquoise, GC, while *I* take my turn to sleep.)

Dearest Subjects, we *do* wish we could visit *all* towns that apply! A shout-out here to Bonfire, another applicant in the Farms. I'm sure it would have been a hoot to visit, and we were intrigued by word of its Pyramid of Pumpkins, but never mind . . . ! (We hear that a stray attack from a fifth-level Gray prevented the selectors from even stepping off the train into that town. How dismal for Bonfire.)

Well, here we must love you and leave you! Oh, but one last thing, a minor matter of state (i.e., foreign affairs) — we were sorryful to hear of the plague outbreak in the southern Kingdom of Rialto! It gladdens our hearts that Queen Lyra (aka Mother) is perusing her way there in the Royal Ship, so she can issue forth boatloads of helpfulness. Anyway, hugs from us, Rialto! Get better soon! [*Editor's note: The plague outbreak is actually in the southeastern Kingdom of Sergendop, and has, to date, killed over 6,000 people. We have been assured that the Queen will remain a safe hundred yards from its shores when she delivers her "helpfulness."*]

Thus concludes our splendid Royal column!

Yours with Royal Vigor and Pomp,
HRH, the Princess Jupiter, and HRH, the Princess Ko *xxx*

Hector sat back, chuckling quietly.

"They seem kind of . . . young, don't they?" Jimmy ventured. "You think you might have been a little . . . disappointed? If we *had* got selection? If they *had* come here after all?"

"Ah, they seem young 'cause they are young. They're just kids, Jimmy, and sweet ones at that. Don't forget their language doesn't do them justice, brought up like they were all over the shop. They've got dialect from half the provinces in their little princess heads." •

He reached for the glass on his desk and found it empty.

"Can*not* believe that Applecart burned a sweet-potato pie!" He slammed the glass back down.

Jimmy regarded him thoughtfully. Then he shifted his gaze to the shelf across the room, the one that held Hector's collection. A souvenir album from the royal wedding; several volumes of *The History of Royal Tradition*; four or five royal teacups hanging from hooks; and a framed portrait of the royal family. In the portrait, which was a few years old, King Cetus and Queen Lyra were seated on high-backed chairs, their four children gathered around them. Prince Chyba, who had had braces on his teeth at the time, was smiling cautiously; the Princess Sisters, Ko and Jupiter, had caught each other's eye and were giggling; and little Prince Tippett, his expression serious, was holding up a large toy frog.

Jimmy turned back to the window. "What's the fax?" he said.

"It's from Jagged Edge," Hector replied, flicking through the papers. "Ha! Another one for you, Jimmy. Up for the challenge?"

Jimmy shook his head. "Hector, when are you going to stop telling the whole Kingdom they can send missing persons reports my way?"

Hector grinned. "It's your own fault for being so good at it. Stop solving them and I'll stop asking for them."

He scanned the fax, breathing in through his nose — it was a sigh, or concentration. "Guy been missing six months," he said. "Electrical engineer. Last seen heading out to work — blew the wife a kiss. She remembers that distinctly, she says. Never got to work. Colleagues say — You listening, Jimmy?"

"Who's this, then?" Jimmy turned side-on to the window and squinted down the darkening street. Two people walked through the rain along the path; each held an umbrella in one hand and a suitcase in the other. They were walking oddly: leaning their umbrellas toward each other while their suitcases kept tilting them apart.

The Sheriff looked up.

"There's a kid," said Jimmy. "It's two people with a kid. They're holding their umbrellas together to shelter the kid."

Hector flicked through the fax again.

"Seems he was caught up with some shady computer page, some kind of a — can't figure out — gambling is what they mean, I think." He turned a few more pages. "Got in over his head — they're trying to say the loan sharks got him and he's dead in the harbor. Just come out and say it, then!" He rustled the papers angrily, winced, and touched the bandage on his hand. His face was white.

Jimmy crossed the room. "You need a refill," he said. "A refill and a rest. Attack from a fifth-level Gray? Most people would still be in the hospital, and here you are back at work."

With one hand he poured whiskey for Hector; with the other he took the fax.

The Sheriff leaned back and closed his eyes.

Jimmy rested an elbow on the counter, studying the papers.

The room rustled quietly; the rain fell hard outside. Hector reached for his glass, sipped and swallowed.

Then the door to the station opened with a whoosh, a creak, and a burst of rain, umbrellas, and suitcases.

The door slammed shut. A man and a woman stood on the carpet, shivering and dripping. They were both short and plumpish, pale hair slicked down on high foreheads.

"Is it not ever raining out there like to a tantalizing foghorn!" exclaimed the woman.

So now they knew that the woman was from Olde Quainte. It is a province with curious turns of phrase, many of which make no sense.

"Call yourselves a good evening from us, will you not, as good as the owl with sooty elbow suggests, and hello, we are the family Twickleham."

So the man was from Olde Quainte too — even more so than the woman.

A shape emerged, a little girl of maybe six, and the room seemed keen to hear what she might say.

"She doesn't speak," the woman stage-whispered — a whisper so loud it seemed to rattle windows.

Sadness slid over the girl's face, and she stared at Jimmy and Hector, wide-eyed. Both the man and the woman placed their hands, gently, on her shoulders. The child's hair was damp and tousled, fine strands springing up with static.

"The family Twickleham!" cried Hector, leaping to his feet and then stumbling a little — his right knee could hardly hold him. "Jimmy, you know who this is? It's the Twicklehams! Here to take up the lease on Abel Baranski's shop! Well, welcome to Bonfire! Welcome to the Farms! You *are* from Olde Quainte, of course you are! But hey now, weren't you expected a few weeks from today?"

Hector was embracing each of the Twicklehams as he spoke.

"Indeed, and so we are early," said the man. "I'm Bartholomew. Here's Fleta, my good wife, and this is our little Derrin. If you will know it, we sold our house sooner than we thought. And as the golden hawthorn sheds its leaves at the scent of the wind-addled skylark, so we set off."

"And here we be, wet through to the dandelions," Fleta took up the story, "and nowhere to stay!"

"We thought, surely the local sheriff will tell us where the nearest inn might be. For isn't," and here Bartholomew paused, "isn't a sheriff exactly like a warthog's ingrown toenail?"

At this there was a brief, startled silence. For some reason, both the Sheriff and Jimmy looked toward the little girl; something about her silence, maybe, seemed to hold an edge of the rational.

She obliged them by shivering violently.

"What are we thinking?" cried the Sheriff.

"Come by the fire," offered Jimmy. "We'll get you towels and hot chocolate. And some of Hector's famous oatmeal cookies."

"I'll call Alanna at the Watermelon Inn," said Hector. "If she's full, there's the Bonfire Hotel, of course, but I'd recommend the Watermelon — prettiest rooms you'll ever see, little stenciled flowers all around the skirting boards. And I can personally guarantee that Alanna does the best breakfast in this province!"

Everyone bustled, making phone calls and switching on kettles, until they were all pulling chairs around the fireplace to drink their chocolate.

The little girl, Derrin, chose a chair, seemed dissatisfied, chose another, and changed her mind again. They all watched until she had settled on one.

There was friendly quiet, everyone taking great breaths, to demonstrate to one another what good chocolate it was, then Bartholomew Twickleham turned to the Sheriff and said, with curious reverence, "Can it truly be that you have sampled *every* breakfast in the province? What a feat!"

Again, there was a loud, silent moment of confusion. As one, they recalled Hector's guarantee that the Watermelon served the best breakfast in the province.

"Well, now," began the Sheriff, and he paused and touched a finger to the bandage on his forehead. A pair of frown lines ran straight through it, like train tracks disappearing into heavy snow. Was the man serious, or making a joke? Or was he being snide?

"Now, we've arrived early as you know," said Fleta comfortably, as if her husband had not spoken, "so the lease on the Baranski shop has not officially begun. But what do you think? Would Mrs. Baranski let us move in early? From what we've heard, her husband only used the shop itself, not the upstairs flat where we intend to live, so —"

"We hear it's been vacant a year," Mr. Twickleham interjected. "So perhaps it is ready? Much as a horsefly —"

The Sheriff interrupted. He glanced at Jimmy, and both his voice, and Jimmy's gaze, were heavy.

"What you might not know," he said, "but ought to know, going into the Baranski shop as you are, is that there's a hole in this town. A hole the size of the Inland Sea."

The little girl, who had just lifted a cookie to her mouth, paused and stared at the Sheriff.

The Sheriff stood and walked to the window. He looked out into the heavy rain and almost-night.

"Abel Baranski, as you know, used to run that electronics repair shop," Hector began. "His brother, Jon Baranski, co-owned the Watermelon Inn with his wife, Alanna. And Mischka Tegan was a high-school physics teacher. A year ago, we woke one morning, to find all three were lost."

The Twicklehams gasped, the little girl most loudly. Her parents frowned slightly, looking down at the child and back up at the Sheriff.

"I'm sorry to say this in front of your little one," the Sheriff said. "But she'll hear it at school anyway — in gruesome detail, no doubt. Now, young Derrin." The Sheriff crouched awkwardly by her side.

"What happened that night was an attack from a third-level Purple. But I don't want you to be afraid. Our warning tower's one of the best in the province, and that I know for a fact." Here his voice rose slightly, taking on a sharpness, but he caught it and turned back to Derrin. "When you hear the bells, you get inside. All right?"

He addressed her parents again, his voice low and hoarse.

"Jon Baranski was found dead out on Acres Road," he said. "But Abel, our electronics guy — could fix anything even *looked* like a circuit board — and Mischka, the teacher — well, they were gone. Abel's truck, engine still running, abandoned by the side of the road."

They stared.

"The Purple had taken them, as Purples sometimes do."

"Oh, now." Bartholomew's forehead seemed to sag; Fleta's mouth did the same.

"And that's why the electronics shop is vacant," whispered Fleta.

"We've been insensitive," said Bartholomew firmly. "As to the shedded teeth of a lionsnake."

"We have," his wife agreed. "Can you forgive us?"

The Sheriff limped back to the window. "You think I told you that to make you feel bad? How could you have known? You'll be staying at the Watermelon tonight, is all. It's run by Alanna, and she lost her husband, Jon. And her tiny girl, Corrie-Lynn, well, she lost her daddy."

"We'll be more tactful from now on," said Bartholomew. "Thank you for sharing." He stood and formally shook the Sheriff's hand.

"And then too you'll be seeing Petra Baranski tomorrow, no doubt." The Sheriff withdrew his hand, turning so they could not see his grimace at the handshake. "Asking if she can clear out Abel's things sooner than planned. And why shouldn't you, but —"

"But it will be difficult for her." Now Mrs. Twickleham stood, nodding, and she also grasped the Sheriff's hand. He flinched this time, but her gaze was lost to tears. "We see that now."

"Difficult for her," Jimmy agreed. "And for her boy, Elliot."

"And Elliot," the Sheriff said firmly, "is a very fine lad."

They were all standing now, by the window.

The Sheriff spoke again. "As for how Elliot feels about his mother re-letting the shop," he said, "well, there's something else you should know. Everyone knows that Abel and Mischka are never coming back — there's not a Purple in the Kingdom that'll get you in its talons, or take you to its caverns, and let you live. But Elliot? He's already taken five or six journeys in search of his dad. He's been to the Purple Caverns of Nature Strip, and to the ones in the Golden Coast, and the Purples have nearly killed him — tore him up anyhow — and he's planning on taking another trip, right after the deftball finals next week."

There was a sad quiet.

"He's got it in his head that he's bringing his dad home, see? And while he might not blame his mother for renting out his dad's shop, well, he could easily blame *you* for being there, if you see my logic."

Mr. and Mrs. Twickleham nodded. "We'll be prepared," said Fleta.

"There's more." The Sheriff hesitated. "Elliot's a popular kid. He's got a group of friends, see, grew up together, most of them. And, well . . ."

The Twicklehams waited.

"If Elliot doesn't like you, neither will those friends."

Now the Twicklehams smiled. "Oh, but they're just kids. Teenagers, yes?"

"Kids raised on farms," the Sheriff said bluntly, "are not exactly kids."

Jimmy nodded his agreement, and the Twicklehams, all three of them, raised eyebrows.

There was silence, and Hector's face softened.

"Used to be," he said, "Elliot'd come to the high school every day around this time and practice throwing ball with his dad. He's a champion deftball player, is Elliot, can throw a ball so high it'll bruise the sky. Now you know what he does? He practices against the wall."

He pointed through the window to the shadowy figure in the high-school grounds across the road.

They all peered into the darkness. Little Derrin rose on her toes so she could see.

Each time Elliot threw the ball, he also threw himself onto the ground, rolled, then jumped to his feet and held up a hand to catch it.

"We should be going," said Fleta. "It's late."

"I'll give you a ride," Jimmy offered.

They all moved toward the door, but the Sheriff turned back to look across at Elliot again.

That wall was getting trounced.

6.

*T*wo days later it was summertime in Bonfire again.

"Fifth time in a month!" Clover Mackie, town seamstress, called from her porch. "Each one hotter than the last."

She had a glass of orange juice in one hand and a battery-powered fan in the other.

Elliot was approaching. He wore jeans and a faded gray T-shirt. Old sneakers without socks. A baseball cap shadowing his face.

"You reckon you could get the town to dig a swimming pool in the square?" Clover continued.

Elliot grinned briefly, pushed through the gate, and ran up the three steps to the porch. He swung his backpack onto the empty chair and opened its straps as the clock tower started up its chiming.

"Eight o'clock in the morning," Clover continued, "and already I'm drooping like a tea bag. What have you got there?"

Elliot placed a small burlap sack on the table, alongside Clover's jug of orange juice. The juice swayed, its pulp jittering, then it stilled.

"Bananas," he said. "Overripe so we thought you might like them for that great banana cake of yours."

"Ah, you're a fine pair, you and your mother. You should both come by tomorrow and I'll run you up a new pair of gardening gloves each. Stay and have some orange juice for now! School won't start for a while yet. It's fresh squeezed."

But Elliot was already standing and re-strapping his backpack.

"Gotta get over to the shop," he said. "That family, the Twicklehams, from Olde Quainte. They came to town early."

Clover let her finger slip from the fan, so the whirring noise stopped abruptly.

"I heard," she said. "That'll be rough on you. Clearing out your dad's shop. You want any help? I'm stronger than I look, you know." She held up her bare right arm and clenched a fist to show off her muscles.

"Never doubted you were a tough one, Clover." Elliot smiled as he headed down the stairs. "But we've got it under control."

He raised a hand briefly, then turned back. "I hear this summer's supposed to be shorter than the last," he called. "Spring expected day after tomorrow."

Then he walked out into the heat.

Abel Baranski Electronics Repair was on Broad Street, two blocks east of the square. It was right between the veterinarian and the barber's shop.

The truck stood at the curb outside, shining fiercely in the sun.

The shop door was ajar, the blinds raised.

First time in almost a year.

At street level, there was the one big room. There was a counter and, a few feet behind that, a high workbench. A televisual machine (or "TV" as they called it) lay facedown on the bench. The other side of the room held rows of wide shelves crowded with appliances.

Shafts of sunlight were blinking their way into the room now, and the dust was in a panic. A vacuum cleaner and a couple of buckets stood just inside the door. His mother must have brought them in.

"That you, Elliot?" she called now, from upstairs.

At the top of the stairs, there was a little flat. Kitchenette attached to living room, with a good-size window overlooking Broad Street. Down the hallway, a tiny bathroom and two bedrooms, each piled high with junk — old toolboxes, a broken circular saw, pieces of TVs, crowbars, and hammers — and, at the back of the smaller bedroom, Elliot's mother.

She was washing the window.

Elliot watched her a moment.

"Funny place to start," he said.

"I know." She turned, wringing a cloth into a bucket as she did. "But I've never seen a window so coated with grime — and when I brought them through here yesterday, the little girl came right up to this window. She can't speak, you know, so she ought to be able to see through her window."

"Can't argue with that," said Elliot, turning to go. "I'll start downstairs."

"They seem like good people, Elliot," his mother said. "The Twickleham family, I mean."

Elliot hesitated. He scratched at his eyebrow.

"Of course," she murmured, almost to herself, "they're from Olde Quainte, as you know, and they did inform me that this place is 'exactly like to a jittering horsetrap,' which," she paused, looked around, "well, I don't see it."

"Indeed, and do you not?" Elliot's eyes sparked now. "For here in my quickening early-morning mind I see *much* that is like to a cascade of turtles and a veritable basket of toadstools."

"Isn't it not?" agreed his mother, getting into character as she reached for the water spray and dazzled the window. "And isn't my stomach now rumbling like to what one of my son Elliot's blueberry muffins might cure if he would only fetch one from the truck for — Hey, there's your buddies, Elliot."

She interrupted herself, leaning closer to the window.

Down below, across the street, a group of five teenagers walked toward the high school. Two boys — one tall and lanky, one shorter — and three girls. One of the girls was holding the end of her own long red braid and pointing it at the taller of the boys, talking fast as she did so. The others were laughing. Just as they reached the corner, another of the girls — thin and dark, a saxophone case over her shoulder — turned, and looked straight toward the window. She paused a moment, her eyes wandering over the Baranski shop and the truck parked on the curb outside. Then she carried on.

"She's keen on you, Elliot," his mother told him. "I saw it clear as you like the other day when they were over."

Elliot was quiet now, watching his friends disappear around the corner.

"Don't go starting something, will you? You'll just go and break her heart. You're perfect, see," his mother explained, "and that can be a flaw of its own."

Elliot laughed. "Ah, perfect is like to a runaway palm tree with a head cold, or a dandelion uprooted in some other bizarre, unrelated thing. I'll get you the muffins from the truck."

He took the steps two at a time, still grinning to himself.

But crossing the shop, he paused and glanced at the TV on the workbench. A panel had been removed from its back so you could glimpse a tangle of wires.

"Who do you belong to anyhow?" he said aloud.

His voice was interested, neutral. He imagined somebody in this town, somebody sitting on a couch, gazing at the empty spot where their TV should be.

He moved to the side of the workbench and looked more closely at the clutter. A circuit board sat patiently alongside the open-backed TV, and beside that, a soldering iron, a multimeter, and a pair of snippers.

The snippers were so familiar Elliot had to turn away.

Hanging on the wall behind the workbench was a corkboard. It was covered with printed papers, photos, and postcards — and one tiny note in his father's handwriting. Something jumped in Elliot's chest and he moved toward the paper fast — but it only said:

Peripheral connectors are: Pin 1: +12, Pin 12 and 13: Gnd.

He'd done the exact same thing a year ago. He and his mother had come into the shop then, a few days after it had happened, and he'd seen that very note, and his heart had startled — but it had been nothing. Technical details.

His eyes wandered over the postcards instead; he knew these as well as he knew that pair of snippers. They were from every province in the Kingdom. Elliot's father had traveled years before; he and his brother Jon had run away from home when they were kids, heading out exploring for a year.

Pinned to the far right of the corkboard were a couple of old casings from spells that Abel had collected at the Lake of Spells on the same trip, their symbols worn and fading.

In the center of the board was a photograph of Elliot himself. He was about ten in the photo, and playing deftball. He was leaping into the air, his shirt lifting up with the leap so you could see his bare stomach, the ball just beyond his fingertips.

Someone outside the family must have taken the photo — probably Jimmy, actually; the shot had the vibrant look of Jimmy's photographs — because both his parents were in the crowd on the sideline, blurred a little, but clear enough so you could see the laughter on his mother's face, the concentration on his father's.

Elliot turned back to the workbench — and again to the TV — "Where *is* my TV?" he murmured, in the imagined voice of that imagined person sitting alone in an imagined living room.

He laughed at himself, and headed out the door to the truck.

7.

*T*here were five of them — two boys, three girls — sitting at a table outside the Toadstool Pub in the square. They were Elliot's friends.

The summer light was fading, but the air was hot, still, languid.

"Gotta hit the road," said the taller of the boys, Gabe Epstein. He was at the table's head, leaning back so his knees rose up like a grasshopper's knees. His cap was inscribed with the fading words *Bonfire Antelopes '07.*

"Give me a ride?"

They all turned to the girl who had spoken. Shelby Ryerston wore her red hair in a braid, a studded black band around her left wrist, and a frayed and graying cast on her right. She had two tattoos on her neck: one, a skull and crossbones; the other, a small reindeer.

"You still haven't got your driver's license? You can fly a crop duster but you *still* haven't got your driver's license?"

The studs on Shelby's armband clanged against the table, defensively.

"Why's there got to be a written test?" she complained. "Been driving since I was two years old. I don't need to write a *book* about it."

"Two?" said the darker, thinner girl beside her, a saxophone case under her chair, beaded bracelets sliding up and down her arms. That was Kala Mansey. "You have not."

"Ah, well, five, anyway. I drove the ATV when I was two."

"Test is easy," said the other boy. Cody Richter had a head wild with curls, and dried flecks of paint on his knuckles. Cody's head was tilted at a thinking angle now, but a slow smile was forming as he spoke. "It's multiple choice."

"Ah, I never learned to read. Grew up in a grain silo."

They laughed, and she added, "The Farms should be exempt from written tests," and they laughed again, their chairs scraping in the evening quiet.

The fifth person at the table was Nikki Smitt, hair the white-gold of a zephyr nectarine.

"He might still come," she said. "We should wait." The muscles in her arms tightened as she reached into her bag for a pencil case. The zipper on the pencil case was broken; she used her nail to slide it open, took out a pen, and handed it to Shelby, who stuck it underneath her cast, to scratch.

Then a figure entered the square from behind the clock tower.

It was Elliot. Faded gray T-shirt smudged, streak of mud on his jeans, old sneakers with no socks.

They watched him approach, and he stopped and said, "Hey," and they all said, "Hey" back. Then they asked him questions, long pauses between each while they waited to see if he had any more to say.

"You get it done?"

"Just took the last load."

"Hot day for it. Where'd you put it all?"

"Shed. Back of the shed."

"It fit okay?"

"Yeah. Broken TVs and program players and stuff. Twicklehams were keen to try fixing them — get their business started that way — but they didn't buy the business, just took over the lease. I figure I'll look up the paperwork and take everything back to the owners. Should've done that sometime back, I guess."

Now the quiet carried on for a while; someone slapped at a mosquito and the table shook.

"You missed the thing in History — the test, the test thing," said Shelby, pulling on her braid.

Elliot looked across at her. Everyone's face was in shadow now.

"He's not in your History class," somebody said, and she said, "Oh, yeah," and they all laughed.

Then Gabe reached out and dragged a chair across from another table.

"Have a drink," he said.

"I need a shower," said Elliot, but he sat down anyway.

"Someone get this guy a beer."

Nobody moved. There were a couple of pitchers of fresh-squeezed lemonade on the table.

"They let us drive at fifteen," said Nikki. "They should let us drink now too."

"Yeah," laughed someone. "'Cause drinking and driving, they're kinda hand in hand."

"Ah," shrugged Nikki. "You know what I mean."

"We could cross the river into Jagged Edge," someone else suggested, and a few of them said, "Yeah," and somebody said, "Why do the Edges get to drink younger than us anyhow?" and somebody else, "'Cause they need alcohol to cover their own stench," and somebody else, "'Cause they're not actually people, they're holograms," and another, "Yeah, we should go."

But nobody meant it.

They all had to be up at dawn. Normally they'd be home by now, but today they'd been waiting for Elliot.

Elliot was clicking his fingernails on the table.

He looked at his watch.

"Train comes through in ten," he said. "You want to hitch a ride down to Sugarloaf? Pick up some hooch at their local — guy there never checks ID."

Elliot pushed his chair back. There was a single beat of hesitation, then they were all standing too, picking up their things, dropping cash onto the table.

The train was heading out of Bonfire Station, but they were fast runners — Elliot and Nikki, the fastest — and they chased it down the track into the deep blue dusk.

Then they leapt, one at a time, and fell into the back carriage.

It was empty and unlit. The six of them formed vague shadows moving inside, breathless, tipping into one another, holding on to the backs of seats in the rattling speed.

There was a squeal of brakes then, and the train shuddered, slowed, and stopped altogether.

Kala leaned out of the window. Her saxophone was lying on a train seat.

"Cow on the track," she said.

Shelby scratched at the edge of her cast and said, "We ran for shit," and they all laughed at their own breathlessness, then the cow wandered off the track and the train started up again.

Later, slick and wet from swimming, Elliot was standing apart. He'd just pulled on his jeans, but he was shirtless. He was drinking from a bottle, looking around at the shades of gray, thinking about the colorlessness of night, watching the blackness of the water with its ripples of moonlight, and then Kala, thin and dark, moved from somewhere nearby and stood behind him. Her arms reached around his shoulders; her long fingers clasped together against his chest.

He was still for a moment, then he turned, loosening her hold, touched her cheekbones with the tips of his fingers, held the bottle to the side, bent his head, and kissed her, underneath the high, dark stars.

8.

*T*hat same night, Jimmy called the Sheriff.

Hector was home, making grilled cheese sandwiches for a snack to eat with his favorite true-crime TV show.

"That missing persons report from Jagged Edge?" said Jimmy. "The fax you got the other day?"

"Guy with the gambling habit," recalled Hector. "Blew his wife a kiss, then the loan sharks got him. You solve it already?"

"Loan sharks never got him. He's run off with a coworker. They're someplace in Olde Quainte as we speak, running that very gambling page."

"You sure about that?"

"Ninety percent," said Jimmy.

The Sheriff limped across the kitchen, his phone cord untangling behind him. He grabbed a cloth and pulled out the grill. Cheese was getting nice and brown and crisp, the way he liked it.

"What's the story, then?" he said.

"He and the coworker had been having an affair the last few years," said Jimmy. "They started up the gambling business together on the sly. Things heated up and they ran away to a seafaring village in Olde Quainte called, if you can credit it, Why."

"Why?"

"Just plain Why. A village called Why."

"No, I mean, why? Why'd they go there?"

"Ah, its registered Hostility's as high as you can get. Sky-high. It's officially Ferociously Hostile."

"I'm with you," said Hector. "So it's exempt from Cello laws."

"They can run their gambling pages from there without getting into any trouble, *and* it's a tax haven. They're rich and in love —"

"And living in Olde Quainte," laughed Hector. "I'll take poor and lonely over that any day."

They both chuckled awhile.

"How'd you figure it out?" said the Sheriff.

"Got them to fax me work records and bank statements — in Jagged Edge, they just about never pay cash, see, so it's all right there on their bank statements."

"Sweet," breathed Hector.

"The guy bought flowers same day every year — date matched up with this colleague's birthday, so I looked at *her* records, and seems she quit her job a week after he disappeared. The rest I got from the network — passwords on the gambling page matched our missing guy's dog's name. That kind of thing."

"You can work it?" said the Sheriff. "The network?"

"Ah," said Jimmy, "I'm just tinkering."

There was an admiring silence from Hector. He had the phone under his chin now and was cutting his grilled cheese sandwich into triangles.

"Thing that got me thinking," said Jimmy, "was that bit about the kiss — the guy blew his wife a kiss when he set off to work. Now why'd she mention that to the police?"

Hector nodded. "Hadn't happened in a while," he guessed.

"He was saying good-bye," Jimmy said.

"Sad story."

"Sad," said Jimmy, "but *it happens*."

The way he said it — *it happens* — that emphasis made Hector straighten up.

"It happens," he agreed, "but it's *not what happened here*. Not here in Bonfire."

"Hector," began Jimmy, "Abel Baranski was always a player. His boy, Elliot, takes after him. I don't think there can be a girl in that school Elliot hasn't gone and broken her heart. *Nobody* expected Abel to stay with his wife. I don't like it any more than —"

Hector interrupted. "Abel Baranski did not run away with that teacher," he said. "He was a good man. He loved his wife and his boy. Setting that aside, how'd you explain the dead body of his brother, Jon, and Abel's own truck on the side of the road. How'd you explain that?"

"He and Mischka took the train where they were headed?" suggested Jimmy. "Gave Jon the truck to take home to the family?"

"Now why would they do that?" said Hector.

Jimmy sighed. "All right," he said. "So let's say you're right and all three of them were in the truck, and the Purple's chasing them. Why get out? Why not just put up the protective shutters on the truck windows?"

"Shutters must've malfunctioned. They pulled over and tried to run. Purple killed Jon, then took Abel and Mischka away with it."

Another silence.

"We've been through this before," Hector added.

There was a clamorous silence, then Jimmy spoke again. "Hector," he said gently, "you think anyone in this town really believes that Abel and Mischka were taken by a Purple?"

Hector took a bite from his cold grilled cheese sandwich and spoke rough and firm through the chewing.

"That's the story," he said, "and I'm sticking to it. I'll fax Jagged Edge about their missing guy tomorrow. Night, Jimmy."

He hung up the phone.

9.

$\mathcal{T}$he Kingdom whispered.

Moonlight sighed across the ice fields of the Magical North, glinting in the eyes of bears and wolves. It wound through the battlements and turrets of White Palace and glanced off the fishing poles that lined the Lake of Spells.

Farther south, it caught the buckles and harnesses of night-shift workers in Nature Strip. It pooled over a pair of sleeping leopards on the Cat Walk and flared against the white of a snowy owl's wings.

To the east, the same moonlight hushed along the cobblestones and lampposts of the seafaring villages of Olde Quainte; farther south, and to the west, it crept across the creaking Swamp of Golden Coast. It skirted ships in harbors, mingling with lighthouse beams, then blinked in surprise at blaze after blaze of city lights.

On a lonely stretch of highway in the north of Jagged Edge, ten black cars trailed an emerald horse-drawn carriage. Streetlights caught the royal crest on the carriage roof, then lost it, caught it, lost it again.

The cars and carriages slowed, and slowed, and stopped.

The doors of the first car swung open, and a man and woman emerged. Both rested their right hands on holstered pistols. They stood at the side of the highway, looking up at an exit sign:

GREGORYTOWN 8

Just above the *Gregorytown*, a spray-painted *H* was encircled with sketched daggers: the Cellian symbol for Random Hostility.

The man shone a flashlight at the sign. He and the woman spoke briefly. They looked up, down, and around. The woman walked the curve of the exit ramp awhile, then came back. They spoke again. They returned to their cars.

The cars and carriage started up again. The procession resumed. As the horse-drawn emerald carriage passed the exit sign, one of the horses snorted, and a princess's face, eyes large, pressed itself up against the glass.

In downtown Bonfire, chairs were stacked on tables in the empty square. The pyramid of pumpkins hulked in shadow.

In her spearmint green house, Clover Mackie lay beneath her patchwork quilt, fingers threading needles in her sleep.

Two blocks east on Broad Street, Jimmy Hawthorn had fallen asleep on his couch. His feet, his camera, and a plate of pastry crumbs were all lined up on the coffee table.

Next door, Isabella Tamborlaine, high-school physics teacher, stood at her front window. Her hands held the pendant that hung around her neck. She was breathing mist onto the window glass; outside, the faintest snow was falling.

A few doors down, a ladder leaned up against the electronics repair shop. Someone had scraped off the words *Abel Baranski* and replaced this with a larger, whiter *Twickleham*. Upstairs, the Twicklehams slept, suitcases open on the floor. Little Derrin, who was sucking her thumb, suddenly sat up in bed. She climbed to the floor, turned a complete circle, and climbed back into bed. Still sleeping, she curled up against the pillow and returned her thumb to her mouth.

Two miles down the Acres Road, an umbrella stood open, drying on the front porch of the Baranski farmhouse. Swimming trunks hung damply from the railings. Faint snow melted as it hit the ground.

Petra Baranski sat by the fire in her living room. She was eating dry-roasted almonds. A book lay open on her lap, but a flash of moonlight had caught her eye. It was sitting on the bookshelf by the window — this moonlight flash — alongside a framed photograph of Petra's husband, Abel. In the photo, Abel was at his workbench. He was leaning over a radio, his snippers poised, the faintest smile of self-consciousness: He knew the camera was there. Petra kept her gaze on the moonlight a moment, then turned back to her book.

Upstairs in his bedroom, Elliot Baranski was sitting on the floor by his bed. Like his mother, he was eating dry-roasted almonds. Scattered across the floor were papers, receipts, manila folders, postcards, instruction manuals, user guides, notebooks. They were from his father's shop — from the filing cabinets, drawers, and the corkboard.

Elliot was sorting through them, matching up customer receipts. Now and then he stopped and made a note in a table he had drawn up for himself. He was going to return the unrepaired appliances to their owners.

If they wanted to take them to the Twicklehams to finish the job — well, that was their decision.

The Twicklehams had asked if they could see his dad's paperwork, wanting his client list and supplier addresses and so forth. Elliot had said he'd think about that, and he thought he'd probably keep on thinking for some time yet.

He paused now and looked at his clock. It was after two. He rubbed his eyes. There was something bothering him. Something wrong about his father's things. Tools and appliances were stacked up in the shed now; the paperwork was here in Elliot's room. But something was askew — like a painting on the wall that is hanging slightly crooked, or an accent that you can't quite place.

He was too tired to figure it out.

His hand landed on a curling paper.

Peripheral connectors are: Pin 1: +12, Pin 72 and 13: Gnd.

The handwritten note from the corkboard again.

It was so real, so mundane, so neat, so blue, so empty, so irrelevant now. He pressed it fast between the pages of a notebook, the moonlight stinging at his eyes.

10

*N*o sign of snow the next morning.

The sun was warm, the sky blue, the ground bright with freshly damp grays, greens, browns.

The parking lot of the Watermelon Inn was full. Sprays of water rose madly from the sprinkler system, swamping the already muddy flower beds.

Elliot grinned, left the truck on the street, and walked across to the inn.

In the front room, it was breakfast time, and crowded. He found Alanna standing on a chair, reaching up to change a bulb.

"Do me a favor," she said when she saw Elliot, "and refill the orange juice? Be with you in a moment."

Elliot held up a hand to take the used bulb from her.

The sideboard was colorful with cereals, fruits, pancakes, waffles, pastries, syrups, jams. A middle-aged couple, loading their plates, were exclaiming, "Would you look at this spread?"

Elliot headed to the kitchen with the empty juice jug. In an alcove in the corridor, he passed his little cousin, Corrie-Lynn.

"Hey, kid," he said. "Whatcha making there? Another wooden puppet?"

"Nope," said Corrie-Lynn. She blew the hair out of her eyes and looked up at Elliot, hammer in one hand, nail in the other. "My window ledge is already too full of puppets. This is going to be a doll's house."

"Best carpenter in the Kingdom," said Elliot, "and only six years old."

"You betcha," agreed Corrie-Lynn, sizing up a plank of wood.

Elliot tossed the used lightbulb in the kitchen bin, refilled the juice, and returned to the front room.

Alanna was chatting with a table of guests now, telling them the best route to Forks from here, and how they should be sure and not miss the Antique Tractor Show in Dewey on the way.

"This is my nephew, Elliot," she told them, putting her arm around his shoulders. "Isn't he a handsome one?"

"Isn't he just!" the table agreed, and Alanna led Elliot back to the sideboard.

"You want some breakfast?" She scraped spilled cereal from the cloth onto her hand.

Elliot shook his head. "Meeting the guys for breakfast in the square," he said. "Just swung by to let you know I've been going through the things from Dad's shop, broken appliances he hadn't got to fix. Found a couple of program players that the records say are from here. Anyhow, I've figured them out so they work okay now, and I left them at the front desk for you."

Alanna stopped fussing with the breakfast things.

"You can fix electronics like your dad?"

"Nope," he said. "Most things, not a chance. But program players can be easy. When I saw they were yours, I gave it a shot."

"Well, that just makes me want to hug you," she said, and she paused and studied his face, and it kind of looked like she *would* hug him. But she was interrupted by a guest who wanted advice on how many pancakes he ought to have today.

Elliot smiled to himself about the pancakes and headed back out into the corridor.

"I'll come back one day soon, Corrie-Lynn," he said, "and see how the doll's house is shaping up."

"Come back later today," she said. "It'll be done by then."

Elliot crouched beside her. "You skipping school?"

"Nope, just work fast. I'll go to school today. Our teacher's all right," she said, then reconsidered. "Well, I *don't* like the way she's always crying. Not exactly crying, but her eyes fill up with tears whenever *anything* happens, sad or happy or anything — like one time when Ben Montessori pulled Susi Wong's hair and she saw all the hair in Ben's hands. And another time when Ethan Crowhorn got all his spelling words right, which he never usually does. But she comes from Jagged Edge so her way of talking is funny, and I like her name. Miss Hattoway. It's funny too, right? 'Cause it's like: 'Get your hat out of the way!' That's kind of funny. Or maybe, 'Put your hat away.' Not so funny, but still."

Corrie-Lynn paused. Her voice was as calm and practical as her hands.

"And we got a new girl named Derrin Twickleham," she continued, "which sure *is* a funny name. I don't even need to *explain* that one. She comes from Olde Quainte and she can't talk."

Elliot was silent, watching his cousin work.

"This doll's house," he said, "it's going to be for your puppets?"

"Nope," said Corrie-Lynn. "For the Butterfly Child."

Elliot laughed.

"If you find the Butterfly Child," Corrie-Lynn said sternly, "you've got to take care of her. And they like to live in dolls' houses, see?" She reached for a book that was lying on the floor beside her measuring tape, and flicked through the pages.

It was *The Kingdom of Cello: An Illustrated Travel Guide*.

"You should stop reading that," Elliot told her, but she ignored him, found the page she wanted, and handed it over.

Elliot read.

The Butterfly Child

The Butterfly Child is so small she can fit into a locket. She likes to ride on butterflies and prefers to reside in a doll's house. I have never been fortunate enough to meet a Butterfly Child, but this is not surprising: A single Child appears, trapped in a small glass jar, once every twenty years or so, and only ever in the Farms. Once the jar "manifests," the lid must be removed immediately, otherwise the Butterfly Child will suffocate. The jar, moreover, is fragile and can manifest anywhere in the province: Tragically, the most recent Butterfly Child appeared on the edge of a mantelpiece. The jar toppled, crashing into the fireplace and killing the Butterfly Child instantly. The family could only watch in helpless horror.

(This happened about twenty years ago. Thus, as this edition of the *Guide* goes to press, there is much talk buzzing around the province of the Farms as to when and where the next Butterfly Child will arrive.)

Butterfly Children are timid, and even the person who releases the Child can have difficulty winning her trust. I have a friend (Barney) who recalls moving to a small town in the Farms when he was young, and discovering, to his immense excitement, that a Butterfly Child was in residence! However, he never got to meet her. She apparently hid behind the tiny chaise longue in her doll's house whenever a stranger approached.

Any number of magical abilities have been attributed to the Butterfly Child — she has been said to be able to conjure invisibility spells, compose nocturnes, and much more. *None* of these claims has been verified, but it *is* generally accepted that: a Butterfly Child can speak both the language of humans and that of the insects; when a Butterfly Child is happy, the crops in the surrounding area will flourish; and, at any moment, she will vanish, never to be seen again — sometimes after only a matter of hours.

Elliot closed the book again and looked up.

"You plan on finding her?" he said.

"People say it's time for one. And it'd fix the farming problems, right? I heard that everyone's selling their grandma's pearls that they'd hoped to give to their daughter someday 'cause otherwise they'll starve 'cause nothing's growing."

"Corrie-Lynn, people are having a tough time but nobody's starving, and whoever you overheard complaining about their grandma's pearls, well, their daughter probably prefers showing pigs at the provincial fair to old necklaces anyway." Elliot reached across Corrie-Lynn's head to the wall, and pressed down a stray flap of wallpaper. "As for the Butterfly Child," he continued, "she could show up anyplace in the entire province of the Farms."

"Exactly," said Corrie-Lynn. "So why not right here?"

Elliot laughed again, standing up.

"I plan on finding the Butterfly Child." Corrie-Lynn leaned forward so her hair fell into her eyes. "And I plan on making friends with that Twickleham girl and teaching her how to talk."

"Well," said Elliot, "I like your attitude."

11.

*A*ccording to the paperwork, the broken TV from Abel Baranski's workbench belonged to Jimmy Hawthorn.

"Hey, Jimmy," Elliot called.

He'd caught up with his friends in the square for breakfast and now they were heading into school. Across the street, Jimmy was opening the door to the Sheriff's station.

Jimmy paused, ran back down the stairs to the edge of the street, and shielded his eyes against the sun.

"Got your broken TV in my truck," Elliot said. The street was empty, so his regular voice carried across easily. "It was in my dad's shop. He was halfway through fixing it."

Elliot's friends shifted closer to him. Jimmy watched them, his hand still at his eyes.

"Thanks, Elliot," he said. "I've got myself a new TV in the meantime, but I'll take the old one off your hands if you like. Maybe I'll get it from you at training later on? Unless you can use it yourself?"

"If you don't need it, I can take it to the dump for you," said Elliot. "Bunch of other stuff I've got to take."

There was another quiet. Elliot's friends were looking at the pavement.

"You don't want to offer it to the Twicklehams?" said Jimmy, even-voiced. "See if they can't use it for the parts?"

Now the chins of Elliot's friends lifted abruptly, and Jimmy could have sworn that a camera flash was going off in each one's eyes.

They spoke one at a time, voices almost overlapping, calm as water:

"Broken televisual machine you don't want, Jimmy?" said Kala, long dark hair shifting with her words. "School might need it for teaching electronics."

"Could come in handy for storage of your files and such," said Gabe, gesturing toward the Sheriff's station just beyond Jimmy's shoulder. "Police files, I mean. You just take out the internal workings and you've got yourself an empty box."

"You can make a broken TV into a picture frame, Jimmy," Nikki suggested, tilting that pretty face of hers. "Cut out the glass and put one of your best photos in there."

"Might make a good fishbowl," grinned Shelby, playing with her leather armband. "Take out the wires and stuff, like Gabe said, and then pour in a bunch of water and a fish."

Then Cody Richter shook the curls from his eyes. "Ah, let me have it, Jimmy," he said. "Just what I need for the sculpture I'm doing for art class. *Exactly* what I need, actually. I plan on putting it in the schoolyard right over there." He pointed, and they all turned and looked.

Five different uses for a broken TV in just over five seconds. Jimmy regarded Elliot and his friends, their backpacks slung over their shoulders. They turned back and stared at him, challenge in their eyes.

He would have liked to photograph them.

"You bet, Cody," he said. "Help yourself."

Those Twicklehams didn't stand a chance.

12.

*T*wo days later, the sculpture was done.

Elliot's friend Cody believed in speed. It was part of his personal theory of art — once you got an idea, you executed it. Right away. Without even stopping to sharpen your pencil, let's say the art in question was a pencil drawing.

The art teacher sometimes talked to him about planting ideas in the soil at the back of his mind, nurturing them, seeing how they grew, but Cody said he spent enough of his life farming without having to harvest his *art* as well.

Faint rain was falling — not falling so much as trembling — and Elliot was crossing the schoolyard, heading back to his truck after deftball training.

In the corner of the yard was Cody's sculpture. It was a pile of cement rising up out of the asphalt, the broken TV jammed on top. It was a mess, that was Elliot's first thought. But he'd been friends with Cody long enough to set that thought aside. Cody always had a point.

TV as trash, Elliot thought, but that was too obvious.

The cement was pale in the moonlight and he thought maybe it resembled a snowman, the TV as its head. In Cello, snowmen lasted as long as the winter, and winters could be anywhere from an hour to a couple of weeks. (Once, there'd been winter for just over a year, but they'd torn down all the snowmen eventually, in protest.) So the sculpture was a comment on the fickleness of seasons — the TV representing what? The weather news?

Elliot moved closer. He circled the sculpture. The back panel of the TV was still missing, he saw now, but in the darkness it looked like a patch of blacker black.

It felt good, the TV being here. The last appliance his dad had worked on — the final, unfinished repair job — and now it was an artwork. Not one of Cody's prettiest, but still. It was not in the dump yard, not under the magnifying glass of those Twicklehams, not even in a shed at the back of Jimmy's house.

It was here. Set in concrete. In the schoolyard.

Ready for his dad to come back for it.

That was the moment when he saw the corner of white. As the thought ran across his mind — *ready for his dad to come back* — he caught sight of it. The corner of a folded paper. Somewhere deep inside the back of the televisual machine.

At first he thought it must be part of Cody's sculpture and tried to adjust his theories to include semi-concealed paper, but then he wondered if it might have fallen in. Maybe it was supposed to be fixed to the outside of the TV? Cody sometimes wrote notes of explanation.

Or maybe — and this thought had been there from the moment he first glimpsed it, playing deep in the darkest darkness of his mind — maybe it was something of his father's.

He reached his hand into the darkness and drew it out.

His head was chanting: *Peripheral connectors are: Pin 1: +12, Pin 72 and 13: Gnd.* To remind himself that even if the paper really was his dad's, most likely it was more of that same thing. Dry electronics. Not something personal or sweet. Not something that would somehow speak to Elliot, or explain where his dad was right now.

He walked away from the sculpture, to the streetlight above the school gate, and unfolded the paper.

It was not his father's handwriting. Nor was it Cody's.

It was a rushed, flat scrawl and it said this:

Dear Parking Meter,

Me too.

I mean, metaphysically speaking I am. I can't figure out how to get away, or get back, and I really freakin' want to, so in that metaphysical sense, well, I am also being held against my will.

If you see what I mean.

And if I'm using "metaphysical" correctly. Not sure.

The thing is, my mother's got us sort of trapped here. In a tower. Or anyway in a flat that's high off the ground. No chance of rescue cause neither of us has hair long enough to let down, let's say our names even WERE Rapunzel, which they're not.

You want to know what I used to eat? Jasmine gelato, lavender cupcakes, frangipane tart, and fine-spun toffee infused with rosewater. That was on an ordinary day.

Here, we eat tinned beans. Specifically: fava beans, white beans, and, on special occasions, baked beans. (They make my mother throw up sometimes cause she's used to the finer things in life.)

Do you know what I USED to hear? Laughter like chime bells, my father playing his double bass, my mother singing, water features gurgling (that used to annoy me, actually, but I see now that it was beautiful), the teeny-tiny ding of the hotel elevator opening at the penthouse floor.

Here, there are tourists saying the same thing over and over, in exactly the same tone, and students ringing their bike bells like scalpels, and the buzz of the sewing machine.

In my life before, I never stayed still. I'd fall asleep in Paris and wake up in Prague. It was like I had wings, I was always flying or cartwheeling or floating. I was a girl who rode in carriages and sleighs, on ships and skateboards and skis, and everywhere I stepped there were white-gloved hands opening the doors to let me through.

Here in Cambridge I only ride a rusty bike, and everywhere I turn I have to Keep Off the Grass. We can't afford the bus fare to London, but my mother buys tickets anyway so she can take useless journeys to see about a quiz show.

So that's my story. What's yours? Life as a broken parking meter. Kinda sucks, I guess.

Yours sincerely,
M.T.

P.S. But if the note was actually left by a PERSON and you're being held against your will? Well, I guess, ignore the above, cause it must sound mad selfish to you. Also, sort of irrelevant, considering your situation.

P.P.S. And listen, you should maybe contact the police rather than leaving messages in parking meters. Just a thought.

Elliot studied the note awhile. He leaned against the school gate. At first the words were like spark plugs, because they were not his father's. Even dry electronics facts would have been a gift, and he'd been hoping for a gift, so this ignited something fierce inside him that scorched his eyes.

But then the words settled into themselves and he began to disentangle a little of their meaning. He raised his eyebrows.

He folded the note, put it in his pocket, drew out the deftball instead, tossed it high and straight into the night, caught it, and headed to his truck.

PART 6

Cambridge, England, The World

1.

*I*t was raining heavily.

Car headlights seemed to scowl around corners. Cyclists scowled back, wiping raindrops from their noses and eyebrows. Drainways and gutters gushed with water; tulips and daffodils trembled; and cherry blossom petals scattered from their trees, forming glowing veils of pink over slick brown mulch.

In the Cambridge Market Square, a man stepped in a puddle and the splash patterned out across a passing woman's skirt. A small crowd of tourists shivered in the entryway to Barclays Bank. The market itself was closed and tightly wrapped, but a fruit-stall owner was still packing up the last of his oranges.

Just off the square, on St. Mary's Passage, cane chairs and tables were soaking in the downpour on the terrace outside a café. In its window was a stencilled image of a buxom woman offering a tray of tea. *Auntie's*, said the flourish above her head, and below, more plain-speaking: *TEA SHOP*.

Inside Auntie's Tea Shop, a girl was squinting hard at her friend. He, in turn, was lost in thought. He was tall and had golden-green eyes, and a wide mouth that seemed ready to form a big wide smile. These were Belle and Jack.

A few streets away, in her attic flat, Madeleine was sitting on the couch. Her mother was at the sewing table. Rain streamed down the windows, and rain-shadows streamed down Holly's and Madeleine's faces and arms. The quiz show played on TV.

Madeleine was holding a closed book.

ISAAC NEWTON, said the cover of the book in big, proud blue and, beneath that, more humbly, the author's name.

Did Isaac have a nickname? Did they call him Zac? she thought. Also: *What does it mean if your name begins with* I*? What effect does that have on your ego?*

She remembered that she'd dreamed about her iPod last night. In the dream, she had seen it on the seat of a passing train. Its music had been spilling everywhere, staining the seat. She'd been in one train, the iPod in another, and there it had gone, heading fast away from her, her hand reaching out through the window helplessly.

Where are they now? she thought. Her iPod, her iPhone, her iPad, the *I*-ness of her life? Her mind stretched around in its memories, searching for her things: She saw her phone on the hotel bedside table in Paris; her iPad in her Louis Vuitton urban satchel; her iPod slipping from her pocket in the restaurant, the night before she ran away.

Then she saw her father's face, and he was pointing out the iPod as it slipped towards the floor.

Madeleine's memory slipped itself, and there was her dad again. He was pushing his chair back from the table and leaping to his feet, to demonstrate the odd way someone walked. The table was laughing hysterically. Other diners turned.

Now she saw her father crouch by her side when she was small: the intensity of his gaze while she herself counted the feet of a millipede for him.

She saw him at a hotel breakfast bar, pushing the collar of his shirt aside to show her a new tattoo.

"Why'd you get that?" she had said.

"To see how it would feel."

That was her father's embrace of life. He did things just to see how they felt. He *felt* things more than most people did. He stopped still to laugh his big, full laugh, not caring if people had to wait or move around him. In an underground cave once, his laugh had echoed out, turning back on him, and he'd paused, surprised, and then laughed harder.

The expression on her father's face when their car hit a dog in Barcelona, the expression when the vet said the dog wouldn't make it through the night. Tears in her father's eyes as he stroked the dog's ears.

In Auntie's Tea Shop, Jack and Belle were sharing the hot banana cake with butterscotch sauce, and drinking tea. The tablecloth was white lace, the chairs were loops of dark wood, and framed prints of Cambridge hung on the walls.

"I had this dream last night," Belle said, her spoon cutting a crescent moon into the cake.

"All right." Jack's spoon hovered. "What was it?"

"I had this dream where I kept kissing people and every time I did it was disgusting. I kept wanting to kiss random people — like the postman and that — but it was all wet, like saliva just pouring into the kiss."

There was a pause. "That's disgusting," Jack said.

"Yeah, I told you that. I said it was disgusting."

Their spoons cut at the cake, fiercely competitive for a while, until Belle said, "Hang about," and she sliced the cake in half, pushed half his way, half hers. "Now we can relax."

They both sat back and looked around. A middle-aged couple pushed open the door with a jangle of exclamations about the rain. A waitress muttered, "We're practically *closed*," but she smiled and seated them anyway. The waitress wore a black uniform trimmed in white at the collar and the sleeves, white apron over it all.

"I love this place," said Belle.

"It must have been drool," said Jack. "You were drooling while you were dreaming, so that's why the kisses were like that."

"I don't drool."

"Of course you do. Everyone does. Especially when you're dreaming. You're paralysed when you dream. You can't move anything, not even your tongue, so you can't swallow your spit."

They both picked up their spoons again, thoughtful.

"That paralysed thing," Jack added. "It's probably why I have so many dreams where I'm trying to run or drive to get somewhere, but I end up going nowhere."

"No. You have those dreams because you *are* going nowhere."

"Thanks," said Jack.

Earlier that day, Jack and Belle had met Holly and Madeleine in the café at Waterstones, when the rain was still high in the grey.

"Begin," Holly had said, "by closing your eyes and breathing in the books."

Belle and Jack did so, while Madeleine went to get extra chocolate sprinkles for her cappuccino.

When she returned, they had opened their eyes, sweet and startled, like small children waking from long naps.

Holly nodded her approval at them, and then she said:

"She walks in beauty, like the night
Of cloudless climes and starry skies;
And all that's best of dark and bright
Meet in her aspect and her eyes."

"Who does?" said Belle.

"It's a nice line, isn't it?" said Jack. *"She walks in beauty, like the night."*

"Do you know who wrote those lines?" said Holly.

"I did," said Jack, smiling with faint pride.

Belle regarded him, incredulous, then her face cleared.

"Oh, right," she said, "so it was Byron." She turned to Holly. "Byron wrote it."

"Hmm." Holly squinted thoughtfully. "I thought so too, Belle, but Jack seems so sure of himself. Maybe Jack *did* write it?"

So all three had explained to Holly about the names in the hat.

"I didn't have to *become* Byron," Jack added, "because I already *am* him, or anyway exactly like him. But without the poetry. Also, girls are not falling over themselves to have my children. As far as I know. If they are, they need to do it more loudly. Apart from all that, I'm just like Byron."

"The similarities are blowing my mind," said Belle.

"Different names too," Jack had continued. "Byron and I have different names."

Now in Auntie's Tea Shop, Jack fixed a critical gaze on the little shelf hanging on the opposite wall. Its edges swirled and curled, the wood getting carried away with itself. A copper kettle sat alone on the top shelf, looking slightly lost. Jack thought that the owner of the tea shop had probably got that copper kettle for a present. And after the present giver went home, the shop owner had said, "What am I supposed to do with this bloody thing?" and someone else had said, "Oh, stick it up there on the shelf."

Jack turned back to Belle, tilted his head towards the kettle, and she raised her eyebrows, agreeing with all his thoughts.

"I still think I'm like Byron," Jack said, suddenly moody. "He had this thunderstorm inside him, see? He was probably an Aries like me."

Belle glanced up at the beams on the whitewashed ceiling. She took another mouthful of the cake.

"Was he?" she said.

"Was he what?"

"An Aries like you?"

"That depends when he was born," Jack said patiently.

Belle blinked once.

"Oh, right." He squinted into his memory, then gave up and riffled through the notes in his bag. "Huh. Twenty-second of January was his birthday, so no, he was an Aquarius. That's all right, though. I was an Aquarius just two lives back."

"You and your past lives," said Belle. "Maybe Byron had an aura like yours."

"You and your auras," said Jack.

"I could read his aura for you if you want. Have you got a picture?"

"You can read auras from pictures?"

Belle shrugged. "Dunno. Never tried."

Jack poured himself some more tea. Everything on the table was white: cake plate, teacups, salt and pepper shakers. The teapot itself, also white, had a sort of attitude about it: tall and fancy, its handle like a hand on a hip, spout curving up and over like a wave, like it was dead keen to get into your cup.

"I'm going to study it at university, you know," Jack said. "Astrology. Did I tell you that? I was thinking, it's what I feel passionate about, so I should. You think you'll study auras?"

"Nope," said Belle. "Auras is a load of bollocks."

Jack was so shocked he nearly dropped the teapot. Belle reached out a hand to save it.

In the attic flat, the rain was thickening against the window, forming curls like drying sheets of bark. Only, the rain's curls were elegant and glassy, turning and turning into themselves until they slid out of the curl and slipped away.

Madeleine herself turned from the window. ISAAC NEWTON was still closed on her lap, and she was looking at the gap between the couch cushions. A thick line of crumbs. The TV quiz show filled the room with questions. A washing machine droned somewhere in the building, blending with the full noise of the rain, and the sporadic buzz of the sewing machine. Her mother shouted answers, and after each shout, when the correct answer was given, there was Holly's thoughtful "Really?" or "Aah, should've known," or just "Tch."

Between the pages of the *ISAAC NEWTON* book was an envelope. Madeleine had stuck it in there earlier, at a random page, and now she ran her fingers along its edge.

She thought: *Who did I used to be?*

Before I was a girl in a rainy flat in Cambridge — a girl who reads books filled with facts, facts that slide around her head like beans in a pot — who was I?

She knew who she'd been, but it felt like a dream. She'd been a girl who ran so fast, even down a hallway to her bedroom, she'd had to skid on her heels to stop. She'd talked like the rainfall. She'd loved the smells of things — cinnamon, coconut, lime; there'd been a special compartment in her luggage for her scented candles. She'd loved loud music, and dancing, and if she was that girl right now, she'd be with her friends and they'd lose their minds, open the window, throw the sewing machine out into the rain. Just to watch it fall four floors to the ground.

She would not be sitting here, watching the leak that spidered down the wall, the strange black splotches of mould slowly expanding. She'd get a sledgehammer and knock a hole in that wall. She'd climb through the window, abseil down the wall, kick aside the pieces of broken sewing machine.

Where was she now, the girl with the thunderstorm heart?

"Yeah," said Belle. "It's bollocks. Did you know that if two aura readers look at someone else's aura, they just about *never* see the same thing? I mean, what does *that* tell you about the scientificness of it?"

Jack gazed at his friend. He shook his head slowly. He said, "I honestly have no idea what to say." He said, "If this is — if you are — well, why have you bloody been talking about auras for the last five bloody years, then?"

"Oh, well, *I* can read them," Belle said affably. "Just, nobody else can, see? So the science of it is total bollocks, which means, why would I waste time studying it, see? But I can read them. Don't worry about that."

Jack's mouth split into its biggest smile.

"Yours is looking sort of peach-coloured at the moment," Belle added. "You're feeling tranquil and dreamy but sort of antsy too."

The smile broke suddenly: He'd had a thought.

"You know what I just realised? You never read Madeleine's aura," he said. "Why's that?"

The waitress took the empty cake plate and put down a glass in its place, bill curled inside.

"We never asked for the bill," said Belle.

"We're closing now."

"Why not?" Jack repeated. "You're always reading mine, and everyone else's, and you're probably about to tell me that the waitress's aura's gone crusty or something. But I've never heard you say a thing about Madeleine's."

"Ah," Belle shrugged. "Madeleine wears too many colours. Clothes have an aura of their own, see, and they interfere."

"Is that a fact?" Jack took his wallet and paid the bill. He looked around dreamily.

"You know what she's like?" he said. "Madeleine, I mean. I've been thinking she's like someone from a music video. You know in music videos, the way they'll do fast cuts between shots? Like a wide shot of the band playing in a hayloft, then a kid in a school bus, then someone rolling a pen between their hands — that kind of thing. And they keep repeating the same shots in a loop. And they've got this one shot — say, the drummer's a girl and she's mostly in shadows, but there's one shot of her looking down and just starting to laugh, with her eyes behind her hair, and then they cut away, before she gets to the full laugh. And each time you see it, you get this feeling like *that* shot, *that's* the real sort of chorus to the song. That's the tantalising bit, and you watch harder and harder, wanting more, and you get the feeling she's really pretty, but you never see her face or hear her laugh. That's what Madeleine is like."

Belle looked away from the table.

"Madeleine's always laughing," she said. "And we see her face all the time. Don't pay yet. I haven't finished my tea."

That morning, Madeleine had gone to retrieve the note she'd left in the parking meter. She'd been thinking how crazy it was, that she'd put her heart on the street for anyone to find. Sure, it was well hidden, but *what if somebody who knew her had found it?*

For a smart person, she'd thought, *I can be kind of stupid.*

She'd cycled fast, wondering at what point your stupidity undermined your smartness.

There'd been a car parked alongside the meter. The car had had a smug look about it. *The parking meter's out of service*, it had seemed to say, *didn't have to pay, did I?* Or maybe it had been a defensive look. *I WOULD have paid but I couldn't — the parking meter's out of service, see?*

Her letter had been gone.

An envelope had been in its place.

A long, thin envelope marked with a red *M.T.*

Inside the envelope there had been two folded papers. One had been her own letter; the other had said this:

Dear M.T.,

I think you meant this to go to a Parking Meter, but it's come out here in Cello. It seemed like the best thing was to send it back to you, so here it is.

Now, your letter made as much sense to me as a fireworks display in a horse trailer but, setting that aside, I think you must be in the World.

It was those places you mentioned — Paris, Prague, and so on — they jarred my memory, and then I got it. We talked about them in World Studies. I only took the introductory course — the compulsory one — not the elective. (It's been over 300 years since we last had contact with the World, so it seemed kind of a waste to study more.) (No offense.)

Anyway, I guess this means there's a crack in the Bonfire High schoolyard. The crack must be right where my friend Cody put his sculpture, so your letter came through and got caught in the sculpture. Not sure of the science, to be honest.

We're supposed to report any suspected cracks to the authorities, so they can close them up right away — that's some kind of strict law or something. I won't, though, 'cause I don't see how it's doing any harm, and I don't like the idea, to be honest. If there's a way to get a message through or across, well, it seems all wrong to me to shut that down.

But listen, I'm heading out in a few days — on a trip to the Magical North — so if any more of your letters come through, I won't be here to send them back to you.

Before I go, can I say a couple of things? First off, in relation to the foods you eat. What's wrong with beans? Maybe spice them up with some garlic or thyme leaves. You could add chorizo sausage, or wood-smoked bacon.

As for tarts and cupcakes, etc., I guess if you had fine baking once, and now it's gone, that's got to be tough. So, I'm sorry to hear about that.

The other thing — my mother's excited about you. She's always had an interest in the World. It was her best subject, she says, when she was at school. She particularly wants me to ask if you've had any more trouble with republicans. Oliver Cromwell was the name, she recalls, but she says he'd be long dead by now.

Anyhow, you take care, and if you want to reply and answer my mother's question — in the next three days, if that's okay — you'd make her day.

Yours faithfully,
Elliot Baranski

Madeleine ran her hand along the side of the envelope. She thought about the poet Lord Byron.

She knew he was born George Gordon Byron in 1788, and that his father married his mother for her money, then stole it, spent it, and gambled it. When Byron was still a baby, his parents unsurprisingly split up.

She knew that when Byron was small, his father, who lived around the corner at this point, invited him to stay. The next day, he returned the little boy. "That's enough," he said, "I want no more of him."

She knew that his mother was frantic and vicious.

That he was born with a twisted foot, a limp, and was always being bound up in metal contraptions, supposedly to untwist the foot, but they twisted him pale with pain.

She knew that he wrote poetry, and that this was his way — his own way, his different way — of getting the message across. Of clearing a path through it all, clearing the cows from the tracks.

Madeleine looked at the edge of the envelope again.

The stranger who found her letter, the one who called himself Elliot Baranski — *If there's a way to get a message through or across*, he had written, *well, it seems all wrong to me to shut that down.*

Right in the middle of this strange letter, there it was.

"Traditionally," said the quiz show, cutting into her thoughts, "what is the colour of royalty?"

"Orange!" cried Madeleine's mother.

"Purple," said the TV contestant. "Or royal blue."

"Tch."

Madeleine looked up.

"Can we change the channel?" she said.

Her mother laughed. So did Madeleine.

She thought of Lord Byron running through his life.

Byron didn't climb like Charles Babbage, frowning back down at the rest of the world. Byron ran helter-skelter, always looking up at trees and skies. If he'd had a skateboard, he'd have skated fast down hills towards highways.

Only, his life was riddled with potholes, and he kept falling. Falling and falling into potholes of love — everywhere Byron turned there was a beautiful woman, or a man with liquid eyes, and his heart thudded madly for them all. For baker's wives, chorus girls, countesses, and cousins.

She also knew this about Byron: that he felt the loss of love so hard he turned white and lost consciousness.

The door to the tea room opened again and another group of rain-huddled tourists rushed inside.

The waitress was out the back.

"You know the kid in that show, *Two and a Half Men*?" said Jack. "Guess how much he gets paid for every episode."

"Can't."

"A *quarter* of a million dollars," said Jack. "A *quarter*. Of a million."

"Why do you keep saying '*quarter*' like that?" Belle said. "Like that's the important bit. A quarter's not that big of an amount, you know. It's not like a *half*, or a *full*, *total* million."

"It's a lot but, eh? Considering it's not even that good of a show."

"What is that in pounds?"

She had to raise her voice. The newcomers were talking loudly. They were exclaiming about everything — roof beams, shelf unit, copper teakettle. Everything was darling; it was all exactly right.

"I'm going to get the scones with clotted cream!" cried one of the women, and the others overlapped her with agreement, their voices clotted with enthusiasm. They passed the phrase back and forth, as if trying out a new language.

Jack and Belle widened eyes at each other.

"I don't know," Jack said. "It's changing all the time, isn't it? The exchange rate. It's a lot, but. That's my point."

"Your emphasis was wrong," Belle reflected. "A *quarter* of a million. So what?"

"Let's change the channel," Madeleine said again. "Can we? For my sake. I just want something else."

"Sake," said Holly. "That's a Japanese drink."

"You pronounce it sah-key." Madeleine looked for the remote.

"You eat it with sushi and sashimi," said her mother. She rubbed her arm. "This arm keeps going numb. What's that about? Too much TV?"

"You don't eat it. You drink it." They both laughed, and Madeleine took the remote from under a swatch on her mother's sewing table. She changed the channel.

"Your arm went numb the other day too," Madeleine said. "And you keep getting headaches and getting — confused." She pointed the remote at the TV.

Holly was quiet, watching the stations change. "What's this, then?" she said after a moment.

"It's that Australian soap. *Neighbours.*"

"Australia," her mother repeated uncertainly.

Madeleine laughed, and her mother did too.

"We went there once," Madeleine said. "To Sydney. Remember, we saw the opera house? We came into the harbour on a cruise ship and they had fireworks. And Dad really liked Vegemite."

"Vegemite?" Once again, they laughed.

"It's like Marmite. Nobody likes Vegemite except Australians who grew up with it," Madeleine explained. "It's disgusting. But Dad decided it was perfect with single malt whisky. He kept putting it on crackers, and making people try a sip of Balvenie, then a Vegemite cracker, and saying, 'Isn't it sublime?' Remember?"

The waitress reappeared.

"Oh, I'm sorry," she said to the table of tourists. "We're closed now."

"Why does *she* not have any money?" said Belle. "How can you go from being as rich as all that to having nothing? Why's she so poor?"

Jack was standing up. "You mean Madeleine? Her parents separated."

"But that doesn't mean the wife ends up with nothing," Belle persisted. "The wife's supposed to take the husband for everything he's got, and that." She tried the teapot again, but it was empty, so she stood too.

The tourists' faces were wide with disappointment. "It doesn't *say* you're closed," they argued with the waitress, and she repeated, "Sorry, but we are."

Jack was pushing open the door.

Belle was behind him, and she took a step into the rain, but then she turned and stepped back in.

She glared at the waitress.

"Ah, let them have their scones with clotted cream!" she snarled, and the room snapped into stillness as she pushed back out into the cold.

Madeleine was standing now. She was reaching for her jacket.

"I think I'll go out for a bit."

"But it's raining!" Her mother laughed and held her right arm in the air. "Can you see that?"

"See what?"

"My leg."

"That's not your leg, it's your arm."

Holly nodded and turned back to the television.

There was an ad for flights to New York.

"New York," said Holly. "Now *that's* the Big Apple."

Madeleine had opened the door. She smiled at her mother.

"It is," she agreed.

"Is it a crunchy one? An apple with a crunch?"

Madeleine laughed. She was standing in the open door and words were stepping out from behind her laughter. "You need to go," she said, and the words surprised her as she said them. She thought they would stay at this calm, even level, at the level of the laughter, but they didn't. They surged up into a terrible kind of shriek: "You need to go *and see a doctor!*" and she slammed the door behind her.

The slam ate the last half hour of laughter.

Bonfire, The Farms, Kingdom of Cello

2.

*T*hursdays, six P.M., the Bonfire Antelopes trained on the high-school deftball field. Jimmy Hawthorn was the coach, and today he'd invited his neighbor, Isabella Tamborlaine, to come along and watch.

Deftball was invented in the town of Clark, the Farms. Clark's primary crop is a root vegetable called deft, greenish in color, a little like a turnip. Unlike a turnip, however, when defts reach full maturity — and fields of them do at the same time — they shoot themselves out of the ground, curving high into the air. The catch is that you have to catch them. Hundreds of little defts flying into the air — and if they fall back to the ground, they will shatter or bruise.

These days machines catch the falling vegetables, but traditionally, deft farmers arranged for teams of contract workers to run about with outstretched hands. Workers competed to catch the most, leaping to intercept defts.

The game of deftball is loosely based on traditional deft harvesting. The playing field is ridged and furrowed; two teams, each holding small green balls, line up along the edge. When the starting gun cracks, each player tosses his or her ball into the air, attempting to curve it as far as possible ahead of the starting line. The idea is to race across the field, leaping over furrows, tossing the ball as soon as it is caught, and, whenever possible, intercepting the opposing team's balls. Once you reach the end you turn and run back. Players on the sidelines, meanwhile, interject more balls into the mix. The scoring system is complex, and it's largely a game about strategy, speed, peripheral vision, and the collection of small green balls.

Although it is played throughout Cello, deftball is not as popular in the eastern province of Jagged Edge. In fact, it is often mocked there. Hence, Isabella Tamborlaine, a Jagged-Edgian who had arrived in Bonfire just a year before, had never seen the game.

Now she watched the players stretching, and leaning into conversations, or sprinting up and down the furrowed field. She knew most of them from the school — a few were in her classes. There was Gabe Epstein, tall as a basketball hoop; Nikki Smitt, one of those girls who is so athletically self-assured they don't seem to notice that they're also beautiful; and, across the field, Elliot Baranski.

Jimmy was snapping pictures of the kids warming up. His hobby — apart from deftball coaching — was portrait photography. He noticed Isabella, dropped the camera so it fell loose on its strap around his neck, and joined her on the sideline.

"I can see why people say Elliot Baranski's the best player," Isabella said, watching the precision with which Elliot threw the ball.

Jimmy nodded and looked sideways at Isabella. She was tall and thin, eyes like fern fronds. She always wore a green pendant around her neck.

"You know something?" Isabella continued. "I feel guilty whenever I see Elliot. The only reason I'm here — the only reason I got this teaching post, I mean — is because the teacher, Mischka Tegan, went missing. And she went missing along with Elliot's father on the night that Elliot's uncle was killed. So, do you see what I mean? It's like Elliot's loss led to my gain. You could turn that around. My *gain* led to Elliot's *loss*. I have this strange algebraic sense of backward causation."

Jimmy watched his players awhile. Then he breathed in deeply.

"Well," he said, "I can see how you could think that but it makes no sense at all."

Isabella smiled, then grew serious again. "I know the official word is that the missing two were taken by a Purple, but the teachers in the staff room have a different story. They say the Baranski brothers were wild their whole lives. That Jon and Abel had grown close to Mischka in the months before it happened. Something about drinking together at the Toadstool Pub every other night? They tell me Abel ran away with Mischka. Do you think that's what happened? Or do you think they were really taken by a Purple?"

Again Jimmy was silent.

Eventually, he spoke: "It was Elliot that found his uncle, you know."

Isabella turned, her hand on that green pendant, and looked at Jimmy's face. In his low, slow voice, he told her that Elliot used to jog along Acres Road every morning, early. One morning, he'd seen blood on the grass. Followed its line with his eyes, thinking a dead deer. Found the savaged body of his uncle. His father's truck nearby, both doors open, engine running, his father gone.

Now Isabella nodded, understanding Jimmy's message: *What matters here is Elliot. The aftermath, his loss. Not causation, not the details.*

Elliot himself was approaching now, from across the field. He and Nikki Smitt carried a basket of deftballs between them.

They stopped nearby, dropped the basket on the ground, and both reached in.

"You planning on doing any coaching tonight?" Nikki called to Jimmy.

He laughed.

"I'll take the blame," said Isabella, then she joked, "But listen, Nikki, do you and Elliot want to demonstrate those pitches for my calculus class next week? We'll calculate the angle of the curves."

Elliot turned, his hand in the air. "I'll be gone again next week," he said.

Nikki, beside him, watched his face.

"Heading out again," Elliot explained. "Soon as the finals are over."

Isabella glanced at Jimmy, and the thoughts ran through the air between them: *But if it really was a Purple, then your father is dead. But if he ran away with that teacher, does he want — or deserve — to be found?*

They said nothing.

Elliot and Nikki turned back to their training. They crouched and threw, crouched and threw, until the damp, dusk sky was alive with small green balls.

3.

*T*he following day, Elliot was at the Bonfire Library, doing some last-minute research.

He sat at a desk near the card catalogues, writing in a spiral-bound notebook. Books and papers rose and fanned around him. He wrote fast, making lists of bullet points, linking these with arrows, sometimes underlining three or four times. *Treat dragon burns with fish oil or the skin of a ripe pear*, he wrote. *GET A WHISTLE for use in werewolf territory.* He read another paragraph and added *????* to his note about the whistle. *Can PROVOKE werewolves if pitch too high — try stamping boots in constant rhythm.*

Large windows lined the east wall of the library, and afternoon sun soared through the glass. Elliot's heel bounced on the carpet. He reached for a magazine, took notes on provincial pastimes in the Magical North in case that might somehow be useful. He scribbled about bear wrangling, snow attire, and the entrance fee to the Lake of Spells. Today's *Cellian Herald* was trapped beneath some books, and he pulled it toward him, catching the toppling pile before it fell. He studied the front-page headline.

RISING HOSTILITY, it said, and beneath that, in low bold caps: CELLO'S ROYAL DILEMMA.

Elliot paused. Hostility was something he was hazy about. It had never affected Bonfire directly, and never been an issue on the other journeys he'd taken this last year. In the Magical North, however, he was actually more likely to come across a gang of Wandering Hostiles than a dragon or a werewolf. What did you do, did you stamp, blow whistles, play dead, or look them squarely in the eye?

He smiled faintly. Politics was something that he'd always found tedious or pointless, so he'd never paid much attention. He guessed he should at least try to understand the issues now.

Page four of the *Herald* gave a brief survey of the history of Hostility in Cello, explaining the truce that had been reached, almost a thousand years before, between agitators, whose goal was democracy, and Royalists. In recent years, the report said, doubts about the current Royal Family, and particularly about the competence of the King, had sent cracks and fissures running through the truce.

An inset on page 5 defined the relevant terms. That was probably just to fill in space, as these were well known, even to Elliot, but he read them anyway:

> **Registered Hostile: A town (or city, village, etc.) that has decided to opt out of rule by Cello's Royal Family. Once it has registered as Hostile, the town (and its inhabitants) are immediately considered Hostile. The level of Hostility (mild, moderate, serious, etc.) is noted, at which point elaborate treaties come into play, enabling self-governance on a sliding scale. In exchange, the Hostiles forego Royal privileges. This system is the cornerstone of the truce.**

Below this was a definition of "Random Hostile." Elliot thought of his friend Shelby and half smiled. Some people might describe her as randomly hostile on account of her tendency to randomly blow things up. Dead trees, anthills, watermelons, tractors she was tired of looking at.

He read the definition.

Random Hostile: A town (city, village, etc.) that declares itself to be hostile toward royalty *without* taking any formal steps vis-à-vis the Register. This is a very recent practice, and is apparently related to animosity directed specifically toward the current Royal Family. It is commonly achieved by spray-painting the letter *H*, encircled with daggers, onto all official town signs. Security Forces and Register Administrators remain uncertain as to how to respond to the practice. To date, rather than treating such acts as treasonous, the Royal Family has either turned a blind eye or entered the relevant town into the Register at the level of Moderate Hostility. Again, to date, there have been no reports of militant activity from any Random Hostile.

Finally, Elliot read the definition of Wandering Hostiles. Those were the ones that really mattered to him, since they were the serious problem up north.

Wandering Hostiles: Loosely connected groups whose members openly defy the truce system. Their objective is the complete overthrow of the Royal Family. They are responsible for clandestine, often opportunistic, acts of violence throughout the Kingdom, for which they routinely claim responsibility, inviting the Royal Family to step down in exchange for cessation of hostilities. While these groups have come and gone for as long as the truce system itself, in recent

years numbers have swelled considerably, particularly in the Magical North. Travelers in that region should be extremely wary of Wandering Hostiles.

Elliot sat back in his chair for a moment, and allowed himself to visualize a long line of obstacles. There were dragons, werewolves, bears, and Wandering Hostiles; he saw himself dodging all of these, or vaulting them like furrows on a deftball field. He saw the Lake of Spells in a shimmering distance, saw himself reach it, and set up camp. He saw himself trap a Locator Spell. Here, his imaginings faltered a little. A circle of doubt, the size of a coin, opened in the center of his chest. But he reached his hand out, and placed it on the cool, soft cover of the book that had central position on the desk: *Spell Fishing: Tips and Techniques for Netting the Spell You Desire.* The librarian had let him have it on extended loan. Sure, that phrase, "Spell You Desire," was a little abstract, a little reminiscent of romance columns in magazines — but the book's bindings were solid. And it had a ten-page bibliography.

He trusted it. He shaded in the circle of doubt, and moved on with his imaginings.

Saw the Locator Spell, damp and filmy on the palm of his hand. Saw it guiding him across the Kingdom to a Purple cavern somewhere — where would it be? On the rim of the Inland Sea in Olde Quaint? In a crag in Nature Strip?

It could be anywhere. The point was, he'd break his way into that cavern. He'd skirt the Purples, shine his flashlight deep into the darkness. There'd be a hoarse call, a whisper maybe, the sound of quiet breathing, something anyway — and he'd take a dagger, cut down his father from the Purple trap, untangle him, get him out of there. Bring him home.

Something rose from the pit of Elliot's stomach, ran down his legs to the soles of his feet, clouded his eyes.

He straightened his shoulders against that surge of emotion, looked toward the sunlight — and saw his friends.

Cody, Gabe, Nikki, Shelby, and Kala were all lined up along the window, foreheads to the glass, looking in at him. They must have been walking along Aubin Street and spotted him here.

They were dark shadows out there, but he could see enough of their faces to know they all had the same expression. It was smiling, like glad to see him, and half laughing too — at themselves, for lining up in that way. At the same time their eyes were sad, because they knew he would be leaving again soon.

Nikki and Gabe tipped their chins a little. They meant Elliot should come out and race with them. Their favorite thing was street racing on motor scooters. The Sheriff was not as keen on this as they were.

Shelby clapped her hands together and let her fingers fly backward, away from one another. She meant she wanted to go blow something up on a paddock with Elliot.

Meanwhile, Kala and Cody were giving Elliot their fierce looks, the ones that meant he should quit the research and come and have a coffee with them.

Elliot laughed at them all, and next thing they'd opened the door to the library and were heading inside.

They pulled up chairs or sat on nearby desks, turned over his books, flicked the back of his head.

"What do you do if you come across a Wandering Hostile?" Elliot said.

"Run," said Gabe. The others nodded.

"Run fast," Nikki amended.

"Don't," said Kala. "*Don't* come across any."

"Helpful," Elliot murmured.

Cody took the *Herald* out of Elliot's hands, and began to leaf through the pages.

"Here it is," he said, and he must have just been telling the others about this, because they leaned in right away, saying, "Where?"

It was on page 47, in tiny print, under the heading, "Sporting Events."

Provincial Deftball Championship:
Bonfire Antelopes vs. Horatio Muttonbirds,
Bonfire Oval, Bonfire, the Farms, Saturday, 2 P.M.

"In the *Herald*," said Kala. "You've hit the big time."

"Sort of makes me wonder why you guys are not training right now," Cody mused. "Day before the game. Isn't that what people do?"

Elliot, Gabe, and Nikki, who were all on the team, shrugged as one.

"Can't get any better than we are," said Gabe.

Shelby chewed a fingernail. "And you leave the day after the game, Elliot?"

Elliot nodded.

"Let one of us come with you this time," she suggested.

"Let *all* of us come with you," Nikki said. "You didn't let us come on your other trips, but you can't do Wandering Hostiles on your own."

There was a moment then, when they were all talking at once, about what they would pack, and how much money they had in their savings accounts, and how they'd always wanted to see the Lake of Spells or take on a werewolf — a moment when, behind their talk, their lives together seemed to move between their eyes. All the things they'd shared — fruit picking right across the Farms; towing one another downriver behind trucks; the year that Nikki's farm did so well they'd all worked day and night, only turning the tractors off for an oil change; the year the dewbirds were swooping and they'd walked everywhere as a group, paper bags on their heads, faces drawn on the backs by Cody to scare the birds away.

Elliot shook his head.

"None of your farms can do without you," he said.

"Mine can," said Kala. "I'll make my sisters cut down on ballet classes and start working on the farm instead."

"My family's farm's gone to hell anyway," Shelby said.

Cody was still turning pages in the newspaper.

"Forget Wandering Hostiles," he said. "Watch out for the Princess Sisters, Elliot. They're still on tour." He was scanning a page as he spoke, a grin forming around his words. "Listen to their column," and he put on a Princess voice and began to read:

Well, trample me underfoot and call me a lyrebird, this tour is *the bomb!*

Dearest, sweetest, most collateral inhabitants of this! our fine and beauteous Kingdom of Cello! — Hello!!!

And we hope you will forgive the rather "informal" opening to this! our fifth, or what is it, seventh? [*Editor's note: ninth*] column for that sweet bean of a newspaper, the *Herald*. It's just that we feel so close to you all now! Having spent so much time with your shy gazes upon us, it's just as if *you,* our totally munificent subjects, are now our friends!!

Oh, listen, about the opening line? We should explain our use of GC slang. For those who have not spent time in Golden Coast, as we have these past few days, when you say that something is *the bomb!* you mean that it *goes off!* [*Editor's note: "goes off" is itself GC slang for a "fun" event. The Princess Sisters seem to be saying they are enjoying the tour.*]

As for Golden Coast, it is a sparklewhirl of starshine! A dazzlespin of haywire! We were unplussed! yesplugged! *clothespegged!*

Writing now from the Emerald Carriage, Ko and I (for it is I, Princess Jupiter, who writes this passage) — are thrown back and forth, our glasses of bubbling teakwater spilling so — ah! there goes a drip smudging the paper! — can you see it?! [*Editor's note: For obvious reasons, you cannot.*] It behooves me to say that Queen Lyra (our mother) suggested we *not* partake of bubbling teakwater —

but luckily we foreswore! (is that the word?) and we partook, and partook, and still partake!! Where were we? Yes! Getting flung from side to side as the carriage takes tight corners! Thus too as we try to decide on our favorite part of Golden Coast, we are flung from side to side inside our minds!! Because we can't decide! The whole place is the livin' circumcision!! [*Editor's note: The Princesses here seem to have misunderstood a GC phrase that is generally used to connote a highly unpleasant experience.*]

We have swum with dolphins, and gasped at cliffbells. We have attended movie premieres, and I (still Jupiter) was honored to do a guest spot at the Dkveira Awards. Of course, we are already close buds with the movie-star likes of Bram Rickstein and Cynt Latte, and it was swanning to catch up with them again.

To put it bluntly, Golden Coast is naught but surprises — none more startling, of course, than the Swamp. Pray tell, by the peeling bark of the long-snouted pug, what is that Swamp *doing* there?! It is naught but dangerous crea-tures and patches of slime that expand (we are told) if they sense you nearby! Aiming to slip into your sneakers and creep up your legs! (Ew.) We only flew *over* the Swamp in the Emerald Helicopter, rather than visiting it, but even so we almost collided with one of the hovering Hideums!

It is our humble declaration that the entire Swamp should be *banished* forthwith from this, our fine and beauteous Kingdom! We intend to take the matter up with King Cetus (known to us as "Dad") the moment he returns from his royal botanical expedition to the Cranes. [*Editor's note: We have been informed that the King is actually studying the flora of the Creens at the moment: islands not far west of the Cranes.*]

. . . Just had to pause for a visit to the city of Pearl, where Ko admired the famous shadow effect (while I rested in the carriage). Due to a quirk in the topography, shadows *remain* for up to an hour after the person or object that made them has gone! Ko's own shadow is no doubt still there, in various places, as we write! She says it's not quite so exciting as she thought it would be as there's often just a total mess of overlapping shadows, and it just looks like someone's spilled a whole lot of buckets full of water. Never mind.

However, Ko was also able to make an announcement in Pearl, and I will make it again now!

For the remainder of our Tour, sweet and noble subjects, we are going to be on the lookout for certain young people! That's right! You heard it here first! [*Editor's note: Presumably, unless you already heard it in Pearl, from Princess Ko.*]

You see, we have been thinking about how splendid the young people are, whom we've met on tour, and we thought: Why not select *three* to form a sort of elite royal youth alliance (only with capitals; so, you know: *R*oyal

*Y*outh *A*lliance)! It will meet with us regularly, this Alliance, and share thoughts on Issues affecting Young People in our Kingdom today. (If we've already visited your town, or we're missing it altogether, don't despair. Simply write a letter explaining what *you* can offer the Alliance, and why *you* best represent your particular province. You might be in luck.)

Ah, long column, long day. We are both somewhat fatigued as we roll past the waving folk of Dreevill — there they go! . . . OK, gone . . . and we miss our sweet parents (known to *you* as King and Queen) and our gorgeous brothers (Prince Chyba and little Prince Tippett), and I feel the need to stretch out this final paragraph with nothing but a series of *zzzzzzzzzzzzzzzzzzzzzzzzz*!

(good night!)

By the time Cody had reached the end of the column, the five were laughing so hard that the librarian approached with a frown.

"Oh, you're reading the Princess Sisters' column," she said, her frown transforming to a smile. "Isn't it a hoot?" and she laughed too.

Cody pulled the page out of the newspaper, made a paper hat from it, and stuck it on Elliot's head.

4

S eems like tambourines are clashing and jangling, but they're not; it's just the atmosphere.

It's the next day, and the morning of the deftball finals. The sky is high with summer blue, and the Town Square is lined with trestle tables. These are loaded with hats, scarves, T-shirts, streamers, noise-makers, and huge foam hands (fingers and thumbs in various states of celebration), all in the Bonfire Antelopes blue and gold.

The pyramid of pumpkins is gone, and in its place is a fiberglass antelope, painted in blue and gold stripes and mounted on a stand. Kids are climbing on the antelope or tossing deftballs high across its head. A couple of very small kids carry a crateload of tomatoes in the direction of the grocery store. They slow down, watching the flying deftballs. With a glance at each other, they dump the crate, take a tomato each, and fling these into the air. The idea catches on: Tomatoes fill the air.

Meanwhile, all over the square, little girls are searching under tables and in coffee mugs, and standing on their toes to check window ledges. Someone up north has predicted that the Butterfly Child will arrive in the province of the Farms today, and the little girls of Bonfire are determined that they'll find her if she's here. Some of these girls have pinned chiffon butterfly wings to the back of their denim overalls.

Elliot and his mother are having breakfast at the Bakery. People are calling, "Good luck!" to Elliot, and "We're counting on you, buddy," or "Knock 'em dead." Others shout, "How you doin', Petra?" and "Proud of your boy?" to his mother. And still others stop right by the table to exclaim, "Well, aren't you two a sight for sore eyes! Look how tall you've got, Elliot!!" because people who moved away from town in the last year — trying to find work, their own crops having failed — have come home today to watch the finals.

Mostly Elliot and Petra are just eating and calling back, "Thanks!" or "Fine, how's yourself?" or "Well, if it isn't Sarah-Jane Marshall?! And you've gone and got your teeth fixed!"

Elliot's friends wander into the square in a group and cross to his table. Gabe and Nikki, already dressed in their blue-and-gold uniforms, lean against the table, but their eyes have the edge and self-consciousness of star players on the big day.

Shelby holds up her arm to show Elliot and his mother the antelope that now adorns her cast.

"Cody did it." She points sideways at Cody. "He wants to do a series on casts, so we've all got to break our bones for him."

Cody nods. "I'd appreciate that." His face is painted blue and gold, and he's inked tiny antelopes up and down the bare skin of his arms.

Petra Baranski takes a mouthful of coffee, puts it down, and scolds, "You want to give yourself ink poisoning, Cody?"

"Look at the little guys on his right arm," Gabe points out. "He had to do them with his left hand, see, but they're perfect. That's talent right there."

"So he's ambidextrous," says Petra. "Won't save his life."

"Ah," says Elliot. "Ink poisoning's a myth."

Kala has blue and gold beads braided through her hair. She's wearing a Bonfire Antelopes T-shirt with tie-dyed cotton pants. Now she takes two woven wristbands from her pocket, and hands them to Elliot.

"One's for luck today," she says, "and one's for luck on your journey tomorrow," and she kisses him fast on the cheek. The others watch this silently, and keep watching while Elliot slides both bands onto his left wrist and holds it up to show her.

Then they all talk about the referees who have arrived from Golden Coast, which is where the deftball headquarters are, and about whether GC game rules will apply, and how GC got ahold of deftball anyway, seeing as it started right here in the Farms. They talk about how Sadie Richmond pulled a hamstring last night, chasing down a goat, but she thinks she can still play today, and how they've heard that the opposing team, the Horatio Muttonbirds, maybe hit their peak too early in the season, and what a dumbass name the Horatio Muttonbirds is, and how that gives the Antelopes the edge right there: that name.

Nobody mentions tomorrow's journey again. They tell Elliot to get his butt into gear and finish breakfast, and that they'll see him up at the field.

They're gone, and it's quiet for a moment.

"You're going to break that Kala's heart," says Petra eventually. "Don't you see how her eyes catch fire when you smile at her?"

Elliot plays with the wristbands. "She's gorgeous," he says. "What do you want me to do?"

"Well." Petra scratches at her eyebrow. "I guess you're leaving tomorrow anyway. First train of the morning, right?"

Elliot nods.

"And you think you'll be gone for a few weeks?"

"Maybe longer. As long as it takes."

Petra grows still. She leans forward slightly. Her eyes are full of the things she wants to say, pages and pages of things she'd like to say.

Instead, she says, "Make this the last time."

Elliot also grows still, then, suddenly agitated, he looks behind his shoulder and pulls on his shoelace. He turns back, changing the subject.

"I checked the sculpture one more time this morning," he says. "Still nothing."

He means Cody's sculpture in the schoolyard. Since he replied to the letter from the Girl-in-the-World, he's looked once or twice for a reply, more for his mother than himself.

"I suppose we're not going to hear from her, then," sighs Petra. "Well, it's for the best. If the Sheriff found out there was a crack and we hadn't report —" but then her eyes startle at something just over Elliot's shoulder.

Elliot sees her startle, and his left arm swings into the air.

He catches it. He opens his hand and there's the tomato that was flying straight toward his mother's face.

"Those are some reflexes," says a voice. It's the Sheriff himself, approaching from behind and stopping beside Petra.

"That's my boy," agrees Petra, grinning up over her shoulder at Hector. "And that's why I'd bet the farm on the Antelopes winning today," and as she speaks, she rests her arm across the table. Her fingertips play with the tomato.

They all look across the square to the kid who threw it, slinking now into a store.

"I'll have a word with him," the Sheriff says.

Petra shrugs. "It was an accident. No harm done."

The Sheriff breathes in the atmosphere and also shrugs. "You still heading out tomorrow, Elliot? Heading to the Lake of Spells?"

"First train of the day."

"Swing by the station later. If you catch that Locator Spell you want, and it leads you back to the caverns, well, you'll need a couple of extra protective jackets. I've got some in the station."

Elliot nods. "Thanks, Hector."

"Just saw the team from Horatio," Hector says now. "Their coach is parked up on Main Street and they're all sort of hovering there. Tough-looking bunch."

Elliot smiles. "We can take them."

The Sheriff tips his hat. "See you at the game."

"See you there, Hector."

They both wait until he's shuffled across the square, then their eyes meet.

"That was close," says Petra. "I should be more careful what I say."

"Ah," says Elliot. "He didn't hear." He drinks the last of his coffee and puts the mug down, looking behind him at the clock tower. "I've got time to head home and check on that window catch that keeps stalling. Meet you at the field?"

Petra shakes her head at him.

"You've got less than an hour until the game; you know I can handle the window catch myself, and you *still* plan to go home now to check it? Elliot, you can't do *everything*, you know."

Elliot stands, half smiles.

Petra gives up. "See you at the game."

It's twenty minutes later and Elliot has found the glitch in the automatic window opener, and fixed the stalling window catch, and is crossing the fields toward his house.

There's a great big quietness out here in the fields, and there's something in his chest, an elbowing excitement. The championship is today, and he loves the game of deftball fiercely, the sprint of it, and the catching, always the catching, the feel of those smooth balls falling and falling in the palm of his hand. He holds a hand out now, and it happens, he catches the ball, closes his fingers tight, and then tosses it high again. He can't walk these fields without tossing that ball.

At the edge of his vision there's some patterns of light. He must have been fixing his gaze too tightly on the bolts and nuts of the window catch.

The elbowing in his chest gets harder; he's excited about the game, sure, but more about the journey tomorrow. The edges of him need that train, the clatter and vibration of that train, and how it pauses at stations, and the doors open and shut, then it moves on, and moves on again. There'll be swiftly changing weather, and shifting altitudes, and bridges crossing high over rivers and ravines. He'll be studying his maps and codebooks and his *Spell Fishing*. He'll look up now and then through the windows, and soon there'll be nothing but the blinding snow-white of the Magical North.

He blinks hard now, to clear that smudge of light from his vision; it's like a splinter of the northern snow-white is already catching at his eye.

He can see the farmhouse, and on the front porch, his rucksack, standing up against the wall. It got damp in the Swamp of the Golden

Coast — he only realized last night that mold was growing in its pockets. He washed it out and now it's drying in the sun. Later, after the game, he'll pack it.

That tightening of straps and buckles: He breathes it in deeply, the idea of that.

It's not his vision, he realizes now; it's something up there in the sky. A flash of sunlight on something, maybe an airplane or the eye of a bird. He looks up, sheltering his own eyes with his hands, but a ladybird bug lands on his wrist, and he lowers his arm, shakes it slightly to let the ladybird go, thinking how that's good luck. They'll win the game; he'll find what he needs on his journey.

His right foot almost lands on a caterpillar turning itself over in the grass.

He keeps walking, still tossing the ball into the blue. There's a flurry of moths over the gatepost there. There's that light in the sky that keeps catching his eye like sun on water.

At the sports field, there's nervous energy sparking through the crowds, throwing smiles and banter helter-skelter. The local farmers have set up stalls down the southern end, selling not just cold drinks and baked goods, but every kind of produce they can grow, and everything they can stitch or knock together. Olaf Minski has lined up jars of honey; Petra Baranski's selling quince, beans, peas, and recycled buttons and zips; the Epsteins have baskets of peaches and buckets of old clothes-pegs. There's cash boxes and coconut ice.

They've come from all over the Farms to see the game: They've sailed down the Chokeberry, and up the River of Dray; they've ridden on trains, coaches, and ferries. They're wearing straw hats and applying sunscreen, and someone picks up a jug of ice water and tips it right over his own head.

At one end of the field, Jimmy's taking photos of his Bonfire team while they warm up, lowering his camera now and then to call out advice. At the other, the team from Horatio is gathered close, talking fast. The crowd is mostly Bonfire supporters, and when they're not catching up with one another, they're staring at those Horatio players. Horatio's a lean factory town up in the north of the Farms, where they manufacture clothes, glass, toys, and polyurethane glue. The team members look tough: torn nails, bruised eyes, big shoulders.

The sky is even higher and clearer now, and people look up at it often. There's been five attacks of fifth-level Gray in this last year alone. Townsfolk who've been living elsewhere share stories of increasing Color attacks all over. A man pats the patch over his eye and says, "Gentian Violet, second level," and a woman says she nearly lost her leg to a malicious Green.

"Color attacks up, and crops down," somebody says mournfully, and "Isn't that the truth?" goes drifting through the crowd. There are stories of farms shutting down and banks moving in, and a woman says her sister, been growing carrots all her life, just got herself a certificate in Hygiene Management at the hospital. Not a whiff of interest in hygiene management before, excuse the pun, but what with the carrots turning up green and puny yet again, she couldn't make ends meet any longer.

A child draws an outline in the dust of a Butterfly Child, and someone spots it and says, "Now isn't that exactly what we need?"

There's a wistful sigh through the crowd, and "Imagine that," and "Wouldn't *that* be the answer?"

"I heard they already found her," someone says. "Up at Forks — late last night."

"Ah, it'd have been on the radio if they'd found her."

Then there's a clattering sound and everyone turns. It's the band tuning up — Kala's on the saxophone — and the soundtrack of the day shifts back to excitement once again.

It's like sun on water or on tinsel or coins.

Elliot's squinting up now to see what it is, that flash of light in the sky.

It's something falling. He thinks maybe a leaf, but he can't get the perspective. A bird maybe turning somersaults.

He keeps walking, keeps tossing the ball, his mind still making lists of the things he needs to pack.

Maybe it's a little touch of Silver, he thinks, but Silver's so rare these days. They only seem to get the bad Colors, not the good.

Sunlight on glass, he thinks, that's what it's like. On a glass jug, or a vase, or — and then he's running.

He knows what it is, and he's running. Time changes right away; it's been falling all this time, in that strange slow tumble, but now it's a lightning plummet.

It's beyond the fence, way over to the left, but the gate's to the right. The fence is too high to jump; he has to sidetrack to the gate and then around.

But he knows how long it takes a thing to fall. He knows exactly where and when that thing will land.

He's running and he's thinking, what a damn fool place for a Butterfly Child to manifest, in the sky, in the sky above a field! He's running and he senses, out of the corner of his eye, his own deftball landing in the grass. He's going to have to clamber over the fence, there's no time to sidetrack to the gate, and then run again, and even then he's going to miss it —

He can see it clearly now, falling — the glass jar, and a little tumble of color inside. That's her, that's the Butterfly Child, tumbling around in the tumbling jar.

He knows what he can catch and what he'll miss — and he's running like he never ran before, but this one, he knows he's going to miss.

At the edge of the sports field, there are a couple of kids on bikes riding in circles. They've pegged little squares of cardboard to the spokes of their wheels to make a high-speed rat-tat-tat noise.

The band's playing tunes now, and someone's slicing oranges and mangoes for the teams to eat at halftime. The school principal arrives and shows some of her students how she's painted her fingernails blue and gold.

Isabella Tamborlaine passes just behind Jimmy, and he stops, turns around, and she twirls her dress for him. It's blue and gold clouds, fading one into the other.

"Is that supposed to be ironic?" he says.

"Of course not," she says. "I got Clover to make it for me. I'm a deftball fanatic now that I know it's all calculus. Just be sure and win today, okay?"

There are picnic blankets on the grass, and the Twicklehams are weaving amongst them, handing out leaflets for Twickleham Electronics Repair.

They climb up to the bleachers, sit down, and hand another leaflet to the person beside them, saying, "Like to a dovecote in a gum boot, so are we with your picture-box repair," while little Derrin waves at her grade-school teacher — Miss Hattoway — who waves back and smiles an upside-down smile.

Then somebody shouts that they need tickets to be up in the bleachers, and the Twicklehams laugh, embarrassed, and stand. Derrin's face remains solemn as she makes her way back down the stairs. She pauses when she reaches the grass, and this time she's waving more vigorously, a wave and a grin that fly across the field to her friend, Corrie-Lynn.

Corrie-Lynn is with her mother, both of them leaning up against Petra Baranski's stall for a chat.

Petra shakes her head about her son. "He'll be here in time — he always is — but he sure knows how to cut it fine."

Alanna laughs. "Tell him I said thanks for getting the team into the finals," she says. "The Watermelon's jam-packed. Every room booked. I should be there right now making beds actually, but who needs that when there's this?"

"Well now, it was the whole team who made it to the finals, not just Elliot," says his mother automatically, but they both know that it was mostly Elliot.

He jumps the fence.

He can't jump the fence; it's too high.

But he does.

He's leaping, flying, sailing over that fence, and his foot catches the top ledge as he does, but his arm's out, his hand's out, his fingers are out, he can actually shift his body in the air, and he catches it.

The cold smooth surface of glass in the palm of his hand. He closes his fingers around it.

Time's strange.

There's enough time to think about how beautiful it is, to catch. How catching is the opposite of missing. How the opposite of missing feels so damn good. How this glass jar feels better in his hand even than the winning catch in deftball.

Then he hits the ground.

His head hits the dirt.

He sees it as he hits, the jar rolling slowly from his hand across the grass.

He's flat on his back, and there's the jar, stopped still now, and inside it he can see her, the tiny, tiny Butterfly Child. She's sitting up straight at the bottom, and she seems to be looking at him. She's holding a dress around her, such tiny hands, holding that dress, and the colors of it! Sapphire blue with deep russet spots, and she's holding this dress close around her, like wings.

Elliot lies with his head on the dirt, watching her through the glass. He's thinking about school. *You do one test, but then you've got to do another*, is what he's thinking.

There's always another test, and he can hear the voice of his little cousin, Corrie-Lynn. She's explaining something to him: *You've got to open the lid of the jar.*

She's saying, *You've got to do it right away or she'll suffocate.* Her voice is growing angry. *You've got to do it immediately!*

But there's some kind of a test he has to pass, and he realizes it's this: He has to replay in his mind the way he hit the ground just now. The way his head, in particular, hit the ground and flew back up and hit again. The·thump of his head, the percussion of that thump. So this might be a music exam.

There's the Butterfly Child in her jar, and she's not sitting straight-backed anymore. She's sliding downward, kind of slumping, her tiny little chin, and maybe those are her tiny eyelashes.

His own shoulder is slumping too, and his ankle, now and then, has a wildness about it. That's one thing, before he goes tomorrow, he's going to have to give that ankle a good stern talking-to.

There's a whole lot of Butterfly Children now, a whole lot of jars, with a whole lot of lids, rolling along the grass together, the lids of the jar are the lids of his eyes, and all of them closing tight.

The Mayor is at the field. Someone from the local paper is photographing her; she's standing on her seat, ignoring the photographer and shouting to the crowd. She's got a bottle of GC teakwater in her hand, and she's holding it up, promising she'll serve it at the after-party if they win.

"So I want to hear some *cheering!*" she cries. "I want you all to do some damage to your voice boxes!"

There's cheering and shouting at this, and a lot of chatter, as word gets passed around about what the Mayor has promised. This gets tangled with the rumor that those strangers in red T-shirts are actually deftball selectors from Tyler University in Jagged Edge!

But that turns out to be just a rumor.

However, then it emerges that they *are* selectors, but from the University of Dentwood, which is not such a bad school, really! Even if it is just in the Farms.

Officials in white are doing final measurements of the furrows on the field. Patterns of orange light are rippling across the scoreboards. The teams are moving into formation.

There's an expectant quieting, then almost at once, a new murmur moves through the crowd. *Where is Elliot Baranski?* says the murmur. And focus shifts from face to face; Elliot's mother, who is sitting in the front row of the stands now, shrugs slightly, then fixes her gaze back on the field. Jimmy is talking to his team, but his head keeps swinging away from them, to scan the crowd and the distance. The players themselves are not listening. Gabe and Nikki step away from him slightly, glancing at each other, then lifting their hands simultaneously to shade their eyes and squint around. The band is playing, but Kala, on saxophone, pauses, lowers her instrument, and twists around in her seat, eyes searching.

The Mayor is standing at the microphone, watching the scoreboard. She's supposed to officially begin the game. She looks across at Jimmy with a question on her face, and he makes a decision, strides out across the field himself.

He joins her at the microphone.

"Anybody here seen Elliot Baranski?" he says, and there's laughter at his informality, and because he's turned all their thoughts into words.

The team from Horatio is protesting, though, and so are the Horatio supporters, and an official blows a whistle hard.

"Welcome, everybody," says Jimmy into the microphone, stalling, "to the Bonfire Sports Field on this fine and beautiful day!"

There's an obliging cheer from the crowd, and the Horatio team fold their arms, hostile — and then there's the roar of a truck engine.

Everybody sees it, just over the crest of the hill: It's the Baranski truck.

The cheer fades into the engine roar itself, and there's a pause, and the truck door opens, and here's Elliot. They watch him get out.

Now he's crossing the empty field, heading for Jimmy and the microphone. He's walking kind of slowly and oddly, limping a little, his shoulder askew, and his chin's low, eyes down, like he's studying the ground. Two or three times he nearly trips on the furrows, and each time a shadow flashes across his face. Over at the stands, his mother climbs out of her seat and starts heading fast in his direction.

But he reaches Jimmy first. They speak quickly to each other, and Jimmy's face changes, confusion sliding down from his forehead to his chin. He leans his head close to Elliot, and nobody knows what they're saying, but they're both looking down. Elliot's hand is in the pocket of his shorts, and he's taking something out. Their heads bend low together, squinting.

Jimmy's head swings back up. The light's shining on his face again, and he's got a smile as curved and bright as a wedge of orange.

"Well, here he is, folks," he says into the microphone. "It's Elliot Baranski, and you know what *he* found? You know what *he's* got?" He pauses. *"He's got the Butterfly Child!"*

Some people catch it, the gleam of light and color in the palm of Elliot's hand before he slips her back into his pocket, safe, and Elliot's speaking to Jimmy again — "You think you could pop my shoulder back in?" is what he's saying — but those words are swept and blown away by the roar from the crowd, the whooping and laughing and applauding.

Practically everyone is crying.

Cambridge, England, The World

5.

"You could sew up the hole in your pocket."

Belle laughed at that. "Ah, who sews? You're funny."

"Well," said Jack. "I just think —" but then his knee hit a sandwich board outside a butcher shop. His arms flew up and curved down, body tilting forward from the waist.

"It's like you're worshipping those pork sausages," observed Belle.

Jack regained his balance, stepped around the sandwich board, and looked at her with frank hostility.

"Don't worry about it," said Belle. "I fancy a bit of pork sausage myself sometimes." She laughed hard, stretching the laugh into a chuckle that she carried with her for another block.

"You're sounding like a low-volume jackhammer," Jack told her eventually.

"Ah," Belle shrugged, and let her chuckle go.

Jack and Belle were walking along Mill Road, their eyes searching the pavement and the gutter as they walked, looking out for Belle's lost keys. It was a Thursday morning and they were heading to their ICT class. Or possibly to a Geography lesson. The computer guy who lived downstairs from Madeleine taught both, looping between subjects like a fish between the reeds.

"I don't need to sew up my pocket, because whenever I put something in it," Belle explained, "I keep my hand there as well. And hold on to it, see? So that stops it falling through the hole."

"Didn't stop your keys from falling," Jack pointed out.

"Now, isn't that the truth," Belle sighed, shaking her head at the strangeness of the universe.

They passed Mike's Bikes, a Subway, a dry cleaner's, a pharmacy.

"Sorry to have to tell you this," said Jack, "but your horoscope for today did *not say a word* about finding your lost keys."

"Did it say I'd have Frosted Flakes for breakfast? Did it say I'd hit my forehead on the whatsit thing with the shampoo on it when I picked up the soap in the shower? No, eh? Well, that's weird, isn't it, because I thought I did both those things." Belle's lips made a thoughtful pop-pop sound, like a child imitating a helicopter, and she murmured to herself: "Must have imagined it all."

"What your horoscope actually said" — Jack glanced up just in time to stop himself headbutting a telegraph pole — "was you should take a stand about an issue that's been troubling you, and stop biting your fingernails."

"I don't bite my fingernails."

"That's lucky, then, you've already done that bit."

They passed Spice Gate, Café Brazil, Piero's Hairdressing.

Jack stopped suddenly and crouched down in the gutter — but it was only a bottle lid.

"Everything glints," he said, and gave a philosophical sigh.

They walked in silence for a while.

"My own horoscope said I should dive right in and try the thing I've been hesitating about," Jack chatted. "And Madeleine's said that someone close to her is going to surprise her."

"Maybe her dad'll turn up," suggested Belle. "What race is she anyway, do you reckon? Her accent's so mixed up."

"That's cause she's lived everywhere in the world, and race hasn't got a bloody thing to do with a person's accent, you berk."

Belle shrugged, and looked up, rubbing her neck.

"My keys aren't anywhere, eh? Which is totally your fault for what you said about my horoscope. But listen, don't you sometimes think that Madeleine doesn't exist? Like, she's not real?"

Jack kept his eyes down, flicking them from the double yellow lines in the gutter to the wheels of bicycles that drooped against each other outside shops. It seemed to Jack that he was being very methodical about the search for Belle's keys, whereas Belle herself was not, and that this was why he kept tripping over things while Belle maintained perfect grace.

"'Madeleine doesn't exist,'" he repeated now. "What I sometimes think is, I sometimes think you haven't got a clue what you are talking about."

"Nah, it's just that you can't follow the complicated pathways of my brain. It's like a labyrinth, my brain, and as beautiful as a brain can get. What I mean is, there's too much going on with Madeleine. It's like when you get every paint colour and mix them up, you end up with not a proper colour at all. Madeleine's lived in so many bloody places and she wears so many different bloody colours. You know what I mean? So she's not a proper person anymore, she's just a mess. Like, she doesn't exist."

Jack stopped altogether and turned to Belle.

"You are being racist beyond all my abilities for measuring racism," he said. "You don't say someone who's mixed race is a *mess*, Belle. Do you actually want to know what race she is? She's part Iranian, part Somali, part Polish, part Irish, and a bit of Tibetan, and what she is, she's not a mess, she's beautiful."

"You can't be all those things," said Belle, flicking his words away. "See, that's my point. You can't. That's like five different people had to have sex to make her, which is not possible. Only two people can have sex."

"I'm not sure you've got the hang of genetics." Jack began to walk again. "Or of sex parties."

They were reaching the residential part of Mill Road now, the shops and restaurants disappearing. Neither of them was scanning for lost keys.

"Ah, you know what I mean," complained Belle. "I'm not saying her skin colour's like a messed-up paint tray, you tosser. She's got very nice skin and that, like honey or whatever, and when I said she was a mess I meant because there's so much going on with her past and that, and her clothes. But I'm very glad for people to come from everywhere and that. Although you've got to admit, she takes it too far. And actually, she takes it so far that sometimes I think maybe she makes things up. Like, can those stories of her being so rich *really* be true? Can she *really* be all those different races? I mean, if she is, she's the poster bloody child for racial integration."

"There's something about her," Jack said, "about her essence or her soul or whatever, and it shines with all the colours that there are. And listen, that reminds me, I have to tell you something. You know how I've become Lord Byron?"

"Byron? I'll be honest with you, Jack." Belle studied him. "I still don't see it."

"Well, I was reading about him and do you know what? One time he was mad in love with his cousin, and he said that she had a transparent beauty and that she looked like she was *made out of a rainbow*. I read that line and I just got goosebumps. Because that's exactly what *I'd* been thinking about Madeleine."

He was quiet, and so was Belle. Their footsteps were slowing.

"Apart from anything else," added Jack, "it was proof that I *am* Lord Byron, despite your unsupportive stand on the issue. Both him and me thought that a girl, a particular girl, had transparent beauty like a rainbow."

They reached Madeleine's building right at the word *rainbow*; it blinked in the air between them.

Jack looked up at the windows of the computer guy's flat, and above that, Madeleine's flat, and above that, the sky.

He kept looking at the sky because something had occurred to him, and it was this: Maybe he and Belle were having a fight.

Suddenly, unexpectedly: one of their fights.

Now he turned to Belle, and her face seemed to confirm his fear. She was leaning forward to ring the doorbell, and the ferocity on her face was echoed right there in her index finger. He stared at the finger — straight, taut, the part around the nail turning pink, red, crimson, the rest turning lurid yellow-white, as it pushed harder and harder at the bell, until her finger had an otherworldly glow to it, ringing and ringing the bell — and suddenly, she took her hand away. She shook it in the air.

"Transparent bloody beauty," she said. "You think Madeleine's got transparent beauty like a rainbow? You realise that means you can see through her, right?"

"No, it doesn't mean —"

"Go on, then." Footsteps pounded down the stairs. The air reverberated with the leftover shrill of the bell. "You have a go at it today. See if you can see through her. I'll stand behind her and you tell me how many fingers I'm holding up." She giggled, suddenly hysterical.

There was a shadow behind the door glass — the computer guy downstairs was at the door; and Jack breathed it in, the sound of Belle's giggle, with relief.

The computer guy downstairs had a name.

He was Danek John Michalski, forty-two years old, born in Wisconsin in the US of A, but raised in Kentucky. His interests included computers, travel, judo, and his dog, an Irish setter named Sulky-Anne.

He was asthmatic, which he tended to blame on whatever might be going on in the fields surrounding Cambridge. Belle always told him it was nothing to do with the crops, you berk, it was an allergy to dogs. Let an Irish setter laze about on your bed all day, she told him, you get what's coming to you.

Danek called himself Denny ("No, not Danny, don't be calling me Danny"), and he smiled vaguely and kindly at Belle whenever she suggested the dog allergy.

His flat was one big room and a bathroom, the same floor plan as

Madeleine's upstairs, except that his ceilings and walls stood up straight, whereas hers leaned into angles and slopes.

Also, the chaos in Denny's flat was more extreme than in Madeleine's. Rising from the chaos were two big workbenches that faced each other in the middle of the room. The bed was pushed against the far wall, and that's where Sulky-Anne was always curled, fast asleep.

Denny's teaching method was to follow the same three steps.

First, he made sure there was something baking in the oven when the kids arrived. It was his belief that the fragrance would stimulate their endorphins, making them work faster and sharper in a hedonistic rush towards their coffee break.

Second, he began by having them all, himself included, do ten star jumps (only he called them jumping jacks) to loosen up their minds (and for bonus endorphins). This was even though the star jumps produced the fragrance of sweat, which undermined the fragrance of baking; and even though Denny himself had been told by a physiotherapist that star jumps were *killing* his knees, and even though he was always rasping with asthmatic breathlessness by the time they were done, and (finally) even though the neighbour downstairs (who worked night shifts) frequently put notes under Denny's door saying, *WHAT'S WITH THE STAMPEDING ELEPHANTS UP THERE?!! SOME PEOPLE ARE TRYING TO SLEEP!!*

Despite all this, they always did the star jumps.

Third, still puffing and panting, Belle, Jack, and Madeleine would sit in a row at one of the benches, each in front of a computer. Their assignment for the day would be displayed on the screen. Denny would sit at the other bench and get on with his own work fixing computers.

Today, Denny's face had a shadowed, stubbled look, as if the grey specks in his hair had spilled onto his cheeks and his chin. He was even more asthmatic than usual, his tongue moving around in his mouth looking for air.

"It's the harvest of the rapeseed," he explained, following the just-arrived Belle and Jack back into his flat.

Madeleine was already there, leaning against the kitchen counter.

She was thinking about Denny's accent: It was always so loose and free, as if his voice had started the day with its own star jumps. The kind of accent that made slow smiles rise on listeners' faces.

The opposite of her accent. That made people squint or lean forward: Something's at an angle or askew, something needs straightening or pinpointing.

The room smelled of baking pecan-and-banana muffins; they did their star jumps, and then they sat at the workbench and looked at their computer monitors:

Construct a message board (or Internet forum) on the topic of hurricanes. Start by drawing up your goals and your rules. Comment on one another's message boards *as if you YOURSELF have experienced a hurricane.*

"How do you know we haven't?" said Belle.

"Have you?" Denny paused, his inhaler almost at his mouth.

"No." She shrugged. "But I bet Madeleine has."

They all looked at Madeleine. In fact, she'd experienced three typhoons and a cyclone, which were the same things as hurricanes, but there was a strange challenge in Belle's voice, so she shook her head no, and they all started work.

For a while, they worked happily. Now and then Denny would say something like, "Now, what *do* you call the unique web address of every page on the net anyhow?" or "I'm just sitting here trying to recall what a phreatic volcanic eruption might be."

He liked to make his pop quizzes appear as if they had grown, naturally and organically, out of a nonexistent conversation.

Once, Sulky-Anne sat up on the bed, clattered to the floor, and wandered moodily around the room. There was something disapproving in the elaborate care with which she moved through the chaos: the old motherboards and modems, boxes of socket spanners and wire cutters, baskets of tangled cables. She pressed the side of her head against Madeleine's knee for a moment, slurped from the water bowl in the kitchenette, then headed back to her place in the centre of the bed.

They kept working. Denny wondered aloud just *what* the relationship was between Java and JavaScript anyway, and all three of them told him there was no relationship.

Then Jack announced that he hadn't even done his intro yet, so maybe Denny could give them a break from interruptions.

"Don't say that," said Belle.

"Say what?"

"Intro. Say 'introduction.' I hate people who abbreviate."

Madeleine and Denny both looked up from their computers.

"What do you mean you hate people who *abbreviate*?" demanded Jack. "Everybody bloody abbreviates."

Belle blinked rapidly. "I don't."

"You just did. What do you think 'don't' is. It's an abbreviation of 'do not.'"

"It's a contraction. That's different. Ah, where are my house keys anyhow?"

There was a surprised pause in the room and everybody raised eyebrows at Belle, who laughed, swerving into her new topic. "I thought I must've dropped them on Mill Road somewhere, but they're not there anymore if they were. Did you accidentally take them home from my place yesterday, Madeleine?"

"I doubt it," said Madeleine. "That would've been kind of a strange thing to do."

"Could you just check your backpack maybe?"

Now there was a curious quiet. Denny picked up a pair of tweezers and leaned over the open computer he was working on. Jack gave Belle a questioning look, but she refused to look back.

Madeleine reached for her backpack and opened it.

Over at his workbench, Denny worked and wheezed quietly.

"Don't just rummage around like that," said Belle. "Take everything out so you can be sure."

Madeleine shrugged slightly. "Whatever." And she began to place the objects onto the desk beside her. Books, notepads, a pencil case, a bruised banana.

Belle watched closely.

"Your keys aren't here," said Madeleine.

"Tip your bag up and shake it out," commanded Belle.

Madeleine looked up. "No," she said.

"Seems to me those muffins must be ready!" Denny stood and moved across the room. "You know what we ought to have? A bake sale! Schools have them, right? To raise money for my travel fund!" He pointed to the jar of pound coins that stood against the wall, alongside two old bikes with missing wheels and half a dartboard.

"I don't think teachers are supposed to use bake sales for personal benefit," Jack pointed out. "They're supposed to be for charity or new instruments for the school band or whatever."

Denny opened the oven. Obligingly, the smell of muffins billowed across the room, and Sulky-Anne sat up and smiled, swinging her tail back and forth. Denny kept up his chatter, now addressing the muffins themselves, "Well, you're looking mighty fine and golden in there, little guys; you feel like coming on out?" and to the others, "I'll put on the coffee, who's for a cuppa?"

Belle turned away from him. Her hand reached towards Madeleine's backpack.

"Seriously," she said. "I need you to tip it up."

"There's nothing in there," Madeleine said.

Belle's hand closed around the frayed strap of the backpack, and Denny took two strides across the room. He picked up a book that Madeleine had taken out.

"Isaac Newton," he said. "You reading this for Science or for pleasure?"

"She's reading it for History," said Jack, and explained about the names in the hat.

"She's supposed to *become* Isaac Newton." Belle let go of the backpack and craned to look at the book.

There was a portrait of Newton on the cover.

"Long nose," Belle said. "You'll have to grow your nose, Madeleine, to be him." She lowered her voice slightly. "You'll have to tell a lie."

"Belle," murmured Jack.

"What do you think of Isaac so far?" Denny returned the book to Madeleine, poured coffee, and tossed muffins onto plates, saying, "Ow, ow, ow," since they were hot.

"I haven't read it yet," said Madeleine. "Don't want to. An apple fell on the guy's head and he invented gravity. So basically he stopped people flying. Who wants to know about him?"

Denny laughed. "Ingeniously flawed reasoning," he said, then he took an apple from his fridge, and moved along the bench, dropping it on each of their heads.

"Any of you come up with brilliant new thoughts about the universe? Gravity or whatnot? Huh! You didn't? Now, see? It's harder than it sounds. A little respect for Isaac."

He returned to his own bench and broke a muffin in half.

"You know what Isaac Newton did when he was here at Cambridge?" he said, facing them across the room. They waited.

"His second year of university," continued Denny, "he sat down with a notebook, and he opened it somewhere in the middle. Left a few blank pages and started writing — he changed his handwriting to a whole different style from what he'd used before. And he started writing questions. Questions about mysteries in the universe. Air, meteors, reflections. Heat, cold, colours, and the sea. Forty-five topics, he wrote questions about."

Madeleine, Jack, and Belle watched Denny, not touching the muffins, not looking at one another.

"He did it again a couple of years later," Denny continued. "This time he just chose twelve problems and made a promise to himself that he'd solve them in the next twelve months. Now *here*," said Denny. "Here's a spot assignment for you."

"Isn't this our coffee break?" said Jack.

"You can drink your danged coffee while you do this. Just don't go spilling it, or getting crumbs in the keyboards. This is what I want you all to do. I want you to open a new document and type up a list of *three* problems in your life. Not the universe's life — your own. Underneath, type the solutions."

"If we know the solutions," said Belle, "they're not problems."

"Exactly," said Denny. "You *do* know the answers to most of your problems. Somewhere deep inside, you know. That was more or less what Isaac was getting at when he wrote questions for himself. And changing his handwriting — you see how that could work? How he could find another part of himself that way, the part that might know the answers?"

There were faint shrugs; the remnants of tension still in the air.

"You know, of course," Denny said abruptly, "you know that computer monitors generate and store a whole lot of voltages of electricity? And you know those voltages can still be around even when the equipment's been switched off for a whole lot of time?"

They stared at him.

"Electrical safety," he shrugged. "I'm supposed to cover it — see, right here in the syllabus?" and he got back to his own work.

Madeleine opened a new document.

Three Problems, she typed.

Then she spent a while trying out new fonts, looking for one that would release the problem solver inside her.

Three Problems:
1) I need to get my old life back.
2) My mother won't go to see a doctor.
3) I think Belle hates me.

She went back up to Problem Number 1, and right away she wrote the answer.

Write Dad a letter!!! Explain things in the letter so he has to understand!! Mark the envelope "personal" so his assistant won't read it!!!

Now she looked at the next problem, and again, before she knew it, she was tabbing in from the margin and writing a solution.

Trick her into going to the doctor with me.

She was laughing now, quiet breaths of laughter. Who knew it could be so simple? At the computer beside her, Belle made an exasperated noise, her fingers clattering and flying. Beyond Belle, Jack was gazing at his screen, pulling at his lower lip.
Of course.
The person who knew Belle best was Jack.
Madeleine typed her third answer.

Ask Jack why Belle hates me.

She paused for a moment, then added:

IM Jack right now.

Obeying herself, she did. She IMed Jack, asking him to come over to her place later that day so they could talk.

She watched him blink as her message flashed onto his screen, then his hands reached to the keyboard, and his response appeared:

You bet.

At that moment, Denny said, "You know what? We've got time for one more spot task before lunch."

"But I haven't solved all my problems yet," complained Jack.

"Fast as you can," said Denny, ignoring him. "Fast as you can, tell me: Is it true? The story about the apple hitting Newton on the head? Is that true? Did it really happen?"

"What do you mean, is it true?" said Jack. "It's *history*."

Madeleine was typing into Google: *Did an apple really fall on Isaac Newton's head?*

· *I've heard that this is a myth*, said someone on Answers.com, and somebody else had added, *No, an apple didn't fall on Isaac Newton's head. He didn't really like to be outside.*

"This is how Isaac told it," Denny began, and they looked away from their screens. "One day, he was out near the apple orchard and he saw an apple falling from a tree. It made him start thinking about gravity. Everybody knew about gravity already, of course — it wasn't like he *invented* it — but he started thinking about how big it was, how far it went, the patterns to it, about *universal* gravitation."

"So it didn't fall on him?" said Belle. "You did that whole thing with dropping the apple on us for nothing? Thanks for that. I've still got the headache."

"An apple falls," continued Denny, "and Isaac sees it fall, and suddenly he thinks about the moon. He thinks: If an apple falls, then the moon is falling too. And if the moon is falling, why doesn't it hit the ground like that apple just did? And Isaac thinks about how the moon is flying through space but it's falling at the same time. The fact that it's flying forward is what stops it from hitting the ground. The fact that it's falling towards the ground is what stops it from flying out into space. See? Without gravity, it would fly forever, flying away from us, away into the nowhere. Lost. So, you see . . ."

Denny had been packing his tools away as he talked. He leaned under the workbench and flicked a switch.

"So, you see," he repeated, and this time he looked directly at Madeleine. "Sometimes it's not really flying, it's just being lost."

There was a pause in the room, then Belle said, "Ah, it's all bollocks. Isaac probably made up the story about even *seeing* an apple fall."

Denny nodded slowly. "Why, yes," he said. "He might have."

"You never know when people might be making things up," Belle continued, her tone so loaded that Jack turned and squinted at her, "making things up *about their lives*."

On Belle's screen, Madeleine saw, was a heading in huge, 24-point font: THREE PROBLEMS. And underneath, Belle had repeated the words, *three problems*, over and over. All the way down the page: *three problems, three problems, three problems.*

Belle shut down her computer and its low hissing noise abruptly stopped.

Later that day, Madeleine was sitting on the sloping roof of her attic flat.

Jack was beside her. It was evening, the sky still pale, but trees and buildings almost black.

There were two or three stars out, and Madeleine's eyes swung from star to star. She felt that the stars were folding into her chest; those sharp, shining, agitated pieces of excitement in her chest: They were stars.

As soon as she'd left Denny's place, she'd started taking action. The actions had tumbled one after the other, so simple and slick!

She had written the letter to her father and posted it. He travelled constantly, but letters were always forwarded to him from a central post-office address. It might take a while but it would find him.

Then she'd come back and mentioned to her mother that there was a strange pain in her side. Over the next couple of days she planned to keep talking about the pain in her side, until her mother insisted on taking her to the doctor's. At the doctor's, she would say, "Huh, actually, *I'm* better now, but listen, my *mother* . . ."

So that was the second problem practically solved.

Then, because she'd still had another couple of hours before Jack's visit, she had run back to Denny's and borrowed a computer. She'd lost all her email addresses with her iPad, but she still remembered Tinsels's. It was Tinsels33@gmail.com.

She wrote Tinsels an email.

She told her old friend about Cambridge and the attic flat. She made jokes about the beans, the damp, the winter cold, the rain, and how she and her mother had concussions from bumping their heads into the ceilings. She typed faster and faster. She said, *Sorry it's been so long! It's been totally BIZARRO!*

She said, *But I've written to my dad so I should see you guys* REALLY SOON. She told Tinsels about home schooling, about Jack and Belle, about her mother *SEWING* for a living!!! The more she typed, the more she exclaimed and capitalised, the madder their life in Cambridge seemed and the better she felt. It was like she was shrink-wrapping Cambridge. Now here it was in the palm of her hands, and she knew, at last, what it was.

It was impossible!

Therefore, it could *not be true*!

Her euphoria paraded around the room.

Here she'd been thinking that this was their new life, but *they* were the ones who had run away! They'd locked themselves in a tower; they were playing at being trapped princesses, taking themselves at their own words.

They'd lost themselves in her mother's charade!

Her real life was just a postage stamp, a Send button away!

It's not EXACTLY a holiday, she wrote to Tinsels. *It's more like one of those Survival Adventures people go on to the Amazon, or whatever. (No, I don't mean the Amazon where you buy books, lol.) Or maybe it's like a reality TV show, only without cameras? Like where they find out just how much people can stand?*

She wrote, *Can't wait to see you guys again, especially Warlock! Are you seeing much of him? How is the little guy? He must be getting so big! Tell me EVERYTHING you've been doing. LOTS AND LOTS OF LOVE FOREVER.*

She hit Send and ran back upstairs.

Her mother had gone out.

She stood on the couch, jumped to the floor, and then did it again. Her excitement had nowhere to go.

While she was waiting for her dad to come rescue them, she thought, she may as well embrace her time here. Now that Cambridge was just a quirk or a glitch, a curious patch in her story, rather than the story itself.

She would read about Isaac Newton! He wasn't such an anti-flying monster after all, he was a problem solver! She'd read everything there was to know about him, and she'd make Federico happy by *becoming* him.

Her backpack was on the floor and the Isaac Newton book was still inside it. She flicked it open, and it fell at once to the envelope, the one she'd found in the parking meter, from the boy called Elliot Baranski.

Now she re-read it.

Ah, she thought, she might as well reply. It was some kid probably, a fantasy geek. He was lonely. Since he'd written his letter, he'd probably been back to that parking meter every day — whenever he could take a break from Call of Duty or whatever multiplayer computer game was big these days — hoping for a response.

When she'd first found the letter, it had seemed like part of the psycho-madness that was Cambridge. But now, well, it was just some poor schmuck trying to be clever. She felt free to make fun of him, but she also felt free to be kind.

She wrote a reply. She was reasonably kind in her reply.

She ran out and slid it into the crack in the parking meter, leaving just a tinge of white — then she came home, and Jack arrived.

So, now, here she was with Jack on the roof.

The earlier chill had settled in and they both wore hoodies, hands in the pockets for warmth.

He was explaining about Belle.

"See," he said, "it's not about you. It's about Belle and me — it's something that goes back to when we were kids."

Madeleine wasn't really concentrating. Now that she had reconnected with her real life, it was all theoretical, the Belle problem. It was irrelevant. She kept turning to Jack as he talked and letting smiles spill from her mouth, and then assuming a solemn expression again. Jack smiled back at her each time she did, smiling through his serious words.

"The thing about Belle and me," Jack was saying, "is that we fight about once a year. She always starts it. She gets sort of strange and suddenly she hates me. I can never figure out what I've done. I always try to ignore it but eventually it gets under my skin and I end up hating her back. Then we spend a week or so snapping like alligators, then we shout on a street corner and then we both cry. And make up."

Jack leaned back and looked at the crescent moon, so Madeleine did too. They were sitting side by side.

From inside the flat, they could hear Madeleine's mother sewing and watching her quiz show. Only, she was not calling out any answers.

"It never gets personal," Jack continued. "Unless saying, 'I hate your guts and I wish you would die in a pool of maggot blood' is personal."

He paused, sighed, and added, "Which I don't think it is."

Madeleine considered this.

"So the thing is," Jack finished, "the way she's been around you lately — it's not you, it's just our thing. Or anyway, Belle's thing. She flares up sometimes."

They watched the stars.

"Well," said Madeleine eventually, "a flare is what people send up into the sky when they're in trouble."

"That's true."

"So maybe it's her way of saying she's in trouble?"

"Could be."

"Only," said Madeleine, and now she glanced sideways at Jack, "if you're in the way of a flare, you could end up getting burned."

"I guess," agreed Jack. "I don't really know the true nature of a flare."

"I think it might be made out of fire."

They were both smiling a little — glinting at each other — and they were speaking in odd, lilting voices. As if they were playing at wisdom, or at psychology, even though they half meant what they said.

"So you've got," said Madeleine, "to be careful."

Jack leaned over and kissed her.

His hands were in his pockets, her hands were in her pockets. Their heads turned sideways and the angles were perfect. Then he took out one hand and put it on the back of her head.

To Madeleine, the whole thing was startling. For one thing, she'd never kissed a boy before. She always *acted* like she'd kissed boys, so her first thought was that she had to maintain the illusion. She couldn't let Jack know she was a beginner.

Her second thought was that his lips were kind of like snails, exactly like the texture of a pair of snails (only without their shells). That was a shock. She'd always thought boys' lips would be like caramel.

After a moment more, though, they stopped being like snails and started to feel softer and more interesting.

Around then, the kiss ended. They stayed close for a minute, looking at each other.

It was suspenseful. She didn't know what you were supposed to do.

"Well, you see," Jack said eventually — chattily, "it was those three problems. For one of mine I wrote, *I want to kiss Madeleine.* Then I wrote: *Kiss her, then.* So I had to."

"Uh-huh." Madeleine nodded.

"It was, like, part of an assignment or something."

Madeleine nodded again, more slowly, making him smile. He stroked her face with the side of his hand, but one of his fingernails caught the skin of her cheek and scratched her, just slightly. It felt good, though, the scratch, like the edge of a tiny star.

"Also," continued Jack, "it said in my horoscope that I had to do the thing I've been afraid of, and *yours* said somebody close would surprise you. What else could that mean? I had to do it."

"Practically compulsory," Madeleine agreed.

"And we both had our hands in our pockets. . . ." He shrugged, and added, "I won't do it again, though."

"Why not?" she said.

Surely that couldn't be the end of her first kiss? It seemed sort of pointless, to do that once without doing it again.

When she'd learnt to ice-skate, as a very small child, it had been strange at first. So slippery and awkward! But there'd also been a faint sense that this could turn out to be great.

Kissing seemed exactly the same.

So she kissed Jack herself, taking her hands from her pockets and crossing them together around the back of his head, looping her fingers through his hair. That felt sophisticated. Also, his hair was soft, thick, and coarse all at once; and even better was the sense of him shifting, murmuring, some echo from behind the kiss.

It was part of the same singing in her heart, was what it was.

It was part of the same truth. That all of this — Cambridge, Jack, Belle, the teachers, this flat, this roof, this sky — it was all just an interlude. A game!

So it might as well be fun.

Bonfire, The Farms, Kingdom of Cello

6.

In a way he was still falling, still flying over the fence, his hand around that warm glass jar, still falling.

A festive hospital room, crowded with overlapping talk. They had lost the deftball championship, they were all too excited. The Butterfly Child right here in Bonfire! Turned out that Elliot had a concussion and a dislocated shoulder and a fractured ankle! *How* had he driven the truck to the game in that condition? A red wooden house walked right through the door into the hospital room. Elliot kept falling. They'd all been drinking GC teakwater at the after-party, and doesn't it go to your head?! The red wooden house moved across the room and settled on the bedside table. It was a spiral fracture of the fibula, but the doctor said she thought she wouldn't operate; she'd just now put it in a cast. Cody spoke: "I wasn't *serious*, Elliot, when I asked for you all to break some bones," and someone else: "He's too obliging is the trouble, is that Elliot." Then there was his mother's voice, somewhere across the room: "What sort of extra damage did you do anyhow, pushing your foot down on the clutch to change *gears*, is what I want to know?"

So they were back to him driving the truck, but Elliot was still falling. Cody was telling Shelby what he planned to paint on Elliot's cast and how he'd redo Shelby's to match it. Shelby said she was just about ready to take her own cast off with a chain saw. Never mind the truck, how did Elliot even get up from the ground and open the lid to let the Butterfly Child breathe, is what they wanted to know, what with all his injuries? Ah, he's a tough one, isn't he? It goes to show what adrenaline can do. And did you see when Jimmy popped his shoulder back in, how Elliot went so pale! In all her life, said his mother, she'd never seen him look so *white*. And did anybody notice how, once the shoulder was back in, Jimmy glanced down at the ankle, and the words slipped off the edge of the microphone, and what did Jimmy say?

A faint sound like a low-down whistle was running through Elliot's head. Maybe the sound of a train leaving without him. Nobody paid it any attention; they were all still reciting the events of the day.

"What the heck have you gone and done to yourself, Elliot?" Jimmy had said — or something like that, but mostly those words had been lost. He'd beckoned the doctor over, the ambulance came and went, and everything had tumbled into jubilation.

Then the deftball finals had begun.

Nobody could concentrate, it was nearly hysterical out there — nobody except for the Horatio Muttonbirds, of course, who concentrated fine — and anyway, Bonfire's best player was in the hospital! So. They didn't win, but there'll be other championships, and there's just *one* Butterfly Child! Right here in Bonfire! The Mayor gave them the party with the GC teakwater, even though they lost, and now everybody's planning. The whole town's planning more parties, and what they'll do with the surplus crops, and how they'll have to put on extra markets and contractors, and how they might end up exporting to other Kingdoms!

Because look at her, look at that sweet Butterfly Child. Look at her sleeping in an empty tissue box on the shelf just above Elliot's head. Alongside the chart that says his blood pressure and so on. She looks more like a teenage girl than a child, though, doesn't she, let's say a teenage girl could be shrunk to the size of a cork.

Corrie-Lynn was opening the front of the red wooden house. It was the doll's house she'd built: She'd brought it into the hospital room and placed it on the bedside table. Now she gently scooped up the Butterfly Child from the tissue box, and there was quiet while she lifted her across to the doll's house, and positioned her, still sleeping, on a tiny wooden bed lined with a handkerchief.

Then they were talking again, about how much pain he was in, poor Elliot, and what a hero he was, and he was falling through it all, but through the fall he found a way to speak.

"But I've gotta get the train in the morning," he said. "Train to the Magical North," and the room laughed.

"Not a chance," they said, and he kind of knew that anyway, so he gave back his half smile. He said, "Well, as soon as it's better, I'll be taking the train. How long does a broken ankle take to heal?" and there was quiet.

Someone ventured: "You won't be able to put any weight on that ankle awhile." Someone else: "When my cousin broke his ankle it took eight weeks to heal." And: "We'll ask the doctor when she's back."

He was falling faster: Eight weeks was too long. A plummet toward the ground.

"Ah," he said. "I'll get crutches. I can take the train on crutches."

Then Corrie-Lynn, standing alongside the doll's house, right by Elliot's bed, spoke in a big, clear voice.

"You can't go, Elliot," she said, and she swung her elbow sideways, indicating the doll's house. "The person that finds the Butterfly Child? He's got to stay and take care of her for as long as she's around. And that could be a year, maybe two. Did you not know?"

His head cracked hard against the dirt.

7.

*T*wo weeks later, Petra Baranski watched from the porch as a pickup truck pulled into her driveway.

Elliot negotiated his way out of the passenger door. He grabbed his crutches from the back of the truck and gave Kala a thumbs-up to say thanks. Then he waited, leaning on the crutches, while she reversed, gunned it down the driveway, and was gone.

It was summer again in Bonfire, but a good sort of summer — long days, balmy nights, breezes that touched your shoulder blades just when you needed them. The celebrations had quieted and everyone was waiting. So far, no sign of any change in the crops, but it can be weeks, people said, before a Butterfly Child takes effect.

Petra had been doing paperwork at the porch table, and now she straightened the edges of papers while Elliot got himself up the porch steps. Five or six butterflies were lined along the porch railings, and a dragonfly was hovering above Petra's pen. She waved it away gently.

Elliot stopped beside his mother and pressed his forehead against the window to look inside.

The doll's house was on the sideboard in the living room.

"She gone out?" he said.

"Sleeping. How was school?"

"She sure does sleep a lot." He rested the crutches against the wall of the house and sat down, breathing in the quiet afternoon. There was a smile about him, a spark in his eye, and Petra waited, watching his face.

Then he took an envelope from his pocket and set it on the table.

"Elliot Baranski," said the envelope in bright red marker. There were fat quote marks around his name like little balloons.

Petra raised an eyebrow.

"From Cody's sculpture," he said, his smile open now. "I'd forgotten all about it, but I was walking by today, so I looked, and there it was."

"A letter from the Girl-in-the-World!" exclaimed Petra. "Did she get *your* letter? Is she answering you?!" Then she quieted. "Nobody saw you? You didn't tell Kala or any of the others, did you? I looked it up the other day, and turns out the penalty for not reporting a crack is banishment to the Undisclosed Province, or even *death*. It's kind of hard to believe in this day and age, but still."

Elliot shrugged. "That must be an old law. Wouldn't be enforced anymore. Read the letter." He leaned back, closing his eyes.

His mother opened the envelope and read.

Dear Elliot Baranski,
You're unstable or you're high or you're a kid who wants to write fantasy.

I'm thinking probably the last one. And finding a note somewhere weird like a parking meter inspired you, so you invented a place called Cello. (Or maybe you've got an imaginary Cello in your head all the time, and you went with that right away?)

Anyway, since you're the kind of person who puts your fantasy in parking meters, I'm thinking you'll be back to check on my reply. I'm happy to play along if you want, but I feel compelled to say that I have issues with your world-building.

These are my issues:

(a) The use of the word "cracks" to explain the way between our worlds. It's not original. And the bit about a sculpture catching the letter but you're "not sure of the science"? Are you for real? You've got to get your "science" figured out up front!

(b) You're way too hokey and sweet. You need an edge.

(c) You say you're about to go on a trip to the "Magical North." Well, I guess you want to narrate an "epic journey" of some kind, but maybe you could change the place name? "Magical North" makes me think of reindeers and Santa Claus and that maybe you're planning to rip off Philip Pullman's *Northern Lights*.

But I like how you just got right into it, without trying to set things up. Even though it was confusing, it felt more real that way. The republican thing was kind of funny.

Also, thanks for your suggestions about beans.

And listen, what I said in my letter about cakes? Well, there's homeless people and refugee camps and then there's me crying about frangipane tart. So. Just forget I said that.

(PLUS, the computer guy downstairs is great at baking.)

Cheers,
M.T.

P.S. I'm not sure how much longer I'll be in Cambridge, but if you want to write more about your imaginary kingdom, why don't you leave your next letter in the Trinity porter's lodge? The parking meter doesn't seem like such a safe place. You could address it to "M.T., c/o Federico Cagnetti." He's a porter there. I'll tell him to watch out for it.

P.P.S. I know Elliot Baranski is not your real name, but it's a good one. I like that too.

Petra finished reading and widened her eyes, and they both laughed.

"I don't know where to start," said Petra through her laughter. "Honey, she's *critiquing* your existence. She thinks Cello is —"

"I know." Elliot picked up the empty envelope and balanced it on the palm of his hand. "She seems harmless enough, I guess, this *M.T.*" They both laughed again.

"Now, what do you think?" Petra shook her head thoughtfully. "Has the World forgotten about Cello? Or is this girl just ignorant? Will you write back to her?"

"Well . . ." Elliot put his hands behind his head, looking out over the fields. There was still that grin at the edge of his mouth. "It seems to me that if I do start up a correspondence, it'll just end up as a whole lot of me trying to persuade her that I'm real. Which could get —"

"Tiresome," his mother agreed.

She reached over, across the table, to brush the hair out of his eyes, and there it was beneath her fingertips — the faintly damp forehead, the sun-warmed hair, the sweet, complex realness of her son.

But later that night, he did write a reply.

He'd finished his homework; the Butterfly Child was still asleep; and there was a pecan pie baking in the oven, which he planned to give to Kala the next day.

"Don't go baking her pecan pies," scolded his mother. "She'll just fall for you harder than she has."

Elliot wasn't listening. His ankle was playing up. Taking all his attention.

"Ah," he said eventually. "She's driving me to and from school every day. Least I can do is bake a pie."

Then, because he couldn't run across the fields to the greenhouse, or play deftball, or pack his rucksack for a journey north, he sat down and wrote.

Dear M.T.,

I'm sitting here wondering why you don't know about the Kingdom of Cello. Or are you pretending not to know?

I'll tell you what I recall from World Studies, but keep in mind I'm rusty on that. Used to be, there was some movement back and forth between Cello and your World, especially around the 1600s, and especially from your cities of Cambridge and London.

Anyhow, but you guys had a sickness called the plague, which came across here, spread over Cello, and spilled across the Kingdoms and Empires. That's when they made the decision to close up the cracks. (There's still occasional plague outbreaks, although not in Cello, on account of Cello's Winds.)

Now and then little cracks reopen — never often, and never big enough for people to get through, just matchboxes or orange peels. But the World Severance Unit seals those fast, and anyone who finds one has to report it right away.

As for your issue with the word "crack," well go ahead and take it up with the Department of Etymology, I guess. Let me know how that works out for you.

(My mother just said she seems to recall it was people in YOUR world who named the "cracks." Bunch of scientists in London in the 1600s called the Royal Society? They were keen on Cello, apparently, and visited a lot.)

Not sure who you should talk to about changing the name of the Magical North. They're kind of proud of their province and its name — still, try the MN Provincial Council. Maybe bring along a security guard when you do, and have an escape route in mind. They might have sweet-as-honey magic up there but they sure as hell don't sugarcoat their tempers.

I haven't got a clue what "hokey" means or who Santa Claus or Philip Pullman are.

Thanks for being nice about my name. (My mother says she wants the credit for that, since she did the naming.)

Got to go check a pecan pie.

Yours,

Elliot Baranski

P.S. Forgot to say: had to postpone my trip to the Magical North on account of a broken ankle and a Butterfly Child. So if you want to write back, I guess I am around after all.

P.P.S. I guess I should check. Have you got the plague?

A few days later, the Girl-in-the-World replied.

Dear Elliot Baranski,

Oh, it's a KINGDOM. I should have guessed. Always with the kings and the queens, you fantasy guys. Why not a republic for once? I'm guessing, next there'll be dragons. Also, some kind of a strong-willed princess with rebellion on her mind? Or a physically unattractive older woman who wants her pitiful son to be king so she's plotting to poison the rightful heir with a brew made out of frogs' warts?

So, how far have you got with your Kingdom? Can you outline the political system for me? Class structure? Oppressed minorities? What about foreign relations, primary industries, and your GDP?

And what about your sky? Is it like ours? Do you have a single moon? (I bet you have three and one of them's a triangular prism, right?) I like stars — I hope you've got stars. Talking about the heavens, what about religion? Seems like you don't have Santa Claus, so you're not a Christian nation. Do you celebrate any religious holidays? Ramadan, Chanukah, Valentine's Day?

Where are you at with technology? Have you had an industrial revolution or are you still hanging out on the land? Or in caves? If on the land, what do you grow on your farms? Do you even have them? (Farms?) Or do you eat holograms? Do you use winnowing baskets, sickles, and horse-drawn ploughs? Or do oxen draw your ploughs? Or technotrons? Or do you, Elliot, pull the ploughs in the Kingdom of Cello?

It's funny you mention the Royal Society — and nice one, making them the people who "named" the cracks (touché) — because I've been reading about Isaac Newton, and turns out he was in that group, or club, or whatever. They were sort of like the first group of scientists in England, right? He even ran it for a while. Turns out his special skills went beyond gravity: He was also great at telescopes, calculus, colours, and problem solving.

Anyhow, do you guys have any special skills or are you just basic humans? I mean, can you walk through walls? Fly? Go invisible? Read minds?

Do you dance? Do you have a sense of humour, and if so, is it witty, sarcastic, slapstick, ironic, or crass? What's your Kingdom's position on sexual freedoms, gay rights, abortion? Do you have animals? What languages do you speak? Can your ANIMALS speak? Are you magic (or is that just for the sweet-as-honey "Magical North" — I still think you should change that name). What's your life expectancies there? Same as ours?

Finally: What's the wind got to do with the plague, what's a Butterfly Child, and how'd you break your ankle? (I broke my ankle snowboarding once, and I still have nightmares about this feeling I got, about a month after it was broken, like I could feel bones shifting and grinding around in there, and it was like I wasn't real anymore, or I wasn't me, or my body was out of my control. Like something had got inside my ankle, and wanted to taunt me. It hurt like hell. In addition to creeping me out.)

I'll send more questions later, gotta go.

M.T.

Elliot read the letter.

"Ah, for crying out loud," he said mildly. He crumpled the paper and threw it in the trash.

Shelby was flexing her fingers, twisting her wrists in their studded leather armbands. The cast from her broken arm had been removed that morning. She was reacquainting herself with the arm now, gazing at it as she walked.

"It didn't heal properly," she said. "I tried to take a swing at some-one earlier and I couldn't connect."

The six were walking down Broad Street, heading to the Town Square for cold drinks, Elliot swinging high on his crutches.

"It'll take a while," Gabe suggested, "to get your normal strength back. Maybe longer for you, Shelby, your normal strength being what it is."

"Who'd you take a swing at?" said a voice.

They were passing Jimmy Hawthorn's place, and the Deputy Sheriff was home, working in his front garden.

"Who'd you take a swing at?" he repeated patiently.

"Can't say a thing around this town," sighed Shelby, "without somebody hearing." ·

Jimmy shrugged and went back to his trowel, and the six of them kept walking.

"What's that whistling sound?" said Elliot.

"It's me," said Nikki. "Whistling."

"No. It's more than that — it's like a lower sound, like the wind."

"Ah, then, it's probably the wind."

They passed Isabella Tamborlaine's place, and now they were on the commercial part of Broad Street. A door swung open just ahead of them, and out came Norma Lisle, town vet.

She was holding a program player to her chest, its cords and cables dangling.

"Just taking this next door," she said. "Seized up in the middle of *The Greenbergs* last night — *right* at the bit where that plumber — the one that's always so handy when the characters' toilets block up — when he's about to kiss the schoolteacher with the temperamental kitchen sink. Any of you kids see the show?"

"He went ahead and kissed her," said Cody. "But don't let it get you down that you missed it, Norma. It wasn't such a great kiss. And I kept wondering if he'd washed his hands."

"Ah, Cody," laughed Norma Lisle. "It's the best thing there is in the televisual waves, isn't it, though I can see from your friends' faces here that we might be alone in that opinion. I'll just pop in and see if the Twicklehams can fix this, but listen, Elliot, before I do, how's that Butterfly Child?"

Elliot swayed slightly on his crutches.

"She doesn't do much except sleep, Norma," he said. "There's butterflies and other insects hanging around day and night, and sometimes she heads out for a ride on one of them. But when she gets back she falls straight asleep. Couple of times she *has* been awake and I've tried to say, 'Hey,' and 'How's things?' but she just stares at me."

"Huh," said Norma. "Well, I cannot *wait* for the crop effect to start working. Not that I *have* any crops, of course, but I've got my lemon trees and my little herb garden — just some pots on my patio. I'm that excited about the day they're going to start thriving! For everyone else, of course, not just me," she amended quickly.

"It'll happen," said Kala. "Always takes a while."

Then, as Norma reached a hand toward the door of Twickleham Repair, Shelby said, loud and clear: "Give your program player to me."

Norma stopped, surprised, and turned back.

They could see through the glass into the repair shop. Fleta Twickleham was standing at the workbench, leaning forward, ready with a smile.

"There's a supermart in Sugarloaf does repairs cheap," Shelby explained. "I'm heading out there later today — got a broken player of my own."

She held out her arms, one paler and thinner than the other, ready to take the program player.

"Oh, well, now," said Norma, and she turned away again, pressing on the door so that its bell jangled. "That'd just be a nuisance for you!"

"No, it wouldn't." Shelby wrenched the player right out of Norma's arms. "You always take such good care of my dogs when they're sick," she added. "Least I can do is take care of your program player."

Norma let the door thud closed.

She studied the faces of the six teenagers. Then she shrugged.

"Well, that's kind of you, Shelby! Guess it'll save me time, and I *have* got an arthritic pig crying quietly in my waiting room!"

The others all agreed that the pig needed Norma more than her program player did, said their good-byes, and waited while the door to her vet's rooms closed behind her.

Then they turned to Shelby.

"You really taking a player into Sugarloaf tonight?" Nikki asked.

"Nah. Don't even *have* one. I'll fix this for Norma myself. Taught myself how to fly the crop duster, I can figure this out."

"Call me later if you can't do it," Kala said. "I'll see if I can track down a manual."

"The way you took that thing out of her arms," said Gabe. "Guess you got your strength back after all."

They laughed, heading up the street again. Behind the glass of Twickleham Repair, Fleta's face creased with confusion.

She slept on her side, the Butterfly Child, little hands clasped together, knees drawn up under the sapphire blue dress. Elliot wasn't sure anymore that it *was* a dress; seemed like it might be part of her, a sort of skin.

It was late, past midnight, and he'd woken with the moonlight splashing on his coverlet and come downstairs. The moonlight was more composed here, shining in neat shafts and bars, lighting up the windows of the doll's house.

She was maybe as long as his index finger, but the tininess was more in her features, and now, in his half-asleep state, Elliot felt a surge of something — of how confounding it was, that tininess. Those little hands, little fingers, little bare feet with their tiny, tiny toes. The lashes of her closed eyes, the sweetness of her nose, the soft breath of pale yellow hair across the pillow, the bend of her elbow, tilt of her chin.

What was it about littleness that made it catch at your heart like this? Elliot's mind ran with little things — snowflakes, hailstones, raindrops, the pin you put through the hole when you clasped your watch. You could say she was as tall as his finger, sure, but how to describe the size of that dimple in her cheek, and the knuckles of her hands?

He thought of raspberries — the separate little globes, or pockets, on a raspberry. He thought of the tiny bubbles that form around the edges of a glass of fresh-squeezed juice. The hesitant *x* that Kala added to her name when she wrote him notes. Smaller than that. The dot on an *i*.

It came to him, a memory of a day when his cousin, Corrie-Lynn, was just a few weeks old. So he, Elliot, must have been about nine. Uncle Jon and Auntie Alanna had been visiting, new baby in a sling around Jon's shoulder, and they were talking about how they'd just cut the baby's fingernails for the first time. How frightened they'd been of hurting those little fingertips.

Alanna had saved the clipping from the pinkie nail; she'd taped it to a piece of black notepaper, and they'd all laughed at her about that, but she hadn't minded; and she'd taken it out of her purse to show. They'd all exclaimed. Just *look* how tiny that is. That little sliver of fingernail. Can it be real?

The Butterfly Child: She was that kind of tiny. She should be taped to a piece of black notepaper and folded, safe, into somebody's purse.

His mind kept tumbling with thoughts of tiny things: those miniature nuts, bolts, screws, washers, springs — the ones that his father kept in empty margarine containers and used tweezers or magnets to pick up.

He rubbed his face hard with both his hands and looked at her sleeping face. Her eyelids! How small were those little eyelids? And could they be twitching a little? Was she dreaming behind those eyes?

It was wrong to keep watching; he was spying, but he wanted to look even closer. What he needed —

Then it came to him.

The thing that was missing from his father's possessions, the thing that was wrong or askew.

*   *   *

In the Sheriff's station, Hector and Jimmy were both typing at their desks.

"Now did I tell you," said Hector, leaning forward to frown at the report in his typewriter, "that I heard from the folk in the Golden Coast? About that missing persons report you figured out for them the other day?"

Jimmy hit the space bar twice. "The sound technician," he recalled. "One with all the money from the prize win. No, you didn't tell me."

"You were right," Hector said.

"Ah, that's a shame."

"It is. They found his body at the nephew's place, just like you said they would. Now *how*, Jimmy, did you know that?"

Hector looked sideways once, then turned the handle, winding the completed report out of the machine.

"I did background checks on them all, not just the ones who stood to inherit, and turned out the nephew had spent years bending Colors in Nature Strip. For one thing, they've got some loopy hereditary laws in Nature Strip — up there, the nephew *would've* got the fortune. I figured, he maybe got it into his head that the same would be the case in GC. See, bending Colors for too long can bend your mind a little. You start to mix things up. You start to *see* Colors, always there, just at the edge of your vision."

"Don't we all?" Hector said, surprised.

"Well, now —" Jimmy began doubtfully, but the door to the station jangled, and they both looked up.

It was Elliot Baranski.

Jimmy ran to open the door wider, so Elliot could hop his way in on his crutches.

"Well, if it isn't Elliot Baranski!" said Hector, studying the cast on Elliot's leg. Cody had painted a complicated pattern there, diamonds overlaid with scorpions.

158

"Look at that decoration!" Hector exclaimed. "It's just like —" but he found he could not think what it was like, so he asked after the ankle bone instead. Then he and Jimmy asked after Elliot's mother, and the farm, and the Butterfly Child.

Eventually, Elliot said, "Anyhow, the reason I came here was — Hector, remember when we made the list of things that might be missing from Dad's stuff? Well, last night — in the middle of the night — I remembered something else that was missing."

Hector and Jimmy both blinked.

"His magnifying glass."

"His magnifying glass?"

"It was special to him. My mother ordered it from the best glass makers in Jagged Edge, for his birthday a few years back. He used it all the time, and I've been thinking lately that something was wrong about his tools, something missing maybe, and finally, I realized — his magnifying glass is gone."

There was quiet in the station for a moment. Hector's face shadowed. The bandages were gone now, so you could see the healing welts crossing his cheeks. You could see the shapes the scars were going to be.

He scratched at the scabs on his hands.

"Well, now," he said. "You think that's the kind of thing he might have been carrying home from work? In the pocket of his overcoat maybe?"

Elliot shook his head. "No. He had tools at home, including a cheap magnifying glass — he'd have just used that if he needed one. And this magnifying glass, it was big." He held out his hands to demonstrate. "Had a special case, sort of a tartan green."

"And you're sure it's not with his things?"

Elliot shrugged. "I'm sure."

"Could he have loaned it out to someone?"

"Doubt it. He wouldn't even let *me* use it, not unless he was watching over my shoulder."

"Could it have been left behind in the repair shop when you packed it up? Maybe fallen off the shelf and got under something? You want to ask the Twicklehams about it?"

Elliot's gaze was steady for a moment.

"We did a pretty thorough job," he said, "cleaning the shop out. Don't think we would have left anything."

Hector nodded slowly. "All right," he said. "Let me add it to the report and have a think about it. About what it might mean." Then he paused and fixed Elliot with his own gaze. "What do *you* think it means?"

Elliot shrugged. "I guess it doesn't mean anything. I guess he did have it with him that night, after all. In the pocket of his over-coat, probably. Anyhow" — Elliot swung around on his crutches, and Jimmy stood again to hold the door — "just wanted to let you know."

He turned back, though, when the door was almost closed, used a crutch to hold it.

"I guess," he said, "there's been no news?"

"Soon as there is," Hector said firmly, "I'll let you know."

Elliot nodded and the door closed behind him.

It was quiet in the station for a moment.

"Don't you say a word," said Hector, not looking at Jimmy.

So Jimmy didn't. They both started typing their reports again, every click and clack a kind of punch.

When Elliot got home from the Sheriff's station, the house was big with quiet.

His mother was still out at the greenhouse, he guessed. He checked the doll's house and the Butterfly Child was asleep.

In the kitchen, he made himself a cup of coffee, cut a piece of chocolate-coconut cake, took a pile of homework from his backpack, and sat at the table.

There was a faint rustle and clatter. A bird landing on the porch railing. The fridge buzzed. The bird flew away again. He opened his mathematics textbook, then closed it.

"Ah," he said, looking down at his plastered ankle.

He pushed the chair back and limped upstairs, leaning and pulling on the banisters all the way. He found painkillers in the bathroom cupboard, took a couple, and headed to his bedroom.

He opened the bottom drawer and dragged it all out: folders, books, notes, photocopied articles, newspaper clippings, official documents. He dumped them on his bed and leafed through the documents: **Missing Persons Report: Abel Garek Baranski; Missing Persons Report: Mischka Elizabeth Tegan**; and there it was.

Coroner's Report: Jonathan Kasper Baranski.

The report on his Uncle Jon.

To look at it, he had to breathe himself sideways. He had taught himself this trick of shifting, inside his head, so that only part of him saw the words. Even doing that, he had to skim fast — past phrases like, *lacerations to the face, neck, torso* and *severed carotid artery; severed spinal cord* — and then he found what he was looking for.

In a box in the bottom-right corner, the coroner had written her **Conclusions**.

Injuries consistent with attack from a Color in the Gray-Purple range; most likely a third-level Purple. Injuries are also somewhat consistent with the attack of a wild animal (tiger, cougar, bear, dragon, wolf pack), but I have ruled these out as unlikely since no evidence of teeth marks or "feeding" on the victim; also, no evidence of scorching or singeing (highly common in dragon attack). Again, it is not impossible that a person, or group of persons (perhaps Wandering Hostiles), wielding daggers, machetes, trench knives, etc., could have inflicted the injuries, but in the absence of evidence of human involvement in the attack (blood at scene is that of victim alone, no traces under fingernails of victim, etc.), and noting that no Wandering Hostiles have claimed responsibility, which would be the norm, third-level Purple seems the likely cause of death.

In the adjoining box for **Additional Notes**, the coroner had written:

The victim was found in the vicinity of the abandoned truck of his brother, Abel Baranski; victim was last seen leaving the Toadstool Pub in the company of both Abel and a woman, Mischka Tegan. I have been asked to comment on whether these other parties may have been involved in the victim's death, either as perpetrators or possibly (unconfirmed) fellow victims. In relation to the former, see my previous conclusions re human involvement; in relation to the latter, I note that Purples are occasionally known to slay one victim and abduct others, carrying them away from the scene. Accordingly, one could speculate as follows: The Purple attacked the truck carrying Jon, Abel, and Mischka; they pulled over, hoping to flee into the woods; the Purple slaughtered Jon, and then carried Abel and Mischka away (in which case, I would ordinarily expect their remains to be found somewhere in the vicinity of the original attack); however, in the absence of any further evidence, this is pure speculation.

Elliot returned the report to its manila folder.

This is pure speculation, he thought.

There were people in this town — not many, but a handful — who were convinced that Elliot's father and uncle had both fallen in love with Mischka and fought over her. That his father had killed Jon, leaving him dead on the side of the road and fleeing with Mischka.

There were others — most of Bonfire, probably — who thought that, more likely, Abel and Mischka had decided to run away together. Taking the train, or maybe a boat upriver. They'd asked Jon to take the truck home to Abel's farm and pass on the news, but the Purple attack had happened while Jon was en route.

The rumors had started right away, and Elliot, hollow with shock, had felt their poison pouring into him.

Then the Sheriff had sat him down one day. It was in the Bakery, in the Town Square, he remembered; autumn chill in the air; the Sheriff in that black corduroy jacket he liked so much.

Hector had taken out this very coroner's report and made Elliot read it.

"This'll hurt like the blazes to read," he had said. "But look here now," and he'd run his finger hard under the phrase *absence of evidence of human involvement.*

"I've seen my share of love triangles," Hector had said. "And yes, a man could kill his brother over love. It happens. But when it does, it's a fistfight got out of hand, not machetes and hunting knives! You don't slash your brother to pieces over a girl. I'll tell you categorically, Elliot. Your father did not do this to your uncle."

Elliot remembered the heat of his coffee mug at the time; the Sheriff said those words and Elliot realized his hands were ice-cold and held them around his coffee mug.

"As for running off with the teacher." Hector had shrugged. "I'm not saying they *were* lovers, but let's say, hypothetically, they were. Well, I've seen my share of that too, lovers running off. But they make plans. They come up with the idea, get cold feet, get more determined. Inch their way toward it. Never heard of someone deciding in a pub one night and asking his brother to let the family know. They write a note. They take money out of their bank account. And listen, they *pack*. Now, tell me again what you think might be missing from your dad's things."

"Well," Elliot had said. "Like I said, there's his overcoat and hat. He'd've been wearing those. And the other things he was wearing. His wallet. His watch. We thought maybe a framed antique map was missing, one he used to have on his workshop wall, but turned out he'd given that to Jon and Alanna for the front room of the Watermelon. So, that's it."

"No medications? No photographs? Not those spell casings he got from the Magical North that he was so proud of?"

"No. Like I said, they were still on his corkboard."

"No clean underwear? No favorite pair of boxer shorts?"

"Not sure he had a favorite pair," Elliot said with half a grin.

"You know what I mean. People don't run off with nothing — they take a keepsake. A memento. A photo at least. You do know what I mean?"

Elliot had nodded, and that's when Hector had leaned forward and run his thumb under the words on the coroner's report.

One could speculate as follows: The Purple attacked the truck . . . they pulled over . . . the Purple slaughtered Jon, and then carried Abel and Mischka away.

"It's ugly," Hector had said. "It's ugly and distressing, and I wish I *could* say they'd run off together because much as that would hurt you — that betrayal of you and your mother — well, at least we'd know he was alive. But it seems to me that *this* is what happened. Like it says right here."

"And if a Purple took them," Elliot had said, looking Hector full in the eye, "if it did, they might still be alive. Alive and held prisoner in a Purple cavern somewhere."

Here Hector had paused for a long time.

"Again, I want to talk straight with you, Elliot," he'd said eventually. "Purples don't carry people away and let them live."

"But until we find them, until we find their bodies," Elliot had persisted, "we don't know for sure."

Hector had tilted his head, not a nod, but not a shake either.

"Elliot, I'm not giving up. Like you say, until we find the bodies, we don't know for certain. In a lot of ways, that's the toughest kind of loss you can have, the one where you don't know for sure. You can be 99.9 percent sure, Elliot, that your father isn't coming back — but yeah, until there's proof, there's always going to be that glimmer. That *tiny, tiny* glimmer of hope. I can see it in your eyes all mixed up with the pain. And I'm not going to lie and tell you I don't feel it too."

Then Hector had leaned forward.

"The tough thing," he had said, "is how to live with that."

For that meeting, those words — for Hector's straight-talking — Elliot had been grateful.

It was different from the gratitude he'd felt back on the day he was seven years old and he'd stolen his mother's new quad bike — which she was crazy about — taken it for a spin and ended up in the river. He'd got himself out, but the quad bike was lost under the water. He'd known the trouble he'd be in, but worse, he'd guessed, would be the disappointment on his mother's face.

He'd run all the way to his dad's repair shop and confessed.

Without a word, his dad had got up from behind the workbench.

He'd led Elliot out to the truck, waited while he buckled up his belt beside him, then driven to the river, speaking only once to check with him: "You mean right here? This is where it went in?"

And he'd pulled it out. He'd pulled out the quad bike, dried it down, hauled it into the truck, taken it back to his workshop, and fixed it up. It took him hours. Hours of work, while Elliot watched silently — and he fixed it, good as new.

The gratitude he'd felt! The hug he'd given his dad! And his dad had leaned down into the hug and said, "Ah, we all make mistakes — that's one you won't make again."

That had been pure, incredulous gratitude, whereas what he'd felt toward Hector was complicated, of course, and sharp-edged. Nevertheless, it was powerful: Hector had believed in Elliot's father.

He'd cleared away those rumors just as surely as if he'd taken his arm and swept the mugs and pie plates from the table.

Only, now there was this.

A missing magnifying glass.

The ruefulness in Hector's voice at the station today.

Jimmy's silence.

A favorite possession. A keepsake, a memento.

There was an urgent voice in Elliot's head saying: *So maybe he HAS run away with Mischka, after all. Well, that's GOOD news. It means he IS alive, that he's okay, and one of these days he'll be back and begging our forgiveness.*

But another thought hit back at once, like a child having a tantrum: *It WAS a Purple, and it's not touched a hair on his body, and he's alive and okay, trussed up in a cavern somewhere now, and as soon as I can get out of here, I'm going out to bring him home!*

"Ah," Elliot said aloud, and it came out a growl. He swept it all off the bed — the coroner's report, missing persons reports, papers, books, and folders. They tumbled quietly to the floor.

Then he reached for a notebook and, sitting on his bed, wrote a letter.

Dear M.T.,

You asked if we had farming here in Cello, and yeah, we do.

And you wanted to know something about technology here? Well, that depends on the province. In Jagged Edge, they're all wired up. They've got whole cities made out of holograms, and computer programs that practically raise children. Golden Coast is similar, though they use it all for fun.

In Olde Quainte they don't even have the telephone or electricity. And in the Magical North and Nature Strip they've got most things, only their magic messes it up all the time.

Here in the Farms we're sort of coming around to computers. Some people use them to send messages but mostly it's still faxes or just regular mail. Our TVs are still boxes that you set on a cabinet in your living room, not images that fly through the air like in Golden Coast.

Farming's getting more mechanized too. Like, we've got automatic openers now in our greenhouse to lift the windows and let out the heat. And the furnace that blows the heat in when it's cold, that's state-of-the-art.

As for what we grow, well, some people in Bonfire raise livestock, especially pigs, but most of us here are agriculture based. It's mainly greenhouses because of the weather.

That reminds me, I think you guys have rotating seasons in the World? Like seasons that come and go at the exact same time every year? Farming must be a dream. Seriously, you must grow stuff in your sleep.

(Cello has a roaming climate: Seasons drift across the Kingdom, moving on whenever they get bored.)

On my farm, we grow bananas, raspberries, quince, beans, and peas. We keep bees too, for pollinating.

Other people around here grow pecans, macadamias, mandarins, defts, potatoes, wheat, and maize.

When I say that we grow these things, well, the word "grow" is used loosely. Maybe PLANT is a better word — we PLANT them, but lately, mostly what comes out of the ground is weeds. Or crumbling, twisted pieces of nothing that die before they see the sun.

Or nothing at all. Just soil that spills from the palm of your hand.

Now, people will tell you the Butterfly Child is going to fix this. That everything'll grow like wildfire any day. But I'll tell you this, and keep it to yourself, we've had the Butterfly Child four weeks now, and all she does is sleep. Goes on adventures now and then, sure, goes off for a ride, which I imagine is plenty of fun for her, and then she comes back home and sleeps.

She should have made a difference by now, I'm sure. She's cute and all, but she's either a dud, or she's sick. All that sleeping, she might be sick, and you know what else, if she is sick, it's probably my fault. 'Cause she was in that jar a long time. I watched her through my double vision, I saw her crumple up in there, I saw her little eyes start to close, and I still couldn't make myself get up. It was like my snapped ankle was using up all the space. I tried, but I couldn't. And when I did, when I finally crawled over there and got the lid off, really slow, like the useless piece of junk that I am, well, who knows how much time had passed and what effect it had had on her?

Who knows? It took a good minute, maybe more, before she unrumpled, looked me in the eye, and bowed her tiny head.

I'll be honest, the only reason I'm writing to you now is that the hurting in my ankle is just how you described in your letter — like a jostling, like somebody's in there wanting to mess with me. That's the only thing I remember from your letter, apart from your question about farms and technology.

But you're right about the ankle, and painkillers don't do a thing.

One last thing, if you decide on writing back, you've got to at least pretend that I am real.

'Cause I'm not in the mood for being treated like I don't exist.

Yours sincerely,
Elliot Baranski

Cambridge, England,
The World

8.

"She has the kissing disease! You had better not come in!"

Olivia Pettifields, mother of Belle, and their teacher for both French and Citizenship, was standing with her back to her front door, breathless, giggling. She'd seen them through the window and rushed out, pressing the door closed behind her.

"*Vous feriez mieux de ne pas entrer!*" she translated, remembering herself, and then repeated: "You had better not come in!"

Madeleine and Jack stood in the front yard of Belle's house — it was on Ross Street, way out near the station — holding their bikes by the handlebars.

They looked sideways at each other. Jack rolled his bike back and forth slowly in the mud-grass.

"She has glandular fever again?" he said, doing his own translating. "Is she okay?"

Olivia Pettifields shook her head. Her lips were the same glossy red as the paint on the front door.

"Belle is all right," she said, with more giggles in her voice. "But she is sick as a dog!"

It was tricky, figuring out how that made sense. And also what was funny about it.

They looked up at the windows, which were curtain-drawn.

"Should we come in and see her?"

"You would catch it! Are you mad?!" Olivia's laughter fountained, then she drew her mouth together, pulling the laugh back in. Still, she could not help a smile curling. "Here is your assignment for today! You must go away and speak French to each other! Or, no, no, I know it! I have it! Go into a café and *order some things in French!!!*"

Jack and Madeleine gazed at her steadily.

"But this is England."

"What should you order? Hmm. Yes, you must order a *pain au chocolat*! Ah! Cheating! I just told you the French. You kids," she scolded. "Always tricking me! I know — order the snails with garlic and the chicken with red wine and the crème brûl — ah, they will almost certainly have none of these things. In a café here at nine o'clock in the morning. Pfft. This place. And you will not be hungry enough yet anyway. I have a better idea! You must go to Luton, to the airport at Luton, and you must take a flight to Paris! There, you will speak French to your heart's content! An excellent educational opportunity!"

She flung her hands outwards. "Go! Shoo with you! Fly away!"

"Tell Belle we hope she feels better," said Madeleine, turning her bike, while Olivia laughed and called: "Do not forget to be *citizens*! In Paris! You will be *citizens*, won't you?!"

That was one thing that Olivia Pettifields had never stopped finding hilarious: the idea that they had to learn Citizenship. In fact, that's why she'd offered to teach it.

Jack and Madeleine wheeled their bikes slowly along the path, talking about Belle and her glandular fever, and Belle and her barking-mad mother.

She had first got glandular fever when she was twelve, and it had come back twice since then. As far as they knew, she had always had the barking-mad mother. She had a father too, who seemed slightly more sane. Mostly he was bemused by his wife, but sometimes he found her almost as amusing as she found herself, and then he fell about laughing with her.

Belle tended not to get the joke.

"What'll we do? You want to get something to eat?" said Madeleine.

"You're hungry at strange times," Jack observed. "It's like you're constantly jet-lagged. Did you know that Lord Byron had a thing where he couldn't eat if there was a woman in the room?"

"Cause he had bad table manners or issues with women?"

"Well, he's dead now, isn't he, so I can't ask him. But I think it was a sort of an eating disorder. He used to do things like starve himself for days then go and eat plates of potatoes. I'm so much like him."

They had stopped at a corner and were waiting to cross the road.

This was a strange time for Madeleine and Jack. Just the Thursday before, they had kissed on the sloping roof of Madeleine's flat.

It had seemed like the start of something but, ever since, they'd pretended nothing had happened.

It was Belle's fault. She was always around, and she was so real and sharp, and they had their pattern of being together. It felt impossible to shift.

"Are you trying to say you've got an eating disorder?" Madeleine said. "Or that you like potatoes?" Her voice had an odd, angry challenge to it. She couldn't figure out where it had come from, that voice. The road was clear, but they stood still anyway, looking at each other.

Then she realised. She was trying to be Belle. There was a gap where Belle should be and she had sidestepped into it.

"I'd never starve myself for days," said Jack. "I'd get hungry. No, but, it's seriously true that Byron and I are the same person. He used to talk a lot, yeah? Like, all night long. It was his favourite thing to do, which, you've got to admit, is an uncanny similarity with me."

The road was still clear, so they wheeled their bikes across.

"I know what we could do," said Madeleine. "We could go look at the statue of Byron. I think they've got one in the Wren Library."

"Byron's in the Wren?!" exclaimed Jack.

"Well, you're the one who's him, so you tell me."

*　　*　　*

So they rode to Trinity and found the statue, and Jack actually trembled, he was that excited.

"That's him," he breathed. "Yes, that's me. You see that soft drapey cloak thing he's wearing?"

Madeline nodded.

"Well, I'd wear that too, if I had one."

He then pointed out that Byron was looking very thoughtful, which was something that he himself did on occasion: think; and that Byron was holding a book and marking its place with his finger, which also was something that Jack had been known to do, let's say he was reading and got interrupted; and most of all, that Byron had curly hair!!

Which Jack also had. Or at least, he would have if he let it grow. Although the curls on the Byron statue, well, they were sort of unlikely. They looked like seashells or seahorses, which you wouldn't want crawling around on your head, would you —

"They're like giant slugs," said Madeleine.

She was still being Belle. Acidic and wry. She tilted her head and slapped at her ear, like somebody trying to get water out after swimming. Trying to get Belle out.

"They're pastries." Jack was still gazing at Byron's hair. "Little croissants on his head."

Then Madeleine's voice changed. "He's got a beautiful nose," she said, and she turned to study Jack's face. "And so do you."

Her hand floated towards Jack's nose and she startled suddenly. "I thought you were a statue!"

That was Madeleine back; they both knew it. The strange Madeleine who forgot herself sometimes, and who liked stars, beautiful noses, and odd dislocations of reality.

Jack caught at the moment fast. He took her hand from the air, ran his thumb over its palm, and let it go. They both smiled.

*   *   *

So that was the real beginning of the Jack-and-Madeleine romance. It was also the beginning of a blue-sky June.

For the next few weeks, while Belle was sick at home, they saw movies at the Grafton Centre, went to antique book shops and the Corn Exchange. They went to Pizza Express and practised doing double takes, because Jack said he'd read somewhere that the hardest thing for an actor to do is the double take. Not that they wanted to be actors, just for the challenge.

They sat by the river, sharing Jack's iPod and arguing in a pleasant, non-combative way about music.

They went to their home-school classes (although not to French and Citizenship), and the teachers either ignored the shift or didn't notice it (except for Madeleine's mother, who was disapproving, teary, and delighted — she took turns of each).

* * *

In Madeleine's mind, it was exactly right. A holiday romance. A summer fling. Everything clamoured happily. June grew warm and festive. The Cambridge students had finished their exams and were having garden parties, planning May Balls (which, confusingly, took place in June), drinking champagne, and Pimm's & Lemonade. Girls wore summer dresses and strappy sandals, boys had swinging ties and pink spots high in their cheeks. The mood was just the thing.

Everything was solved, and Madeleine felt like a ballet dancer. The letter to her father would find its way to him any moment, she was sure. She wondered if he would reply, or sweep into Cambridge unexpectedly. That was more his style: He'd open the letter, and even as he scanned it he'd begin to roll his eyes and click his fingers for a jet.

She kept catching glimpses of him emerging from a splash of sun, or punting up the river towards her. What would happen was, he'd fix his gaze on her and raise the pole into the air in mock exasperation. Then he'd leap from the punt to the shore and take her in his arms, his navy linen jacket buckling against her, his beard scratchy as he

kissed her cheek. (In her imagination, he'd grown the beard again —
for comfort, probably, in the absence of her and her mother.)

Speaking of her mother, it was now clear to Madeleine that Holly
did not need a doctor! She was just misplaced. Like a swan that has
flown from its glassy pond and is trying to set up house in a car junk-
yard. The swan would also grow vague and absent-minded. Its feathers
would rust as it tried to sleep on the ripped leather of car seats, and
it would have occasional headaches too.

Nobody would be at all surprised if the swan had difficulty answering the questions on a quiz show.

(Also, most likely, Holly had never been as good at quizzes as
they'd thought: That sewing-machine win had been a fluke.)

Madeleine dropped her plan to trick her mother into going to the
doctor. All Holly needed was a rescue and a salt scrub for her feathers.
And if she *was* unwell, then Madeleine's father would find the best
physician in the world. (Not a doctor, a *physician*.) (She wasn't really
sure of the difference, but still.)

And meanwhile, as she waited, there was the romance with Jack.
Madeleine was so giddy, she sometimes found herself confusing
Jack with Lord Byron, falling for Jack's claims that he and Byron were
one and the same. She would be swinging Jack's hand — he often had
a Band-Aid or two on his hand, and the edges of these, their soft
coldness, seemed somehow more intimate than the hand itself — she
would be walking along with him, swinging his hand, and she would
actually believe she was with Byron.

When they kissed in Jack's room, or when they kissed outside on
her sloping roof, or when his hand stroked her bare arm, she would
close her eyes and think of poetry.

She knew more about Byron than Jack did. She knew that when he
was eight years old, Byron had loved a girl so much he would sit for
hours gazing at her. He felt sorry for the girl's sister, for not being as
pretty as she was.

Years passed. He never saw this girl. Then he heard that she had married someone else, and it hit him like a thunderbolt. He nearly choked on the news.

To the astonishment of all of those around him.

Later, when he was still a teenager, Byron fell in love again — with an older girl, one of a superior class, named Miss Chaworth. Again, he loved her with his own profound madness. Only, one day he overheard her talking to a friend. She said, with a sneer, "Do you think I could care anything for that *lame* boy?"

Meaning Byron with his twisted foot.

Again, years later, his mother said to Byron, "I have some news for you."

"Well, what is it?" Byron said.

"Take out your handkerchief first," she suggested. "For you will want it."

"Nonsense."

"Take out your handkerchief," she insisted.

He did so, holding it up for her to see.

"Well, what is it?"

"Miss Chaworth is married!"

The strangest expression crossed his face, and he returned his handkerchief to his pocket, exclaiming: "Is that all?"

"Why," said his mother, "I expected you would have been plunged in grief!"

Byron did not reply and, after a moment, changed the subject.

So, when Madeleine and Jack lay side by side on his bed — with the door open, at Federico's insistence, and with Federico complaining his way through a pasta in the kitchen — staring at the glow-in-the-dark stars that Jack had stuck to his ceiling (so that they corresponded to the signs of the zodiac), and Jack explained that, as an Aries, he had courage, fire, and fertility, Madeleine would laugh, but as she laughed, she would smile to herself, and think, *Behind that bravado you've been hurt, haven't you? Over and over, by girls in the past. You've loved with intensity and passion, and have learned to hide your heartache, learned to press your handkerchief back into your pocket and pretend that you are okay.*

And she would look at his legs in their blue jeans, wondering which one was lame. Then frown slightly in confusion, remembering neither was.

On the street, she'd approach Jack from behind, touch his shoulder, and he'd turn around with that expression he got when he saw her these days. It was startled, embarrassed, happy, bold, and uncertain all at once. She liked him when she saw it, she felt a rush of fondness, and then, maybe seeing her fondness, he would relax and start talking.

He did talk a lot.

In that way, he was like Byron.

I'll miss him, she thought sometimes, *when I go home.*

But they could email.

Speaking of email, her friend Tinsels was taking a while to reply. But that was not a surprise. Tinsels was always floating around in pools reading books, or else out riding horses. She hardly ever checked email, and when she did, she forgot her password, or how you opened Gmail, and she'd often fling computers across rooms, demanding tech support. "I am *endearingly hopeless* with technology," she liked to say.

Eventually, Tinsels would figure it out and reply.

As for Jack, the disbelief in his chest was like brooms jostling in a closet. That's how much it confused him. He kept thinking of things to make the smile dazzle across Madeleine's lovely face: He'd bring her raspberry slices from Fitzbillies, or a takeaway coffee with a peppermint chocolate resting on the lid. He found her a second-hand bike basket and secretly attached it for her. The smile would come, and deep in his mind, somewhere behind the toppling brooms, he would whisper to himself in wonder: "She actually likes me."

The words seemed to play on a chime bar.

She talked a lot about her life before, and her chin lifted in the air as she remembered. She'd skated and paraglided. She'd been expelled from boarding schools for running away on weekends. Her dad has always been angry about the running away: He sometimes wouldn't talk to her for weeks. He must be *furious* right now, she said, sounding nostalgic.

But when her father wasn't angry, she explained, it was like a light seemed to shine from inside him. People would turn and look at him when he passed. He was good at life, she said. In one night he could give a speech at a reception, play pool, get drunk, do a multi-million-dollar deal, go dancing, come home, and start again. He never got hangovers. It was true he was always busy, but he never stopped thinking of ways to entertain her and her friends. He'd climb up behind the puppet show to explain to her how the strings worked. Or, at the start of a meal, he'd shove something up his sleeve like lightning ready for a trick that he would play to entertain her, seven courses later, at the end of the meal.

"*Seven* courses?"

"It was a degustation," she explained.

Jack felt like he had to run to keep up with Madeleine's conversation.

Definitely, he had to be funny. The way she laughed at his jokes, it was like she was catching on to them with both hands and holding tight. Sometimes, her eyes seemed to move around his words, searching for the humour, and he thought it was like she was sizing up a shredded old tissue to see if she could use it for an origami rose.

It didn't always work. Once, he was quoting lines from the movie *Monsters, Inc.*, which she hadn't seen, and she was falling about laughing, and he told her how he and Belle used to have this thing where they'd look at each other and shout, "Mike Wazowski!" — the name of a character in the movie — and Madeleine laughed even harder.

Then she stopped suddenly and reflected. "That's not actually funny," she said.

"No," he said, "I guess it's not."

"I mean, I can see how it was funny at the time, but here? Now? It's not."

"You're right," he apologised.

She had those bright eyes, that way of twisting her foot, and often when they'd just sat down somewhere, she'd be jumping up again ready to go. She was always looking around, waiting for something.

He thought maybe she was waiting for her dad to come and whisk her away, and he worried about this. He'd dig his nails into his palms as a wish to the stars that Madeleine's parents would never get back together.

He felt quite guilty about that.

It seemed unlikely, though, after all this time, that the dad would suddenly turn up. So that was a comfort.

Madeleine and Jack were not always together.

Madeleine spent time with her mother too, and reading. She was reading about Isaac Newton these days.

Also, although Jack did not know this, she rode her bike to the broken parking meter to send letters to Elliot Baranski.

Dear Elliot Baranski,
Yeah, okay, you can exist if you want.

Well, that sucks about the Butterfly Child not fixing the crops for you! She's teeny-tiny, right, though? So . . . maybe a bit too much to ask of her? Could make more sense for you FARMERS to look into the problem. More likely to have the expertise, right?

Have you tried fertiliser? I hear that can work wonders.

Maybe it's a pest control issue. Is it organic farming? If not, use pesticides. If so, well, try them anyway but do it at night.

Well, I'm not really the girl to ask, seeing as I've never even SEEN a farm (except on TV) — and maybe neither is the Butterfly Child.

Especially if she's sick!

But your only basis for thinking she's sick is that she's sleeping? That could be because she's tired.

When she goes out with her insect companions she's probably partying hard, getting blitzed, loaded, tanked (etc.), coming back, and passing out? Do you have Alcoholics Anonymous for Insect People in your Kingdom? If so, sign her up.

What else? OK, it seems like you have guilt because you think it's your fault if she is sick? I doubt that it is. I THINK, if I'm understanding you right (and your letters confuse the hell out of me) — but, anywayz, I THINK you were saying that the reason you couldn't get up and take the lid off the jar (?) was that you had a broken ankle?

Well, don't beat yourself up over that.

When I broke my ankle, everyone was like shouting at me, "Don't get up! Stay still!" which they didn't need to, cause it freakin' well KILLED. So I just lay there in the snow till the huskies came with the sled. And I can guarantee that if someone had said, "Oh, Madeleine, by the way, there's a little butterfly-fairy thing inside that jam jar over there, would you hop on over and open the lid?" I would have said, "Tell the *%$ butterfly to open her own &^# lid."

Those little marks indicate choice language (in case you don't have that convention in your Kingdom).

Also, when Tinsels (she's my best friend) broke her FINGER (with the blender when she was making a Long Island Iced Tea, and forgot she was blending it, and put her finger in to taste it), she had to lie down in a hammock for a month.

Hang on, I have to go, meeting a friend. We're going to the Trinity May Ball — seeing the fireworks in a punt even — it's a surprise he arranged for me —

Okay, I'm back. It's the next day. And I've been thinking some more about your issue. I just looked at your letter, and you seem in a STATE about it, so I wanted to tell you that I recently discovered that the way to solve a problem is to write it down. With, like, a question mark, and then WRITE THE ANSWER.

Try it. It totally works.

It's the Isaac Newton approach.

Isaac was also a big believer in thinking about a problem. Just thinking. Here's a nice quote from him about it:

"I keep the subject constantly in mind before me and wait till the first dawnings open slowly, by little and little, into a full and clear light."

But wait, listen, I just remembered that my therapist, Claudia, once told me that sometimes you can solve a problem if you STOP THINKING ABOUT IT. Think about other things. Or just, like, go to bed. And tell your subconscious or whatever — your dreaming mind, maybe — to sort the whole thing out for you.

k, it's 3 a.m., better go.
catch you,
M.T.

P.S. Sorry about the conflicting suggestions for problem solving, i.e., think all the time or don't think at all. I guess it's a choice between genius of all time Isaac Newton, or my (very nice and often quite sensible) therapist, Claudia Tilmaney.

P.P.S. In making your choice you might like to keep in mind that:

• Someone famous once said that you could split up the entire history of mathematics into two halves — the first half is all previous mathematics from the beginning of time; the second was Isaac Newton. And Isaac Newton was the better half.
• When Tsar Peter of Russia visited England back in the days of Isaac Newton, the things on his must-see list were: shipbuilding, the Greenwich Observatory, the mint — and Isaac Newton.
and
(most important of all)
• Isaac Newton invented the cat flap.

By comparison:

• I remember once Claudia telling me she was useless at her multiplication tables (it bothered me a lot — from then on, I was always kind of like wanting to say to her, "Nine twelves?" or "Eight sixes?").
• To the best of my knowledge, Tsar Peter of Russia never once asked if he could meet Claudia.
and
• Claudia doesn't even OWN a cat.

A few days later, Elliot Baranski replied:

Dear M.T.,
Thanks for your thoughts on the Butterfly Child.
She's still sleeping, crops still dead in the ground, but my ankle's on the mend and I feel like an ass for complaining like I did in my last letter. Sorry about that.

A wave of Reds is on its way — we get Color attacks here, not sure if you know about those. I think I recall that you don't get Colors in the World.

Most often, you don't have a clue that a Color's coming until the warning bells ring (or until it's on you), and most Colors travel alone, but Reds travel in waves, and in the open. So you get a week or two's notice of them (towns up the line call it in).

Anyhow, if I write you a letter that's sort of off-kilter in the next little while, don't take it personally. Fourth-level Reds mess with your mind.

But then they'll be gone —

— and I've gotta go myself.

Elliot

Madeleine could see him clearly, the writer of the Elliot letters. He was probably around her age. Shy and awkward, teeth that criss-crossed at the front, a high freckled forehead, round glasses, an awkward way of laughing at all the wrong times. Or a laugh like a snort that made him blush. "Elliot Baranski" was his alter ego — his avatar, his escape.

Who did it hurt to play along?

One thing about all this — the correspondence with "Elliot," the romance with Jack — it felt truer to her previous self.

She had never even suspected that Jack liked her until the night he kissed her on the roof, but as soon as he did, it made sense.

Because that's how it used to be. In her previous life, there were always eyes on her. People wanting her attention, just because she was rich and pretty. And mostly she'd be hanging with her own friends, but sometimes she had liked to meet these other people, answer their questions, ask *them* about themselves.

So now it was happening again, and she was having fun.

She liked them both, Jack and the letter writer, but even more, she liked their alter egos: Lord Byron and Elliot Baranski.

Around this time, Darshana Charan asked Jack and Madeleine to come over early to babysit.

Darshana was their Science and Mathematics teacher, the former microbiologist who now cleaned students' rooms.

Her daughters were four and three: Rhani, the elder, was wild, loud, and passionate about robots and aliens; Chakiki, the younger, was sweet, obliging, and loved fairy wings and princess crowns.

"You are no child of mine!" Darshana often said to little Chakiki.

On this day, Jack and Madeleine arrived at the same time. They could hear the sounds of Darshana and her elder daughter impersonating monster roars, and the high voice of Chakiki explaining that their noises hurt her feelings.

"Remind me I have something to tell you," Jack said as he knocked.

"Tell me now," said Madeleine.

But the door flew open, and there was a tumble of little hands dragging them inside, while Darshana shouted instructions to everyone at once, and then was gone.

Some time later, the girls were watching TV side by side on the carpet, while Madeleine and Jack sat on the couch. There was a careful space between them; their fingers tangled once and then drew apart.

"This is what I have to tell you," Jack said to Madeleine. "I'm *not* Byron after all."

On the TV, a dinosaur roared, the sound like bathwater sucking down a drain.

"I've figured it out," Jack continued. "I'm not him, but I met him once. In one of my former lives. That's why I felt like I *was* him — because I knew him so well. We used to shoot the breeze, Byron and me."

Madeleine turned back to the TV. "Oh, yeah," she said. "Me too. We had a blast, eh? You, me, and Byron."

"I knew you wouldn't take me seriously. I did! I did know Byron. And not only that but I was a guinea hen at the time."

Madeleine laughed, and the two little girls turned and held their fingers to their lips with a sharp "shhh."

Obediently, they stayed silent for a while, then Madeleine curled her feet beneath her and turned sideways to Jack. "Do you actually believe in reincarnation?"

"Of course I do. Have you not listened to a single word I've said? All of us are reincarnated. We all come back under the twelve different signs of the zodiac so we get to draw on the twelve different elements of our character, and I happened to be a Scorpio when I was hanging with Byron."

"I thought you were a guinea hen."

"Not a *scorpion*, a Scorpio. A Scorpio guinea hen, and there's nothing hilarious about that, a guinea hen is a noble creature and I held my head high when I was one. It's true that I don't have *exact* memories of my former lives, but I've got glimpses and sensations and so on, and if you would ever, sort of like, listen to your heart, you might get glimpses of your own past lives too. You might even *meet* yourself from a former life, so, you know, be ready to be polite."

"Okay, that part makes no sense."

"Sure it does," said Jack. "You never listen when I talk, do you? Time is crumpled, see. I've told you that before. It's sort of folded on itself — there's really only one time and it's now, and Rhani's goldfish there could easily be you from a former, or even future, life."

They regarded the fish. It ignored them, lost in its own thoughts.

"It's not a goldfish," said Madeleine. "It's blue. It's a fighting fish."

"That's beside the point."

"Well, don't let them forget to feed me," said Madeleine. "And maybe you could get me a castle or something for my fishbowl."

The dinosaur cartoon finished and *Sesame Street* began.

"Oh, *Sesame Street*," said Rhani, turning to Jack and Madeleine. "We always get a chocolate biscuit when this comes on."

Chakiki also turned. "Yeah, we do. We get the kind with the white bit in the middle, and we get two ones each."

The only thing the little girls had in common was a swift ability to lie.

"You can look me in the eye," Jack said, "and tell me that your mother flies to the kitchen to get you a couple of chocolate biscuits whenever *Sesame Street* starts?"

"She doesn't *fly* to the kitchen," Rhani withered. "She just kind of like strolls in."

"I can look you in the eye," offered Chakiki.

"I'll call her and check, shall I?" Madeleine suggested, and the girls sighed noisily and turned back to the TV.

All four watched *Sesame Street* for a while, then Madeleine said: "How do you know you were a guinea hen? In your former life with Byron, I mean. Does a guinea hen *know* that it's a guinea hen?"

"Well," Jack conceded. "I'm not totally sure. I've just sort of pieced it together. See, I've figured out I was a small domestic animal in *all* of my former lives. Like a cat or a possum. And once, I was a Tasmanian devil in a petting zoo with a zookeeper that loved me."

"Okay."

"I remember being lower down than other people — there were always ankles around, see? Also, I remember they used to pick me up sometimes and cuddle me. So that's why I know I was a small domestic animal."

Madeleine considered this. "I think you're remembering being a baby," she said.

"No." Jack shook his head. "I remember chasing pigeons. I remember kind of scrabbling away when humans tried to cuddle me. I remember this sensation of being helpless and *wanting* the things humans had, and I remember the noises I made. They were animal noises, like shrieks and things, and I felt good when I did that, but I also sort of scared myself. Plus I remember being a bear cub in a pit somewhere in Florence in the fifteenth century."

"Okay."

"That was lonely. In the pit."

"I'll bet. And you remember meeting Byron as a guinea hen?"

"It's like this," Jack said. "I was reading about Byron the other day, and did you know he lived in Italy for a while? Anyhow, he had horses, dogs, monkeys, cats, an eagle, a crow, a falcon, peacocks, guinea hens, and an Egyptian crane. I was reading this and the words *guinea hens* sort of caught at me and said: *'Jack!'"*

"Ah, then," agreed Madeleine.

"He let all his animals live in the house. Peacocks and monkeys wandering up and down the stairs. Oh, except the horses. They weren't allowed inside."

"Poor horses," said Madeleine. The girls were transfixed by the TV, so she leaned over and kissed Jack's cheek. "I liked it better when you were Byron," she murmured. "As sexy as a guinea hen can be."

Jack turned back to the TV and sighed deeply. "Actually, now that I think about it, that's all bollocks. Everything I just said. I was never a guinea hen. I *am* Lord Byron."

He touched her thigh with a curled fist and she let herself lean into him.

"The letter of the day is *J*," both girls shouted, suddenly turning and catching her quick shift back.

A key turned in the front door and a voice shouted, "The letter of the day is *J*, is it? But what is the *name* of the day? YOU DON'T KNOW, DO YOU?"

The girls ran down the hall, and Jack and Madeleine unfolded themselves from the couch.

There was Darshana's voice at the door, but also another voice, an extra voice, laughing.

"Look who I've found, and she's come to have morning tea with us," called Darshana.

Holly Tully moved into the hallway light, smiling.

"We'll have Science later," Darshana said. "Or another day. Who cares. But, you small people who live in this house with me, you still have not told me the name of this day!"

"Saturday?" tried Rhani.

"Friday," asserted Chakiki, confident.

"Ah! You are no children of mine!"

Madeleine looked beside her at Jack, with his smile and his cheek lit up by curtain-speckled sun. She looked down the hall at Darshana, still at the front door, still thundering; at the two little girls, swinging from mood to mood as if on a jungle gym; and finally, at her mother, straight-backed and bright, a spark in her eye, whispering fiercely to the girls out of the side of her mouth: "It's *Tuesday.*"

There was that lift again, that surge of *holiday*, of blue-sky June — that certainty that everything was going to be all right — and then there was a curious sound, like a handful of pebbles spilling to the floor.

As Madeleine watched, the strangest quiver ran across her mother's shoulders and down her right arm, and Holly Tully fell to the floor.

Bonfire, The Farms, Kingdom of Cello

9.

$\mathcal{I}$t was autumn dusk in Bonfire, shadows closing in on themselves in the empty high-school grounds.

Elliot stood by Cody's sculpture, reading the latest letter from the Girl-in-the-World:

Dear Elliot,

Strange day.

My mother fainted this morning. I was at my Science teacher's house and there was a noise like pebbles falling, which turned out, actually, to be exactly that.

Still haven't figured out why Mum walked into the house with a handful of pebbles.

Anyhow, it was bad. There's my mother on the floor, and the teacher's little girls thinking she's playing a joke, so they're both HYSTERICAL, falling flat on their backs, jumping over her, squealing. The TV was counting blue hippos behind me. Darshana's face seemed to snag on its own surprise so she just stood there with her eyes wide open (which really scared me — she's usually a human iron lung), and my friend Jack started saying my mother's name over and over, in this scary, questioning voice that gets louder and louder — "Holly? Holly? HOLLY?" like a dad about to bust a kid.

I just stood there, counting blue hippos.

ANYHOW, she's fine.

When Chakiki (the younger of the girls) realised Mum wasn't getting up, she emptied a flower vase over her face. (She's still got half-dead tulip petals stuck in her hair, actually.) Right away, Mum choked, opened her eyes, and said a word that practically choked the little girls with the shock. They were still shouting it at each other an hour later, and using it as the punch line of jokes and the chorus of songs. (Darshana kept telling us, "Ignore them and they'll stop," and saying to the girls, "I'm not impressed, you know! I'm not bothered! I'm ignoring you and you will stop!" But they didn't.)

Mum explained that she'd forgotten to eat breakfast this morning, and then she remembered that she'd ALSO forgotten dinner last night (I'd been at Jack's having pasta, so I didn't realise this), and everyone was like: NO WONDER YOU FAINTED, YOU STUPID IDIOT.

So we all ate masala dosa and drank tea, and my mother started to look less like a corpse.

I am now at home, and I've just made tofu fritters, which were okay. And she's back at her sewing machine.

Anyhow, so, listen, I'm thinking you should choose something else for your "villains" (or "monsters" or whatever they are) in your Kingdom of Cello. Something other than Colours, I mean. Because, seriously, "a wave of Reds is coming"? Do you realise how racist you sound? (I'm thinking of the history surrounding Native Americans.) Even the word "Colours" sounds too close to another word, also from American history, right?

Or are you doing it on purpose? Like an ironic cultural reference?

Anyway, I don't like it.

I guess, though, if you do keep them, it's kind of funny that the colour Red travels in "waves." Cause, well, all colours do that, right? Travel in waves, I mean.

I know this cause I've been reading about colours. My guy, Isaac Newton, was into them.

Have you done the research? I mean, got your colour science right? Because, okay, as I see it, there are two different kinds of colours, and I want to know which you have in mind.

There are true colours, and those are made of light. They come from the sun, and if they hit the rain in a certain way, that's a rainbow. If you could take light in both your hands and fan it out, you'd see true colours, lining up, blending at the edges. (You can make your own rainbow. Just let the sun shine through water or glass. Did you know?)

Then there are what I call flat colours. They're the kind we see around us. Like that bag over there is red and white striped,

189

and that banana is (partly) yellow (mostly black), and the tiles in the kitchen are an unbelievably disgusting mottled pink, like a salmon that got old, died, then ate a boiled beetroot.

Now, if I'm understanding it properly, what the flat colours are is just a sort of conversation with light. Cause when light hits an object it's like it offers the object its handful of *true* colours, and the object says yes to some and no to the rest. So, some it absorbs (eats, takes in, loves, whatever) and the others it throws right back.

The colours that it throws back are the ones we see. The banana is yellow because the banana ate all the other colours but did not want the yellow.

It's sort of ironic, yeah?

Anyway, I'll finish this letter by sharing with you something that I can't get out of my head. Isaac Newton once said this about fire:

"The flame is of several colours, as that of sulphur blue, that of copper opened with sublimate green, that of tallow yellow, that of camphire white. Smoke passing through flame cannot but grow red-hot & red-hot smoke can have no other appearance than that of flame."

So, why can't I stop thinking about that? I guess it's kind of poetic — sulphur blue, copper green, tallow yellow — but mostly I think it's the way he talks about smoke and flames. Smoke goes through flame and turns red-hot, and red-hot smoke appears like flame. You can turn that inside out. You can say, smoke makes flame makes smoke makes flame. So what is smoke and what is flame? They're looping in and out of each other, separate but also the same thing.

Like I said, that's my final thought for the letter. But I want to know more about you. Like, what do you do for fun,

Elliot? Got a girlfriend? Got any thoughts about smoke and flames?

Cheers,
M.T.

Elliot folded the letter, feeling strange. He felt free but clumsy, tall but childlike: It was his first day without crutches. The cast had come off his ankle a few days before, but today the doctor had said he should try walking on it. The red haze of the sunset seemed to echo the mild blaze, the low-level excitement, in his chest.

Except that, he saw now, that red haze was not sunset at all.

It was the first of them, the first one on its way, and Elliot was already pushing the letter into his pocket, half running, half loping, half limping, half tripping, as the warning bells spilled through the air.

With most Colors, the warning bells seem to suck people inside of their houses, or into the nearest shelter or shop — into anywhere with a door and lock-down shutters.

But a second-level Red (grade 2(b)) has the opposite effect. Doors and windows fly open and people pour onto the streets.

It's the most luminous of all Colors, and it filled the sky over Bonfire that night like a dazzling fireworks display. Almost at once, the streets and square and rooftops were alive with people. The Sheriff had been taking a shower and he half ran, half limped down the pavement in bare feet and a bathrobe. A group of small ghosts and skeletons swarmed by (children from a fancy dress party); then came the Mayor — she'd just been having her hair colored and was still in the black salon smock, her hair folded helter-skelter into silver foil.

High above the town, the Red burst again and again — the heel of a hand slamming down on a giant raspberry, or enormous stoplights shattering. Light showered from each explosion, scribbling the sky, swerving in every direction.

The tricky thing, for the people of Bonfire, was to tear their eyes from the beauty of the sky, so they could concentrate on what they had to do. They had to find hoses, buckets, and watering cans. They had to drag safety tarpaulins over electrical units and fuel stations. They had to gather extinguishers, blankets, and coats; pull on boots; scatter themselves throughout the town, its gardens, parks, and fields, and watch.

Within moments of the first Red explosions, the sparks began to rain. Autumn had been hovering in Bonfire for a fortnight or more, long enough for the gold-red leaves to form drifts and piles, and these were the first things to catch. The sparks fell, flames leapt up, and the people of Bonfire moved. The local firefighters took up the corners and shouted orders. The fire truck spun around corners, dealing with the biggest outbreaks; but the entire town — children, the elderly, the sick — had to work.

Elliot Baranski stamped and stamped at sparks with his good leg as he tripped through the streets. He saw a ballet class in leotards passing buckets hand to hand from the fountain in the Bonfire Gardens. There were Gabe and Cody, running along rooftops, punching out fires in gutters and eaves. Freshly delivered newspapers flared up one after another, and little Corrie-Lynn ran from one to the next, her friend Derrin Twickleham beside her, each smothering fires with their coats. Derrin was more methodical, but also more whimsical, so sometimes she'd get distracted and stop with the fires altogether. Corrie-Lynn would step in at that point. They were a good team.

Litter caught fire — cardboard coffee cups and candy wrappers — and so did patches of overgrown grass, and dried bark, and a pile of discarded telephone directories, and the corners of wooden paling fences. A banner over Main Street announced the upcoming Craft Fair, and Elliot watched as it crackled alight, but before he could reach it, Jimmy Hawthorn was clambering up a telegraph pole and tearing it down. On the street below, Isabella Tamborlaine was ready with a tin can full of water. She and Jimmy gave each other a thumbs-up.

Elliot darted from spark to spark, and it was dangerous but, still, it was hard not to let your heart go wild. There were bursts of rust red, paprika red, cinnamon red, and Elliot thought that as the sparks fell they formed other colors too — sulfur blue, copper green, tallow yellow. They swayed and bent like comet tails, star bursts, cattails, cottonwood trees, or like stems of straw snapped in two. He was kicking at cinders and charcoal, exhilarated by the mischief of the sparks; the ends of his hair were singed, the acrid smell of that, the smell of smoke, flames, wet burnt leaves, the heat on his cheeks.

Nearby, the edges of a woman's frayed jeans caught, and Elliot pressed his own ankles against her legs, extinguishing the fire, and she grinned her thanks, then used her bare hands to clap out Elliot's coat collar.

He looked up at the gold-silver edges of the sparks, the not-quite-there of them, the falling fireflies. He heard the crackle of flames, the shouts and warnings, the crumple-stamping and frightened laughter; and he saw behind his eyes an image of his father welding, visor down, impossible spray of sparks.

Then, abruptly, there was a quieting.

The Red had gone. The sky was musky gray with smoke, but blackening and brightening as the smoke drifted and the stars studded back into place.

There were occasional shouts and flurries still, as fires were spotted and put out, and then there was the engine of the crop duster — the little flying machine low and high then low again — swooping above Bonfire.

That was Elliot's friend Shelby, flying rain over the town and surrounding fields, showering the last of the sparks.

In Elliot's nose there was the smell of smoke, and behind his eyes was the afterimage of feathering flames. The words of the

Girl-in-the-World ran through his head: *Smoke goes through flame and turns red-hot, and red-hot smoke appears like flame. So what is smoke? And what is flame?*

It was a strange coincidence, his reading those words — or her writing them — just before the Red arrived.

Around him, the people of Bonfire were turning to one another with breathless laughter, wide-eyed relief, startled and proud. They had done it, they'd saved one another and the town. Elliot shook the girl's words from his head and smiled back.

The next day, he wrote a reply.

Dear M.T.,

I'm sorry to hear about your mother fainting. That must have been scary for you. But I like the sound of the little girl being inventive with the flower vase.

She's got to eat better, your mother. You're right about that.

Okay, you asked about Colors.

Well, I'm not so sure about this "true" versus "flat" divide of yours, but maybe it kinda works. We've got regular colors here, which I guess you'd call flat. I mean, my hair is dark blond and my jeans are dirty-blue — but we've ALSO got Colors with a capital *C*, and yeah, since they're not a lie, I guess they're true.

No, all Colors don't travel in waves. Just the Color Red.

We got the first of the wave last night, and I'll be honest, it was wonderful. It's one of the original Colors, Red (along with Blue and Green), and there's something kind of magic — and strong and dangerous — in all three. You can't bend the originals — protective gear and shutters are useless against them.

To be honest, I don't think you could change their names either. Doesn't seem likely to stop YOU from trying, though, 'cause you sure have a thing for name changing. What's that about, you think?

Just occurred to me that you might not know what Color bending is. There's Color Benders in Nature Strip, and some in the Swamp of the Golden Coast, and here's what they do: They go into the sleeping lairs (caverns or hollows or tree stumps or whatever that particular Color's preference is), and they steal the newest Colors — the babies — and bend them. If you bend an agreeable color, like Orange, say, and you bend a dangerous Color, like Purple or Gray, and you graft them together, that gets you a vaccination. Those are injected into protective gear and shutters. They don't last more than a couple of years, though, so we're always having to replace them.

And that's if you don't use them. Use protective gear in an attack and it'll wear out faster than a tap drips.

Anyhow, let's move on from Colors.

You asked if I have a girlfriend.

Her name is Kala and she's the smartest girl I know. Lately she's been thinking about applying for scholarships to boarding schools in Olde Quainte — they're the best in Cello, and if you go to one of them you've got a good chance of getting into Brellidge University.

Her family moved here from Jagged Edge when she was nine, and they started a macadamia farm. Not long after they arrived, Gabe was cycling past one of their fields, and he stopped to let Kala know she was plowing in the wrong direction. They got into a fight 'cause Kala had researched the pants off farming, and she was sure she KNEW the right direction; but Gabe's always had the instinct for farming — he could grow a ladder in a kitchen sink if you needed one. They ended up friends anyway, and now she's one of us.

She's got two little sisters who are always ballet dancing. She plays the saxophone and makes her own jewelry, and you can see both those things in her hands — she's got hands that move so gentle and graceful, soft and free. And when those hands push against her long, dark, shimmering hair, or press the keys of her saxophone, well, that's art is what it is, right there.

As for smoke and flames, no, don't have any particular thoughts on those.

Hope your mother's feeling better.

Take care,

Elliot

She was sleeping again, the Butterfly Child.

The weather had turned wintry, and Elliot watched her in the doll's house a moment, wondering if she might be cold. The fire was quiet, so he added another log, pushed it around a bit, sparks and smoke flaring, until the flames grew tall and busy. A pair of his gray woolen socks was hanging on the grate. He closed his hands around them. They felt crusty-warm, maybe a little damp around the toes still, but dry enough. He folded one in half and gently draped it over the Butterfly Child. She stirred in her sleep and turned over twice, so the sock slipped off.

He replaced it, straightening it so her little face and shoulders were free, and there it was again, a kind of catch in his throat. She was so tiny!

He thought of flakes of coconut, grated chocolate, granules of sugar, dustings of cinnamon or cloves.

He thought suddenly of how his father used to cut his hair. Elliot would sit at the kitchen table and his father would start off flamboyantly with the scissors, but then he'd slow, and slow, and it seemed he would never finish. "*Almost* done," he'd murmur, "not quite yet," concentrating, leaning forward, feathering the edges, snipping so finely it was almost not snipping, the touch of the scissor blades faint moments of cold against Elliot's neck, the touch of those fine, fine hairs falling past his cheeks to the floor.

In Elliot's backpack was a book he'd borrowed from the library that morning. It was a Saturday, and he'd finished the farmwork. So he moved away from the doll's house and sat on the couch by the fire, the book in his hands.

The cover was dusty pink. Its title, in elegant mauve, was: *The Butterfly Child: A Cellian Treasure.*

Beneath the title was a deep purple lithograph of a Butterfly Child clasping a rose. Quite possibly, she was waltzing with the rose. Across the bottom of the cover was the author's name, *Daffodil A. Hazel*, in a shiny foil font.

Elliot regarded this cover for a while.

Ah, what have I got to lose? He shrugged. There'd only been this one book in the library on the topic.

He opened it and scanned the contents. These, also, made him pause.

- *Whence comes this fragile angel? Musings on Her Origins . . .*
- *Exquisite Friendship: Tales of the bonds between the Child and her Finder . . .*
- *Her sweetest tastes: Her eating habits and her hobbies . . .*
- *All this from one so small? Myths surrounding Her magical skills . . .*

And so on.

Elliot had been thinking more along the lines of "Dealing with a Dud."

He found the index, and there were about twenty references to "the Crop Effect," but every single one told wide-eyed-wonder anecdotes of branches breaking beneath the weight of apples, wheat fields growing to the height of buildings, and honey darn near flowing down the streets.

The Crop Effect begins within days of the Butterfly Child's arrival, said the author confidently, *although it may take up to four weeks.*

Well, that deadline had passed.

Elliot turned to the index again, but there was no entry for *Sleep* or *Rest*. None for *Excess* of either sleep or rest or lying around either.

There *was* an entry for *Illness*, which excited him a moment, but it only took him to the chapter on *Myths surrounding Her magical skills* and the legend of how, centuries ago, Butterfly Children had spun healing beads that supposedly cured human sickness.

He flicked through the pages at random, and occasional phrases jumped out: *Some think that the fable of the genie in the bottle arose from early Butterfly Children*, and *In a way, she does grant wishes — just not necessarily the ones that you want*.

In the eating habits chapter, there was a claim that the bark of the sycamore tree was a delicacy for the Butterfly Child.

She likes to read about current affairs, asserted a section on *Hobbies*. *A thoughtful Finder will leave newspapers casually strewn about in the vicinity of Her doll's house. How the heart swells to catch sight of the dear little thing struggling to turn those enormous pages with her tiny hands! (A thimbleful of honeydew is excellent for washing off the print stains.)*

The book was a waste of time.

He snapped it shut, and there was the faintest sound from the doll's house. Then quiet again.

He stared at the tiny shape and as he did, the words of the Girl-in-the-World came to him:

> *I keep the subject constantly in mind before me and wait till the first dawnings open slowly, by little and little, into a full and clear light.*

Okay, then, he thought, and he kept watching.

He sat and stared at the Butterfly Child for half an hour, and just as his neck was aching and his legs getting agitated — just at that point, it came to him.

Like a curtain shifting. *Little and little, into a full and clear light.*

A dreaminess stole across him.

It was words he'd read about the Butterfly Child in the Cellian guidebook — the time Corrie-Lynn had shown him — they pinned themselves up before his eyes, slow and graceful.

When a Butterfly Child is happy, the crops in the surrounding area will flourish.

He opened his eyes wide.

"You're not *happy?*" he said into the stillness of the room. "*That's the problem?*"

The Butterfly Child lay still.

What's not to be happy about? he thought, suddenly annoyed.

What did you do about a depressed Butterfly Child? Get a therapist like the Girl-in-the-World used to have?

He sat back on the couch and raised his eyebrows.

Leaned forward to stoke the fire, and sat back again.

Now this was strange.

The warmth of that fire was running down his spine, and more than that, it was *inside* him. Like hands around a mug of something hot, only the hands were in his chest, at his heart, warming his heart.

Somehow he wanted to weep with it, that warmth. Wasn't it just a moment ago he'd been so annoyed with that sugar-sweet book and that dozing, miserable Butterfly Child? Now his fingertips brushed against the cover of the book and he smiled tenderly at the author's name, *Daffodil.* There was a sighing sound, sighing in, sighing out — the room was breathing, the world was breathing — then he realized, no, it was him that was breathing. He *was* the world.

Ah, that Butterfly Child, he thought, and he felt the tears touching at his eyes. He looked across at the doll's house and realized his mistake was trying to compare her to physical objects: No object could ever be small enough to describe her sleeping lashes! She was as small as that sound — was it a sound he could hear? That Butterfly Child, she was as small as the sound of a page turning, in a distant room in a house.

Elliot shifted ever so slightly but only so that this soothing warmth could find another part of his heart. His thoughts seemed to sigh their way together, and then a single word emerged. Kala! Ah, Kala. Now the warmth seemed an actual physical force, pressing at him so his eyes burned, and tears fell, and the warmth of those tears on his cheeks was an echo of the wonder in his heart.

To have Kala in his life, to be allowed to kiss her, hold her, touch her, listen to her voice, and catch her eyes with his. That was all there was. That was the essence.

He watched the fireplace, and he thought of sitting side by side with Kala on the roof of the barn, holding her hand. He thought of the essence of Kala herself, and he got the crazy idea that she was one of those fold-up postcards, the kind where you get ten picture post-cards all joined together, but folded into one. He could fold her up, unravel her, fold her up again, their legs swinging side by side on the old tin roof.

He let the butterfly book fall to the floor and took a notepad and pen from his backpack instead.

Kala: (he wrote)
  Your face,
    Your mind,
      Your heart,
        Your beautiful hands

Then he drew a little sketch of Kala's hands, and underneath: *I love you — Elliot.*

He looked at the paper and knew he had to take it to Kala immediately.

Outside, there it was: the fifth-level Red, and the faint sound of warning bells. He nodded, not surprised. This Red was rich and warm, a lighter red, almost orange, and it misted at the height of tall trees, drifting in broad boatlike shapes.

It was the Red that was making his heart fill up, he knew that now, but still, he did not hesitate.

It might be the Red, he thought, *but it's also the truth. The Red is just illuminating truth.*

He took his bike and rode slowly into town — the truck would be too noisy for this mood — and he put the note into Kala's letter box.

Meanwhile, all around town, the fifth-level Red washed through the air, and people caught their breath and placed hands palm-down on their chests. Women climbed into attics to find old hats, old paintings, old love letters. Men wept quietly and tenderly. Children stared through windows at fields or ran outside to stroke their pet rabbits. Little Corrie-Lynn set to work on a new wooden puppet for her best friend, Derrin Twickleham.

Jimmy Hawthorn walked out of his front door, down the path, through the gate, and knocked once, twice, three times, on his neighbor's door. When Isabella Tamborlaine answered, he said, "I think you ought to know — well," and they fell into each other's arms.

In the Sheriff's station, Hector Samuels was sitting on the floor behind the counter. His face was a wreck of scars, lines, and tears. He was holding a gold ring so tightly that it was aching a mark into his palm. "Ah, Simon," he rasped, meaning his lost love, his first love, who died of an illness twenty years before. He'd hardly thought about Simon this last decade or more, but here he was again, snared on Hector's heart.

Back at Elliot's home, Petra Baranski was curled on her bed, turning the pages of the family photo album, touching the photos of her lost husband. *Your face, your mind, your heart, your beautiful hands.* Over and over, she mouthed the words, her own face streaked and stained with sobbing.

The following day, the fifth-level Red was gone.

Bonfire's residents moved through town, stilted and awkward, bowing their heads to hide their red-rimmed eyes.

It was a Sunday, and Elliot started the day by repairing the lock on the shed door. He guessed his mother must have broken it while trying to get inside — maybe wanting to see the old junk of his dad's that was stored there, so she could hold it and weep.

Then he headed to the square to meet his friends, but detoured via the schoolyard first, to check for a letter in the sculpture.

There was a new one. He glanced around — sometimes he almost forgot that this was illegal — but the schoolyard was still, and empty, so he opened it and read.

Dear Elliot,

Okay, so, you win, Colours are the bad guys there.

(But they DO all travel in waves. You're wrong about that.)

It's funny, the way you've got red, blue, and green as the "original" colours, cause they're the primary colours, right?

I've been thinking about it, though, and you know what? THEY'RE NOT REAL.

Now, listen, science was never really my thing, so you can ignore all this if you want, but I THINK what the books are trying to say to me is, like I said, that they're not real. They don't really exist. For two reasons.

The first one is this. They're just made of light. So, you know, in the dark, they're gone. Switch off the light or put up a black curtain and they're gone. Objects have no colour in the dark, did you realise that? It's only the light hitting them that sets off this chemical reaction with their pigments or whatever, that makes them turn a particular colour. Otherwise, it's kind of like, "If a tree falls in a forest and nobody sees it, does it really fall?"

Yeah, sure it does. The tree falls. But with colours? Well, if a red violin is sitting in the dark, is it really red?

Nope. Not in the dark it's not.

So, that's the first reason.

The second reason is this. Our brain invents colour. It's this tricky thing our eyes do, which I won't get into, except to say that our eyes have teeny-tiny things called "cones" and "rods." The cones see red, blue, and green, and the rods figure out shapes. So, these cones and rods send little electrochemical messages to our brain, and the brain puts them together and invents colour.

Who knows if all our brains are inventing the same thing? I mean, how do we know that the thing YOUR eyes see and call "red" is the same thing that I call "red"?

Instead of saying, "Look how green the grass is," we should actually say to each other, "Huh, that grass is absorbing light rays with wavelengths blah to blah nanometres, and reflecting light rays with wavelengths blah to blah nanometres, which the cones and receptors in MY eyes are seeing as a certain shade which we have chosen to label GREEN and I realise that your brain accepts the label GREEN, but I wonder what you actually think GREEN is?"

Anyhow, all this is leading to my suggestion for how to deal with dangerous Colours in your kingdom.

It is this:

CLOSE YOUR EYES.

And the Colours won't be there.

My mother seems okay at the moment. I'd kind of like her to see a doctor, but she just looks confused or irritated when I suggest it, and remembers some sewing job she's forgotten or something she wanted to ask the computer guy downstairs. I'm not too worried cause my dad should be here soon, to get us, and he's the kind of guy who knows how to fix things. Like, he'll look at her and he'll KNOW right away what she needs, and how to get it.

Whereas I'm kind of like, one day, OMG, SHE'S REALLY SICK, and the next day, um, is that my imagination or is she sort of off-colour? And if she IS sick, will she get better on her own or does she need antibiotics? Or just to eat better and that?

And so on.

When my dad does get here and takes us back to our usual life, I'll be able to see my real friends again — Tinsels, Corrigan, and little Warlock.

Anyhow, I liked your letter but I'm not sure that the "Kala" girl is working for me.

She's kind of too much? If you know what I mean. The whole "artist and musician" thing — can't she just be one or the other? And she can plough a field! And she's so smart! I just sort of find I don't like her that much. And does she have to have long glossy hair, or whatever you said? Next thing you'll be telling me her eyes sparkle like dewdrops.

Get a new girlfriend.

And get back to me soon — like I said, I don't know how long I'll be here.

Take care,
M.T.

As Elliot finished reading the letter, he looked up and there was Kala herself, walking toward him across the schoolyard.

He hadn't seen her since he left the note for her yesterday, and now, as he watched her approach, he saw that her face — especially her eyes — was sending him a complicated message. She was smiling but the smile had a tilt that told him that she knew his note had been brought on by the fifth-level Red. Her eyes laughed about this, but there was kindness too, and something deeper that said: Even if it *was* the Red, it was special, Elliot, and it kind of transcended Color.

She meant she wouldn't hold him to it, but she liked it all the same.

Ah, thought Elliot, seeing all this, *she's amazing — and I'm sorry, but her eyes* do *sparkle like dewdrops.*

Over the next few days, winter snowstorms blew through.

Then, late one night, an abrupt summer.

Elliot was sitting on his bedroom floor, his research sprayed around him. The window was open to let in the hot breeze, and he was shirtless. Outside, the snow was in a frenzy of melting.

Eventually, the Butterfly Child would fly away for good — maybe sooner rather than later, seeing she was so sad — and the moment she did, Elliot would fly away himself. But lately he'd been wondering exactly where he'd go. His idea about the Lake of Spells and catching a Locator Spell was starting to wear thin, to fray around the edges — it even seemed childish and unlikely.

So he'd ordered some new books on Colors, and these were stacked beside him now, alongside all his usual research.

The Hunting Tactics of Third-Level Purples was the title of the first book. The next asked, *Feeling Blue? Reimagining Cello's Cooler Colors.* Then: *The Palette of Cello, or How to Paint the Sky* — and so on.

He sorted through the books and wondered why he'd ordered them at all — none of them seemed remotely helpful. A thin book called *Thrupp's Comprehensive Guide to Locating and Opening the Seams of Purple Caverns* was followed by an even thinner volume, asserting that every word Thrupp uttered was demonstrably false.

There was a long, chatty article written by a Color Spotter (a person whose hobby is tracking down Colors, taking photographs, and ticking them off lists — a little like an extreme bird-watcher) — who claimed he'd seen a concentration of third-level Purple caverns on the coast of the Inland Sea. Behind that was a manual put together by a Color Bender, which said there was not a single trace of Color in the entire Inland Sea.

And now that Elliot looked closer, *The Palette of Cello* was actually an art manual. Nothing to do with Colors at all.

*   *   *

So he let the stack fall, and turned back to the official documents. There was the coroner's report on his Uncle Jon, the missing persons file on his dad, and the other one, on Mischka Tegan.

He pushed these aside, and then he stopped, and pulled the latter back.

Missing Persons Report: Mischka Elizabeth Tegan

He touched the sharp-edged papers and gazed steadily at the name for a moment:

Mischka Elizabeth Tegan

He flicked through the papers. There were lists of details about Mischka: her age, height, weight, build, hair, complexion, occupation, address.

Her hair was dark brown, it said, and just touched her collar.

Her address was Apartment 4 (Directly Above the Bakery), Town Square, Bonfire. Her housemate was Olivia Hattoway, Grade 2 teacher at Bonfire Grade School. That was Corrie-Lynn's teacher this year.

There were pages and pages of interviews too, mostly the same people who'd been interviewed about his dad, although here was an interview with Olivia Hattoway herself, and a number of teachers at the high school.

All the same questions. Tell me your full name. Tell me when you last saw her. Tell me what she was wearing. What did she say to you when she left? Did you hear from her? Did she call? Where do you think she might have gone? Did she say anything about where she was going or why? Did she take anything special?

Seemed like it could keep going on forever, the Sheriff blowing air on it, making it thin out in different directions. Questions trailing off, starting up again.

His eyes fell on phrases: *Nothing special missing.*

No evidence of bank accounts having been used since the disappearance.

Mood in days leading up to disappearance was cheerful, maybe a little distracted.

Last seen at the Toadstool Pub with Jon Baranski (dec'd) and Abel Baranski (missing).

He stopped reading.

Down the hall he could hear the sound of his mother taking a cold shower, trying to cool down in the heat.

The classic text on Colors — *The Origin of Cellian Colors* by Enid Thurgood — was always on his bookshelf, bristling with his own Post-it notes.

It practically fell open at the page he knew so well — the chapter on third-level Purples — and there, in tiny font, was footnote no. 7, the footnote that had springboarded him all over Cello.

7. There is anecdotal evidence that a third-level Purple once took its victim all the way to its cavern, and, rather than slaughtering him immediately — which is the Purple custom — held him prisoner for as much as twelve months (the exact length of time varies between tellers).

There it was again. The slight, fragile chance, as small as an eyelash of the Butterfly Child, that his father — and maybe Mischka too — might be alive somewhere.

But what could Elliot do, trapped here in Bonfire?

And with *nobody* who thought he should keep looking, and nowhere to turn for advice.

Outside, the snow seemed almost violent in its melting, racing and shoving in drips and clumps and half-melted icicles past the open window to the ground.

Ah, well, he thought, smiling suddenly. *There's ONE person who seems keen to give advice.*

He meant the Girl-in-the-World.

Her suggestion had more or less worked with the Butterfly Child — or anyway, given him a starting point.

Keep the subject constantly in mind.

Well, he'd been doing *that* with his missing father for over a year now.

May as well try her other suggestion — her therapist's suggestion. Stop thinking about it. Go to bed. Tell your dreaming mind to find an answer.

He kicked the books and papers halfheartedly across the room, dragged the blankets from his bed, lay down on the sheets, and fell asleep.

Two things woke him the next morning — a hammering sound and a shout from somewhere deep in his own head.

Go to the Watermelon Inn and put up those coat hooks! shouted his head.

He scrambled out of bed, his heart shouting just as loud and fast as that voice in his head.

Write a letter to the Girl-in-the-World! it cried next. *Why have you not done your Chemistry homework yet?* And then, *First thing you've gotta call the glass-repair guys over in Appletown and get that crack in the greenhouse fixed!*

He was skidding around his room amidst these shouts, throwing on his clothes, dragging on his sneakers, running his fingers through his hair, and all the time there was an odd sense of familiarity. Another voice, somewhere quieter and farther back, was saying: *You know what this is.*

Ah, yes. He did. There it was, outside. Air filled up with the shafts of a fourth-level Red, and they were coming in through his open window too. Flying around at waist level in long, straight bars, about the size of his arm. It looked like these ones were grade 6(d), but a fourth-level Red could shift grades at any moment.

No warning bells — he must have missed them while he slept.

He jogged down the hall and leapt down the stairs. In the kitchen he saw the cause of the hammering sound. It was his mother, dressed in trackpants, sprinting on the spot, weights in both hands.

"Why have I not been exercising?" she bellowed.

"It's the fourth-level Red!" he yelled back, grabbing at a knife and wildly hacking at a loaf of bread.

"I know! But why have I not?"

"Well, why haven't I gone to the Watermelon to hang the new coat hooks yet?" Elliot cried. "I promised Alanna I'd do that *weeks* ago!"

They grinned madly at each other. Sweat poured down Petra's temples, dripping to the floor. Elliot threw bread in the toaster, sliced oranges, and squeezed juice, did his Chemistry homework, phoned the glass-repair place, and wrote a letter to the Girl-in-the-World. All within five minutes.

M.T.,

You gotta spend some time rolling rosemary and sage into the lids of your pastry pies! You gotta stand on the tractor seat now and then! Scrape toffee from the apples in the trees! You've got your lava and your chestnuts and the tree falls in the forest, and the violin IS red, if it's waiting to be red, if it's ready to be red, then it's RED, it's just better at hiding than most — and you know what? YOU'RE THE ONE WITH YOUR EYES CLOSED!

'Cause your obsession with Colors and collars and ruffles, and with telling me what's what —

I kinda like it. I've gotta say you're kinda

Bye,

Elliot

"You sure you want to send that?" cried his mother, half reading over his shoulder. She'd stopped exercising and was wrenching open all the kitchen drawers, clattering their contents onto the floor. ("Gotta polish the cutlery! Gotta sort out the stationery! What have I been *thinking*?!")

"You bet I've got to send it! Right now! But *first* I have to cheer up the Butterfly Child!"

He skidded into the living room shouting, "Cheer up! What's to be down about?" He did some humorous spins and dances, then paused for a split second, watching her. He couldn't be sure, but it seemed to him that the Butterfly Child might be squeezing her eyes tighter.

"Ah well, I tried." Elliot shrugged, then ran from the house, slamming the front door behind him. That old whistling sound was playing in his mind again, but he whisked it away.

He ran right by the truck and by his bike.

Who needed them? He could take on the world! He could *fly* there if he wanted to! Why not? He held his arms high and the Reds swooped under and over them, and he flapped his arms, waiting to fly, while a quiet voice in his head said: *Uh, no.*

Okay, not fly, but he could run!

His ankle throbbed a little and "That'll teach you, ankle!" he shouted as he ran, "that'll teach you to go breaking on me!" He ran faster.

Downtown, everyone was out.

Ladders leaned against buildings, and people shouted instructions at one another and themselves. Paint cans were opened, nails were hammered, wooden structures rose up out of lawns.

"We've always wanted a garage! Why not just *build* one?!"

"Look, children! You don't need to live in our house anymore! Here's a little house of your own!"

Clover Mackie, town seamstress, was sitting on a park bench surrounded by papers.

"Doing my taxes!" she called to Elliot, punching furiously at a calculator. "Haven't done them in twenty years or more!"

The Reds swerved up and down the streets, swooping around corners.

Isabella Tamborlaine jogged past Elliot, swinging her ice skates.

"The lake won't be frozen!" Elliot cried. "It's summer, see?" pointing to the warm blue sky.

"I'm a Science teacher! Surely I can freeze it myself!" Isabella picked up her pace.

Elliot hurdled the school fence, passed a huddle of teachers — they were urgently grading exams at the same time as making plans for a *complete overhaul* of the school syllabus — and ran to deliver his letter to the sculpture. Everyone was caught up in activity and nobody paid him any heed.

A Red brushed his arm, and he turned and sprinted from the school and on through the town.

At the Watermelon Inn, the parking lot was crowded with people spray-painting their cars ("Who chose white anyway? I always wanted a black-and-orange-striped car! Just like a tiger!") or taking out the engines ("Surely I can fine-tune this myself!") or moving around the plant pots, adjusting the sprinklers.

In the front room, Alanna was standing amidst piles and piles of bedsheets. "Going to refold them all!" She grinned at Elliot. Guests and visitors were in a frenzy of agitation, the bars of Red weaving amongst them. Some people were shifting the couches into new positions; others were busily unpicking the seams of their coats. He saw the Twicklehams leaning together by the fireplace, talking up a storm. "As to a puff adder in a hint of olive oil!" Mr. Twickleham prattled, and "Call yourself a screwdriver and be hooray!" responded his wife.

Nearby, little Derrin Twickleham was playing a clapping game with Corrie-Lynn, their hands slapping together so fast the air seemed to vibrate around them.

Then, suddenly, there was a shift. The color of the Red darkened ever so slightly, and the atmosphere changed at once. Waves of anger swept across the room. Couches were shoved aside, brows crumpled, and mouths snarled in rage.

"It was the idea of a cockerel in a malt house!" shouted Mr. Twickleham.

"And *you'd* have thought of something twittering better?" she hollered back.

Corrie-Lynn and Derrin continued to clap hands together, but now it was more like pounding, and Corrie-Lynn was bellowing: "JUST TALK! JUST *STOP NOT TALKING*!"

A sound like someone ripping aluminum seemed to tear right out of Derrin's mouth.

"IF YOU CAN MAKE THAT NOISE," Corrie-Lynn screamed, "YOU CAN TALK!"

Elliot found himself crossing the room. His face was alive with heat, the blood knocking wildly at his temples. Those Twicklehams. He would kill them. He would pick them up by the hair on their heads. He would hurl them through the air, they would smash through the picture window.

Those Twicklehams.

He stepped over the rolling bodies of two elderly men, locked in a wrestling match.

Those Twicklehams.

In his father's shop.

Stealing his father's business. His customers. His place in Bonfire. His place in Elliot's —

And then suddenly Elliot stopped.

The Reds had changed again. Their hue sharpened and darkened further. The rage fell from the room like a dropped towel.

Instead, there was profound, piercing silence. Eyes widened and found one another. The wrestling men untangled themselves and drew back, unblinking. The fourth-level Red was now at grade 9(d), and everything, every thought, every object, had intensified.

Elliot found himself turning, backing from the room. He moved with careful clarity toward the lobby.

Everything he saw had redrawn outlines — *fiercely* redrawn outlines.

Here was the lobby.

Here, he knew now with vicious certainty, he would affix new coat hooks for Alanna.

Objects asserted themselves. The guest book. A pen. An empty coffee mug.

Behind the desk, the leaflets and notices on the corkboard. Breakfast Serving Times. Tours of the Farms. Maps of Bonfire. A small handwritten note in the bottom corner.

He would nail the coat hooks beside the corkboard.

His gaze seemed to lift itself up with its own certainty, and to shift, a careful shift, then another careful shift, until it stopped. It was on the corkboard, again. His vision aimed directly at that handwritten note in the corner.

That was his uncle's handwriting.

That was Uncle Jon's tiny script:

Guest Room Heaters: Pin 1: +12, Pin 72 and 13: Gnd.

Elliot stared. At the corner of his mind he was aware of a new change: the Red had switched back to grade 6(d), and people were once again restless with ambition, agitated with plans.

But Elliot stood still, let his heart pound without him, and the words and numbers continued sharpening, the focus turning and turning until it seemed to be a light so bright that it burned right through his eyes.

In the Sheriff's station, Hector was climbing on the furniture.

"Gotta change *all* the lightbulbs! Gotta make this station shine!"

Jimmy was spinning in his chair, fanning out papers as he did so.

"I'm solving them all," he muttered feverishly. "All five of them. Right now!"

"No!" The Sheriff jumped from his desk, stumbled on his bad knee, and snatched at the papers in Jimmy's hand.

Jimmy ducked away, reading eagerly.

"Shred them," ordered Hector, and he swung himself onto his own chair, dragging the typewriter across his desk. "I'm sending out an urgent notice! *No more missing persons reports for my deputy!* Enough! I've had enough!"

"You're the one who *asked* for them." Jimmy frowned fiercely at the papers. "What's the connection? I *know* there's a connection, I can *see* the connection! I just can't catch it!"

"Never asked for these ones! They're from Cellian Central Intelligence! It's your fault, Jimmy — you're too darn good! They heard about you and sent you *five* of their unsolved!" Hector was typing as he fumed. "I'm telling them now, *Solve your own missing persons! We've got better things to do!* I'm saying, *You're supposed to be the best, aren't you? Or anyway, the most central!*"

"What's the connection?" Jimmy's eyes swerved from report to report.

"There *is* no connection!" Hector swiped his letter out of the typewriter and rapidly turned it into a paper plane. "That's five *separate* missing persons from all *over* the Kingdom that they've sent us! Nothing to do with one another! Nothing to do with us, more to the point. Nothing to do with you!"

He looked down at the airplane in his hand and frowned in consternation. Then he threw it across the room.

The door to the station swung open and Elliot Baranski skidded in. The paper airplane flew toward his nose.

"It's the *same!*" Elliot shouted, catching the plane and hurling it right back. "Hector, it's the same! There's a connection!"

The Sheriff looked up. Jimmy looked up.

There was a pause and in the pause, everything seemed to slide away.

It was the bars of Red: They were fading.

But Elliot's voice still clamored: "It was in Dad's workshop! A note on his board that said peripheral connectors are pin 1 plus 12, something, whatever, and just now I saw it at the Watermelon Inn! Uncle Jon used the *exact* same sequence, only for heaters. The guest room heaters! It's gotta mean something! It's gotta be connected to the night it all happened. It'll maybe even tell us where he is!"

Hector and Jimmy gazed at Elliot.

He shouted the story of the two notes again and again, until they understood.

"What do you think it means, Elliot?" Hector ventured.

"I don't know! But —" and Elliot himself was abruptly aware of the volume of his voice, the quiet around him.

"Might be what you call a coincidence," suggested Hector. "Or, no, more likely, your dad fixed the heaters one time for your Uncle Jon, and he wrote that sequence down for himself *and* for Jon, just for technical reasons. Or maybe, like I said, it's plain coincidence."

Jimmy was staring around the station. Paper chains hung from windowsills and paper lanterns were strung across the desks.

"Seems like we decided to redecorate," he said ruefully.

"Ah," sighed Hector, looking closely at one of the lanterns. "Used our paperwork to do it too."

Their bewildered, sheepish quiet seemed to spread out of the station, down the steps and right across the town.

"It's fourth-level Reds," said Jimmy, his eyes on Elliot. "They make you do crazy things. They make you see things that aren't there."

"But it was there," whispered Elliot.

"You know what I mean. A connection that's not there."

The quiet kept drifting, and then it was filled with the sound of ringing bells.

"It's the all clear," Jimmy said. "No, it's more than that. That's the code that means the whole wave of Reds is through."

"It's over," Hector murmured, and Elliot stood in the center of the station, his forehead crumpling so hard he had to close his eyes.

Cambridge, England, The World

10.

*O*ne Friday morning in the first week of July, Belle came back.

She arrived at Madeleine's flat for the lesson with Holly, and she looked exactly like herself, but her voice was dry and hoarse.

Outside, it was raining quietly and efficiently, and inside the electric lights and lamps cast a soft glow. They stood around at first, welcoming Belle, and there was a strange physical awareness. A sense of the shape and closeness of their bodies in the small golden space surrounding Belle.

Belle took on the character of her low, dry voice, her eyes almost sultry, her words lethargic.

"The only thing," she said, "is it hurts to talk. Otherwise I'm better." Then, with a shrug and a quick lift of her eyebrows, she said: "Of course, if you people could learn to read auras, we wouldn't *need* to talk. We could just, like, glance at each other's auras and know everything in all our heads." As she spoke, her eyes shifted from Holly to Jack to Madeleine, studying the air above their heads.

"Or we could learn telepathy," suggested Holly. "No need to interpret colours. Cut to the chase." She moved into the kitchen, announcing she was going to make Belle ginger tea with honey.

"If you'd all just keep up with your horoscopes," Jack said, "we wouldn't even need to *meet*. We'd just go, oh, right, so that's what's going to happen, may as well sleep while it does."

Madeleine was laughing, but she had the curious sensation that her body was too small. Too neat and rigid compared to Belle, who was somehow more present and at ease in the room. But this was

Madeleine's flat, and that was Madeleine's boyfriend beside her. The feeling made no sense. She tried to rattle it out of her head, but instead, looking sideways at Jack and Belle, she felt sudden, intense embarrassment.

She felt as if she had spent the last few weeks accidentally wearing someone else's coat. Now the owner had returned and was gazing at her with shrewd, wry amusement, astounded that she'd never noticed her mistake, but ready to forgive if she apologised.

At the same time, watching Jack joke with Belle — he was touching the centre of Belle's forehead, telling her she should just *close* her third eye sometimes, out of respect for privacy — as Madeleine watched this, she saw him.

Suddenly, and for the first time, she saw Jack.

And what she saw was this: that he was complex, imaginative, funny, and kind, and that he had, in addition to his beautiful nose, golden-green eyes like a tiger. That he was smarter than anybody realised, and that, behind those tiger eyes, he was Byron.

He *was* Byron, just like he claimed. He was reckless, passionate, scared, hopeful, and, in his soul, a poet.

Helplessness washed over her; she wanted to get Jack out of here, get him alone. She wanted to tell him what she had seen, to speak in an urgent voice, or to write a letter to him. She wanted to praise him and praise him. There was an ache to have him touch her and gaze at her in wonder, only this time she wanted to gaze back in the same way. But even as she had these thoughts, she knew she was too late. She'd had her chance, and missed it.

Belle's return would signal the end of the summer romance, and this was all Madeleine's own fault. She had designed their relationship *as* a summer romance, and Belle, seeing that, would make Jack see it too. It would be over.

Holly handed Belle the tea and returned to the kitchen.

She switched on the kettle.

"I'm just making Belle a cup of lemon tea with ginger," she called.

Jack and Madeleine turned to look at her. Belle drank from the mug in her hand and faced the window.

"You already made one," said Jack.

Holly smiled.

Then she pressed her fingers to her forehead, very carefully and methodically, as if she was looking for something that she'd left inside her head.

"Sinus headache," she said. "They're bad in the morning, although they *usually* get better once I walk around." She reached for the kettle. "I'll just make Belle a . . ."

Then she lowered it again.

"Do you know," she said with a surprised tilt, "I think I might lie down for ten minutes?"

Jack, Belle, and Madeleine talked at once, suggesting painkillers, herbal remedies, antibiotics, and promising to leave her alone, but Holly waved her hands in the air.

"Stay here," she said. "All I need is ten minutes — and it'd be nice to hear you chatting while I doze. Then, when I get up, I will *teach* you something."

She walked across the room to the bed. All three were silent, watching her. Holly wrapped her arms around one pillow, put her head on the other, and closed her eyes.

"You should change into your pajamas," Belle said. "I hate lying down in jeans. We'll face the other way while you change."

Holly smiled without opening her eyes and snuggled into the mattress like a child.

Jack and Belle sat on the couch, and Madeleine took the sewing-table chair.

They raised their eyebrows at one another.

"I think we should get out of here," Jack said across the room to Holly. "You need quiet."

Again Holly smiled, her eyes closed. "I told you to stay," she murmured. "I would've *said* if I wanted you to go. Don't you have *homework* or something?" Her voice faded into a yawn, and within moments her breathing slowed and deepened.

"She's asleep," whispered Belle.

"Should we go?" said Jack.

Madeleine looked across at the small, curling shape of her mother on the bed.

"I want to stay with her," she said.

"Well," Jack whispered, "she told us to work. I've got stuff to do on my tourism project for Denny. Maybe I'll run downstairs and print it out. You want me to get anything for you two?"

Madeleine asked him to print out an attachment to one of her emails, giving him her password so he could, and Belle explained that she was so far behind in everything that there was no point trying to catch up. She'd just watch them work.

They listened to Jack's footsteps, his knocking on the door downstairs, the door opening, Denny's voice.

They looked at each other

"You get glandular fever a lot?" Madeleine asked, even though they'd already covered this when Belle arrived.

Belle sniffed, ignoring the question. Her eyes were moving around the flat, her foot tapping slowly.

"So," she said, turning back to Madeleine. "You and Jack, eh?"

This time Madeleine did not reply. She felt a sudden surge of something — of her own self, her pride, her past — and she found herself holding Belle's gaze. She'd do what she could to keep Jack.

Belle watched this, and twisted her own lower lip thoughtfully.

There was a long silence — sudden intakes of breath from Holly; the rain outside; traffic; a motorbike revving — and more silence.

Then voices downstairs, and the sound of Jack running up the steps.

His footsteps pounded quickly and then slowed and slowed, an almost comical slowing, like a machine winding down.

There was silence in the stairwell.

Belle and Madeleine glanced towards the door, then back at each other, and widened their eyes. The quiet out there continued.

"What's he *doing*?" said Belle. "Putting on his Superman suit?" And it occurred to Madeleine that it might be okay. Somehow she had passed Belle's test.

The door opened slowly and Jack came in.

At first, Madeleine did not notice the change. Her focus was on the papers in his hands, and the fact that he was moving towards her, holding out a single sheet.

"Printed this for you too," he said, his voice an even murmur, his eyes on Holly, asleep across the room. "I noticed it in your inbox, and I knew you'd want it right away. I saw the name Tinsels, so . . ."

Madeleine grabbed the paper.

But when she looked down, there were just three lines.

Hi, I just found this in my junk mail, and I don't know you so I think you must be thinking of another Tinsels (who knew there'd be more than one of us?). So I'm just letting you know so you can find the right one. T.

In Madeleine's head there was a tangle of confusion (how could she have remembered the address incorrectly?) and disappointment (the jump in her heart when Jack said Tinsels's name), and anger (with *this* Tinsels, for being the wrong one), and then confusion again (she was *sure* she had the email address right), and then at last she became aware that something was wrong.

She looked up. Jack was leaning against the kitchen bench, the papers in one hand and a curious expression on his face.

Madeleine felt her heartbeat panic while her mind rummaged for an explanation — and then, almost at once, she knew.

Her own email to Tinsels was right there beneath the reply.

Now her eyes fell on the phrases she'd written weeks before, and as they fell, she knew that he had seen them.

Standing on the staircase outside, Jack had read this.

Sorry it's been so long, she had written to Tinsels. *It's been totally BIZARRO!* Then she'd complained about rain, damp, cold, and beans. She'd said life here was a survival adventure. She'd said, *it's like we're in a fairy tale, locked in a freakin' tower trying to spin gold — only, if this were a fairy tale, I guess I wouldn't say freakin', and I'd know HOW to spin, or at least sew.*

She had said:

You should see what I'm wearing — these mad combinations of colours — it's like I'm ADDICTED to colour and you know why? It's cos I'm desperate for it. Cos, honestly, there are no colours here! There's like a blankness — it reminds me of those paintings Warlock used to do when he was three or four, and he'd just use whatever dried-up paint was left on the brush and a lot of water. So it was just faded, washed-out greys. That's exactly what it's like here. And that includes the people — like, I'm home schooling with people named Jack and Belle and they're nice and all, but seriously, they're both just, kind of like, colourless voids.

Her hands clapped over her paper, as if she could stop the words now, and she looked at Jack, shaking her head.

"I didn't," she started. "I couldn't —"

"Yes, you did," said Jack with a small smile.

"You weren't supposed to see this — I didn't . . ."

It was worse because they had to be quiet, contain it at the level of whispers.

"What is it?" said Belle. Her eyes moved from Jack to Madeleine to the paper in Madeleine's hand, and she snatched it before Madeleine could stop her.

Belle scanned the letter.

She lowered it.

"Now I understand," she said, almost to herself. Then she smiled at Madeleine: "You move to England, then you sit around feeling sorry for yourself and trashing the place. It's funny how it never sort of occurred to you that there's people in the world who might think that Cambridge is special, like maybe even *more* special than a princess like you?"

"I know," whispered Madeleine urgently. "I don't know what to say. I'm so —"

A terrible expression, a savage sort of sneer, replaced Belle's smile, and she spoke in an everyday voice.

"I know what to say," she said. "And it's this. All this time I thought you were sort of rubbish and full of yourself, but I also believed that you really were our friend — me and Jack's friend. So stupid of me! Do you know why I never read your aura, Madeleine? Do you know why I always make excuses not to?"

She was looking for her bag as she spoke, moving towards the door. Her head tilted at Jack, and he dropped the papers onto the sewing table and grabbed his own backpack.

Belle opened the door.

"It's because of what your aura's like," she continued. "It's never once changed since I met you, Madeleine, and you know what it is?"

She paused.

"It's black," she said. "I can honestly say I've never seen an aura so full of deception."

Then she walked through the door.

Jack glanced back once. "You don't always have to eat beans, you know," he said. "They've got cheap frozen sausage rolls at Sainsbury's."

He held her eyes a moment, then closed the door behind him.

The sound of their footsteps faded down the stairs, and in the distance, the front door opened and closed.

Bonfire, The Farms, Kingdom of Cello

11.

*I*n the Sheriff's station, Hector was typing. Every few clatters, he'd stop and press the heels of his hands against the desk so that his chair rolled backward. Out in the open, he'd spin from side to side, chewing gum, thinking. Then he'd smile, propel himself back with his feet, and type again.

At his own desk, Jimmy sipped coffee, humming and leafing through papers.

The sun shone hard through the windows, picking up the dust and cheerful mood.

One final clatter, then Hector wound the paper from the machine, adding it to the small pile on his desk.

He swung his chair sideways now, sidling up to Jimmy and handing him the whole set.

"Feast your eyes," he recommended, and leaned back, smiling.

"*This* is what you've been doing?" Jimmy shook his head, leafing through the pages. "It goes on forever, Hector. You sure there's not any stray Reds caught up in your shirtsleeves?"

Hector ignored him.

"Read it," he said. "It's a letter."

"I can see that." Jimmy could be dry as bark sometimes. He sighed and began to read.

To the Right Hon. Splendid and Harmonious
Royal Tour Selection Committee

Dear Sirs and Madams,

Now, it's true that there are only a few short weeks left in the Princess Sisters' Tour of the Kingdom.

It's also true that what I'm about to ask is unorthodox in the extreme.

However, here I am, asking it.

What if the Princess Sisters *skipped* part of their tour in Jagged Edge and, as a substitute, headed back to the Farms, to visit another town here??

The town I would suggest for this honor is:

Bonfire.

Incidentally, Bonfire is my town.

Now, you might recognize its name, on account of we already applied for selection. You might also recall that you didn't get a chance to stop here, since a fifth- level Gray arrived just as you did.

But I think you should return and think again!

The reasons I'm suggesting this are compelling. They are:

1. Now, no offense, but the Jagged-Edgians can be downright derisive about the Royal Family. That's not just Hostiles I'm talking about; there's a whole lot of people in JE who think they're better than the Royals, even people who are otherwise quite nice. No disrespect to the Edgians, but they're a bit overeducated, and it does their heads in.

2. Therefore, why put the Princess Sisters in line of that sort of attitude? Why not just do a small part of the official itinerary there, by which time I'm sure their royal sweethearts will have had it up to HERE with the mockery — then head over to.the Farms to visit us!

3. Now, as charming as Applecart is, there's not a chance in heck that anyone in Bonfire would burn a sweet-potato pie. When I heard that'd happened when the Royals went to Applecart, I just about lay down for a week. (I didn't, though.) Seems to me that the Farms deserves a chance to redeem itself. (Might seem a bit much, to call a burnt piecrust a catastrophe, but here in the Farms there's not much we hold in higher esteem than baking.) (Other than farming, I suppose.) (And the Royal Family. But that goes without saying.)

4. The Princess Sisters were keen to see our pyramid of pumpkins! I read it in their Royal column!

5. Now, it is true that our pyramid of pumpkins has since been dismantled (weather conditions; the usual decaying ways of nature, etc.); however, we have something else here now, and some might say it's even better. I will give it a new number.

6. The Butterfly Child!

7. Yes, as you may have heard in the newspapers and so on, the Butterfly Child is RIGHT HERE in Bonfire.

8. Our Butterfly Child was caught in her jar by a local resident, name of Elliot Baranski.

9. Why do I mention this? Well, because Elliot Baranski may be only fifteen years old, but he's a legend in these parts, and some might say that HE is an additional reason for the Princess Sisters to visit.

10. Here is what Elliot has already achieved, despite his young years, aside from being known as very fine-looking, and with a

kind heart but no nonsense about him, and a good sense of humor, and one of the best pecan-pie and blueberry-muffin bakers in the province — what else has he achieved? Well, he has been captain of the local deftball team, taking them all the way to the provincial championships this year (which, however, they did not win, but you can't blame Elliot for that); his grades, I hear, are very good to excellent with occasional slips into average, but those can be forgiven. Also, he has suffered a serious personal tragedy a year ago, in that he lost his uncle and his father (along with the high-school physics teacher — although I should say that I don't think that Mischka Tegan was actually Elliot's teacher, she taught the senior grades; however, the loss of ANY teacher at a school has a ripple-down effect) in an attack by a third-level Purple, yet he has continued to be a very nice kid; and, as I just mentioned, he caught the Butterfly Child, but I did not yet mention that he broke his own ankle in making sure he caught her, which just goes to show. The sort of personal sacrifice Elliot Baranski will make if need be, is what I mean.

11. It therefore seems to me that the Princess Sisters might like to meet him and give him a medal, or at least pat him on the back for good Cellianship. The best way to do that would, of course, be to come to Bonfire.

The above eleven points strike me as excellent.
The facts are: We are a fine, neat, clean-living town of humble and hardworking folk; we've had it tough this last year, what with the crops failing (as have most of the Farms, it's true, but I get the sense that Bonfire's had it especially tough — and the Butterfly Child has not yet reversed that problem, which is strange, but we are all being very quiet and patient about that, and despite her excessive sleepiness and slowness re: the crop effect, the Princess Sisters will LOVE her!).

Finally, you might have heard that I myself was caught in that fifth-level Gray attack that prevented you from stopping in our town, but I assure you that it has not hindered my capacity to function as Sheriff, and that things have not slipped in any way in Bonfire as a result. On the contrary, it has only served to heighten my awareness of danger, which, when you think about it, is a good thing in a sheriff.

Well, thank you for your time in reading this.
I look forward to your answer.

Yours with great affection and hope,

Hector Samuels,
County Sheriff
Bonfire, The Farms

Jimmy looked up from the letter in the manner of somebody gazing over the tops of their spectacles at a well-meaning but difficult child.

"That'll persuade them, eh?!" Hector said.

"No," said Jimmy. "I doubt it."

He ignored Hector's cries of protest, running his eyes over the pages again. Eventually he looked up.

"It's a good letter, Hector," he said, "although I don't know that 'their royal sweethearts' is the technical term." He scratched the back of his head. "And you think maybe you should leave out the bit about Elliot? It's not . . . kind of taking advantage of him?"

"Nah." Hector retrieved the letter and rolled his chair back to his desk. "Elliot's gonna *love* it when the royals come to town!"

Jimmy laughed and turned back to his own work. He reached for a mandarin and dug his nails in to start peeling.

"You know what I'm working on again?" he said to Hector. "Those five missing persons reports. The ones that Central Intelligence sent through. Still got me stumped. All five of them."

"Huh." Hector grew thoughtful. "Me writing letters to royal tour committees, you doing missing persons for Central Intelligence. Makes you wonder how we ever get any *real* police work done around here, doesn't it?"

Jimmy paused and spat out a mandarin seed, looking equally thoughtful.

"I guess it is a Saturday," he began, but at that moment the door jangled open and they both straightened up in their seats.

"Here we go," Hector said, rubbing his hands together. "Police work."

But it was just the Twicklehams, come to apply for some money from the Red Wave Damage Fund.

The signage out the front of their shop had been scorched when the second-level Red (grade 2(b)) came through, they said, and two windows had broken when passersby, enraged by the fourth-level Red (grade 8(a)), had hurled hammers at each other and missed.

Hector began talking through details with the adult Twicklehams, while Derrin sat down on the carpet. She always wore a leather pouch on her shoulder, stenciled with a butterfly, and now she flipped this open, drawing out a pencil case. It had a row of little plastic windows spelling out her name: D E R R I N, and was otherwise decorated with butterfly stickers. She took out a notebook and green marker and began to draw.

The application was done in a few minutes, and Hector added it to the pile, and moved from behind the desk to say his good-byes. Jimmy also stood, politely.

"Either Jimmy or I will swing by in the next day or two to check out the damage," Hector said, "but seems fairly cut-and-dry to me. How are you finding Bonfire these days anyhow? Apart from the flying flames and hurling hammers, I mean!"

The Twicklehams laughed, and Derrin looked up from her drawing.

"Oh, well, and if it isn't the picture of a town!" exclaimed Mrs. Twickleham.

"The square is of excellent proportions," agreed her husband. "And the Gardens are a tissue to the soul."

"Folks here treating you right?" continued Hector. "Given you a proper Bonfire welcome?"

"Indeed and they are!" began Mrs. Twickleham. "We often partake of tea with Derrin's grade-school teacher! Olivia Hattoway, she is a dove! Perhaps you have seen us together in the square? As to a —"

"If you will know it," Mr. Twickleham said at the same time, his voice gruff, "the town has not —" His wife touched his shoulder.

"Now, then," she murmured gently. "Shall we not bother these good folk with such things?"

Derrin continued drawing. Her picture was entirely in green: a green wind blowing across a green field, a green man and green woman, each with green tears and sad green mouths.

"People here *aren't* treating you right?" ventured Jimmy.

"Ah, you warned us," sighed Mr. Twickleham. "It is the young people, the friends of Elliot Baranski. They find ways to jib at us — nothing we can *actually* complain to — but at least a dozen occasions we've seen them accost customers about to enter our store."

"And the leaflets we make," added Mrs. Twickleham, glancing at her husband. "To advertise our specials and such? We put them under screenwipers on cars, but each time, within half an hour, they are gone again. Snatched by the breeze, I thought at first, and was unplussed, but then I saw one of those young people — I think it was Cody — gathering them up and throwing them away!"

"It's such things," nodded Mr. Twickleham. "A hundred examples we could give, but we seem petty! As to that poor young Elliot Baranski — why, there he is now!"

He pointed toward the window, and both Hector and Jimmy startled. Then they all looked across the road to the schoolyard. It was empty, being a Saturday, but there, indeed, was Elliot Baranski.

"What is that odd and disastrous contraption he investigates?" exclaimed Mr. Twickleham.

229

"That's a sculpture." Jimmy smiled. "Cody made it. That's my old TV on top there. It was broken, so Cody used it for his sculpture."

"A broken televisual machine," sighed Mrs. Twickleham. "*We* could have fixed that for you, Jimmy. We're good with electronics, you know. As to a —" But her voice drifted away and she turned her attention to Derrin, still on the floor.

"Of course you're good with electronics," Hector agreed heartily. "That's why you've got an electronics shop!"

"Ah, my little Derrin." Mrs. Twickleham was crouching. "We're not so sad as your picture depicts, my sweetsnail. We'll be all right, I promise."

Derrin pushed her hair behind her ears. In her elfin face, her eyes were large and unblinking. She shifted these around the room, from person to person, then settled on Hector. She handed over the green picture.

"This is for me?" he exclaimed. "Why, it's so pretty! I'm going to put it right here on the wall. Wait! No, I'm not." With a flourish, he reached for his own satchel — it was leaning up against his desk — and pointed out a plastic window on its front. "I've got a window here, like you've got little squares for your name on your pencil case! But mine is the right size for a picture!" He slipped Derrin's picture into the plastic cover. "Now I can carry your masterpiece everywhere I go!"

Derrin seemed essentially to have forgotten about Hector as he enthused about her artwork and where to put it. She was packing her pencil case into her pouch, standing and adjusting its straps onto her shoulder.

The Twicklehams smiled grateful and embarrassed smiles at both Hector and Jimmy.

"Business will improve," Mrs. Twickleham said. "There's that Bonfire Trade Fair coming up, and we've plans for a stall, such as we'll build in the shape of an *appliance* of some kind! Or anyway, we'll make it very pretty. And we'll bake little deliciousnesses and give these away, along with coupons for 'one free repair.' The plans we have! It will save us. The fair will save us."

"The fair will save us," agreed Mr. Twickleham. "And in the meantime, Jimmy" — he pointed again to the schoolyard and the sculpture; Elliot appeared to be leaning against it — "what if I gathered up your broken TV and fixed it for you?"

Jimmy breathed in through his nose and clicked his tongue.

"You know," he said, "I feel like maybe that's *not* the solution to your problems in this town?"

"Ah, the kids'll get over it," Hector said. "You just give them time. They're too loyal, is the problem, but in this case they've got their loyalty all in a tangle. I'll have a word to them on your behalf, is what I'll do."

The Twicklehams thanked him, at the same time as exclaiming that he should do no such thing, then they smiled their gentle smiles, and the door to the station closed behind them.

Jimmy and Hector watched them through the window for a moment.

"Sad," murmured Hector.

Jimmy shrugged. "The fair *might* save them," he said. "But in the meantime they want to take Cody's sculpture to pieces? That'll *sure* improve the situation."

Hector laughed, and they both returned to their desks.

In the empty schoolyard, Elliot had found another letter from the Girl-in-the-World. He sat on a bench to read it in the sun.

Dear Elliot Baranski,
Your last letter was crazy and I liked it, and then I remembered you warning me that a "Red" might mess with your mind — and that made me like it even more.
   Cause that was kind of clever.

231

I know your letter wasn't supposed to make sense — the lava and chestnuts and that — but you know what? One thing you said, you actually got right. *"You're the one with your eyes closed!"* you said.

You put it in capital letters actually, which, you'd think would've been enough of a message from the universe that I should take notice. But no. I just kept on closing my eyes, and now it's too late.

I guess there are things a person doesn't see, even with their eyes open. Like, did you realise there are more colours than we realise? We've got that handful from the rainbow, but just outside that range, there are more. Just past violet, there's ultraviolet, and in the other direction, past red, infrared, and they are THERE but our eyes can't see them.

Rattlesnakes can see infrared, and birds can see ultraviolet. Some birds even have patterns in their wings that only other birds can see cause they're in ultraviolet.

Makes you think, doesn't it?

Specifically, it makes me think that you can walk around with another person for weeks and months, never seeing the beautiful patterns on his feathers, and just when you finally do see, you realise you've torn them to pieces.

So he flies away with shredded feathers.

Anyhow, that's kind of morbid, and my metaphor got slightly shredded too, so let's leave that.

Although, the whole colour thing makes me wonder — do you have invisible "Colours" in your Kingdom too? Colours off the edges of your vision so they attack you but you can't see them coming? Like tear someone to pieces in the middle of the night! You should totally think about introducing those.

Bye.
M.T.

P.S. The UV thing makes me wonder if bird-watchers have UV vision? (Very confused about how ultraviolet can be a colour and burn your skin.) (So do the UV patterns on a bird's wing burn the sky?)

P.P.S. I'm asking you this because I feel like you might know the answer to bird-watching questions.

P.P.P.S. Okay, I've got an idea. Do you want to meet up? I know you might be a crazy old guy so, you know, don't meet up if you are. And just in case you ARE, maybe somewhere in the open and in public. But I THINK you're young and normal, right?

Elliot replied later that day.

Dear M.T.,
See, the thing is, I can't meet up with you, 'cause I can't get through to your World, 'cause here I am in the Kingdom of Cello.

Like I might've mentioned once or twice before.

And it's true there's a crack that lets our letters get through, but it definitely wouldn't be big enough for people. Hasn't been one that big in over three hundred years.

I wish I could help because you sound sad, what with your troubles with tearing up your friend's feathers, and wanting to see colors that aren't there, and reading messages "from the universe" into my fourth-level Red letter.

Sorry about that letter, and I can guarantee, there wasn't any "message" there, just madness.

I'm sure your eyes are open at all the right times.

What else?

Okay, seems to me, if I'm reading you right, there's a boy you like, and you didn't realize how much you liked him until now, but it's too late 'cause you've done something to hurt him? And now he's run off?

Ah, just tell him you're sorry, and he'll come around. He's probably even forgotten by now — girls are always imagining things into boy's heads that have long gone. We're tougher than you think — and more forgetful.

Speaking for myself, if you're looking pretty and your hair's all shiny, and there's a glint in your eye, and you say sorry like you mean it, and then kiss me on the mouth and let your hand kind of slip under my shirt so it's on my back, well, I'd sure forgive and forget.

(And if I've misread your letter about what's actually happened, and I'm way off the mark on all this, that's your fault. You're too cryptic.)

Anyhow, like I said, there's no way through, and to be honest, I'm not all that keen on risking the plague.

One more thing.

M.T.: It's good corresponding with you, but maybe you could give the talk about Colors a rest.

Take it easy,

Elliot

P.S. Can't help with your bird-watching question either, mainly on account of I have not the faintest stirrings of a clue what you are on about. No offense.

Clover Mackie, town seamstress, was sitting on her porch doing a crossword puzzle. Every now and then, she straightened up to think about an answer, her eyes running over the square.

Here came Elliot Baranski in the Thursday afternoon sunshine, stopping at the doorway to Le Petit Restaurant and handing over a big cardboard box. He ran back across the square to where his truck was parked, and emerged with a second box, this time handing it over at the grocery store. For a third time, he ran across the square toward his truck, calling "Hey" to a friend in the Bakery, and jumping to touch the eaves of the Toadstool Pub with his fingertips as he passed.

Now he was back in the square again, a smaller box under his left arm, and he was running his right hand along Clover's own paling fence, opening her gate, and leaping up the stairs to her porch.

"You seem happy," Clover said. "Tell me first, what's a seven-letter word that means shy? And after that, tell me if you've got time to sit and have a coffee and a fresh-baked croissant, and share some of that good cheer with me?"

"Word that means shy? No idea," said Elliot. "Hang on, seven letters? *Bashful.* And I'd kill for one of your croissants, Clover, but I'm meeting Kala any minute."

"Ah, that explains the good mood," said Clover. "She's a sweet girl, your Kala, isn't she?"

"She is," agreed Elliot, "and a whole lot more. Just been dropping off some raspberry deliveries, and we've got some extra for you." He placed the cardboard box on the table.

"Here she is now," said Clover, pointing across the square with one hand, and holding up a raspberry with the other. "These look delicious! How's things with you, Kala?" she called.

They both watched as Kala approached the gate, grinning up at them.

"Actually, things are sort of great, Clover. I just got news." Kala turned her grin on Elliot, her hands brushing over the fence posts. "Guess what happened?"

"Can't."

"I got a scholarship to Demshield College."

Elliot's hand reached across to the box of raspberries.

"The boarding school in Olde Quaint?"

"It's the best one there."

"Didn't know you'd applied." Elliot was studying a handful of raspberries.

"Sure you did." Kala smiled back. "Well, you knew it was my plan anyhow."

"I guess," he agreed. "When's it start?"

"In a couple of weeks! It's a third-round offer, that's why it's so last-minute. I wasn't smart enough to get in with the first two rounds. But it's good anyway, it's a full scholarship."

"Well, how about that," said Elliot, his voice low and easy, dropping the raspberries back into the box. He nodded at Clover, jumped down the steps, put an arm around Kala's neck, and kissed the top of her head.

"Not smart enough," he murmured. "Smartest girl in all the Kingdoms is what you are."

A few days later the Girl-in-the-World wrote again.

Hey Elliot,

You know the poet Byron? He went horse riding in the rain when he already had a chill, and ended up dead.

So anyhow, there was this other poet, Tennyson his name was, and he was only fifteen at the time. He was a big fan of Byron — I guess poets were the rock stars of the day — and the day he heard that Byron had died, he went to pieces.

He talked about it later. "Byron was dead!" he said. "I thought the whole world was at an end. I thought everything was over and finished for everyone — that nothing else mattered. I remember I walked out alone, and carved 'Byron is dead' into the sandstone."

I'll tell you what I saw in my friend Jack's eyes when he walked out the door of my flat after I hurt him.

That something was dead.

His recklessness, his hope, the poetry inside him.

Byron is dead, I thought, *and everything is over and finished.*

I guess what I'm saying here is, I don't think brushing my hair is
gonna fix it.

Why don't you write me into your story? Give me a role to play
in the Kingdom of Cello, cause turns out I'm useless right here.

M.T.

Hey M.T.,
You guys die from riding horses with a chill?

You need to get yourselves some better doctors.

Sad story, but I still think it's not so bad as it seems, kid.
Betcha one of our quince trees it'll turn out okay if you say sorry.

Elliot

Dear Elliot Baranski,
You remember once I was talking about how to solve problems?

And I said it's really easy, and gave you, like, suggestions?

Ha-ha.

Today I was reading about Isaac Newton (again) and turns out
I was totally wrong.

Okay, so Isaac had this obsession with light and colours — how
they work, how our eyes see them, that kind of thing — and he
wanted to figure them out. (I know you asked me to stop talking
about colours, but why? I like them.)

So, yeah, he did all the simple problem-solving things — he
thought about it, wrote it down, probably even told his dreams
to sort it out for him.

But do you know what else he did?

He stared at the sun.

He looked directly into it.

He stared for so long he nearly went blind. He had to sit in a
dark room for three days to cure his vision. That's a true story.

Also:

He stuck a NEEDLE into the side of his eye. A huge needle —
it was called a bodkin — and he actually stuck it into the edge of
his eye and moved it around, to see what effect that would have
on his vision.

Do you see what I'm trying to say here?

Turns out, if you really want to figure things out, you have to
look straight at the sun and stick a needle in your eye.

It might send you blind, and it'll hurt like hell, but at least it'll
be the truth.

Like maybe if you can't get in touch with your family or
friends, it's because they don't WANT to hear from you; and
maybe if you've lost the people you love, it's your own fault.

M.T.

Late afternoon, Elliot's mother watched him cycle down the driveway, park his bike, and join her on the porch.

She was sitting on the top step shelling peas, and she tilted her
straw hat at Elliot to say hi.

Elliot sat beside her, grabbing a pea pod and getting to work.

"Got another letter," he said.

"Can I read it?"

"Ah." Elliot shifted the bucket of pods a little. "It's just words."

His mother accepted that. She snapped the ends from a pod.

"You're still careful, right?" she said. "Make sure nobody's around
when you look for her letters?"

"It's Saturday. Nobody's around."

"The Sheriff station's right across the road. All he'd need do is look
out the window."

Elliot held a handful of peas to the light. "Some of these look perfect," he said. Then, after a moment: "You really think Hector would
turn me in?"

"Elliot, you beautiful boy, I'm not sure you get how serious this kind of thing can be. Hector'd *have* to turn you in, he'd have no choice."

Elliot shrugged. "I think our letters are winding up, so you can stop worrying." Then he smiled. "Anyhow, Hector sees me in the schoolyard from his window, what's he gonna do? Arrest me for an unnatural interest in sculpture?"

Petra smiled faintly but *tched* at the same time.

"You see Kala today?" she asked.

Elliot nodded.

"When's she leaving anyhow?"

"Next week."

"Seems so sudden," his mother said. "You'll miss her, won't you?"

Elliot scratched the back of his neck. He stood up, moving across the porch to the front window. "Might go inside a moment." He reached for his backpack. "I've just collected some sycamore bark for the Butterfly Child to try to cheer her up. Apparently it tastes good. Who knew? She in there now?"

He looked into the shadows of the living room. There was the fireplace, the couches, the doll's house — but something was odd. A kitchen chair was standing right beside the doll's house, and — he pressed closer to the window — a person was sitting in the chair.

"It's Corrie-Lynn," said his mother, still shelling peas. "She's been coming by now and then. Just sits by the Butterfly Child."

"I never knew." Elliot knocked on the glass. Inside, Corrie-Lynn shifted in her chair and turned toward him.

She turned away again at once.

Elliot raised an eyebrow.

"She not talking to me?"

He sat by his mother again and reached into the bucket of pods.

The sun was slipping lower in the sky, light glaring their way. Petra raised her head, blinked, and lowered it again.

"It's your friends. Corrie-Lynn's mad at you because of what they've been doing to the Twicklehams."

Elliot looked up and was caught by the sun too. He sheltered his eyes with his hand.

"My friends aren't doing anything to the Twicklehams," he said.

"Ah, you know exactly what I mean. They're driving them out of business, Elliot. Things being how they are, nobody's got spare cash for fixing electronics, so they've started on the back foot as it is. The Twicklehams might end up leaving town, you know. We'd lose the rent on the shop, which is one thing, but more to the point, Corrie-Lynn would lose her little friend."

Elliot squinted. The fields were lighting up in silvers and golds, fences running shy and dark through all that magic light. In the distance, the greenhouse was practically a starburst.

"Shame if she loses her friend," he said, "but if they have to leave, well . . ." He shrugged.

"Elliot." Petra stopped, collected her face, and tried again. "Elliot, it's not the Twicklehams' fault that they're in your dad's shop."

"Sure it's their fault," Elliot said lightly.

Petra scraped peas into the bucket of pods, then gathered them back and put them in the pea container instead.

"Okay," she said, her voice taking them in a whole new direction. "Okay, here's the situation as I see it. About your dad, I mean — and so forth."

Elliot stopped moving. He closed his eyes.

His mother continued talking.

"As I see it, there's two possibilities. One is that all three of them were driving along in the white truck, and the Purple killed your Uncle Jon and then took off with Dad and Mischka Tegan."

A pod sat still in the palm of Elliot's hand.

"As for that story," continued his mother. "I know the Sheriff believes it, but listen, what were the three of them *doing* in the truck? Headed down the Acres Road toward here? In the middle of the night? Why would they even've *been* there? And how come there's been no . . . trace of Dad or that teacher? Which you'd usually expect."

She sensed Elliot move again, and talked faster. "I know, Elliot, I know, it's because the Purple took them to a cavern someplace and it's keeping them prisoner now. But, honey, the Purple that got your Uncle Jon, did it seem all that patient to you? It's cruel of me to ask, you having seen what you did. But there it is. The chances of that particular Purple carrying somebody all the way to its cavern, well, seems to me the chances are about as small as —"

She reached for an unripe pea pod, and split it, holding out the barely formed seeds.

"Smaller," she said.

Elliot sheltered his eyes again. The wind rustled leaves. Far away, the shadow of a deer crossed a tree.

"The second possibility," Petra continued, snapping pods, quick and rhythmic, "is that your dad and that teacher ran off, and Jon was bringing the truck home to let us know when the Purple got him." Her voice had changed again and it reminded Elliot of the way he himself read the coroner's reports. She was shifting away from herself, talking side-on, or as if she wasn't really there. "As for that possibility," she said, "well, yeah, I know they didn't pack their bags or make plans. Didn't take anything special. Haven't used their bank accounts. But listen. Listen, Elliot."

The evening breeze picked up. In the distance, a truck changed gear.

"Your dad was wonderful, we both know that. But we also know that he's always been a . . . wanderer. He and Jon ran off to see Cello when they were still in school! Nearly killed their parents with the worry. And he's always been a heartbreaker too. Nobody believed for a moment he'd stay with me as long as he did — and that includes me."

Now Elliot looked at his mother.

She kept her head down, ducking the sun.

"Yes, that includes me. I knew he wouldn't stay, Elliot, and he did play around when we were first married. Stopped when you were born, but that was because of you. Lately, though, well, you were growing up, so I guess . . .”

She was rising a little as she spoke, shifting positions, adjusting her hat, tilting it forward then raising it, trying to balance the sun.

“That teacher, that physics teacher, she was so pretty and bright. Interested in Dad’s kind of things — electronics and suchlike. Going to the pub together just about every night, him getting home later and later. The whole town was talking, Elliot. It was only —”

She caught her breath, struggled with a pod a moment, then snapped it hard.

“It was only a matter of time. As for him not packing, well, spontaneous is just like your dad, Elliot. You know that too.”

She stopped, and half laughed.

“He *did* take his magnifying glass.”

“You knew that?” Elliot said.

“And their not using any bank accounts,” she continued, “well, Elliot, if a person wants to start afresh, if a person doesn’t want to be found . . . the person will find a way.”

There was a powerful silence. Petra’s voice turned inside out, and urgent. “You’ve got to stop taking these journeys,” she said. “I know you’re just waiting for the Butterfly Child to be gone, and then you’ll be off again yourself. I’ve been letting you go because I knew you needed to do it — for yourself — and maybe I kind of hoped too — I wanted that tiny chance to be true. But you *cannot* put yourself in danger again. Not one more time.”

She was almost crying. “He loved you so much, Elliot, you know that he’s the crazy one, right? That *he’s* made the terrible mistake in leaving you behind, that wherever he is, he’s missing you like mad, that this is none of your fault, that . . .”

But Elliot wasn’t listening.

He was staring straight and hard into the glare of the sun. His hand was in his pocket twisting at the letter from the Girl-in-the-World.

Two days later, another letter arrived.

Hey Elliot,

You haven't replied to my last letter, which I don't actually blame you for, cause I was kind of melodramatic, right?

Anyhow, I was thinking, seriously, why are you afraid of meeting me? It's either because you're a mad old guy or cause you're shy, right?

So, I've decided not to give you a choice. I am going to be at Parker's Piece, standing under the lamppost this Sunday at 2 p.m.

I honestly don't care what you look like — it'd just be nice to chat, cause I like your stories. This might seem very strange to you, but the fact is, you're kind of my only friend.

My imaginary friend is my only friend. Ha-ha.

Anyway, I'll be holding a book about Isaac Newton, and I'll be wearing a black and white headband. You can't miss me.

See you there,

M.T.

M.T.,

Suit yourself.

Elliot

Cambridge, England, The World

12.

*P*arker's Piece is an enormous square of green near the centre of Cambridge.

It's bordered by trees and fences, but just beyond these you can see buildings: the green turrets of the University Arms Hotel, the steeples of the Roman Catholic church, houses and shops.

Two paths run diagonal across Parker's Piece, forming a giant X, and in the centre of the X, there is a lamppost.

On this particular Sunday afternoon, the sky over Parker's Piece was overcast. In the northeast corner, there was a straggling cricket game. Opposite were two groups of picnickers, one of which was playing reggae music. Two girls sat cross-legged looking at photos on an iPhone. Nearby, a boy read a newspaper, his bicycle sprawled on the grass.

Leaning against the lamppost was a girl. Her dark hair fell around her shoulders but was held back from her forehead by a black and white headband. There was a spot high on her cheek, near her ear, and she'd covered this with makeup. Under her arm was a book (*The Life of Isaac Newton*), and over her shoulder was a backpack with a broken strap. In her eyes was a light that was defiant, ironic, amused, defensive, frightened, and hopeful all at once.

Now and then she stared at the boy with the newspaper, and when he looked up, she lifted her chin ever so slightly. The boy returned to his paper. The girl looked up at the lamppost. It was hung with four lanterns, and scratched into its base was the word *Reality*. A slow smile formed on her face.

The girl was remembering that the lamppost is known around Cambridge as the "Reality Checkpoint." *Funny place to meet an imaginary person*, she thought.

Then it occurred to her that this lamppost was the first electric lamp in all of Cambridge; that Parker's Piece was named after Edward Parker, a college cook who used to farm on it; and that she would share these facts with her imaginary friend.

A frown flickered. She was changing her mind about sharing these facts.

Reminding herself that she used to be kind of cool.

Striding along the path towards the girl came a man with a deeply lined forehead, wearing a T-shirt that said *Beer Belly Under Construction*.

Panic crossed her face. But he carried on without looking at her.

The girl looked down at the palms of her hands and saw a memory inside a memory.

The outer memory was herself under apple trees at Grantchester, eating scones with jam and cream, and talking to Jack and Belle.

Inside that was the memory of herself losing control on a skateboard: a highway just ahead, her father watching from the side of the road.

But what was the point of that memory?

That she used to have summers in Genoa? That she used to fly down hills and cause collisions?

That her father had watched and waited to be sure she was okay?

She let her palms fall to her sides, and realised what the memory meant.

It was the lines her father had traced in the air with his fists, the ones she joked were to show how long he planned to grow his beard.

He had meant to remind her of the speech he used to give her every time she ran away.

"We must think outside of *ourselves*, Madeleine," he'd say, and he'd wave his hands over the space of his body. "Live for *others*, not just yourself."

She'd been spinning down that street on her skateboard without thinking. She could have killed herself, but worse, somebody else. Cars had swerved, crashed, and skidded sideways.

"If you do not learn this thing," her father used to say, "people will give up on you. You only get so many chances."

He meant, "One day, I will give up on you."

The letter is taking a while to find him, she told herself fiercely. *He has not given up on me.*

Her body trembled. She stilled it, pressing her lips together: *I just need to wait.*

The cricket game wound up.

Several more people biked along the path, some with wire or wicker baskets, some with handlebars strung with shopping bags. A few caught her eye, most ignored her, but all of them rode past.

When the rain started, it was unconvincing. The picnickers gathered things together slowly. Cyclists pedalled a little faster, hunching forward. The boy folded his paper and rode away. A woman pushing a baby in a pram stopped to click a plastic rain cover into place and carried on.

The rain became more persuasive. Water ran down the lamppost and spilled onto the girl's neck. She pressed the book more firmly beneath her arm, and waited.

*

Bonfire, The Farms,
Kingdom of Cello

13.

$\mathcal{K}$ ala's family had stopped downtown to pick up coffees for the road.

Now they stood around their open car doors in the frosty afternoon, having one last chat with Elliot and his friends.

"Good time to set off," Shelby said, glancing up at the darkening sky.

"Isn't it perfect?" Kala's father agreed with bitter gusto. He tilted his head toward Kala's little sisters. "Couldn't miss their ballet classes, could they?"

At once the little sisters began to dance on the street. Their mother scolded one for not wearing her jacket in this weather, and the other for pirouetting like soap stuck down a drainpipe.

Kala leaned against the car, examining the woven bands on her wrist.

"Sell your jewelry to those rich kids at Demshield," Gabe advised. "Make yourself a fortune."

"You're coming back for the holidays, right?" Cody squinted through his cigarette smoke.

"If you put out that cigarette I will."

Cody took another drag. "Ah," he said. "Too cold."

"We should get going." Kala's mother reached her hands toward Elliot, as if she was thinking of hugging him, and then let them fall. She smiled instead. Then she scolded the little girls into the car.

Nikki tugged on the rope that was holding luggage to the roof racks. "Mind if I just retie this for you?" she asked, "Seems a little loose," and Kala's dad nodded, "By all means."

Kala stepped toward Elliot a moment. She tilted her head, and her hair, which was loose, caught the streetlight.

Elliot touched the light in her hair. He took her right hand, turned it upside down, studied it a moment, then let it go — raised his eyebrows, and stood back.

Kala and her family got into the car.

At the intersection down the street, the car stopped behind a pickup truck, and Kala and her sisters lowered their windows, leaning out from either side of the car to wave.

Then the lights changed, the pickup truck gunned it, and the car disappeared in a cloud of exhaust fumes, windows shooting closed.

Shelby wound her arm around Elliot's neck. "Let's go blow something up," she said.

Two blocks east on Broad Street, Jimmy Hawthorn, Deputy Sheriff, was opening his front door.

Isabella held up one hand; with the fingertip of her other hand, she was writing her name in the mist of his front-door glass.

"Done?" he said.

"It's a long name," she explained.

Her cheek felt cold when he kissed her.

They were a couple now, Jimmy and Isabella. The Red had brought them together and they'd stayed.

In the living room, the fireplace was glowing, the coffee table scattered with papers.

"You're working again?" She stood with her back to the fire, holding her hands behind her to warm them.

Jimmy opened a bottle of wine and poured them both a glass.

"It's those missing persons reports, the ones that Central Intelligence sent." He gathered the papers together. "Look at this." He was leafing through them. "There's a man went missing in Golden Coast. There's a woman in Golden Coast too. A teenage boy in Nature Strip. A teenage girl, Golden Coast again. And a little boy in the

Magical North. A whole heap of witness statements, and I've followed every path I could, but I haven't got a single one. Five missing people, you'd think I'd have got *one* by now." He glanced at her. "I'm usually okay at this sort of thing."

"I know." Isabella smiled. She sat down, sipped from her wine, closed her eyes. "Well," she said, "if Central Intelligence sent them to you, it means they can't figure them out, right? And if *they* can't do it, maybe they just can't be solved. How did they end up with Central anyway?"

"That's the thing." Jimmy sat beside her, returned the neatened papers to the coffee table. "There'll be some reason — it'll be drugs or witness protection or foreign affairs or something. And darn if I can figure why a seven-year-old boy in the Magical North could be connected with any of that."

"No *wonder* you can't solve them," Isabella exclaimed. "You're missing vital information. The drugs or whatever it is, it's probably pivotal. They're wasting your time! Am I allowed to look at them?"

"Go ahead."

Isabella leafed through the files.

"I see why you keep trying, though," she murmured. "This is a thirteen-year-old girl — and the seven-year-old boy — I suppose they have parents."

Jimmy stood. "I've got some nice cheese and bread," he said, heading to the kitchen. "Let me know if you solve them while I'm in here," he called.

"What I want to know," Isabella called back, reading fast, "is whether this waitress ever found her earring. And why she thought she should include that in her statement."

"That's the seventeen-year-old boy? Went missing from the restaurant in Nature Strip, right? Yeah, and the waitress says something about how the back of her earring fell off, and she was crawling around on her knees looking for it?" Jimmy leaned out of the kitchen door. "They get them to include every little thing 'cause you never know what might be relevant. But the earring, that's what you call *ir*relevant."

He returned to the kitchen, got the breadboard, and started slicing bread. It was soft on the inside, gold and crunchy on the outside, flakes of crust scattering as he sliced.

Then he put the knife down.

He walked into the living room.

"You think it's going to snow tonight?" Isabella wondered. She was sitting on the couch again, the files high on her lap. "Because if it is, I've got this experiment I'm working on at school, and —"

"Wait a moment," said Jimmy.

He took the files from her.

He flicked through one, stopped, put it back.

He flicked through a second, paused with the same narrowing eyes, then replaced that too.

Then the third.

The fourth.

The fifth — and back to the first one again.

He looked at Isabella.

"I know where they are," he said.

It was late and cold, and the banks of the Sugarloaf Dam were scattered with cigarette butts; also with the charred remains of explosives. The field nearby was torn up with tire marks from motor-scooter racing.

The others had gone home now, but Elliot and Nikki sat on the darkening grass. They were rolling an empty bottle back and forth between their feet in a slow, idle game, leaning into each other against the cold.

"What's up with your Butterfly Child anyhow?" Nikki said. "The sycamore bark didn't cheer her up?"

"Nope," said Elliot. "She ate it all, though." He gazed across the water of the dam. "Which is weird enough," he added.

"It is," Nikki agreed. "But she's got to do more than sit around eating bark."

"Well, she heads out with her insect buddies now and then."

"Okay, more than that too. She's gotta fix the situation here in Bonfire, I mean. Get the crops going and so on. Isn't that her job?"

"That's what I hear," Elliot agreed.

"'Cause everyone's hanging by a thread. You know the bank moved in on the Whittakers last week? And I hear that Marcy Tam's closing up and moving out."

"You sure are helping my state of mind here, Nikki," Elliot said.

Nikki had a giggle that was low and unexpected, rolling across the air between them like marbles.

"Ah," she said. "It'll be okay. The farms'll come good eventually, with or without the Butterfly Child's help. Maybe crops are not her thing. Who said they all had to have the same tricks?"

Elliot looked at Nikki sideways, blowing on his hands. It was getting colder.

Nikki held her own hands toward him. "Blow on those for me too."

They shifted closer and Elliot took both her hands into his and rubbed them hard.

"But if she *can* do it," Nikki added, thoughtful, "but she's not, because she's just depressed, well, I guess we've got to cheer her up. You tried telling her any jokes?"

He laughed a breath of mist into the air.

"Okay, what's she need?" Nikki was getting determined. "A self-help audiotape? Or maybe it's more of a practical problem. It's school vacation in a couple of weeks — you and I could spend the time renovating her doll's house. A new coat of paint can do wonders for your mood, is what I hear."

Elliot wound a finger through Nikki's hair. It was that pale, it shone like milk under the moonlight.

"Or could it be boyfriend troubles?" She leaned forward, and the hair slipped out of Elliot's fingers.

"Boyfriend troubles," Elliot repeated. "You never noticed the 'child' in 'Butterfly Child'?"

"How do we know she's a child? People just call her that because she's small, right? Or maybe it's 'cause she's supposed to be the *child* of a butterfly? You ever asked her how old she is? Come to think of it, you ever asked her *why* she's not happy?"

"She doesn't talk."

"Well, the time I saw her, she didn't look like a child. More like a young woman, maybe. Only freakishly tiny. Maybe that's what's got her down — her own freakish smallness." Nikki leaned back again, resting her head on Elliot's shoulder. "Or, like I said, boyfriend troubles."

"She does go out a lot," Elliot said. "Could be she's got lovers all over the province. Never thought of that."

"Ah," Nikki nodded, her hair scraping against Elliot's jacket with the nod. "Trying to juggle them all. Tricky."

Their hands were intertwined now, their faces so close their cheeks were touching. An owl murmured nearby, and in the distance there was music. Somebody in Sugarloaf was having a party. Behind the music was the high-pitched sound of an ATV engine, and behind *that* was the sound that Elliot kept hearing, that faint, low fluting. People always shrugged when he mentioned it, so he'd stopped asking. It must be in his head — maybe some residual Color poison in his ear canals.

A stray touch of icy wind, and he and Nikki tried to shift even closer, coats pressing together, and then they were kissing.

It felt so much like a natural part of their shifting, or like the next step in the conversation, like defense against this cold, dark night, that they almost didn't notice what they were doing. Then they noticed, and it felt so good his hands reached around her waist, rotating her toward him, and she followed the trajectory he'd started, climbing onto his lap, and then, abruptly, she stopped.

She climbed right off him, sat herself a good distance away, and said: "What are we doing? She won't even be out of the province yet."

Elliot scratched his head.

"We're drunk, I guess."

"We are." Nikki jumped to her feet, offering her hand to pull him up too, but he stayed. He looked at his watch.

"If they're not out of the province yet," he said, "they drive too slow."

Then she did drag him to his feet, and as he stood, he looked for his own reflection in the water. Couldn't see it there; the water was too black. Moon must have slipped behind a cloud.

The telephone rang and the Sheriff regarded it a moment.

He was working late at the station, trying to get through the Red Wave Damage Fund applications.

Drinking whiskey, eating crackers, lost in paperwork, and that shrill, repetitive sound took him by surprise.

He answered it anyway.

"You there? I tried you at home first." It was Jimmy.

"I am here," confirmed Hector, nodding.

"Well, I know where they are."

Hector waited. "Who?" he asked eventually.

"Those five missing people. The Central Intelligence reports? There *is* a connection, Hector. Guess where they are? Guess where they all are?"

Hector waited again.

Jimmy sure wanted to draw out the suspense.

"Where?"

"*They're in the World.* All of them. All five of them — they've gone to the World."

Hector swung himself into his chair, holding the phone closer to his chin. He was grinning. "How do you figure that?"

"I remembered World Studies classes from school — something Isabella said made me remember. Back in the days of cracks big enough for people to go through, there used to be a kind of displacement when they went. A tremor in the air. An adjustment of reality. Small things would go wrong. A picture would fall off a mantelpiece. Or a branch would shift its position in a tree. It stayed in my mind because I liked the idea."

"Sounds familiar, I guess. Yeah. And?"

"Well, every one of these reports gets me nowhere. I've never seen such a series of dead ends. There is *no* explanation. Or there wasn't. But tonight I realized that in *every* one of these reports, there's something. A waitress loses her earring. A guy has to retie his shoelaces. Somebody else says the radio switched itself on so she turned it off. There's even a guy says the commas in the letter he was typing suddenly fell down a line. That one I dismissed as plain craziness; the rest I paid no attention to, thinking they were just asides — those irrelevant details people stop and look at when they're making their way to the point."

"Okay." The Sheriff scratched at some dried paint on the edge of his chair. "But seems to me you're drawing a heck of a long bow here. There haven't been cracks big enough for people in hundreds of years. Just a handful of *tiny* cracks all this time, and those get closed before you can take a breath. Penalty for not reporting a crack is death. Penalty for even *suspecting* a crack and not reporting it is banishment. What are the chances that there are five people-moving cracks across the Kingdom and nobody knows? Seriously?"

"Small as the toenail on a Butterfly Child," Jimmy agreed at once. "But there must be, because that's where these missing people are."

"And what's more," Hector continued. "If these people went through the cracks, why didn't they turn around and come straight back?"

"I think somebody's *moved* them across. Without their choice, I mean. Maybe closed them up right after they went."

Hector sighed. "I'll tell Central your theory."

"It's not a theory," said Jimmy. "It's a fact."

"I'll also tell Central to solve their own darn missing persons reports from now on," Hector continued. "In fact, I'm telling police departments right across the Kingdom — I want my deputy back. I'm at the station working and it's nearly midnight!"

There was a smile in Jimmy's voice. "Don't want to be the one to say this, Hector, but . . ."

"I know, I know." Hector sighed again. "I asked for them in the first place. You've been patient with all this, Jimmy, which makes me feel even worse about the truth of the matter. I'm just about to admit that truth, Jimmy, but before I do, can you promise you won't make too much noise? When you hear it? I'm too tired for noise."

"Can't promise anything." Jimmy grinned. "I'll do my best."

"When I asked them to send in their missing persons reports, I only wanted a *specific* kind. I wanted missing people in the electronics field. Remember the first few? That electrical engineer? The sound technician? Where it went wrong was, you solved them so fast, word got around you were genius at it. So they started sending anything and everything."

"All right," said Jimmy. "Why'd you ask for missing people in electronics?"

"Because of Abel Baranski."

"Ah, Hector."

"Well, now, I'd almost prefer you to make a lot of noise than to go all soft-voiced like that."

Jimmy blew air out of his cheeks and it came down the phone line like a breeze.

"I knew it wasn't a Purple," Hector admitted. "Purple got Jon, sure, but not the others. Thing was, I didn't want it to be the alternative — those two running off together, Abel running off on his wife and his boy. Leaving his brother to tell the truth, and getting his brother killed for it — not intentional, of course, but still. What a shameful thing for a man to do, and I *liked* Abel. He was my friend."

"I liked him too," Jimmy said.

"So I stuck to the Purple — the idea that it had taken them alive, and in the end they'd find their way back. At the same time, I looked for a third explanation. Got to thinking about the fact that Abel was in electronics and Mischka in physics — sort of related, right? Maybe some Hostile group was snatching up people with those skills. Maybe we'd find a pattern if we looked at unsolved cases in that field across the Kingdom. That's why I asked for the reports. Trouble was, like I said, you solved them, so they *weren't* being snatched by Hostiles after all. No big conspiracy. I was wrong."

"Ah, Hector," Jimmy said again.

"Worst thing," Hector continued, "the worst thing is, my Purple story gave Elliot false hope. Should never have done that. It's 'cause of me he's been off across the Kingdom, putting himself in danger everyplace he turns. Never figured he'd do that."

"You know, if Abel and Mischka went off of their own free will, they're not even technically missing, Hector. It's not police business."

"I know."

"I'm thinking," Jimmy said, "that *any* strange disappearances from now on, we should consider that they might have been sent across to the World like these five people. But Abel and Mischka? That wasn't strange. I've told you this before, but I'll say it again. The night before they disappeared, I saw Abel and Mischka walking out of the Toadstool Pub together. The strap on Mischka's dress fell from her right shoulder, and Abel reached over and fixed it for her. His hand reached out like the next step in a dance. The way he did that — the way his eyes fell on her shoulder as he did so — well, it seems to me there was nothing strange at all about the two of them being gone the next day."

Jimmy's last few words disappeared into a cough.

"Coming down with a cold," he explained.

Hector waited for the coughing to finish, then he spoke slowly. "Well," he said, "there's still a part of me thinks Abel fixed the strap on Mischka's dress because he's thoughtful that way. But a bigger part is finally inclined to think you're right. I'll talk to Elliot. This one I got wrong."

"You lost your mind, Hector. It can happen to the best of us."

"You're a good man, Jimmy. Occasionally you're off your tree — people going across to the World, for example — but still, a good man. I'll tell Central your theory about these five missing persons, and it might help to dry up the reports that keep coming your way. Meantime, I promise: Any more that do come in, I'll send them straight back."

"It's a deal. Night, Hector."

"Night."

The fax machine started up just as Hector put down the phone.

He reached for his whiskey and watched as page after page whirred through. Eventually, he picked up the cover sheet.

To the Good Sheriff of Bonfire in the Picturesque Province of the Farms,

We here in Gwent Cwlyd, in the Startling Province of Olde Quaint, have heard tell that you there in Bonfire have a Deputy Sheriff whose skills in missing persons are like to a flower in a staple box. Hence, we have here a missing persons report — or if not TECHNICALLY a missing persons report, it is, at least, a missing cat report — and we would be grateful beyond —

"Oh, for the love of . . ." Hector murmured.

He was crumpling the fax, ready to throw it away, when he noticed a postscript to the letter.

P.S. We're also sending through another unsolved case — a child has been missing for some time, and it is our hope that your deputy might solve it. Herewith.

Hector's shoulders softened. He leafed through the pages.

The child was of a sweet and lively nature, said the report, *and had no cause to vanish.*

A few paragraphs on:

The child's mother was known for her whistling — ah, she would go about so gaily, whistling more than she spake, and many it was that mocked her! But not now; not since the little girl set forth.

Hector stopped at that line.

He put the fax into his briefcase.

"Shame to waste a talent like Jimmy's," he said to himself. "Just this one last one."

Then he knocked back the last of his whiskey, switched off the lights, and headed home.

The clock tower was striking twelve midnight, and Elliot Baranski was knocking on a door.

It was Apartment 4 (Directly Above the Bakery), Town Square, Bonfire.

The home of Olivia Hattoway, Grade 2 teacher; formerly, also, the home of Mischka Tegan.

Elliot knocked through the striking of the clock, and then knocked again into the silence.

Silence drained the air. Then a muffled thud. Slow footsteps. A pause. She must be looking at him through the peephole.

The door opened wide, and there she stood, Olivia Hattoway, smoothing down her curls. Her flannelette pajamas were patterned with hot-air balloons.

"I've woken you," said Elliot.

"How did you guess?" Miss Hattoway smiled, which made her eyes disappear more deeply into sleepy lines. She was curvy in just the right way: as if a sculptor had smoothed her at the very point before curvy becomes plump. "Come in, Elliot," she said. "I know we've never met but I certainly know who you are."

"You teach my cousin, Corrie-Lynn." Elliot followed her in, half smiling as he remembered Corrie-Lynn's pronouncement that Miss Hattoway had a funny name. He tried to think of her as Olivia, but found he could not. She was Miss Hattoway.

There was something else, something Corrie-Lynn had *not* liked about her teacher, but he couldn't remember that part.

"It's small," Miss Hattoway was saying, holding both arms up, and pivoting slowly to display the apartment's living room. "But the location's wonderful. Right above the Bakery. You can smell bread and pastries twenty-four hours a day! You smell that?" She breathed in deeply, closing her eyes, and Elliot raised his eyebrows.

Truth was, all he could smell was coffee and burnt cheese and something vaguely fishy, maybe sardines.

"Let me get you a glass of milk and a piece of hazelnut slice — I've been baking today myself." She ducked into the kitchen and Elliot watched as she opened the fridge. He wondered, as any good Farms boy would, why people from other provinces thought they ought to bake. It made his heart sink, the idea of her hazelnut slice.

He glanced around the living room. There was a window that looked over the square, a small table beneath it. Rugs in primary colors crisscrossed the carpet; three or four mismatched throws were flung over a short, fat couch.

On the wall was a huge painting of a vase, flowers spilling over its side. There was something smudged and childish about that painting, something askew about the perspective maybe, or could be the flowers were out of proportion with the vase.

"Mischka painted that," said Miss Hattoway. She was standing by his side holding a tray, which she placed on the coffee table. "We did an art class together, back when we were at teachers' college. Mischka got this idea that we ought to stretch our artistic minds, or some such rubbish. Everything we painted was terrible! But we both agreed that *that* one deserved to be on the wall."

She beckoned Elliot to sit beside her on the couch.

"Although now that I look at it again, well, it's quite awful really, isn't it? I bet that's what you were thinking."

Elliot smiled faintly. He was thinking that Miss Hattoway seemed soft and warm, bright and giddy, like a grade-school teacher should, but there was also something perspicacious about her. She had slid the conversation straight to Mischka. She knew, even half asleep, that this was why Elliot was here and she'd smoothed the way to the point.

He appreciated that.

(Then, too, she had guessed his thoughts about the painting.)

"That's where you two met?" he said. "At teachers' college?"

"Yes, we were roommates. And when we applied for our first posts, we decided to try for the same town, which was a long shot. But we got it! Listen, is it just me or is it freezing in here?"

She stood up and switched on an electric heater, hitting it twice to make it work.

Elliot took a bite of the hazelnut slice. It wasn't so bad. A little dry maybe, but the hazelnut flavor was both rich and subtle at once.

"I have to tell you," she continued. "This is a super town, of course, but it was so good having a friend from home. Did you know Mischka at all? Did she teach you? No? Well, the thing about her was, she seemed very shy and reserved, but she could be so ironic and witty. We used to play board games most nights — she always won, of course. Or we'd watch *The Greenbergs* together and eat marzipan. . . ." Her voice faded and she gazed around the room.

Elliot also looked and caught more details. There was a bookshelf, a framed print of the Lake of Spells on the top shelf. Through the door, he could see the fridge in the kitchen, scattered with magnets, and he could just make out a handwritten note, headed: *Healthy Foods You Must TRY to Eat!* with a smiley face. On the window ledge was a jar of gold stars, and on the table, a scattering of papers, scissors, and glue.

"I try out all my craft activities at home," Miss Hattoway explained. "Mischka was so much better than me at crafts. Better fine motor skills."

A sudden memory came to Elliot. At school, he'd known Mischka Tegan's name, and he must have seen her around, but all this time, he hadn't had any clear memories of her. Now he recalled an announcement she'd made at assembly once. Something about a class excursion. She'd read from a small piece of paper. Most teachers didn't do that; mostly, they just leaned in to the microphone and talked, remembering what they had to say and not caring if they got it mixed up.

The paper had slipped from Mischka Tegan's fingers while she talked and had fluttered very slowly through the air, and she'd watched it flutter for too long. Elliot remembered thinking that the fact that she'd dropped it must have stunned her. Then she'd snatched it from the air.

That's where the memory ended. Elliot must have stopped listening.

"I guess you miss her," he said now.

"Anyway," Miss Hattoway continued, ruffling her voice back into place. "Anyway, we had some lovely nights. Although, of course, that more or less stopped when she took up with the Baranski brothers." She glanced over at Elliot. "I mean with your dad and your Uncle Jon, of course."

"How did they get to be friends anyhow?" Elliot asked, just as if they were chatting about neighborhood acquaintances.

"Oh, Mischka borrowed some equipment from your father, for an experiment at school. I'm not sure of the details. Anyway, they hit it off, and they started going to the Toadstool Pub every other night. I suppose Jon just joined the party. I used to watch them from here while I graded schoolwork."

She pointed to the window, and Elliot stood, moving closer so he could look out.

Down below, the square was mostly dark and quiet, but the Toadstool was still open. There were clusters of people huddled around tables, coats on, collars up. By looking out, Elliot seemed to be fishing up sounds from below. Now he could hear small murmurs of laughter, a woman's aggravated voice, the deep voice of a man curling into a joke, another murmur of laughter.

He looked away from the Toadstool, and there across the square was Clover Mackie, rugged up in blankets on her front porch, a blue mug beside her as usual.

Elliot smiled at that and turned back to Olivia, feeling stronger.

"It was always the three of them?" he asked. "Dad and Jon and Mischka?"

"No, on occasion it was just your dad and Mischka. I suppose Jon had work to do back at the Watermelon. When the Toadstool closed, they'd come up here sometimes. I'd usually be in bed by then, and they'd listen to music and talk and talk. I'd have to put my earplugs in to get to sleep."

Elliot turned away again, staring at the window. The room seemed to swim with unasked questions.

"You've been drinking tonight, haven't you, Elliot?"

Elliot turned, startled. There was that perspicacity again. But she was smiling in her warm, grade-school-teacher way.

"You look like your dad," she added gently.

He stared at her.

"Most people," he said, "say I look more like my mother."

"No, no. You've got his eyes. And the lines across your forehead when you're thinking hard, when there's something you want to say, those are your dad's."

He asked then, and the effort was like wrenching the plug out from a huge basin of water.

"Were they planning to run away together?"

Olivia Hattoway did not say anything. She looked at him and her eyes clouded with tears.

For a moment he felt himself swaying with heartache, then there was a hit of irritation in his chest. What was that supposed to mean? Silence and teary eyes? What did she mean by that?

He asked a different question instead.

"There was nothing missing from her things? That's what you said in your witness statement."

"That's right," agreed Miss Hattoway, and she sipped from her glass of milk. "That's what I said. But do you want to know something ridiculous? I forgot all about her teddy bear."

"Her teddy bear?"

"Yes, she had this teddy — from childhood, you know — used to keep it on her bed at college, and the same thing here. I would never have teased her because there's the issue of my own fluffy rabbit." She paused, but Elliot did not laugh, so she continued. "Anyway, a few days after I talked to the Sheriff, I realized it was gone. The teddy bear was gone. I didn't think it was worth wasting police time — amending my witness statement or whatever — because it was just an old teddy. Elegant in its way, and sweet too, which is just like Mischka actually."

"Is it," said Elliot, only not as a question. He looked around the room one more time. "I think I'll go home now."

"All right," Miss Hattoway agreed. "I'm glad you came by." She walked toward the door and reached for the handle, then stopped.

"Oh, and one other thing," she said. "Well, Mischka always wore this bracelet — it looked a simple thing, but she once confided in me that her dad gave it to her on her sixteenth birthday. The stones in it came from the Dark Caves in the Swamp of Golden Coast — worth a fortune, stones like that. So, she'd have been wearing that on her wrist, of course. I mean, that wasn't left behind."

Elliot nodded, and he reached for the door handle himself. But Miss Hattoway's hand remained in his way, twisting the knob slowly.

"The funny thing was, I was looking at Shopline — that network thing where people buy and sell things — I was looking at that a few weeks after the . . . the disappearance, and somebody was selling a bracelet just like Mischka's. I thought to myself: *If that's Mischka selling her bracelet, she'll be set up for life.*"

She took her hand away from the door and half turned to Elliot.

"I suppose I should have mentioned *that* to the Sheriff, but who knows how many similar bracelets there are in the Kingdom? Could

263

be hundreds. And if it *was* her, if it *was* them, well, I guess it was kind of clear they didn't want to be found."

Elliot looked at her, and she was gazing at him with something like compassion, those tears welling up in her eyes again.

Now he remembered what Corrie-Lynn didn't like about Miss Hattoway. It was the fact that she was always crying.

Elliot didn't much like it either.

He closed the door behind him.

He drove the truck home. He went right up to his room, pulled out his folders of research about Purples, carried them downstairs, and dumped them in the trash.

Cambridge, England, The World

14.

*M*adeleine waited for almost two hours in the rain on Parker's Piece.

Then she went home.

Her mother was sitting cross-legged on the couch, drinking coffee. There was an envelope in Holly's lap, and as the door opened, she took this into both hands and held it in the air.

But seeing the state of Madeleine, she let it fall again.

Water trickled from Madeleine's forehead and ran rivulets down her cheeks. Her eyelashes were wet. Her backpack was so drenched it was leaking black dye onto her shirt.

She dropped the backpack onto the floor and sparks of water flew up. She drew out the book that was clamped beneath her arm, and it left behind a drooping water shadow. The book cover itself was looped with water stains, its pages clumped together and dissolving.

Holly Tully couldn't wait. She lifted the envelope again. "You wrote to him?"

Madeleine snatched the envelope from her mother's hand. Her body trembled. It was from her father! That was his address on the front in such familiar —

Her excitement unravelled.

The handwriting was familiar because it was her own —

It was her letter to her father, stamped: *RETURN TO SENDER*. He'd sent it back.

Madeleine shrugged. "Yeah? So?" She went into the bathroom and returned with a towel around her neck.

"You went out without an umbrella," said Holly.

"It wasn't raining when I left."

"This is England, Madeleine. Have you written to him before?"

"No." She rubbed at her head with the towel, so her voice vibrated. "I also emailed Tinsels, but she pretended to be someone else. I know I had the right address — Tinsels33 — she chose it cause 33 was the number of her favourite racehorse." She looked thoughtful. "Dad must have told her to pretend not to know me, on account of being so mad at me."

Her mother nodded.

"He must get a lot of unwanted mail," Madeleine continued, "to need a stamp that says *Return to Sender*. Don't most people just *write* that on?"

The mistake was, she tried to smile at that moment. The movement of her mouth sent a faulty signal to her cheeks and eyes, and it all fell apart and she was crying.

"Oh, sweetheart." Her mother reached out but Madeleine covered her face with her hands and sobbed, "I am *not* crying!"

"Okay."

"It's just —" Her voice fought its way between the gasps. "I'm so selfish and stupid, and Dad was right! On the skateboard and his beard, and now we've lost everything! We've lost him and Tinsels and the others and our life, and we're trapped here spinning straw in a non-life! And it's all my fault! Cause I've always been so selfish! Always running away! And I've brought you with me, and I've brought *it* with me too, haven't I? My selfishness! I've killed Byron! And Elliot Baranski isn't real!"

"All right," murmured her mother, standing up now, trying to hug her from behind, until the surges of sobs began to slow and fade.

Then Madeleine sat on the couch. She wiped her eyes with the backs of her hands.

"I wasn't crying," she explained.

"No, of course not," her mother agreed. "You weren't making any sense either. A skateboard and a beard and you've killed Byron. What's Byron?"

"The poet."

"Well, you didn't kill him. He's already dead."

Madeleine burst into tears again.

Holly waited.

"*Tell* me," she said eventually, exasperated.

So Madeleine turned her face into the couch, and began to speak.

She told her mother everything, starting with her father's warnings about her selfishness; the way he was after the skateboarding incident; that she knew it was her fault they were here because if she hadn't run away that weekend, her mother would never have left.

She told how Jack had found her email to Tinsels; that she'd realised Jack was the poet Lord Byron; that she'd been leaving letters for a stranger in a parking meter; and that the stranger had not shown up at Parker's Piece.

When she finished, she was calm again. She straightened up on the couch.

"So you've got a total loser for a daughter," she said. "Who knew?" She scratched the side of her mouth. "I guess Dad did."

"Cut it out now," said her mother. "I'm trying to think. I need to get my thoughts in order and present them in an incisive, persuasive way. Because *I'm* the one with the answers today, which won't always be the case — for instance, if you were weeping about a mathematics problem, well, I'd be clueless and we'd both end up weeping. Not that you *were* weeping, of course."

Holly reached for her coffee, which was now cold. She drank from it anyway. She needed a haircut: Her fringe was so long it touched the coffee mug. She set the mug back down again.

"Okay, I've decided to start simple and work back. So, I am now formally telling you, as your mother, that I want you never to become a smoker, never to own your own motorbike, never to get a chess board tattooed onto your face — and never ever to write to an imaginary friend in a parking meter again."

Madeleine smiled. "It's okay. I'm done with him anyway. He left me in the rain for two hours."

"Although we *could* hide out in the street and watch until he or she comes creeping up to the parking meter, and then we'd — but no. It's dangerous. You know that. Elliot Baranski is imaginary, but the person writing these letters is not. I remember when you were little, you had so *many* imaginary friends. Your imaginary friends had imaginary friends of their own. So. Just watch your tendency to slip out of the real world. Come back and join us here, okay?"

"Like I said, I'm already back."

Holly ignored her, frowning at the ceiling.

"Jack and Belle! That's easy too. It's sad that you hurt them, but we all hurt our friends sometimes. We feel terrible. Then we say sorry. Jack's got a heart as big as a planet, and even with all her weirdness, Belle's a good person. They'll forgive you, I promise."

Madeleine shrugged, but Holly grabbed her shoulders and stilled the shrug. "This is *not* an issue on which you have opinions! Your face must flood with the revelation that I'm right! And then you nod gratefully. Which reminds me. *Jack is not Byron.* He's Jack."

Madeleine almost shrugged again, but stopped at her mother's warning glance.

"And really, why shouldn't you write to an old friend and complain about your life? It's a *huge* change you've had to deal with — why shouldn't you take a while to realise that it's the right one? Or to see that Jack's not just some temporary distraction, but actually a great kid?"

"I should have realised," said Madeleine.

"Hush. Now, about the skateboarding incident. Where was your mother?"

"Excuse me?"

"When you were ten years old and speeding down the hill towards a highway, where was your mother? Where was I?"

"I don't have a clue."

"Exactly!"

Now Madeleine kicked off her shoes and swung her feet onto the couch. "You were doing well for a while there," she said.

"I know! But now I'm doing better! Because that was my brilliant rhetorical swoop. Listen, Madeleine, children on skateboards aren't being *selfish*, they're being children. You were young and a little crazy. That was your thing. I was probably getting my hair and nails done. Or having another meeting where we figured out how to get richer. If you'd flown into that traffic and been killed, I can guarantee nobody would have said: 'What a self-centered little girl!' They would have said: 'Where were her parents?'"

Madeleine bit at a fingernail. "Well, one parent was there. Dad was there. By the side of the road."

Holly stopped. She studied Madeleine's face, then looked away. She was making a decision.

She made it.

"I think I should tell you something," she said. "About your dad. About the night you ran away."

Their eyes met, and the expression on Holly's face was fierce and complicated. Madeleine realised she was trying to send her a warning: preparing her for what she was about to hear.

"The night you ran away," Holly began, "we were in the penthouse suite and I was about to get in the shower when we got word that you were at the station buying a ticket for London. Well, I was annoyed, of course. Of course I was. Your dad was already dressed. He was at the mirror. I remember he was brushing his cuff links or putting on his hair — that was the wrong way around but whatever. Anyway, so I said, 'We'd better go get her ourselves.' I said, 'What is this, fifteen times she's run away now?'"

"Seventeen and a half," Madeleine put in.

"Thanks. Anyway, I said, 'I don't think we should send somebody else to get her. I think we should skip tonight's party and spend the night with her, and figure out why she keeps doing this.' I'll never forget the expression on your dad's face when I said that. I saw it in the mirror. It was like he was right on the verge of a tantrum but caught himself just in time. Something crumpled in his forehead and around his mouth, then he set his chin firmly, and he said, 'Let her go,' and he said in a voice that was almost a whine but that tried to sound perfectly reasonable — he said . . . do you know what he said?"

Madeleine shook her head slowly.

"He said, 'They're serving 1990 Château Latour Pauillac tonight.'" The room was still.

"Did you hear me?" Holly repeated.

"Yeah, yeah, I got it." Madeleine picked at her teeth irritably with her thumbnail. "That's a good wine, right? So then what?"

"He meant it, Madeleine. Our thirteen-year-old daughter was running away and he didn't want to rescue her because they were having nice wine at a party."

"So?" Madeleine shrugged. "He likes wine. He knew I'd be okay on the Eurostar. He thought it'd teach me a lesson."

"You were *thirteen*. You don't let thirteen-year-olds skip off to London to teach them a lesson! You don't risk your child's life because you *like* wine, and if you do, it means you have a problem."

Now the thumbnail caught at Madeleine's gum and she grimaced.

"You're making him sound like an alcoholic," she said. "He did not have a problem! He never even got hangovers! He was running a corporation, so *how* could he have been a drunk? He was right to let me go that night. *You* were the one who was wrong to follow me. And now it's *my* fault that you're here instead of still with him! *I broke up your marriage!*"

She was crying again, but her mother spoke low and fast. "Just because somebody's not passed out in a gutter, doesn't mean they're not an alcoholic. Sure, he was running the show but you can get away with a lot of mistakes with a corporation that size. Especially surrounded by people who are often just as trashed as you are." Holly took a breath, and spoke even faster: "It wasn't just wine, you know, it was dope and pills and cocaine, and he never got hangovers because he never stopped for long enough to get one."

Abruptly, Madeleine's eyes were dry. "This is stupid," she snapped. "If it was that serious — if you really thought he had a problem — you should have *done* something about it, not just run away! Which proves that you *know* there was no problem."

Now Holly's face softened and there was so much sympathy in her eyes and the set of her mouth that Madeleine felt strangely panicked.

"I tried a million times to make him slow down or cut back," Holly murmured. "I shouted, cried, and talked, talked, talked. I wrote him letters, I even wrote him a poem once. I left books about substance abuse all over the house. But he could always point to someone else we knew and say, 'You think *I've* got a problem? Look at him, he was rushed to emergency for alcohol withdrawal last week!' Or he would pretend to agree to slow down, but then a moment later there'd be that glug-glug-glug of wine pouring into a glass. There was always one more night club, one more jazz bar. He was so quick to get angry, but it was more than that — he had this restlessness, this need to move, and it was like he was lost deep inside himself. I think, if you let yourself, Madeleine, you'll realise that a part of you knew that."

Madeleine was shaking her head. "No chance, because you're wrong."

"It's not your fault that we're here," Holly said, ignoring her. "It's *my* fault that we weren't here sooner. We escaped, Madeleine." Holly separated her words, handing them over one at a time. "We're not trapped here, we were trapped there. Sure, we sparkled and glittered and flew through the world, but it was only an illusion of flight. We were trapped in the orbit of a man who was no longer truly there."

"But —" Madeleine waved her arms around at the sloping walls, the cracked floorboards. "But look where we are now!" Her eyes were blurring with tears again, and her mother reached for her hands and pulled her up.

"Look, there's a you-shaped print on the couch. Any other mother would have made you change out of those wet clothes before we talked. You need to have a bath or you'll end up with pneumonia and die, which would be an unexpected plot twist in our lives. Or the couch might get pneumonia. Even more unexpected."

She went into the bathroom and emerged again, talking over the sound of blasting tap water.

"This is too much for you. Don't think about any of it for a while. Instead, let's make this like one of those children's stories where you get cold, wet, and bedraggled, but then you have a bath. And you wash away all terrible thoughts about yourself, and all confusing thoughts about your father, and you just be you. Then we drink hot chocolate, and get on with our brand-new lives."

Madeleine shrugged.

"There you go shrugging again. Listen, England is a perfect place for our new life, and here's why. It's summer but it's so grey and rainy that the whole bath-and-hot-chocolate thing works. Which is not a feature many countries offer."

The bath tub was pink enamel with a crack along its side like a wayward kite string. A rust stain on the tiles outlined the place where a soap tray had once been attached. The cabinet door was swollen, and always stood partly open, releasing a pale damp smell into the room.

Lying in the bath, Madeleine looked around at this, and smiled slightly. Her mother was wrong about her father. To say he had a problem with alcohol and drugs was ridiculous. He just knew how to have a good time. He was not "lost somewhere deep inside himself." He was busy. He would come for them eventually, and so would all the colours, then the three of them would fly away together. Specifically, they'd fly to the luxury spa bathrooms of five-star hotels.

On the floor was the towel that she'd had around her shoulders while she talked to her mother. Beside that, lying in a shallow puddle, was the letter that she'd written to her father. The ink on the RETURN TO SENDER stamp was smudged.

She stared at it awhile, trying to remember what she'd said to him. She reached out of the bath now, picked it up, opened it, and read.

Dear Dad,

Okay, first off, DO NOT RIP THIS LETTER TO SHREDS. Or just, you know, read it before you do that. Thanks.

Now, take a deep Zen breath, and we will visualise ourselves speaking very calmly to each other.

I realise you are feeling angry with me. The word "angry" doesn't even come close, right? You're furious, outraged, incensed, LIVID (that's a word I've never used, which might help to calm you down a bit, seeing as you're keen on my vocabulary extension). You're as angry as a demon out of hell!

(Although maybe demons out of hell are not angry? Cause they're happy to be out of there?)

Anyway, seriously, I am so, so, so sorry for running away again, especially as this time I accidentally brought Mum with me.

I have totally learned my lesson, and I will NEVER run away again. I'm done with it. I promise.

I guess you're probably angry with Mum too, for running out on you, but listen, the only reason Mum is here is that she followed me. Which you can't blame her for, seeing as she's, you know, my mother. She just wanted to protect me. So it's TOTALLY unfair for her to get the blame for my wrongdoing.

Therefore, I am just going to ask you really politely, can you, kind of, like, forgive us? Or anyway, temporarily forgive us while you come here and get us? The address is on the envelope. And you can have a totally touristique time while you're here cause there are historic buildings and flowers and stuff in Cambridge.

It's crazy to let our family fall apart because of my mistake! Mum's not all that well at the moment, and she's probably scared of how mad you'll be, so she's not going to call you, and this could just go on forever, totally unnecessarily. So can you please be the grown-up here?

You know, I have this strange feeling that you're not really hearing me, even if you HAVE set aside how angry you are. And I want you to hear me, because it's the most important thing in the world for you to come here and get us.

I'll try to explain what I mean. This is the difficult bit of the letter so please don't get mad all over again when you read it. The thing is, I've had this feeling lately that you can't quite hear. Not that you're technically deaf, it's more like the real you is hidden somewhere inside you. Like you're wrapped up in layers, or underneath a pastry lid or something. I mean, don't take offence, but sometimes it's like your delays have gone wrong, or like you're a scratched CD and you're skipping important bits of the song.

This isn't making sense, and I don't even know what I mean. Just, maybe you're working too hard? Or maybe going out a bit too much? I shouldn't tell you this but I did a lot of partying/ drinking/drugs and stuff when I turned thirteen and it's true it makes you feel great, but I kind of realised it wasn't real. And it wasn't really ME anymore. Anyway, I think it's probably the stress of work making you not yourself, and maybe you should have a change of direction?

Like, come here and get us, and Mum could start her own fashion design business, instead of just mending other people's clothes, and you could do the promotional work for her, and it would all be fun and colourful but also way more Zen.

I know for a fact that the real you, if you can just get hold of him again, will jump on the first flight to Cambridge.

Can't wait to see you.

Love,
Madeleine

P.S. And can you come soon? What I said about Mum being a bit unwell — I really think she might need a doctor. So can you hurry and come here and get her to go see one? Thanks.

Madeleine held the letter in her hands and felt a coldness fan right across her body.

She reached over and turned on the hot tap. Right away it squealed in that high-pitched way it had, as if it was in a blind panic about having to produce hot water.

She turned it off.

She stepped out of the bath, reached for a towel, and leaned around the door. Her mother was sitting at the sewing machine.

"I need a favour," Madeleine said.

"Okay."

"Promise me you'll see a doctor."

Holly blinked, startled.

"Sometimes, like today, you seem just like yourself, and everything you say makes sense. Sort of. But other times — well, not so much. And the headaches. And the fainting. And . . . forgetting things. You have to see a doctor."

But her mother was already nodding, distracted. "All right. But only if you go and get me some chocolate when you're finished in the bath."

"Make an appointment right now and you've got yourself a deal."

Her mother picked up the phone.

PART 7

ELLIOT BARANSKI

Dear Madeleine,

Some time back, you gave away your name in a letter. It was a joke you made about when you broke your ankle, I think, and someone saying to you: "Oh, Madeleine . . ."

It's pretty, Madeleine, I like it.

I kept on using M.T. out of respect, though, 'cause I thought that's what you wanted.

Ah, that's not true. I was using M.T. to make fun of you, I guess.

Because it kind of sounds like "empty."

That was wrong of me. Just like it was wrong of me to say "suit yourself" when you said you were going to a place to wait for me.

You might have taken that to mean I'd be there, and I hope you didn't.

I was mad at you, Madeleine, and I guess I should explain why.

There's something I never told you about me. It's school vacation at the moment, so I guess I've got some time and I can tell you.

Almost a year and a half ago, my father went missing, and so did a high-school teacher.

The night they disappeared, I found my Uncle Jon dead by the side of the road.

The thing about my dad being gone.

I never knew what it might be like to have somebody missing. Before it happened, I remember thinking that'd be tough — but turns out, the distance between how you think something might feel and how it *actually* feels, well, the Kingdoms and Empires combined couldn't measure that.

One time, years ago, I was playing in a junior deftball game. This was when my cousin Corrie-Lynn was just a baby. Uncle Jon and Auntie Alanna were there with Corrie-Lynn on the sidelines, watching. And a ball went astray.

It was flying — speeding — fast and hard through the air, and everyone could see it was heading for Corrie-Lynn in her baby carriage.

Jon and Alanna were a little way away from her, chatting with my parents. Corrie-Lynn was sitting straight and solemn in that way she's always had, and the ball was shooting right for her face.

I was on the other side of the field.

I could see it flying. I could see exactly where it was going to hit. And there wasn't a thing I could do.

In the end, my mother caught it. She turned just in time and threw herself into the air, grabbing the ball and landing on her stomach in the dirt. The palm of her hand was bruised from the catch, so I don't want to think what might have happened to little Corrie-Lynn if it had hit.

The point is, that feeling you get in your stomach and your throat — in your whole body — as you watch a ball spin toward a baby. The terror of that, the suspense — well, that's how it feels to have my father missing.

The difference is, in real life, someone either catches the ball or it hits and you deal with the consequences.

When someone's missing, the ball is always flying.

Even on my best days, days when I'm distracted by friends, having fun, even then it's like I've left something baking in an oven somewhere. A part of my mind can sense burning every moment of the day.

It's exhausting too, because I can shift facts and possibilities around in my mind forever. A third-level Purple killed Jon and we thought it must've taken my dad and Mischka Tegan too.

But their bodies never showed up. So maybe the Purple had taken them to its cavern and was keeping them alive?

Or maybe my dad had run away with Mischka? Run off on my mother and me as if we never existed. Maybe Dad had killed Jon before he left? Or asked him to drive the truck home?

I've spent the last year wanting to believe a Purple had my dad in its cavern, because it sort of fit the facts, and it meant I could go out there and rescue him.

But there were other facts too — like my dad and Mischka drinking together, my dad's reputation — and they kept leaking in.

It was like, inside my mind, I'd built myself a pyramid of pumpkins but every time I turned my back, its balance would shift — crates start tipping, dirt spilling, rain seeping in between the cracks. So I'd clean up, reconstruct — and turn my back again.

Anyhow, with all this going on, I'm also getting letters from you that say I don't exist, and that family who disappear don't want to be found, and if they do disappear, it's most likely because of me. At the same time as going on and on, like a combine harvester, about Colors.

It's not your fault, but you sure can say the wrong thing.

Anyhow, lately, that pyramid in my mind has come crashing down, and this time I'm not going to rebuild.

I cheated on my girlfriend — on Kala — the day she left town, you know, and right away it came to me: If I can do that, maybe my dad did cheat on us. Maybe he and I are the same.

I already knew he had his magnifying glass; then it turns out *she*'d taken her teddy bear, *and* they had a bracelet to make them a pile of cash.

My dad ran away with that teacher; he's not in a Purple cavern at all.

I looked into the sun I guess, like you told me, and it hurts but at least it's the truth.

Or, to put it another way, the ball hit, but at least it's not that high-pitched suspense anymore.

And he's not dead — it's not like they found his body torn to pieces like my Uncle Jon's, which would be a different kind of hit, more savage and brutal, its own kind of hell — but simpler somehow and more honorable. Not so ugly, complicated, and personal.

And one of these days I can track him down, give him hell, and walk out on him.

Ah, even sitting here on my front porch, looking out over the fields, there's a part of me aches to see him walking. To conjure him out of the sunlight in the distance. The shape of my dad, I can almost see it, crossing the field toward me. Come to put his arm around me, reach out an arm to my mother as well, and I'd close my eyes and just breathe.

Take care,

Elliot

MADELEINE TULLY

Dear Elliot,

So, I wasn't even going to look at that parking meter again.

I was totally going to shun it. Even if the parking meter was, like, drowning and calling out, "Madeleine! Save me!" I was just going to shrug, and go, "Whatever."

Even if it asked me to dance.

And I love dancing.

Cause you stood me up in the rain, buddy.

(Also, my mother made me promise never to communicate with Elliot Baranski again.)

But here I am.

What's *that* all about?

Your guess is as good as mine.

Well, no, I doubt that actually. My guess would probably be better than yours.

What happened was, I was walking along, keeping my eyes away from the parking meter, but there was a car parked in front of it with its two front seats pushed forward. As if the two seats had just got bad news. The driver's seat was resting its head on the steering wheel, like, completely overcome by the news.

I was, like, *Oh, no, guys, what's wrong, what's happened?* but the seats didn't say anything. And then I felt I should respect their privacy and so I turned away from them, and there was the parking meter. Right in front of my eyes.

With a REALLY fat envelope in it.

I had to WRENCH it out of the crack.

But I did. I wrenched it. And I read it.

The first thing I want to say is that I'm embarrassed that I gave away my name. So much for being a supercool, superspy, undercover, code-name kinda girl.

So much for protecting my privacy, I guess.

(And I never in my whole life thought of my initials as sounding like "empty." Great. Thanks for that.)

Anyhow, I read your letter, and I started writing a reply in my head, but then a strange thing happened. Something slid sideways into my mind and said: *I think it's real.*

And for a moment, I believed in the Kingdom of Cello. Seriously.

Only for a moment, though. I'm over it now.

Anyhow, so that happened. And then, I'm walking home and I saw two cats. This was in a children's playground. I stopped at the fence and watched them. They seemed young, like a cat's whisker (ha-ha) past being kittens. They were slender with bright eyes, and they were running side by side, exactly as if they had been choreographed. They slipped in and around the children's play equipment, flying apart then coming back together. One found an old key on a loop of rope, and they tossed that around for a while. The pattern of their play felt symmetrical, and then I realised that the patterns on their fur felt that way too.

One was black, the other dark grey, but they both had a kind of shimmer of white at exactly the same points on their coats. It was like one was the cat and the other was the shadow of the cat.

I was watching them, and I thought of you and me. How we're like shadows of each other, or maybe reflections. I ran away from my father, your father ran away from you, but both things have turned out to mean the same thing. That our fathers betrayed us. I've betrayed Jack, and you've betrayed Kala. We're both secretly afraid that it might be our own fault that we've lost our family and friends. We've realised how flawed our fathers are, and we think we might be flawed in the same way.

It's like we're complementary colours. (Sorry to be talking

about colours again.) You know what those are, right? Colours that make each other disappear? So if you cross red with green — or blue with orange, or yellow with purple — you get a pale, pale colour, almost white. (Isaac called it a "faint, anonymous colour.") (I'm not talking about paint here — red and green *paint* don't cancel each other out, they just make mud-brown.)

Interestingly, though, if you put complementary colours *next* to each other, they make each other shine much more brightly. (They glow with more than their natural brilliance, is how Leonardo da Vinci put it.)

I wonder what would happen if you and I met? Would we kill each other off, or make each other glow? Maybe both.

The point of all this is that even though I can't believe in the Kingdom of Cello, I believe there's truth in your writing. Maybe the essence of *you* comes through behind your stories? It's, like, the things you describe *have* happened to you — or something like them — and you're translating them into a place called Cello. Maybe your father disappeared, and it's connected with the colour purple, somehow? So you've created a monster out of purple? Maybe he was wearing a purple jacket when he left?

(If it makes you feel any better, they used to make purple dye out of the glandular mucus of a sea snail. So, you know, who likes purple? It's just snot.)

Anyhow, Jack and Belle are still not talking to me. Well, they say *words* to me, but they're the kind of words you'd say to a visiting great-aunt who's sleeping in your bedroom and frying liver in your kitchen every morning.

Meanwhile, my mother finally went to the doctor. She got referred to a neurologist at Addenbrooke's, and they've already done a CT scan, which apparently showed some kind of abnormality in her brain, but who knows what *that's* all about? (That's quoting the doctor, apparently — according to my mother. Not sure you can trust her on that.) She's scheduled for an MRI in a couple of weeks, to find out just what *that's* all about.

She says they all just shine lights in her eyes and make her do tests like what's ten plus ten, or tell her to smile then frown, or they make her close her eyes and touch things and guess what they are. I asked her how she was going in her tests, and she said she got an A+, and I was like, "Did the *doctor* say that?" and she said, "Well, no. But I could tell."

So who knows?

She told me that she said to the neurologist, "Well, what *might* the MRI show?" and he said, "That's a multiple-choice question."

I guess we just wait. It feels good to have the professionals take charge. I think the job was kind of beyond me. (And I get the feeling they're actually a lot more professional than my mother's painting them. Plus, if there's an abnormality in her brain, they'll just, like, operate and take it out, right? That would've been totally beyond me. Brain surgery.)

Huh.

Did you catch that?

Something just kind of spun by my eyes, and it was the belief again, that the Kingdom of Cello is real.

(Gone again now.)

Best wishes,
    Madeleine

PART 8

Bonfire, The Farms, Kingdom of Cello

1.

The Cellian Herald

Dearest, Sweetest, and most Quizzically Sublime Subjects of this! our fine and torrential Kingdom of Cello!

Welcome to this, our thirteenth??? (who knows?!) [*Editor's note: yes, thirteenth*] **column for that ratbag of a paper, the *Cellian Herald*!** [*Editor's note: We humbly submit that the Princesses here intended to use the word* ragtag, *meant as a term of endearment; accordingly, we will not take offense.*]

Most apologies, but we are going to be adorably rapid in this column — ah, the fatigue of these last weeks! However, it's all winding up now, much as our dear brother, Prince Chyba, winds *us* up sometimes! (That's Jagged Edge slang for teasing, we believe.)

Oh, Chybs, he's the greatest, and he's been in remote diplomatic talks with our neighboring Kingdom of Aldhibah for *weeks* now, which is good of him (although not surprising, considering how Chybs can talk — the Aldhians have probably packed up and gone home and he's still sitting there at the monitor, oblivious, talking on and on) — but sometimes we wish that those Aldhians would arrest Chyba and lock him in one of their dungeons for the rest of his life.

Hmm, put like that, it sounds kind of harsh.

Sorry, Chybs! We don't mean it!

(Hope no Aldhians are reading this!) (Not too worried as nobody in Aldhibah would read the *Cellian Herald*, right? Cute

as the paper may be.) [*Editor's note: The circulation of the* **Cellian Herald** *in the Kingdom of Aldhibah is around 775,000.*]

Dearest Ones, this, as we said, will be a helter-skelter column — just letting you know that we have completed Olde Quainte (got caught in a strong current while on the seafaring town of Irate, where the coffee was a little bitter for our taste — otherwise, all good) and we're now in the thicket of Jagged Edge — *loving* the excess of night-dwelling here, even if it *has* turned our body clocks upside down! But . . . as we said . . . our tour is almost at an end.

We can't wait to hug and tickle our little brother, Prince Tippett. As for our Royal Mother (Queen Lyra, as she is known to all of you), she writes to us from her retreat on the border of the Magical North and the Undisclosed Province (where she's gone to calculate the Kingdom's finances), she writes that she misses us dearly, and *she* can't wait to hug *us* again!! (She makes no mention of tickling.)

But listen, there's a point to all of this!

IT'S AN ANNOUNCEMENT!!!

A super-awesome, kick-ass announcement [*Editor's note: The Princess Sisters presumably are not aware that the JE slang "kick-ass" is rather coarse.*] —

And it is this!

TWO of the three members of the Youth Alliance have been CHOSEN!!!!

Drum roll!

Number One Selection: a boy named SAMUEL HORACE JURGEND, of Twy Eam Peck, in Olde Quainte!

Number Two Selection: a girl named KEIRA J. PLATTER, of Tek, in Jagged Edge!

In relation to Samuel, that *was* a heart-stopper! We were in the Emerald Carriage, riding past the outskirts of Twy Eam Peck, very quiet and respectful, it being a registered Hostile. Suddenly, there was a shout! Several more shouts. The horses picked up speed! What was happening?

It seemed that Samuel, a mere schoolboy of twelve years old, was *running after the carriage*!

He had prepared an application to join the Youth Alliance, you see, and wanted to deliver it in person!

Unbelievably stupid or brave as a lion, that Samuel — either way, he came *so close* to getting himself shot!!

Anyhow, we were so taken by his pluck — and by his wire-rimmed spectacles, lace collars, and jodhpurs; and by the elegant calligraphy on his application; and by the sheer *randomness* of a boy from Twy Eam Peck (do you *realize* how Hostile that place is?!) *wanting* to join a Royal Youth Alliance (?!?!?) — well, because of all this, we chose him.

So, Samuel is in!

His delight at our decision was heartwarming.

As for Keira, we just chose her today. We were watching an underground motocross championship in Tek here in JE, and Keira was the winner.

Jupiter and I were charmed. She was selected on the spot.

She seemed surprisingly unim-pressed but we take that to be her natural modesty.

WHO WILL BE NEXT?!

Only one more person to choose! Could it be somebody we are going to meet this very day?

Or could it be a certain boy who lives in a certain town in the Farms, and let's just say that the town's name is *hot* and by the sounds of things, so is this boy himself. His sheriff wrote to us about him, which is adorable. He is burning up a line on *my* short-list, anyhow. . . .

Or could it be *you*, sweet reader?! (Assuming you are young. I suppose older people read this paper too. Yes. They would.)

Anyhow, keep the applications coming —

but for now,

we must fly!

more anon.

Yours with Royal Vigor and Pomp

HRH, the Princess Jupiter, and HRH, the Princess Ko xxx

$\mathcal{H}$ector Samuels swung his chair around twice, then three times in the opposite direction.

The newspaper was open on his desk, and he skidded toward it and read it again, laughing aloud.

He picked up the phone.

"Jimmy? You see it?"

"See what, Hector?" There was a crackle and croak in Jimmy's voice, and Hector remembered himself.

"Ah, sorry, Jimmy. Still sick, eh? I guess I forgot. Actually, I guess I'm just *tired* of you being sick. What's it been now, almost two weeks? Come on, just give that flu a stern talking-to and get well already." He laughed.

"Good to hear you sounding so chipper yourself," Jimmy said drily, before losing himself in a coughing fit. "Have I seen what?"

"The royal tour column! The Princess Sisters' column! They're talking about *us*! They must've seen my letter, Jimmy, and they're *talking about it in their column*!"

"Seriously? They talk about Bonfire?"

"Well, it's not a *specific* reference as such, but what else could it mean? They say a town in the Farms with a name that is *hot*. Bonfires are hot! And they mention a *boy* who lives in this town, which *must* mean Elliot, 'cause I talked about him in my letter. They're hinting they want him for their Youth Alliance!"

There was a pause. Another cough.

"You'll get yourself in a world of trouble with Elliot," Jimmy pointed out.

"Ah, he'll be over the moon. Go get the paper and read it! No, hang on, you're sick, so I'll read it aloud to you. Better read the whole thing so you get the context. *Dearest, sweetest, and most —*"

"That's okay, Hector. I'll track it down myself. Listen, you hear anything back from Central Intelligence yet?"

Hector chuckled, still happy. "Not yet, Jimmy. Seems your theory about those five missing people being in the *World* has left them speechless. And now I'm thinking — didn't you come up with that right around the time you got this flu?"

"What's your point, Hector?"

"Fever addled your brain! You want to send a retraction to Central? Try to win back their respect?"

"I stand by my theory. Central should be following up. Maybe check they got your fax?"

"Hang on, Jimmy, looks like someone's coming in. Call you back. Read the column!"

The door jangled open and the Twickleham family appeared.

It seemed to Hector suddenly that the Twickleham family were *always* appearing at his station door. Always in that formation too: two adults with the little one between, like a row of snowmen he'd seen once. The grown-up Twicklehams did have the roundness of the snowman about them.

Of course, snowmen didn't usually wear tunics with tights, or floor-length silk dresses with brooches at their collars, or pointy leather shoes, which is how the Twicklehams were dressed today.

"Call yourself a good morning from us, will you not," said Bartholomew Twickleham, and the Sheriff, as usual, found himself uncertain how to respond. Was he to obey and call himself a good morning?

He grinned instead, and slapped the paper on the desk, being too happy for formalities.

"How the heck are you?" he said. "And little Derrin, now, I *like* that puppet! I'll bet you that's one of Corrie-Lynn's creations, eh?"

In answer, Derrin held up the wooden puppet she'd been hugging to her chest and had it do a jig and bow in the air.

"Ah, she's an angel." The Sheriff smiled at her parents. "And what can we do for you?"

"We've some news," said Bartholomew.

Fleta agreed. "We have," she said, "some news."

The Sheriff straightened, and solemned his face for them.

"It has come to us that we must leave this good town," said Mr. Twickleham, "for the fair was to save us, and as to a serpent in a kiwifruit, it did not."

"It did not," agreed his wife.

"Well, now," said the Sheriff. "I am sorry to hear this."

"And so we have resumed our Olde Quainte style of dress," Fleta added.

"Ah." The Sheriff nodded.

Derrin sat on the floor and played with the puppet, while Mr. and Mrs. Twickleham explained what had happened at the fair.

It seemed that certain young people had been in charge of placement of the stalls — which had surprised the Twicklehams, rather. But it seemed that these young people — Cody and Gabe were their names — had arranged for the Twickleham stall to be placed in the farthest corner, in the shadow of the circus tent, where none but the most *intrepid* explorer in search of electronics repair could find it!

"We waited all day," said Mrs. Twickleham sadly. "With all our baked treats, and our little gadgets meant for the children, and our flyers in multiple colors, so full of hope! But not a soul came by! And when Bartholomew set out, strident, with his megaphone, to shout up interest, well . . ."

"Whenever I tried to shout, music started up! Drowning my words! Every time! Until I had to give up."

"Later," added Mrs. Twickleham, "we learned that it was certain young people — Shelby and Nikki, to be precise — well, they were in charge of the music, if you will know it."

"I will know it," murmured Hector absently.

"And so we have already been out to the Baranski Farm this day, to tell Petra Baranski we must needs leave the shop. And we head off tomorrow."

"So sudden!" cried Hector.

"It is the timing of coincidence," said Fleta. "Our friend, some might think our *only* friend here — aside from you, Hector — our friend Olivia Hattoway, that is Derrin's teacher, is driving home to see her family in Jagged Edge tomorrow. As the school vacation has begun. She suggested we ride with her to Olde Quainte. Not exactly a direct route for her but a visit in our province will break up her trip."

"And she'll have our company," said Mr. Twickleham, "for the ride."

Hector sighed.

"That does make sense," he said, "but I blame myself for all this. I meant to talk to Elliot and his friends, and never did."

"Oh, now," murmured the Twicklehams.

They turned to the window, and both laughed a little bitterly.

"And isn't he always there! Does the boy not know it is the vacation time at the school?"

Hector looked, and sure enough, across the road in the empty high-school grounds, Elliot was standing near the sculpture again.

While they watched, he moved away from it, sat on a bench, took out a notepad, and began to write.

"Well now." The Twicklehams turned back. "So we wanted to let you know this sorryful news, but also, we wondered if our application for money from the Red Wave Damage Fund had been processed. Not to be hurrying you, but . . ."

Hector winced. "Ah, now, I *am* sorry. I'm way behind on paperwork, with Jimmy being out with the flu. What if I promise to get it processed by this afternoon? I could bring the check around to you?"

"We wish you no such nuisance," said Mrs. Twickleham. "We will return at the hour of six if that suits you?"

"You'll be busy packing up," said Hector. "I insist."

But the Twicklehams insisted back, and so it was agreed.

They left with a jangle, and Derrin with a wave from her wooden puppet, and Hector sat at his desk looking sorry for a few moments.

Then the newspaper caught his eye, and the grin lit his face up once again.

*   *   *

Elliot was sitting in the schoolyard, watching the sculpture.

After a moment, the glint of white caught his eye. He looked around fast, and then reached for it.

It was from Madeleine again.

Over the last few days, they'd written long letters to each other, the longest Elliot had ever written. He'd told her about his missing father, and his journeys to Nature Strip and to the Golden Coast. She'd told him about how she'd run away in a train called the "Eurostar," and how her mother liked chocolate, and how she'd met new friends named Jack and Belle.

Now, today, something had happened.

He'd delivered a shorter letter to her, and then turned to go, but for some reason he'd turned back. And a single piece of paper had appeared.

Are you there right now? it said.

Yes, he replied, and waited. A few moments later another note.

Cause the weirdest thing just happened, she wrote. *I was at the parking meter, about to put a letter in it for you, when your envelope just sort of APPEARED. It happened again right now. How are you doing this?*

Elliot grinned.

It's a crack, he wrote. *Like I told you before. No clue about the science.*

This is freaking me out, she replied. *But I totally like it. Keep doing it and I might actually get another one of my surges of belief in the Kingdom of Cello.*

It was a conversation.

He was having a conversation with a girl in the World.

They exchanged short notes for the next two hours.

They figured out that they were both in the same time zones. They told each other about the weather. She told him that this was like inter-Kingdom texting, and he said he had no clue what she was on about. She told him her favorite books and bands, and he repeated

295

that he had no clue. But that stood to reason, he said, her being in the World. She told him her mother had had an MRI, which had shown what looked like a tumor in her brain, and they'd done a fine-needle biopsy, and they were waiting for the results of the pathology, and she was thinking it would turn out all right because it'd be benign, or they could just cut the tumor out, but the doctors looked distracted when she said that, and there was a sort of darkness to the way they talked.

You know what I just thought? Elliot wrote. *I read somewhere that Butterfly Children used to make healing beads. Not exactly sure what they are, but if mine can't do crops, maybe she can do healing?*

Madeleine replied: *If you can get your Butterfly Child to make healing beads — and you can get them to me by tomorrow morning, 10 a.m. — and they cure my mother — well, I'll believe in the Kingdom of Cello for real.*

It's a deal, Elliot wrote.

There was a longer pause, then another note from Madeleine appeared:

Who really knows what's real anyway? I was reading a book the other day (about Isaac Newton again) and it mentioned the "shadow of the rainbow." I was like: what? That's real? Cause, whenever I see that extra rainbow — the one that's just behind a rainbow in the sky — well, I kind of assume I'm imagining it. Like it's a trick of the light. Like my mind is painting that extra one in.

But who says tricks of the light AREN'T real?

One time I had to get my hearing checked — the therapist thought maybe I kept running away from school because I couldn't actually HEAR the teachers tell me not to (she was getting desperate). Anyway, I had to sit in this little chamber wearing earphones, and the doctor or whatever sat outside the chamber, and I had to press a button whenever I heard a sound. At first, it was a really clear kind of GONG, and I was happy to press the button. Then the gongs started getting quieter and quieter, fading away, disappearing, until I couldn't figure out if I was hearing them or not.

It's like, are we supposed to see the extra rainbow? Was I supposed to hear that sound? Was it a sound inside my head or outside the chamber? It's like the blurring point between imagination and reality – something very faint, a reflection.

Elliot thought for a moment, then replied:

That sort of reminds me of the dragons, werewolves, trolls, giants, vampires, and so forth they've got up at the Magical North. See, the thing is, they're only there 'cause kids have gone to the Lake of Spells and caught SPELLS to make fairy-tale creatures. Nobody can figure out why any kid would do a dumb thing like make a werewolf, but they do.

Anyhow, now and then people talk about whether they really exist, those dragons, etc., seeing they're not supposed to be there. Seeing they're just imaginary.

Seems to me, if they are, they are. If a dragon sets you alight or a vampire sucks your blood, well, there's your question answered. And I guess, if you can see a rainbow, or hear a gong, it's answered too.

Before Madeleine had a chance to reply, he started another piece of paper.

If you were so happy in your life before, he said, how come you were always running away?

There was a long silence and when she did reply, she ignored his question:

If you and I are shadows of each other, like rainbows – or like those cats I wrote about the other day – which of us do you think is real and which is the shadow?

Could be we're both shadows, he replied. But I kinda doubt it.

I thought of something, she said, how come 404 never doubted MY existence? If you've had no contact with the World for, like, hundreds of years, why'd you assume my letter really WAS from the World? Not, like, a hoax by someone at your school?

Elliot replied:

People around here are kinda busy for that sort of thing. Gotta go now myself, actually. See you here at ten tomorrow.

He delivered the letter. Touched the sculpture once and walked away.

In her doll's house, the Butterfly Child was asleep.

"That's a surprise," Elliot said drily.

It was later that evening. He stood watching her a moment, then cleared his throat and spoke.

"Hey there," he said, then paused. "I don't want to disturb you," he added.

The Butterfly Child sighed in her sleep and turned over.

"Well, I *do* want to disturb you," Elliot said. "The thing is, you've been here in Bonfire a long time now, and nothing's happened to the crops, and well, okay, if you're sad . . . But I wish I knew *why* you were sad."

He sighed. Then carried on: "Anyhow, setting that aside, I read somewhere that you could make healing beads, and I've promised a friend that you'll make some for her."

He waited. The Butterfly Child breathed steadily.

"So I guess — well, who knows if you're hearing this anyway, but if you *are*, and if you *can* make healing beads, I'd be grateful. If you would make them. I mean."

He sniffed.

"Ah, what's the point?" He sat down on the couch, but almost at once there was a thumping on the front door.

His mother opened it. Corrie-Lynn's little voice sounded, and next thing she herself was in the room.

"Hey," he said.

Corrie-Lynn tilted her chin away from him, circled around the back of the couch, and stopped in front of the doll's house.

"Corrie-Lynn," said Elliot. "I heard about the Twicklehams leaving town, and I'm really sorry about your friend. I guess sometimes businesses just don't work out. And maybe one day I could, I don't know, take you to see Derrin in Olde Quainte? You could write to her in the meantime, right? Anyhow, I hope you'll talk to me again someday, 'cause I miss you, kid."

Corrie-Lynn held her face away from him. Her shoulders trembled and he thought maybe she was crying, but then she swung around and it wasn't tears, it was fury.

"You're '*really sorry*'?" She sure could wither when she tried. "You're *really* sorry, and it's because *businesses* fail?" Now she stamped her foot. "They're *leaving* town because of you and your friends! *I'm* really sorry your dad's away, and I hope he comes back, but if he does, he can get himself a *new* electronics shop, for crying out loud! And you know what, Elliot Baranski? If my dad was still around, he'd give you a serious talking-to, that's what he'd do. He'd say, 'What are you thinking, Elliot, scaring off a nice family like that? Making my Corrie-Lynn lose her only best friend? What are you *thinking?*'"

"Ah, baby . . ." Elliot was by her side, wanting to take her into his arms, but her eyes grew wide and her jaw gripped hard against the tears, and she punched him once, hard, in the stomach.

Then she sidestepped away from him, scowling.

He stood, watching her.

"You're right," he said eventually. "That's exactly what Uncle Jon would've said, and he'd have been right too. I *am* really sorry, Corrie-Lynn, and I want to fix it. I'll talk to them."

"Too late to fix it," she said coldly. "They're leaving in the morning. Now *they* could fix things — electronic things and that, but you and your friends never gave them a chance."

"Like I said, you're right. I'll fix it, Corrie-Lynn. I'll ask them to stay and I'll tell them my friends and I will do everything we can to make their business work. We'll do them a marketing campaign. We'll get Cody to paint billboards for them. We'll get Shelby up in her plane flying a banner that says GET YOUR TVS FIXED BY THE TWICKLEHAMS!"

Corrie-Lynn studied his face. She considered.

"You will?"

"I'll go over to the shop right now and tell them."

"Well," she said, still cold but relenting, "as long as it's something better than that on the banner. *Get your TVs fixed by the Twicklehams!* That's the dumbest slogan I ever heard. It's not even a slogan."

"Fair enough."

Corrie-Lynn was still watching him.

"Don't go over now," she said. "They go to bed early. But they're coming by the Watermelon first thing tomorrow, so Derrin and me can say one last good-bye." Her lower lip trembled, but she straightened her shoulders. "Meet us there at nine, and if you can persuade them to stay, I might just see if I can forgive you."

Then she swung around and walked toward the door.

"You going home already?"

Corrie-Lynn nodded, her back to him.

"Throw your bike in the back of the truck and I'll give you a ride. It's getting dark."

"No," she said. "I need some time alone."

When little kids act like grown-ups, Elliot thought, *it nearly breaks your heart.*

She was in the door frame when she turned back.

"It's 'cause you never listen to her," she said, swinging her thumb toward the doll's house. "That's why she's sad."

"The Butterfly Child? I never *listen* to her?"

"Exactly."

"She doesn't talk!"

"Oh, for crying out loud," muttered Corrie-Lynn. She shouted, "Bye, Auntie Petra!" and headed out onto the porch. He could hear her talking to herself as she ran down the front stairs: "He's supposed to be so *smart*, and *great*, and *brave*, and so good at *deftball*, and he's as dumb as a chain saw. . . ."

Her bicycle wheel squeaked in time with her mutters as she cycled down the drive and away.

The door to the Sheriff's station opened and the Twickleham family spilled out.

They'd collected their check from the Red Wave Damage Fund, said their farewells to Hector, and now they stood buttoning their coats against the evening chill.

They walked down the stairs, silent.

Fleta Twickleham paused at the bottom step. She was squinting across at the empty high-school grounds.

Her husband followed her gaze. She looked sideways at him, raising an eyebrow, and he shrugged. With Derrin between them, they headed across the road and through the school gate.

They stopped at the sculpture.

They studied it, peering inside and out, now and then knocking on the side of the TV.

Derrin swiveled on her heel nearby, gazing up at the stars until her neck started to ache. She rubbed at it awhile, tilting her head up and down.

Mr. Twickleham patted the concrete base and slid his hands over the sides of the TV. Mrs. Twickleham reached right inside.

She frowned. There was a crackling sound.

She held up a piece of paper.

They leaned in close, holding it in various positions to catch some of the light.

Eventually, they could see enough to read:

Hey Elliot,
I think you've gone now, but I wanted to tell you this anyway. I've decided I'm going to say sorry to Belle and Jack today. So, you know, wish me luck.

If it doesn't work out with them, maybe I should just come and live in your Kingdom?

I'm thinking, there's only two obstacles to that. (1) This "crack" is only big enough for letters, right? Well, just, kind of like, STRETCH it! (2) You think I've got the plague. I keep forgetting to tell you, we haven't had the plague here in the world for, like, hundreds of years! (I think.) I think they found a cure. Antibiotics, right?

So, no obstacles.

Oh, except that you have to prove that your Kingdom exists first.

Well, looking forward to that by ten tomorrow morning.

Madeleine

Fleta and Bartholomew Twickleham grew so still that Derrin stopped pivoting and glanced across at them.

But they were only looking at a paper, so she tried to see how fast she could hop on her left foot. When she stumbled and looked up again, they were staring at each other instead of the paper. Then, as one, they turned their gaze toward the Sheriff's station.

Cambridge, England,
The World

3.

*J*ack and Belle were in Auntie's Tea Shop.

She watched them through the window for a moment: Jack was talking and Belle was spinning a teaspoon on the table. They were the only customers.

When Madeleine pushed on the door, they both turned and looked. Their faces held steady for a moment, then Jack smiled a close-lipped smile.

Walking across the empty room felt like elbowing through a crowd.

"Can I join you?" she said.

Belle widened her eyes but Jack nodded.

"So you reckon 'Belle and Jack from outer space'?" Belle said, and Madeleine looked around for the waitress to order coffee.

"It's a blog we're planning," Jack explained to Madeleine. "We're thinking we should do it in the voices of aliens. It'll go viral, yeah?"

Belle's foot tapped quickly, and she turned her profile to Madeleine.

"We're giving free aura readings and horoscopes to anyone who comments," Jack continued.

"You're doing online aura readings?" Madeleine raised her eyebrows. "How's that going to work?"

"It'll work," said Belle, her gaze still on Jack.

Madeleine was quiet.

"I was thinking maybe not aliens," Belle said. "We could pretend we're famous people instead."

Jack turned to Madeleine. "What do you think?" he said, and Belle scratched her chin impatiently.

"Um. Sure," Madeleine said. "But won't the famous people, kind of like, sue you?"

"We could be dead famous people," Jack suggested. "Like I could be Byron! And Belle, you could be — who were you again?"

"Ada Lovelace," Belle said. "The one who made friends with Charles Babbage and invented computer programming."

"Yeah, and so it'd be, like, educational. I'll talk about my day-to-day life *as Byron*, like how my poems are going, and what the kids are up to and stuff."

"Byron didn't have kids," said Belle. "Ada will be way more interesting. Everyone'll be reading her part of the blog."

"Yes, he did. Byron had kids. He had two. First he married a beautiful, intelligent, extremely moral woman —"

"Ada was smarter," Belle interrupted. "She had measles when she was a kid and she had to go to bed for, like, a year. So she had nothing to do with her brain except get intelligent."

The waitress brought Madeleine's coffee. She picked it up and held it to her mouth, but it was too hot. She replaced it on the table.

"Anyhow, so Byron and his moral wife had a little girl. But then he took off and left them and the wife didn't want her daughter growing up to be a loser poet like her dad so she made her study mathematics."

"Yeah, all right, but Ada invented computer programming, so she was obviously even better at mathematics than —"

"You're talking about the same person."

Jack and Belle looked at Madeleine.

"It's the same person," Madeleine repeated. "Augusta Ada Byron. She was Byron's daughter, and he liked to call her Ada. She got measles when she was thirteen or fourteen. Her mother didn't want her to be a poet like her dad so she made her study mathematics. She married the Earl of Lovelace — that's why she became Ada Lovelace. She met Charles Babbage when she was eighteen, and got interested in his computers and wrote an algorithm that was kind of like the first computer program."

"Get out of here," said Belle.

"It's true. Your Ada is Byron's daughter."

"How do you know all that?"

Madeleine shrugged. "I've been reading a lot since I got here."

They were still staring at her, so she breathed in hard, looked just over their heads and said: "Since I got here to Cambridge, I mean. Which I just wanted to say is a very nice place. And I think that you two are . . . very nice people, and" — her voice sped up — "and I just wanted to, kind of like, say I'm really sorry that you saw — that I *wrote* that letter, cause you two were probably the best friends I ever had, and I don't think you would pretend you didn't know me just cause my dad told you to, and I should've realised that, and kind of like realised that *I* was the one who didn't belong in *your* lives, rather than you not being . . . good enough for me, and you two are connected — with your auras and your horoscopes, and your Byron and your Ada — and I should've realised I was the lucky one, cause you were letting *me* join you, but I was all superior, and *I* was the one who didn't belong because I'm just, like, that crazy Newton guy who nobody liked, walking around Cambridge scratching numbers in the dirt and talking to himself and trying to make gold out of fire in his room, and so I'll leave you alone now, and that's all I wanted to say."

Even though she was not a crying kind of a girl, Madeleine was finding that her words were falling at such high speed, and they all sounded so unexpectedly true, that they were gathering into a storm in her chest.

"Also my mum's really sick." The storm broke and she pushed her chair back and ran from the tea shop.

Jack and Belle watched her.

They watched through the glass as her face crumpled and she ran along the path and across the marketplace.

Then they turned to each other, raised their eyebrows, paid the bill, and followed.

They found her sitting on a staircase, her arms folded around her knees, her head resting on her arms.

Jack sat on one side, Belle on the other.

"What do you mean about your mum?" said Jack. "Has she got another headache?"

Madeleine kept her head on her knees and told them about the doctors, the scans, and the biopsy, handing over all those words like sharp-edged stones.

Jack put the palm of his hand on her back. Belle was silent.

"Okay, cut that out." Madeleine lifted her face, which was damp and streaked, and narrowed her eyes. "Don't go quiet like that. Mum's going to be fine."

"She will be," Jack agreed at once. "Addenbrooke's is one of the best hospitals in England. They'll fix her up. But I can't believe this has all been happening and you didn't tell us. Why didn't you tell us?"

Madeleine chewed on her finger.

"Because we weren't talking to you," Jack answered himself. He took his hand from her back and sighed deeply. "See, the thing is," he said, "I shouldn't have read your email to Tinsels. It was private."

Madeleine put her head back onto her knees, wrapping her arms around it as if to protect it.

"And you're allowed to be nasty about your friends in a private email," Jack continued. "I've thought about that. I mean, you were writing to your old friend so why shouldn't you, sort of like, vent, yeah?"

"But I didn't *mean* to be mean about you. . . ."

"Sure you did," said Jack. "I've been thinking about that too, and it must be like culture shock for you. Being rich and then poor. It'd totally seem colourless here."

"It's not, though." She sat up again, wiping her face with her sleeves. "You're not colourless."

"Yeah, I know." Jack shrugged.

Belle remained silent.

"Another thing," Jack persisted. "You do belong with us. If Newton was crazy, well, so was Byron. He kept a pet bear when he was at Cambridge. Well, I think he did anyway. Nobody seems to know for sure. He had rocks in his head. His totally moral wife thought he had fluid on the brain. So, see, we're connected too."

Belle finally spoke. "Ada wasn't crazy, though."

"Sure she was," said Jack. "All mathematicians are. We're like a circle, the three of us, and the best kind of circles are the ones that are sort of squashed — you probably already know this, with all that reading — but the more squashed and oval a circle it is, well, the more *eccentric* it is. That's where the word *eccentric* comes from."

He stopped talking and looked at Belle. "I think I've lost my point. You say something nice now, Belle."

"Ah." Belle shrugged. "All right, Madeleine, you might be smart remembering all those facts and stuff, but you're not *exactly* like Isaac Newton. Cause he was a genius, which you're not. If that makes you feel any better."

Madeleine smiled. "Okay."

"And —" Belle breathed in deeply. "The truth is, your aura's looking a bit better just at the moment."

Madeleine burst into tears again.

Dark Night

4.

O n the stillest nights, you could hear the clock tower from all the way out on the Baranski Farm.

Or maybe he was imagining that.

Either way, it was midnight now, and Elliot's eyelashes kept lowering. He shook himself hard and looked at the Butterfly Child again.

Remarkably, she was awake. But she was sitting on the edge of her bed, poised as if she might, at any moment, curl herself back under the covers.

Ever since Corrie-Lynn had left, Elliot had been trying to figure it out. The Butterfly Child was not helping. He'd been talking, talking, talking. Making suggestions, asking questions, even drawing notes and pictures on paper, for hours. And all she'd done was sit and stare, now and then taking a nap.

"How do I listen to you? Is there a code or something I'm missing? A way you move your arms or legs? Can you nod if I'm getting close?"

Ah, he'd already said all of this. All she did was sit there looking sleepy.

He stretched his arms and heard the clock tower again, so then he knew he must be imagining it. It didn't strike twice in ten minutes.

Or maybe that wasn't the chimes.

Maybe it was that sound he'd been hearing lately — that low flute sound like distant wind through trees, the one nobody else seemed to hear.

It was kind of annoying, that sound.

He might as well just go to sleep and try again in the morning.

He stoked the fire halfheartedly, the sparks crumbling into ashes then brightening again. Thought about adding a log, but closed his eyes instead, leaned back on the couch.

That chiming, long and low, deep in his mind. Seemed it was curling itself like falling leaves. He let it curl and fall, curl and fall, as he fell with it toward sleep.

Then the chime stood up and spoke.

"Sycamore bark is all very well," it said crisply, "but what I actually like is *mulberries*."

Elliot's eyes flew open.

Madeleine was sitting on the edge of her mother's bed.

Holly had woken with a headache, and now they were talking in the dim light of the bedside lamp.

"We should reconfigure," Holly was saying. She was sitting up, her arms around her knees, looking at the shadows of the flat. "We should put *all* of this junk in the attic and start again."

"Great idea," said Madeleine. "Except that we *are* in the attic."

"Hmm. You're right." There was a long silence. They were drinking cocoa, which was making Holly Tully happy. The idea of cocoa at midnight.

"What's your accent anyway?" she said abruptly.

"Whose accent?" said Madeleine.

"Yours?"

"What do you mean?"

"Where's your accent from?"

"It's from all over. My accent's an everywhere accent." Madeleine's voice was rising. "Just like yours."

"Yes, of course. Well, it's lucky you're here now." Holly frowned into her headache again. "You can gather them all together, all those pieces of accent, and consolidate. Find yourself."

"Don't do that." Madeleine was angry now. "I thought you didn't know who I was."

"Madeleine," her mother put her cocoa down, and placed an arm around her shoulder. "No matter what happens with the doctors, no matter what the biopsy shows or what they decide to do, I promise I will *never* forget you."

"You can't promise that. Nobody can. You keep forgetting everything. You used to know everything."

"Sweetheart, you just think I did. Kids always think that about their parents. But you've been overtaking me for a while now, and I think that's how it's meant to be."

Madeleine swung her legs onto the bed, lying down beside her mother.

"I remember when you were three years old," murmured Holly, "and you pointed out a lavender bush. You said to me, 'That's lavender,' and I thought, *So it is.* I thought, *This kid, she's three and she's* already *smarter than me.*"

She adjusted her pillow.

"And I remember when you said 'pieue' instead of 'pillow.' You couldn't make the 'l' sound, see?"

"I was cute, eh?" said Madeleine, relenting.

Belle and Jack were watching a movie at Jack's place, but Federico's snoring was so loud they had to switch off the TV.

"You ought to get some kind of a machine," mused Belle. "Like a soundproofing machine, and use it to soundproof your grandfather. Do they have them?"

"No."

They were quiet for a while, then realised they were both half swaying to the rhythm of the snores, and laughed.

"Holly seemed okay, eh?" said Jack. That afternoon, they had taken Madeleine home and stopped for tea and a chat with Holly. "I mean, it's hard to tell because you can't actually see inside somebody's brain, but she seemed great. Poor Madeleine, though, she must be so worried."

"Yeah." Belle paused. "You think you'll get back together with her?"

"I think she was into Lord Byron more than me. She had us mixed up, and as I am a strong, outdoorsy sort of bloke, and not a namby-pamby poet, well, I'm not her type." He took a handful of popcorn.

"No," agreed Belle, then: "Doesn't your grandfather get fined under some kind of local ordinance against noise pollution?"

"You know what I just thought of?" said Jack. "Normally, when someone's sick, you start going on about how they should stay away from hospitals and do alternative therapies, like, what are those things? Light therapy, and chromotherapy, and acupuncture, or herbs, or whatever, for her aura. But you didn't say a word about that to Holly today."

Belle started scraping up the popcorn that they'd dropped between the couch cushions.

"Don't eat that," said Jack.

"All right."

"And you were weird around her. You kept sort of not looking at her. What's that about?"

Belle let the popcorn spill back onto the couch.

"Well," she said, sighing, "not long ago when I was at their place, and you and Madeleine went to get coffee, Holly showed me this big jar she has. She said it was her jar to get back home. Cause she'd seen downstairs, she said, that Denny had his jar of coins, so she'd decided to start collecting too."

"Well, that's kind of sad that she wants to get home, and it might take her a while, collecting coins, but you can't blame her. She must miss being rich like Madeleine does."

"It's more than that." Belle pulled on her lower lip. "Holly's jar was full of pebbles."

"Oh." Jack thought about it. "Well, that won't get her far."

He pointed the remote at the TV, started the movie again, and sat back.

Then he sat forward and switched it off.

"Hang about," he said. "You didn't answer my question."

Elliot was having a conversation with the Butterfly Child.

Or was he?

It was like Madeleine's rainbow shadow, or the gongs she described from her hearing test.

The voice in his head could be real, or it could be his own invention.

He was standing in front of the doll's house, and the Butterfly Child was still on the edge of the bed, looking up at him.

"You like mulberries?" he said in a low voice.

The fluting in his head turned itself over again. "Right. I love them."

"This is freaky," he said. "And *freaky*'s not a word I often use. Is it really you?"

"Of course it is."

"Well, nod or something."

The Butterfly Child gazed up at him.

"I don't do tricks. You know perfectly well it's me."

Elliot breathed in, and trembled a little with fatigue.

"I'm tired," he said. "I don't know if I'm talking to you or to myself."

"To me," fluted the voice.

"All right, then." He tried to shake himself awake. "Well, why haven't you talked to me before?"

"Are you *mad*?" Maybe he could see a flicker of something in her eyes at that moment. "I've been *trying* to talk to you since I arrived! I've been sending my voice all over this town! Do you realize how *exhausting* that is? Calling you and calling you! Why do you think I sleep all the time?"

Elliot raised his eyebrows. "I thought Butterfly Children were supposed to be sort of timid."

Now her face really did seem to take on a look of scorn.

"We're not all the same, you know."

"You're not wrong there," Elliot agreed. "No offense, but crops around here look as bad as they did when you arrived. Worse maybe."

The fluting went dim for a moment and he pulled at his ear trying to get it back.

"All right." The voice was clear again. "I'm *not* that good at the crop thing, but I blame you for that."

"It's my fault?"

"For not listening."

Elliot sighed. "That again. Seriously, couldn't you have spoken in some other language besides flute?"

"I don't know what you're talking about. Look, for Butterfly Children to be effective, we need to have a connection with our Finder. Our *souls* need to intertwine, if you will. We need to loop together like a skating figure eight."

"Well, I'm happy to go skating with you, symbolically speaking, if you could do something about the crops. And you think you could spin those healing beads as well? If I let you twine up my soul, or whatever?"

"This is not a matter for jest."

"Okay. Well, seriously. Please?"

"I can't do anything."

Elliot chuckled. "Ah, then." He let his eyelids rest a moment, then opened them halfway.

"The *reason* you haven't been hearing me," the voice was saying, "the *reason* our souls have not intertwined, is simple. You do not like me. And that, Elliot, offends my feelings."

"There's a sound missing," whispered Holly, and Madeleine, who was almost asleep, lifted her head.

They had switched off the light to go to sleep.

"What sound?"

"Something I used to hear," Holly said into the darkness. "It's *all* sliding away, you know, like thoughts just before sleep. Like the feeling in my hands sometimes — they go numb, they slide away from me. Have I mentioned that to you?"

Her words seemed to creep into the room, like creatures crawling from the opening of a shell.

"It's a thick sort of custardy grime in my head," muttered Holly. "And my knee does this thing where it wants to dance a jig."

Madeleine was silent.

"You know, of course," Holly added, "that Tinsels and Corrigan and Warlock were just your imaginary friends."

There was a shot of ice through Madeleine's chest.

"No," she said firmly, trying to warm the ice. "They were real. You're just forgetting them."

"They were special, *very* special, to me *and* to you, but entirely imaginary."

Madeleine switched on the bedside light again.

Holly sat up, and looked at her daughter closely. "They were your brothers and sisters," she said.

Madeleine shook her head.

"Or maybe," Holly added thoughtfully, "maybe Tinsels was a cat."

Tears were spilling and spilling, and Madeleine kept shaking her head.

"Of course I like you," Elliot was saying.

"Nonsense." The flute sound struck a new pitch. *"Nonsense."*

"Well." He sat on the couch and looked across at the Butterfly Child. "Look, if I *haven't* liked you, I'm sorry. I guess maybe I blamed you for keeping me here. I wanted to go find my dad, see. I was planning to go to the Lake of Spells the day after I found you and it's not your fault or anything, but you kind of trapped me here."

"I know that."

"Well, then." Elliot tried to lift his hands in the air, but they were too heavy.

"It's more than that. You dislike me for something other than that, but I don't know what it is, and this — the fact of your dislike — it offends my sensibilities."

"No, it was just that. Which I feel bad about, 'cause it was obviously not your fault. I've been blaming all the wrong people lately. See, I was wrong about wanting to go anyway, and now I'm planning to stay. So you know, I like you just fine, and we can intertwine souls for as long as you need me. If you'd explain just exactly how to do that."

"Oh, nonsense."

The Butterfly Child maybe folded her arms at that point, which again matched up with the words. Or maybe he was seeing things through his half-closed eyes. Everything was blurring.

"Tell me," she persisted, the flute notes piercing now. "*Tell* me why you don't like me."

"Ah," murmured Elliot, shifting on the couch, closing his eyes, and he wasn't sure if he was speaking or dreaming. "Just didn't *want* to like you, I guess. Seeing as you can leave at any time. What'd be the point? There's my dad gone. Uncle Jon dead. Now Kala gone too. Any moment, any second, so they say, you'll be gone too. Why would I bother getting to like you? I mean, you're so tiny, you're *already* not here."

And his voice folded itself into sleep.

Belle sighed deeply, and scowled.

"Maybe I don't *want* to answer the question."

"Are you saying you didn't suggest alternative treatment for Holly because she's loopy? Because she collects pebbles?" wondered Jack. "But doesn't pebble collecting make you, sort of like, the perfect candidate for acupuncture, if you get my point?"

"Ah, you haven't got a point, Jack. And it's not that she's loopy, it's something else." Her voice trailed into quiet. She chewed on her nails.

"What?" said Jack.

Belle chewed harder, and looked away from him.

"Just tell me."

"I don't want to," Belle said.

"Yes, you do."

"It's — well, did you notice how I didn't look at her today?"

"Yeah, I just mentioned it."

"It's because . . . it's because she's got an aura like a black hole."

Jack made an exasperated sound.

"That's what you said about Madeleine. You and your auras. Belle, you've got to get over this thing about rich people having bad-ass auras. I mean, those two aren't even rich anymore. So, sort of forgive them, yeah?"

"It's nothing to do with money." Her voice seemed to thump to the floor. He looked at her, surprised, but she turned her face away from him. "This is not like Madeleine's aura," she said. "That one was more, sort of, false, but it's getting better now. But Holly's — Holly's means she's going to die."

Jack stared. "We're all going to die one of these days."

"No. Soon. She's going to die very soon. That's why I hated looking at her. It could happen any moment, and there's not a single thing that anyone, or any therapies or aura healing or anything, can do."

"There must be," whispered Jack.

Belle shook her head.

Her mother was sleeping again, and Madeleine was sitting cross-legged on the bed.

Holly breathed in and out, in and out, and each breath felt like a zipper inside Madeleine's chest, a metallic tearing, opening and closing, opening and closing.

She was thinking about Lord Byron.

When he first came to Cambridge, Byron had hated it. He and a friend used to swim in the river, first throwing objects into the water, like plates, eggs, and shillings, and then diving for them. Byron later remembered that there had been the stump of a tree in the bed of the river, and that he used to cling to this stump and wonder how the devil he came here.

He said it half broke his spirits. He said it was one of the deadliest and heaviest feelings of his life, to feel that he was no longer a boy.

"Some nights," said a voice — Holly was awake again.

She pushed herself up and smiled at Madeleine.

"Some nights," she repeated, "are darker than others."

Then Holly's hand flew sideways and she sagged onto the bed.

PART 9

Bonfire, The Farms,
Kingdom of Cello

1.

Such a bright morning, the sky blue, the sun in one of its energetic moods.

Hector sat at a table at the Bakery and looked around the square. There was a breeze about, which now and then got itself flustered. The flags at the Pennybank Store curled themselves together, and a passerby reached up and unraveled them. A couple of kids crossed the square, carrying a kite between them. From his table, Hector could see Clover Mackie drinking coffee on her porch, hair flying sideways, then settling again.

The Twicklehams had called him the night before and asked if he could meet them here this morning, just before they left.

They had something of *"vital import"* to tell him, they'd said, and they'd summoned the Mayor to meet them. She should hear this too, they'd said.

Seemed like a waste of everybody's time, but Hector figured they deserved a little leeway, what with how the town had treated them.

He was early, but he'd brought some paperwork to do while he ate his pastry and waited. He reached for his leather satchel — there was Derrin's drawing in the plastic window; it made him sad to see it — and drew out a pile of papers.

The breeze wanted to take them, of course, so he put his elbow on them hard and reached for the sugar dispenser to weigh them down. For good measure, he added the salt and pepper shakers.

Somewhere down the pile of papers, a yellowing edge was poking out. What was that? He slid it out.

To the Good Sheriff of Bonfire in the Picturesque Province of the Farms, it began, and right away, he remembered.

It was that fax from Gwent Cwlyd in Olde Quainte. The missing child with the whistling mother. He'd meant to give it to Jimmy, but of course Jimmy had been sick since that night, so it had stayed in his satchel.

He turned it over ready to put away again, but as he did, the concluding lines caught his eyes.

Why should this sweet child have gone? Was it a Green that has took her? For haven't we had the most unlikely influx of Greens in the last year or two — as to a tree in the springtime? But Greens are not known to steal children! Or was it a ferocious Wandering Hostile? For haven't they too traversed our town of late? But what cause would THEY have to kill or take a little child — and one so dear as this?

Ah, it broke your heart, the things that happened to people.

(Not to mention the hopelessness of Olde Quainte law enforcement.)

Hector closed his satchel, thinking he'd drop the report over at Jimmy's that afternoon. Seemed to him that Jimmy had been sick for long enough by now. Although, if he started saying that this missing girl had been whisked across to the World, well, Hector would send Jimmy back to bed.

The clock tower struck eight. Things were picking up in the square. Rows of oranges were appearing in the stands out the front of the Pennybank Store. High-school kids, on vacation, were wandering toward the Candy Shoppe and the Bakery too.

The breeze was lively again; it knocked over the menu on Hector's table, and smack-smack-smack, the menus at the next three tables too.

There was a rattling sound and a woman emerged from the staircase alongside the Bakery itself. It was Olivia Hattoway, the grade-school teacher. Of course. She lived above the Bakery.

She was dragging two suitcases, one in each hand, but paused to smile at Hector.

"Good morning, Sheriff! Just taking these to my car."

"Nice day for a road trip," Hector replied. "And it's good of you to take the Twicklehams along for the ride. Need any help with the luggage there?" He stood from the table, but Olivia smiled and resumed her walk.

"Easy!" she said. "See, they roll? And I'll enjoy the Twicklehams' company, so it's not 'good' of me at all! See you in a couple of weeks!"

He watched her cross the square.

There were voices at the next table along, and he realized it was Elliot's friends — Cody, Shelby, Nikki, Gabe — settling down with their coffees and pastries.

He watched them a moment, and listened. Seemed that Kala had sent Cody a postcard from her boarding school, and they all wanted to hear her news. The Sheriff half listened, then he glanced at his satchel. There was Derrin's drawing again — the sad-faced man and woman all in green — and he couldn't stop himself.

"You kids," he said, and they turned to him. "You proud of yourselves?" His voice grew blustery. "Your shenanigans and whatnot with the Twicklehams? They're leaving town this morning, you realize that? You went and broke them, and I'll tell you something, it just about breaks my heart."

They stared, wide-eyed. They looked so young suddenly. Nikki pulled at her lower lip. Gabe rubbed at his hair. Cody looked down, drumming his fingers quickly on the table.

"Yeah, we heard," said Shelby. She scowled and put her hands in her pockets. "We feel bad about it. But the thing is, Sheriff, what else could we do?"

There was quiet.

He was ready to storm again, to get into a frenzy along with the wind, but then there was a kind of shrug inside him, and he leaned back in his chair and sighed.

He knew what Shelby meant. It was that helplessness you feel when there's nothing you can do to comfort a friend.

Those kids had all wanted to go along with Elliot on his trips to the Purple caverns, but Elliot had refused. He'd let them do this, though. He might never have said it expressly, but they would have guessed: He'd *wanted* them to scare off the Twicklehams, to get them out of his dad's shop.

So what else could they do?

Across the square, Hector could see Olivia Hattoway piling her suitcases into the trunk of her car. From the opposite corner, the Mayor came striding, swinging her hands out in that way she had, as if she was constantly making a point. And walking under the clock tower and into the square were the Twicklehams themselves.

Ah, it was too bad. The things that happened to people. Starting out in a new town, full of hope, and it all falls to pieces like this.

He was pretty sure the kids hadn't meant it to go this far — they were wild but they had good hearts.

It was just the way the pieces fell sometimes.

Broken pieces falling.

And here came the Twicklehams now.

"Wake up."

Elliot woke on the couch.

His eyes went first to the doll's house, but it was empty.

Then to the clock on the mantelpiece, but that must have stopped. Quarter past eight, it said, whereas Elliot woke at the exact same time each day.

Ten before six.

The house was quiet.

There were rustlings around: the wind rattling windows and door, that buzz from the fridge in the kitchen.

Another thing: It seemed brighter than it should.

He went into the kitchen and the clock on the oven said quarter past eight.

Couldn't be.

He switched on the radio, waited through a song, and the announcer told him it was eight-seventeen.

For crying out loud.

He'd overslept. His mother must be out there in the greenhouse, wondering where he'd got to. Ah, he'd promised Corrie-Lynn he'd meet her at the Watermelon Inn to try to talk the Twicklehams into staying. Well, there was still time for that at least, if he moved fast.

It was that Butterfly Child.

He'd been up half the night trying to get her to talk, and then there was that strange —

Well, he didn't know what it had been.

An actual conversation with her? A dream? A sleep-befuddled hallucination?

He stood by the doll's house, looking at its empty rooms. The little pieces of wooden furniture that Corrie-Lynn had built: chairs, tables, a miniature wooden chest. Most of these, the Butterfly Child ignored, concentrating on the bed.

The covers were on the floor at the moment, and Elliot picked them up between his thumb and forefinger, ready to straighten up for her.

But something odd was on the bed.

There were five or six mothballs lined up there. At least, that's how they looked. Little white balls, anyway, maybe pills or candy.

"Wake up."

There was that voice again. It had woken him on the couch. It was the flute voice from last night actually, sounding patient enough, but maybe a little sigh behind it too.

He laughed aloud.

Those weren't *mothballs*, they were healing beads!

"Thank you," the voice said promptly.

"No. Thank *you*," he said aloud, grinning.

Ah, this day would turn out all right after all.

He'd go see the Twicklehams, see what he could do. Then he'd take these little white candies — "Cut it out," chided the voice. Well, that's what they looked like, they didn't *look* like healing beads.

"How exactly did you *expect* healing beads to look?"

He hadn't given it much thought. More magical, he guessed. Like dewdrops, maybe, or at the very least like glass.

"Oh, blah," murmured the voice.

Anyhow, he'd deliver them to Madeleine, and then she would believe in him and the Kingdom.

He found an envelope in the kitchen stationery drawer. Slipped the healing beads into it, folded the envelope, and put it in his pocket.

Got himself an orange juice and a blueberry muffin.

Drank and ate leaning up against the counter.

Thought about taking the truck, but it was such a bright day, and the breeze was so jumpy, he'd ride his bike instead.

It happened just like those menus falling over. Slap-slap-slap. Pieces falling into place so fast Hector could hardly catch them.

Twicklehams approaching him. The usual formation — Derrin between them, the three holding hands.

Looked down a minute, and there was Derrin's drawing on the side of his satchel. Green wind blowing across a green field, a green man and a green woman, each with green tears and sad green mouths.

The Mayor called, "Howdy, Hector!" striding toward him.

Next table along, the kids were talking again. Cody was telling them more about Kala's news. "She's met three different people with the name Twickleham," he said.

"Must be a common name in Olde Quainte," Nikki said.

"And one of them even said they had cousins who'd been planning to move here to Bonfire," Cody continued. "But it didn't work out."

"What are the chances?" Shelby murmured, and the kids were quiet, and Hector could feel the guilt in the quiet.

The adult Twicklehams raised their free hands, waving at Hector. Their faces were solemn. In Fleta's waving hand, a piece of paper fluttered.

He looked back at Derrin's drawing, and the difference jarred.

Three people approaching — but in this picture there were just two. Now why had Derrin not drawn herself in as well?

The wind shifted his papers, even under the salt and pepper shakers.

What are *the chances?* Hector thought, confused. *There were* other *Twicklehams planning to move here?*

They were almost upon him, and slap-slap-slap, it was falling into place.

For haven't we had the most unlikely influx of Green attacks in the last year or two?

Here in Derrin's picture, everything was green.

The child's mother was known in our little town for her whistling — ah, she would go about so gaily, whistling more than she spake —

Here in Derrin's picture, these two sad adults. They were skinny as beanpoles! And weren't those Twicklehams plump?

He looked closer at the woman in the picture. Her little mouth was a circle; he'd taken that to be sadness, but could it be that her lips were pursed? Was she actually *whistling*?

It was falling into place, but the pieces were still tangled, and still he'd have doubted if it wasn't for what happened when he looked up again.

It must have shown on his face.

His slow revelation, his bewilderment, his questions.

They saw it right away.

The Twicklehams saw it, and they hesitated.

"Stop them," said the Sheriff, his voice croaking with effort.

The Mayor herself stopped, surprised by the Sheriff's face.

Suddenly the Twicklehams were running, Derrin still between them so their arms stretched and concertinaed like a chain of paper dolls.

"*Stop* them!" the Sheriff shouted, finding his voice. *"Get Derrin!"*

He was trying to run against the drag of his limp. Behind him, chairs were crashing to the ground.

On her porch, Clover Mackie watched as the Twicklehams ran toward the parking lot; as Gabe, Cody, Nikki, and Shelby sprinted after them; as the Sheriff loped and hollered; as Olivia Hattoway, grade-school teacher, threw open the doors of her car and slid into the driver's seat; as a sheet of paper flew from Fleta's hand, and curved itself high into the breeze.

There were sounds of commotion — engines revving, squealing tires, horns, shouts, even a siren — but Elliot didn't take much notice, riding along Aubin Street toward the Watermelon.

His mood was so high and hopeful.

Then he was at the top of the slope, and there it all was, right before him.

The madness.

A car was speeding up Aubin from the opposite direction.

Three motor scooters right behind it, zigzagging madly. One almost toppled, then rode on. A fourth motor scooter was heading cross-country, across the dirt, toward the Overbrook Bridge. Behind them all came the Sheriff's car, siren blazing.

In the parking lot of the Watermelon, the tiny shape of Corrie-Lynn stood still amidst parked cars, watching in wonder.

The cross-country motor scooter skidded sideways, slammed onto the dirt, and its rider leapt up and ran toward the bridge.

Elliot recognized her. It was Shelby.

He looked back at the speeding car. That was Olivia Hattoway driving, and in the passenger seat beside her was Fleta Twickleham.

Looked like Mr. Twickleham in the backseat, and Derrin too.

And on the other motor scooters?

It couldn't be.

But it was.

Nikki, Gabe, and Cody: What were they *doing*?

"Stop it!" he shouted. *"Stop it!"*

This could *not* be happening! What had he started? What were they doing to the Twicklehams now? Chasing them out of town? What sort of madness had overtaken them?

He tried again, but now the car's tires were spinning as it swerved toward the bridge — the bridge that led to the road out of town — and his voice got lost in the squeal of it.

"Leave the Twicklehams alone!" he shouted, rough with hoarseness. "Let them go!" and right at the word "go!" there was a low, thunderous BOOM!, a blast of black smoke, and a scream from Corrie-Lynn.

The bridge!

She'd blown up the Overbrook Bridge. Shelby had blown up the bridge.

Great chunks of concrete crashed and collided, single bricks fountained, dirt and water flew up from the river.

The Sheriff's car shrieked to a stop.

Olivia Hattoway braked just as her car was about to hit. Almost at the same moment, she reversed, and mud splattered the windows.

Nikki and Gabe swerved to avoid her, but now they'd caught up. They were riding either side of the car, Cody just behind, all of them heading up Aubin now, toward Elliot.

He threw himself to the side of the road to get out of the way, and watched from the dirt.

Nikki was riding alongside the car, using her elbow to smash the back window. Inside, there was a lowering of heads against the showering glass. Gabe reached a hand through the broken window, hit a pothole in the road, bounced twice, and overturned so he spilled onto the gutter. Nikki rode up instead, reached in one hand, her other hand on the handlebar — and next thing, impossibly, she was opening the car door.

It swung back and forth as the car sped, Nikki sped, Cody sped behind her, then somehow, between them, Nikki and Cody were dragging Derrin from the car.

The car raced away.

Its door rattled closed. It disappeared into the distance.

The Sheriff's car flashed by Elliot, siren blasting.

There was another sound — loud and persistent — and the siren stopped suddenly, the Sheriff's car slowing.

It was the warning bells.

Everybody stopped.

The motor scooters. The Sheriff's car.

The warning bells chimed and chimed.

It was the code for a first-level Yellow.

Lemon Yellow.

Most lethal Color of them all.

They hadn't noticed Corrie-Lynn in the parking lot.

They got themselves into the Watermelon Inn: Nikki carrying Derrin in her arms like a baby; Gabe, Cody, and Shelby running; the Sheriff reversing his car down the hill, then racing in after them. The shutters to the Watermelon slammed closed.

That's when they saw her.

Through the gaps in the shutters, swarms of Yellow filled the air. These took the form of bright little darts, each group soaring low and sure.

Lemon Yellows aim for the eyes and the heart. Each one blinds with its first strike, and kills with its second.

They saw her all at once — Corrie-Lynn — still standing in the parking lot, confused, and Alanna screamed and threw herself at the shutters, scrabbling to open them and get out.

Then Elliot was there.

Outside, flying past the shutters, running by the windows, into the parking lot, to Corrie-Lynn.

"He doesn't have anything," someone said.

"There's nothing he can do."

He was there with her. He was trying car doors, but they were locked. He took Corrie-Lynn's hand in his, looking back toward the Watermelon. The air was thick with the Yellow dart swarms; any moment now a swarm would aim at Elliot and Corrie-Lynn.

In the Watermelon, Alanna kept screaming to get out to them, but guests gripped her elbows and dragged her back.

Elliot and Corrie-Lynn were running, hand in hand.

"They can't make it," whispered Hector.

A swarm cut them off from the hotel. Two more swarms drifted closer.

At the edge of the parking lot, Elliot and Corrie-Lynn stopped. They were surrounded.

Elliot put an arm tight around Corrie-Lynn.

"They've given up," murmured someone.

They were going to die. Elliot and Corrie-Lynn were going to die right before their eyes.

But now Elliot was crouching. They could see his lips moving — he was talking and crouching.

He was doing something on the ground. He was at one of the faucets, and was turning it.

Now Corrie-Lynn was on the ground at the other faucet.

Then, all around them, the sprinklers shot up.

Elliot called to her again.

They were detaching sprinklers, and lifting them into the air, the water rising higher.

A swarm of Yellow darts had seen them now.

A second swarm swerved toward them from the east.

They were tilting the sprinklers, lifting them, lowering them. Then it happened. Sunlight hit the water and faint colors wavered in the air around them.

"Stop!" Elliot shouted, so sharply it was audible from the Inn. "Hold it now!"

Rainbows of colors shimmered around them in an almost circle —
The swarms were almost on them. And then the strangest thing.
The Lemon Yellows hit the rainbows and faded.

They struck at Elliot and Corrie-Lynn, but over and over they hit
the rainbows, and dwindled into something pale and listless.

Other swarms attacked, but each Yellow that hit melted away —
melted into something that wasn't quite there, like mist on a window.

Then there was a shift, and the swarms changed direction
altogether.

They swung around, flew away, and disappeared.

Elliot and Corrie-Lynn stood in the parking lot.

The rainbows played in the air around them. The water drenched
them. But still they stood, arms aching, sprinklers held high to catch
the sun.

Cambridge, England, The World

2.

*I*saac Newton liked questions.

In 1704, he published a book called *Opticks,* in which he described
and analysed the nature of colour and light. At the end of the book,
he appended a list of "queries" — questions without answers that
leapt between topics — from air, honey, oil, and sunrays, to comets,
animals, backbones, and atoms. Over the next several years, he

returned to his list, adding to his questions, adjusting them, expanding on them.

Whence is it that Nature does nothing in vain? And whence arises all that beauty that we see in the world? he asked. *To what end are Comets and whence is it that they move all manner of ways?*

And so on.

On the day that the neurosurgeon at Addenbrooke's Hospital took Madeleine aside and explained that her mother's collapse the previous night had been brought about by bleeding in the brain, which itself was the result of a high-grade tumour; that the tumour had probably been growing for several months now; that this explained the irrational behaviour, the headaches, vomiting, confusion, numbness, memory loss; that surgery and radiation treatment might prolong Holly's life for another few months, but that surgery itself could well kill her; that, however, without surgery, she would die within the next few days — on this day, Madeleine found herself ensnared by one of Newton's queries.

The query was this:

What hinders the fixt stars from falling upon one another?

Sometimes the query took the form of a bramble bush that wound itself tightly around Madeleine, muffled her mouth, and scratched her skin, so that it was almost comical, trying to answer the doctors' and nurses' questions, and she actually giggled at one point.

How could they expect her to speak with these thorny branches crossing her eyes?

At other times, the query was more of an intransigent force; a vacuum that dragged her down with it; and then the difficulty was trying to walk or stand or move in any way.

What hinders the fixt stars from falling upon one another?

It was not so much that she had to *answer* the query, it was that *she* herself turned out to be the answer.

She had to stop the stars from tumbling together. The query had given her the job. A sky full of stars was relying on her to keep her back straight, her shoulders firm, her head nodding now and then, her voice calm and polite — when they asked if there was somebody else she wanted to call, her father, for example, or a friend, she shook her head, no, it was just her. Because as long as she could keep the stars in place in the sky for just this day — as long as she did that, her mother would be okay.

Obviously, the doctors were not in a position to take care of the stars.

The choices they offered! Death by surgery, or death over the next few days. Didn't they know about *third options*? They were quitters, these doctors, without vision. They knew nothing of problem solving, the key to which, she had just realised, was finding the third option.

For example, she now discovered that there were *not*, after all, two choices about crying. She had thought of herself as "not a crying kind of girl," but today, neither crying nor not-crying was possible.

This called for a third option, specifically: wailing, shrieking, and smashing of windows. The hospital would frown on that, most likely. They'd sedate her, which was proof, again, that these people knew nothing of third options.

So she did nothing, pressed her lips together and used them to form small smiles.

Anyhow, it was lucky, she thought, while they took her mother's blood, pinned her mother down with tubes and machines, as if they were worried she might escape — like those diamond pins the stylist used to put in Madeleine's hair — they had kept her *head* in place, those pins, but not *Madeleine* herself; no, she had fled, trailing her mother behind her — and now their adventure had taken an unexpected turn; she supposed it had been following this path all along, and it was true that she had urged her mother to turn back, or sidestep, but she'd never tried hard enough. She'd been too busy with her summer romance, or with visions of her father in a punt —

But *still*, it was lucky, she thought, while they conferred about her mother, it was just so *lucky* that she'd been reading Isaac Newton.

Because now she knew about problem solving.

Even though the hospital did not.

And this problem, Isaac had solved for her.

All she had to do was keep the stars fixed to the sky.

At some point that morning, Madeleine fell asleep in the hospital chair. She dreamed that she was a hat rack. The hat rack's job was to hold up the stars; however, various people kept adding extra weight to it. Federico, Belle, Jack, the waitress from Auntie's Tea Shop, two or three doctors — they were hanging decorations from the hat rack, as if it was a Christmas tree.

"No, no," she explained, polite and smiling at first. "I can't take the weight of this. My duty is to hold up the stars." But they smiled blandly at her, and kept on hanging decorations. Colours, lights, calculus, curves, alchemy, chemistry, mathematics, measurements, gravity, magnets — each of these things was an ornament that weighed her down. Then they started adding facts.

"At two A.M. on Christmas Day in 1642," said Jack, "he was born."

"And he was so small," added Belle, "that they put him in a quart pot."

"Two women," said the neurosurgeon who had spoken to her earlier, "were sent to collect items for the baby, but they sat down on a stile along the way, and they said to each other: 'There is no occasion for making haste, for we are sure the child will be dead before we get back!'"

"And he was so weak," piped a voice — and it was her mother! Madeleine rushed forward, elated, spilling ornaments and concepts, but Holly shook her head firmly. "He was so weak," she repeated, "that he had to have a *bolster* all around his neck to keep it on his shoulders." Then Holly pointed to her own neck, which was bolstered with something like a wooden frame, and she gave a wry, sad smile.

"*Who* are you talking about?" shouted Madeleine, shaking herself so that everything rattled, jangled, and began to fall, including the stars.

She opened her eyes and thought: *Isaac Newton, of course.*

*　　*　　*

The dark red in her mother's hair looked like streaks of blood or wine against the pillows. Her face had a pale greyness to it, like concrete. There was a small pimple on her mother's chin, which Holly had pointed out the day before. She had explained to Madeleine, as she always did when she got a pimple, that chocolate was not the cause. It was more likely a manifestation of an unpleasant thought someone in the building had had.

She ate too much chocolate. She had a pimple. She made dumb jokes about the pimple!

It was impossible for her to die. The doctors were wrong.

Madeleine was suddenly exasperated.

She stood up, stretched her arms above her head, reaching absent-mindedly for lost stars, frowning, angry.

"It's twenty to, I think," said a passing voice.

"Twenty to *what*?" responded another voice — they all seemed to talk in that jokesy, blustering way here — their voices looming up and then fading into corridors.

"Twenty to ten," called the other voice.

Not even ten o'clock yet.

There was another reason. It was not even ten o'clock in the morning yet! How could anything so serious happen before ten?

And there it was.

The third option.

She put down the fixed stars and she ran.

She was running in the rain.

It's a long way from Addenbrooke's to downtown Cambridge — she remembered this as she ran, but it only made her run faster.

There were cars, clouds, rain splatters, umbrellas, bicycles, and someone was walking a dog. Her chest was aching, her breath was heaving, her legs were shot through with needles or magnets. The closer she got, the more crowded the footpaths, and she was dodging and swerving. Some people scowled at her and this made her laugh aloud.

My mother is going to die! she thought. *And here I am running to a parking meter!* Each breath of laughter was a spasm in her side.

She almost fell as she slid onto the street, and there it was — the graffiti, the broken parking meter, a car with its hubcaps missing. . . .

Through the rain-blurring, she thought she saw the hint of white in the crack, but no! There was nothing. She was running, skidding toward the parking meter, and there was *nothing* in that crack, and through her gasps of air she was laughing and the rain was hammering her head.

Under an Overpass

3.

*T*he bells were ringing for the all clear, and they were surging out of the Watermelon Inn. Someone was turning off the sprinklers; someone was taking these gently from the outstretched arms of Elliot and Corrie-Lynn; others were draping towels around their shoulders and leading them inside.

They brought them into the front room, and Elliot and Corrie-Lynn were whiter than the Magical North, pale and trembling, but every other face was alive with smiles and wonder, and everyone was asking, "How did you *know* to do that, Elliot?"

Eventually, Elliot shook the trembling out of his body, and half smiled.

"It was something that a friend told me once," he said, and then something seemed to turn over in his face, and his hand reached into his pocket.

"What's the time right now?" he said, and when someone said it was just on ten, he seemed to fly from the room.

They watched through the window as he ran through the parking lot and away.

The rain hammered on Madeleine's head and she stopped laughing, stopped gasping and turned from the parking meter, where there was no slither of white, there was nothing —

And then something happened. It was a fragment of time, a breath of time. It was like being in a car in pouring rain and driving under an overpass, and for just that second there is a profound, powerful sense of reprieve — the utter silence of non-rain.

That was how it was — she was, for a fragment, without rain; she was somewhere silent and warm, and there was the flash of an image — a schoolyard, distant buildings, blue sky, intense quiet, strong sunlight, an odd pile of cement topped with a crooked TV, and beside her, right beside her, a boy in jeans, his head turned away from her; she saw dark blond hair, a sun-brown neck —

Then the rain again.

She was back in the street with the parking meter, the chaos of the downpour, and parked cars again.

But now, in her hand, was an envelope. It was instantly sodden with rainwater, and she sat on the edge of the kerb, let the rushing gutter water swarm over her shoes, soak her socks, let the rain drench and drench her hair, the curling water rush past her eyes and tendril down her cheeks, and opened the envelope.

A handful of little white balls.

Were they children's sweets? Were they aspirins? Were they mothballs?

Whatever they were, she sat on the kerb, folded them tight in her fist, and the sobs gashed their way through her chest, surging against the flesh of her face, bursting out through her mouth and into the rain.

Strange Morning

4.

*A*fter he had delivered the envelope to the sculpture, Elliot returned to the Watermelon Inn, and was just in time to hear little Derrin Twickleham, the girl who could not speak, announce in a strident voice: "My name is *not* Derrin Twickleham."

There was a sudden quiet in the front room.

Derrin explained that her name was, in fact, Libby Adams.

For a child who could not speak, she was very vocal. In an Olde Quainte accent, she told the room that she had been taken from her hometown of Gwent Cwlyd by a pair of Wandering Hostiles who'd brought her to Bonfire, disguised as a family called the Twicklehams.

The real family Twickleham had a small daughter, so they had stolen Libby to play that role. It was her understanding that the real family had been sent a false note, telling them that the repair shop was no longer available.

They had some Hostile mission here in Bonfire, the child continued, but she had not been able to figure out what it was, although she had tried and tried to drop in on their eaves.

"She means eavesdrop," somebody murmured, and the others nodded or agreed.

"There is also this," she said. "That I never got their real names. As to an apple in a seashell, so were they careful to call each other Fleta and Bartholomew, even when I was a-bed."

There was an impressed silence after this lengthy speech.

Then Corrie-Lynn, who was still wrapped in a blanket in her mother's arms, announced: "You can *speak*. I taught you how to speak!"

Libby replied diplomatically: "You did a very good job trying to teach me how to speak, Corrie-Lynn. But actually I think I can probably speak now because the Mute Spell they put on me would now be far away — away from this town it is going, in the back of Miss Hattoway's car."

Everybody nodded. A spell like that would lose its effect with some distance.

"Well, why didn't you write me a note?" Corrie-Lynn persisted. "You're good at writing."

"I wrote a note to Miss Hattoway," Libby said, "on my first day at the grade school. She whispered that she'd help me, and that I had to lie low and not tell a soul. Of course," she added ruefully, "it soon became clear, as to a window in a washhouse when the door is open wide, that Miss Hattoway was actually a Hostile her*self*. And quite good friends with my kidnappers."

"You should've told me," Corrie-Lynn insisted.

Libby shrugged. "But I didn't want you to be in danger. And I *did* draw a picture to try to tell the Sheriff." Here, the Sheriff assumed a deeply sorrowful expression. "But my picture was probably confusing. Also . . ." She scratched the inside of her ear thoughtfully. "Also, on my very first *morning* in this town, I scribbled a note and tucked it into an old TV machine in the repair shop — when we were being shown around, before it was cleared out. I was hoping that Elliot or his mother might find that note and save me."

Everyone turned to Elliot.

"I'm sorry we didn't find it —" he began, and then stopped suddenly. "What did it say? What did your note say?"

"I wrote something like, *Help! I am being held against my will!* But I had not time to write more."

"You put it in the TV that was on the workbench there?" hazarded Elliot. "The one that ended up in Cody's sculpture?"

"Did it? All right. Yes, that's where I put it — they watched me closely all the time, as to a . . ."

But here Libby's voice faded, and she begged that somebody might contact her parents, as she would like to see her mother very much; then she put her thumb in her mouth and two tears slipped from her eyes.

In the consequent hubbub, Elliot slowly shook his head.

In Cambridge, England, the World, an extremely ill patient, her brain effectively strangled by a malignant tumour, lay in intensive care, waiting to die. Her teenage daughter walked into the room, dripping with rain, and was seen to draw a handful of white pills from her pocket. The supervising nurse rushed forward, thinking that the girl intended to give these to her mother for some reason, but the girl simply crushed them between her palms and let their dust sprinkle over her mother's face and neck.

Then the girl sat weeping quietly, a hand on her mother's hand.

Some minutes later, the woman sat up in her bed, pulling tubes from her mouth and her nose, so that the equipment set up frantic alarms and beeps, and requested chocolate.

Later that morning, various scans showed that the tumour had entirely resolved itself, that it had altogether disappeared, leaving behind apparently healthy brain cells — which, it would be fair to say, was an exceptional turn of events.

*　　*　　*

Meanwhile, in Bonfire, the Farms, Kingdom of Cello, the Butterfly Child flew through the streets, riding on her favorite moth.

Several people caught glimpses of her — or at least, glimpses of her russet-colored dress — and, as she flew, there was a whispering and rustling, a bending and straining, an odd tearing sound through the fields. Word rippled out that the crop effect was happening at last!

Within moments, the Butterfly Child had vanished, and some people thought they heard a faint fluting sound, while others swore they heard the words, "good-bye," and also, "sorry."

"The crop effect! The crop effect!" The shouts ran up and down the street.

There was brief jubilation, but it quickly emerged that, in fact, it was not the crop effect.

Instead, the fields, the streets, the Town Square, the school grounds, even Norma Lisle's little herb garden, were all now entirely clogged with mulberry trees.

PART 10

Sheriff Hector Samuels
Bonfire Sheriff's Station
Bonfire, The Farms
By Facsimile

Dear Sheriff Samuels,

We are pleased to inform you that the town of **Bonfire,** in the Farms, has been selected as a **bonus town** on the Princess Sisters' current Tour of the Kingdom.

As you probably know, **bonus town** selection is highly unusual in Royal Tours, and is therefore **truly** an honor for Bonfire.

Your town has been selected as a consequence of reports of an extraordinary **recent event** in Bonfire. We understand that a young person (**Elliot Baranski**) successfully repelled an attack from a **first-level Yellow** using nothing but a **garden hose.** The Princess Sisters have expressed great interest in meeting with Mr. Baranski and discussing his revolutionary approach to **Color attacks.**

We have further been informed that — either immediately before or after the altercation with the Yellow (reports are not clear on the chronology) — certain other young people successfully negotiated the rescue of an abducted child. It appears you have a glut of heroes in your town.

It should be emphasized that the selection of Bonfire as a **bonus town** is unrelated to your recent correspondence in which you suggested, amongst other things, that the Princess Sisters "skip" part of the Tour of Jagged Edge, since they would have "had it up to HERE" with the "mockery" in that province. On the contrary: The Princess Sisters were delighted by Jagged Edge, were treated with the utmost **respect** and **humility** by its people, and are very sorry to be leaving it so soon.

The Princess Sisters intend to spend **twenty-four** hours in Bonfire. As is customary, they will commence their visit by parading through the streets in the Emerald Carriage. During this parade, they will **wave** and **smile** at residents of Bonfire but **will not address the crowd in any way,** and any person who **approaches the carriage** or **attempts to engage one of the Princesses in conversation** or **behaves in a foolish, comical, "wisecracking," or otherwise odd manner** in an effort to get the Princesses' attention will be shot.

After the initial parade, **one** of the Princess Sisters (Princess Ko) will attend the following events, while the **other** (Princess Jupiter) rests:

• **an awards ceremony** at which the Princess will greet, **chat briefly with,** and present a bravery medal to each of the young heroes referred to above;
• **three (3)** visits to town monuments, museums, scenic outlooks, items of curiosity, etc., of your choice, at which the Princess will exclaim and/or nod (please note, however, that the Princess is not particularly interested in *farming*, per se, and accordingly would prefer not to exclaim or nod about crops, irrigation, etc.);
• **two (2)** visits to recently opened hospital wings, orphanages, etc., of your choice, at which the Princess will be glad to cut a ribbon, smash a bottle, etc.;
• **a reception** to be attended by the mayor, high-school principal, sheriff, hospital administrator, post-office clerk, and **Elliot**

Baranski (so as to give the Princess an opportunity to chat with him for three to five minutes), and at which the Princess has requested that baked goods and GC teakwater be served; and finally:

• **a brief meeting** with your town seamstress (which meeting shall be the only event attended by *both* sisters), as the Princesses have requested that certain adjustments be made to their ball gowns, following their exposure to the fashions of Jagged Edge.

Enclosed, you will find:

• a suggested **menu** for each of the meals to be served during the relevant twenty-four hours;
• a list of accommodation requirements. We understand that your town hospitality options include the **Watermelon Inn** and the **Bonfire Hotel.** As the enclosed form notes, the Princess Sisters require **adjoining suites** in the most **luxurious** of these establishments, such suites to be the "presidential suite" or the "penthouse suite" or the "deluxe suite with harbor view" (should you have harbor views in your town), etc., etc. — that is to say, a suite with a grand title.

The Cello Secret Service will arrive shortly to carry out security checks; accordingly, please arrange for accommodation, food, entertainment, etc., for **twenty-five** members of the Service, **ten** members of the Royal Tour Committee, and **ten** members of the Royal Support Staff.

Finally, anything you can do to ensure good weather for the visit would be most appreciated.

We trust that all of these arrangements will be in place in time for the Princess Sisters' arrival in Bonfire, scheduled to take place **tomorrow morning at 10** A.M.

Yours with Royal Splendor and Harmony,

The Cello Royal Tour Bonus Town Selectors

P.S. The Princess Sisters have particularly asked whether your Pyramid of Pumpkins might be *rebuilt* in time for their visit?

PART 11

ELLIOT BARANSKI

Dear Madeleine,

It's moonlight quiet on the porch out here, but the words are rattling around in my head like chains in the back of a pickup truck.

They all want to get written down first, the words, so if this ends up as nothing but a tangle, you'll know who to blame.

(The words.)

First, though, I have to thank you.

You saved my life, and Corrie-Lynn's too. Your Color talk — about water splitting sunlight into rainbows, about complementary Colors, about the fact that yellow and purple are complementary — well, to put it bluntly, it saved us. We made rainbows with sprinklers and sunlight, and somehow the purple in the rainbow killed off the Yellows that were coming for us.

So, like I said, thank you.

The trouble is, now I've got the whole Kingdom wanting to know more. Color Coders, Color Benders, the Cellian Center of Illumination, Department of Color Counterfuge, Brellidge University, Tyler University, Central Intelligence, guy who works in the local grocery store — they're *all* calling up and coming around with questions.

And what can I tell them?

That a girl in the World gave me the idea?

They'd take the medal away and lock me up instead.

Anyhow, my point is, everyone wants to know and I can't tell them.

Even Princess Ko.

Which brings me to the Royal Tour.

The Princess Sisters are sleeping at the Watermelon Inn as we speak — they came here on their tour today, and it's been the craziest day this town has ever seen.

The Sheriff was so happy he was bouncing around like he'd turned into one of Corrie-Lynn's puppets. His head couldn't stay still on his shoulders.

Royal flags were flying, the school band was playing (which made me miss Kala and her saxophone), and the streets were lined with people, a lot of whom had even camped out last night so they'd get front-row views. ("People," my mother said. "They'll never stop mystifying me.")

The Emerald Carriage came trundling through and you got a glimpse or two of princess smiles and princess hands in the air.

The Sheriff had talked Shelby into flying her crop duster over the parade, showering the carriage with silver petals from the blue jacarandas of Golden Coast — which looked pretty, but next thing security guards were shooting at the plane. Someone hadn't got the message through, I guess, and they thought Shelby was throwing down poison dust.

It turned out okay. Shelby was doing some fancy flying, so they couldn't get in a good shot, and Gabe tackled one of the guards to the ground. It all got cleared up, although Gabe ended up handcuffed to a door handle for two hours until somebody remembered him.

That's been the only glitch so far, if you don't count all the joking around of Gabe, Nikki, Cody, and Shelby at the awards ceremony. They're on a high, see, because they'd been feeling guilty about driving the Twicklehams out of town, and then suddenly it turned a corner and seemed the Twicklehams *deserved* to be driven out. Although, the Sheriff keeps saying, "Hmm" about this, and, "The thing is, kids, you couldn't have *known* they deserved it," and, "If they *were* good people, then . . ." Gabe and the others just put on frowns like they're trying hard to follow his logic but can't keep up.

As for little Derrin Twickleham herself — well, her name is actually Libby Adams — her parents are in town now, both of them whistling and hugging practically everyone they see. They're very keen on Gabe and the others, for rescuing their daughter, and for giving the Twicklehams a hard time while they were here. They keep telling the Sheriff that, "No doubt, these young people *intuited* the wickedness of our daughter's kidnappers."

Derrin's the one who wrote the *I am being held against my will* letter, by the way — the one that got through to the World.

Anyhow, where was I? I was talking about the Princess Sisters' visit.

Yes, I was. And how my friends were sort of disrespectful 'cause of being happy.

Not that Princess Ko seemed to notice. Her focus was more on getting herself another baked pastry or a third glass of GC teakwater.

Oh, yeah, and the mulberry trees — I guess they were another glitch in the royal visit. They're everywhere now, thanks to the Butterfly Child. Can't take a step without a mulberry landing in your hair, or falling down your collar. Princess Ko got a mulberry stain on her dress, which was a national emergency for a bit, but, like I said, her mind seemed mainly taken up with cake so we all got over that and moved on.

There was a reception, late this afternoon.

I was invited, so was the Sheriff, and the Mayor, and a few other local people. Princess Ko walked into the room, and she's all sparkle. Exactly like her columns, only slightly more high-pitched, if that's possible. How she can talk — and live, and breathe — at that level, is beyond me. You'd think it'd get her exhausted. Or at the very least make her ears ache.

Anyhow, she whirled around the room, excited about everything from the Postmaster's shirt collar to the Mayor's signet ring. When she got to me, she turned out to be really pretty, in that glitter-sparkle way that she has — and she started talking about the Color attack and how I used the sprinklers, and next thing, she's begging me to *demonstrate* for her, *right this moment*, how I did it, since she thought it would surely look like a *whirlshine* of *prettiness*, a *landscape* of *rainbows*! (Those were her words.)

I was confused for a moment, looking around the Mayor's living room (which is where the reception was held), wondering how I was supposed to get sprinklers in here — not to mention sunshine — and the damage it'd all do to the carpet.

That's when the Sheriff stepped in and saved me, telling the Princess how he'd read every word of her columns, and asking after her folks like they were old family friends. Princess Ko kept wanting to get back to the *heroics* of the *Color Battler* (she meant me), which I was not so much enjoying, so I pointed out that my buddies were the real heroics.

I meant to say "heroes," but she knew what I meant.

She said, "Oh, my, yes — and imagine! You had that Olivia Hattoway living and breathing amongst you all this time! Not to mention Mischka Tegan!"

The whole room went quiet in an instant.

There'd been murmuring, and teaspoons and so on before that, but the moment she said that name, it stopped.

"Hold on," said the Sheriff, and looked at her quizzically.

"Yes," she said, with a concentrating look. "The Security Forces brief me, you see, at each town, and it seems that you've had *four* Hostiles undercover here — Mischka Tegan and Olivia Hattoway and, more recently, the false Twicklehams of course. Now . . ." She stopped a minute, thinking, and the room stopped breathing altogether, it was waiting so hard. "Now, as I recall it, Mischka and Olivia were here trying to infiltrate a branch of the Loyalists, but that fell apart and Mischka left town. Olivia stayed, and then the Twicklehams came with the stolen child. And they worked with Olivia secretly under the guise of parent-teacher meetings. We think they were trying to figure out what the Loyalists — Abel and Jon Baranski, I mean — had been working on."

The silence seemed set to blow the glass out of the windows.

Princess Ko looked around, then took a deep breath and kept talking.

"Yes, you see, Abel and Jon Baranski were working on some secret project to try to assist us Royals against a Hostile plot. Mischka persuaded them she was on their side."

There was a rising murmur in the room. Some people made distressed noises.

Then the Sheriff spoke, and set aside his manners.

"What in the *blazes*," he said, "are you talking about?"

The Princess looked puzzled.

"Oh, didn't you know? No, I suppose you wouldn't. These things are meant for *top-ranked*, highly rated, quizzically over-the-top agents, aren't they? And here I am, chattering. Security will kill me! If only Jupiter were here today instead of me, she's *much* more discreet! Or a little anyway. Waiter! Take this teakwater away from me!"

She giggled.

In a more restrained voice, the Sheriff said, "Jon Baranski was killed by a Purple. And it's our belief that Abel Baranski left town with Mischka for . . . romantic reasons."

"No, no," the Princess said. "Well, we can't be *sure*, but I can tell you what Central thinks happened. Right. Jon and Abel were working on something secret when Mischka joined them. Then, one terrible night — the report didn't use the word *terrible*, that's my innovation — one terrible night, Abel and Jon *discovered* that Mischka was a 'bad guy.' Before they could expose her, she *abducted* Abel, no doubt using a weapon of some kind. Weapons are all the rage. Jon was probably chasing after them in his truck, or perhaps heading to Abel's family's home to let them know what had happened? Anyhow, that's when the Color attack took place. And so, tragically, he was lost."

You can imagine the state of my head, and my heart, while she was talking.

"If this is all true," I said, finally speaking, "where's my father now?"

Then she looked at me, and you could see her linking it up. *"Baranski!"* she said. "You're his son! Oh, well, you *would* want to know that. It's dreadful, actually, that all this time you *couldn't* know the truth. But there it is. That's how Central Intelligence seems to work. Secrecy. Look, the thing is, we're not sure. We do know the particular Hostile organization that has him. We know that."

"How do you know," the Sheriff said, faltering a little, "how do you know that he's alive?"

"If they'd killed him, they'd have let us know." She shrugged. "It's how they work. Gloating. Intimidation. They're probably keeping him prisoner, trying to get him to help them with their plans. Or to reveal the technology or whatever it is. Who knows? Maybe he's even joined them!"

I was trying to shake this all into place, kind of believing her since she was a princess and all, but then I realized that it made no sense.

"No disrespect, Princess Ko," I said, "but you must be mistaken somehow. My dad was not part of some Loyal club or whatever. He was in electronics repair."

Princess Ko seemed to have forgotten her decision to stop drinking; she was looking around for somebody to refill her glass.

"He most certainly was," she said, distracted. "Look around his things — there's a secret code that Loyalists use to let others know who they are. It's a number — they display it in plain sight, disguised as something ordinary."

I was still shaking my head, almost laughing even, and then it came to me.

Peripheral connectors are: Pin 1: +12, Pin 72 and 13: Gnd.

It had been in my dad's workshop, on his corkboard.

Guest Room Heaters: Pin 1: +12, Pin 72 and 13: Gnd.

That had been on Uncle Jon's notice board at the inn.

Just at that moment, the Princess leaned over and murmured in my ear: "1, +12, 72, 13." Then she stepped away and put a finger to her lips.

"Now, what about those rainbows?" she said.

I ignored her.

So did the Sheriff.

"My dad is really out there, being held by Hostiles?" I said, and the Sheriff was saying something similar.

The Princess smiled again. "It was in the report. Central Intelligence are looking for him, of course — they *will* find him eventually, don't worry yourselves. Now, about . . ."

But I was gone.

I was flying from that room.

Heading home with a wildness I never knew I had — to tell my mother.

He hadn't been taken by a Purple. He hadn't run away with the Physics teacher.

It was a *third option* all along.

You think I was going to spend another second without her knowing?

My mother and I talked for hours, both of us crying. We were crazed, happy, frightened, furious. That all this time we hadn't known. The wasted time. The wasted trips to Purple caverns.

But the more we talked, the more we let our anger get out of the way, well, the more it kind of made sense, the idea of Dad and Jon being in some secret Loyalist association. It fits with Dad and what he'd been like in the months before he'd gone; it fits with that spark in him, and how much he and Jon had liked adventure.

Anyhow, all this is to say, the train goes to the Magical North in the morning and my rucksack's packed.

I'm going to the Lake of Spells, and I'll catch a Locator Spell, use it to track down the Hostiles that have my dad, and then I'm getting him back.

Meanwhile, my mother's going to get Central Intelligence talking — no top-level secrecy's going to stop her. She's down at the Sheriff's station right now, to find out all she can about the Hostiles; then she's going to *elbow* her way into the Central files, she says.

And she's got some tough elbows on her, my mother.

So this time it really is good-bye to you, I guess.

I'll miss your letters.

You take care — and thanks again for the Color information.

You know what I just realized? That Color information of yours, it's true it saved me and Corrie-Lynn, but it's also what brought the Princess Sisters into town.

That's the reason they came here, see?

So without that, without that idiot of a Princess coming to Bonfire and giving away state secrets, I still wouldn't know.

Thanks again.

Anyhow, I hope you got the healing beads in time, and they cured your mother, and you believe in us now and —

Lotta love to you, kid,

Elliot

MADELEINE TULLY

Dear Elliot,

I used to think that my dad was a sky full of colour, that Jack was a dead poet named Byron, and that my mother was a swan who, in a mad flight of fancy, got us locked up in a tower here in Cambridge.

Turns out that my dad has issues with substance abuse, that Jack's a super-nice guy who wears Band-Aids on his hands to cover warts, and that my mother's flight of fancy was probably an early sign of a grade IV astrocytoma.

That's a fast-growing malignant brain tumour, if you don't know.

I'm sitting here in our attic flat with the mould in clumps across the ceiling and the floorboards more cracked than a stick of celery, and I'm watching my mother asleep on the bed, thinking how unbelievably lucky I am that she's there.

Also thinking how my overhyped imagination and my dreamy approach to life, well, basically, I'm thinking how close I came to letting her die.

So, I've decided to grow up. From now on, I'm seeing things just the way they are.

Mum and I have been talking a lot, and we've agreed that,

even though it was crazy and irrational to run away on the spur of the moment with nothing but a sewing machine — well, there was truth in what she did.

Because, like I said, I think Dad might have some problems. I still don't *completely* believe it, but I keep remembering things. Like how his reactions were too quick or too slow — his frowns stayed too long, or he couldn't get them off his face, or they came too quickly. And how he had a tilt to his walk, a veering sort of walk — something funny about his waist, or his hips. Like he wanted to dance with somebody. Mum's right that he's gone missing in a way. He's lost somewhere deep inside himself, and a part of me knew that already.

Mum thinks our only chance of getting through to him is to be gone. He has to realise on his own, she says. It hasn't happened yet; he's still sulking. She says he's sending my letters back, and even telling my friends to do the same, as a way of turning all this into *our* fault, so he doesn't have to take any responsibility. So he doesn't have to look at himself, or at the truth. And all we can do, she says, is hope that eventually he'll look.

I'm thinking maybe I'm a bit like him and I don't like to see the truth. So from now on, I'm going to be different. I'm going to sweep away my mad imagination, and *only* see the truth — and you probably think that all this is leading to me telling you I don't believe in you.

But you know what?

At this moment, I totally do.

I believe in the Kingdom of Cello. I believe that you're a boy named Elliot Baranski with dark blond hair, that you persuaded a Butterfly Child in a doll's house to spin healing beads for me, and that these saved my mother's life. I believe that a princess just told you the truth about the night that your father disappeared, that your dad's being held by Hostiles, and that you and your mother will rescue him.

I can actually feel my heart speed up because he wasn't taken by a Purple and he didn't run away with the Physics teacher. I feel so happy for you, but also scared because I guess he's in danger. And you must be scared, and no wonder you're angry that nobody told you the truth before — I'm angry for you too.

But excited and hopeful.

Also, I believe that you used colour information from me to save your little cousin from an attack by a level-one Yellow, and that makes me smile.

I can't take the credit for those ideas, though. They come from Isaac Newton. I'll let him know you say thanks.

I believe all that, and I want to hold on to it, all of that belief, which is why it's good that you're saying goodbye. Cause that's what I'm doing too.

If you do write another letter, I won't read it. I'm moving on, like I said, to the real world, but I want to take the memory of you with me — and if we kept writing letters, it'd all disentangle and dissolve. I'd have to let in some truth, I'd have to start seeing how impossible it is. I'd see the mechanics behind your illusions.

I'd have to admit that healing beads can't cure cancer and that my mother's tumour could come back. The people at the hospital don't trust that it's gone — they want her in once a month for checkups; they're still talking about chemo and radiation and anti-convulsion drugs, even while they try to figure out how the tumour disappeared. Apparently they've never seen that happen before. They're not, like, falling to pieces about it — they talk about how the human body is always surprising you; how there are a million examples of things that miraculously cure them-selves; how pathology might have got it wrong in the first place; how mistakes can be made — and they're also very cautious about being too happy. If it can go this way, it go can the other too.

So I'm being cautious too.

If I read another letter from you, and it talks about Colours, well, what I'll see is the white of my mother's eyes rolling back into her head; the rust brown of the freckles on the ambulance driver's hands; pale blue of the ink on the hospital forms; the grey of her face against the hospital pillow; the tarnished gold of the bracelet on the neurosurgeon's wrist — it slid up and down her arm while she talked to me about "palliative care," about the "team" that would manage my mother's treatment in the last days or weeks of her life — neurosurgeons, oncologists, neurologists, neuropathologists, psychiatrists —

Anyhow, we're not sitting around waiting to be rescued from the tower. Mum wants to find out if she can do some course in fashion design cause that's what she's always wanted to do; and I guess I'll just sort of study hard and maybe get a scholarship to university one day.

I might try to get on that quiz show of Mum's too, cause turns out I can answer the questions.

Well, I hope this letter makes sense. The thing is, Elliot, you were like a piece of magic.

You held the fixed stars in place for me and you stopped them from falling.

If I open another letter from you, I think they might start to tumble.

So, bye,
and thanks,
and
lots of love,
Madeleine

PART 12

Bonfire, The Farms, Kingdom of Cello

1.

Overnight, winter fell on Bonfire.

Elliot Baranski wore his coat and his gray wool hat, rucksack on his shoulders. He was crossing the Town Square, leaving boot prints in the fresh white snow.

It was early. Elliot had said his good-byes to his mother. He was going to collect a new protective jacket that Clover Mackie had sewn for him late the night before. Then he'd have breakfast with his friends at the Bakery, and get the 7:35 train to the Magical North.

The Bakery was the only place open in the square, and even there, chairs were still upturned on tables and coated with snow. But now, as Elliot passed, the door swung open and there stood the Sheriff.

A cloud of steam floated from the coffee in Hector's gloved hands, and he blew out another puff of steam with his grin.

"Elliot!" he called. "Just the boy I want to see."

Elliot paused and grinned back.

"I was going to swing by the station to say bye, Sheriff," he said.

"Not about that!" The Sheriff pulled the Bakery door closed behind him and loped out, sliding on a patch of ice. Elliot reached out a hand to straighten him.

"I was hoping to be the first to tell you!" Hector's face was deep pink, his eyes crinkled with snow-light and excitement.

"Tell me what."

"You don't know, then! They must've missed you at your place this morning! You've been selected, Elliot! You're the third and final member! I got word late last night — they've chosen you for their Royal Youth Alliance!"

Elliot breathed in deeply.

"Ah, for crying out loud," he said mildly. "What's that mean?"

"What's that mean? You don't read the papers? You'll be meeting with the Princess Sisters regularly — their tour finishes next week, so they're having their first Royal Youth Alliance conference in the Magical North in a fortnight!"

"Sheriff," said Elliot heavily.

"I know you're off on another trip to find your dad, but don't you worry about that. I'm working with Central myself. Me and Jimmy, we'll get him back. You go on and have fun with the Royals and the youths and so forth! Be young again, Elliot, it's your time!"

Across the square, the door to Clover Mackie's house clicked open. They both turned and looked. Strange to see her framed by the doorway like that, instead of sitting on her porch.

She waved, and they both waved back.

"Hey, Clover!" called Elliot, then to Hector, "See you in a bit." The Sheriff protested, but Elliot was heading across the square again.

On Clover's porch, he turned back again and shouted to the Sheriff.

"Tell the Princess Sisters I'm taking a train this morning," he called. "Tell them I regret it, but I'll have to respectfully decline their invitation!"

The Sheriff threw up his hands, and Clover Mackie took a step back inside her house.

"Come on in," she said to Elliot, "and tell them yourself."

In Clover Mackie's living room, Princess Ko stood by the fireplace, dressed in a sleeveless ball gown. It was pinned at the hem. The Princess was folding her arms against the chill.

Across the room, facing the mirror, was another golden-haired girl. She was standing on a small footstool and the sleeves on her dress reached down to cover her hands.

"Just doing some adjustments," said Clover. "Help yourself to the pastries and I'll fetch you a coffee." She disappeared into the kitchen.

Elliot let his rucksack slide to the carpet. He hung his coat on the back of the couch.

He rubbed at his forehead.

"Ah, Your Majesties," he said, and bowed, trying to recall the protocol. "Cold morning, eh?"

Princess Ko was gazing at him.

"We don't have long," she said, stepping forward. "Less than ten minutes! So we need to talk fast. I believe the Sheriff just told you about your selection to the Youth Alliance?"

Elliot rubbed his forehead harder. "About that," he said. "I'm really sorry —"

But the Princess was reaching for a plastic envelope that was lying on the coffee table. She sat on the couch, and opened it.

"Take a seat," she told him, patting the cushion beside her.

Princess Jupiter, meanwhile, continued to gaze at herself in the mirror.

"Now," said Princess Ko, "you will not 'respectfully decline,' you will exclaim what an honor it is. And I will now tell you why."

She drew a pile of papers from the envelope.

"Do you realize," she said distractedly, "that your Deputy Sheriff, Jimmy, is the *bomb* when it comes to solving missing persons reports? That means he's a whirlshine of excellence. Anyhow, not long ago, Central Intelligence heard of his skills and sent him some unsolved cases. Here they are." She placed five reports on the coffee table, lining them up side by side, describing each as she did so. "This is a man who went missing in Golden Coast," she said. "Here's a woman, also in Golden Coast. A teenage boy, disappeared from Nature Strip. A girl, gone from Golden Coast. And here, finally, is a lost little boy, vanished from the Magical North."

She sat back in the chair and studied Elliot's face.

After a moment, he felt he should speak.

"All right, then," he said.

Princess Ko reached for a pen.

"Watch what I am doing," she said.

Then she began to write on the documents.

King Cetus, she wrote at the top of the first.

Queen Lyra, she wrote on the second.

Prince Chyba.

Princess Jupiter.

Prince Tippett.

She replaced the lid on the pen and turned back.

"I don't understand," Elliot said.

"Neither do I," sighed Princess Ko. "But there it is. The entire royal family — excluding me, of course — have been missing for over a year."

At this point, Clover Mackie returned and placed a cup of coffee in Elliot's hand.

"It's a shock," she said chattily, "isn't it?"

Elliot scratched his eyebrow.

"But they're *not* missing," he said. "I read about them in the paper just the other day — I'm *always* reading about them. And as for Princess Jupiter . . ."

Here, the girl across the room swung around and faced him.

"Hey," she said, and smiled.

Only it was not a she.

He had fine features, a delicate nose, and long yellow hair — but he was not a girl. He was a boy.

"Oh, that's not Jupiter. That's my stable boy, Sergio. He wears the wig and the clothes, and waves from the carriage. It's all worked *remarkably* smoothly, you know. The great thing is, it's always been tradition for my sister and I to take turns doing official visits. So. Perfect. It's always me, you see — I play the role of both myself *and*

Jupiter. It gets exhausting, but, well, so is running the Kingdom and pretending that my family is still here."

Elliot ran his eyes over the names on the documents. He leaned forward, his heart thudding uncertainly.

Princess Ko picked up a cherry pastry and took a bite.

"I'm sorry but we do have to rush this," she said around her mouthful. "You seem a bright boy, so could you just gather your shock and confusion into a little handkerchief-size and save it for later? Thank you. Anyway, obviously this is a huge secret. The Kingdom would *crash* to its knees if word got out that the royal family is gone! As for our neighboring kingdoms, don't get me started about the potential for invasion. Hence, our charade. Hence, all the false stories about the family's whereabouts, constantly planted in the papers. Most of Central Intelligence don't even know — only a tiny handful. That's why we use Sergio to play the role of Princess Jupiter — you'd think we could have got a *girl* to do that, rather than a stable boy, but Sergio knows Jupiter well, and he's a great actor. More to the point, he already knew about the disappearances — he's my best friend, you see, so of course I told him — and we didn't want to extend the circle of knowledge any further than we absolutely had to. Most of my staff don't even know."

She stood while she was speaking and swirled her dress, raising a questioning eye at Clover, who nodded and came forward.

"Meanwhile," she continued, "I have to pretend that I'm a *total moron*, which is *enormously* tiresome, but there it is. It seems an effective way to hide the fact that I am running the show."

It occurred to Elliot that Princess Ko's voice was not at the same high pitch as it had been the day before. It had dropped at least an octave.

"The columns in the *Cellian Herald*," she continued, sighing. "Well, obviously I write those in my idiotic voice, and make as many mentions of the other Royals as I can. Plus, there's all sorts of codes in there to get word back to my allies — you'll have to get to know the code, when you join us. It's just things like, if I say I'd give away my last peach-nettle candy, I mean that a certain town has Wandering Hostiles at its edges. If I say the coffee's bitter, I mean they're tending toward Hostility. That sort of thing. Oh, the paper itself drives me *insane*! It *is* a ratbag of a paper. But I suppose the editing helps maintain the image."

The Princess brushed the crumbs from around her mouth.

"To the point! I formed this Youth Alliance because I need people with certain skills to help get my family back. And you have been chosen."

She leaned back and studied him.

Sergio-the-stable-boy in the blond wig also gazed, while Clover Mackie crouched down at Ko's knees and threaded a needle.

Elliot looked away. He looked at his coat on the back of the chair and his rucksack on the floor.

He breathed in deeply.

"Princess Ko," he said, "it's hard to put in words how impressed I am. This last year and a half, it's been tough for me, living day to day while my dad's missing, but it turns out you've had your *entire* family gone, and meantime you've been running a kingdom."

The Princess shrugged slightly and watched his face.

"I'd really like to help you," he continued, "but the thing is, I can't. My dad's still missing, see? Thanks to you, I know more about that now, and . . ."

"Yes." The Princess nodded sharply. "I'm sorry you were kept in the dark so long. I find Central Intelligence to be *inscrutably* ridiculous at times — *why* did that have to be a secret? I wanted you, and your whole town, in fact, to know the truth, so I pretended to be drunk. I apologize — both for the delay, and for you having to find out that way."

"Well, that's okay. But I have to find him now. Get him back from those Hostiles, wherever he is. And no disrespect, but I don't really see what I could offer your Youth Alliance anyhow. That thing with the Lemon Yellow, that doesn't make me any kind of hero. That was just luck."

Princess Ko shifted, and from the floor, Clover called, "Whoa, hold your horses," so Ko, obediently, held still.

"I have four and three-quarter minutes," she said. "I'll speak fast. Strange as it may seem, helping me find *my* family will be your first step in finding your father. I see doubt in your eyes." She swung her hand toward the documents again. "But the fact is, Elliot, your Jimmy *solved* these reports. Do you want to know where the royal family is?"

"You know where they are?"

"They're in the World. We knew they'd been abducted by a splinter group of Wandering Hostiles — now, thanks to Jimmy, we know they've sent them to the World."

There was a long silence in the room.

Princess Ko looked at the clock on the mantelpiece.

"I make three points, then I go," she said.

Clover said, "Done," and pushed herself up from the floor. She moved to Sergio and began to stitch his ball gown instead.

"First. As you may have noticed, Cello is in a state of chaos. Color attacks are up. Hostiles are out of control. Crops are failing. Help us restore Cello's royal family, and order will be restored. Chaos like this can only increase the danger that your father is facing."

Elliot looked into her eyes.

"You are doubtful. You should not be. Perhaps you are skeptical about whether my family *could* restore order. Maybe you're even anti-Royal yourself. To this I say that I am inclined to agree that a monarchy is not necessarily the best form of governance — don't look at me like that, I have no time for even your restrained expression of surprise — but neither is destabilization of the Kingdom through abduction and violence the solution to this chaos.

"Number *two*, your father was working on a project to assist my family. Nobody knows what it was, but the Twicklehams obviously wanted it — they moved into your father's repair shop in the hopes that they would find it."

Across the room, Clover finished with the second dress, and Sergio-the-stable-boy began to change clothes.

"Okay," said Elliot, thinking fast, "that could explain why they wanted his paperwork. . . . It could even be them who broke the lock on the shed, the time I thought it was my mother."

"I have no idea what you're talking about and do not care. The fact is, the Twicklehams have gone now. We think they failed to find anything, but who knows? Either way, you of all people are surely in a position to unlock the secrets in your father's work. Whatever you find may help your *father* as much as it helps us."

Elliot sat straighter.

"Three." As she spoke she began to shrug off the gown that she was wearing, and Elliot turned his face away.

"Three — you have a contact in the World."

He turned back.

She was slipping a different dress over her head. She smoothed it over her hips, then tidied her hair.

"Why do you think I'm *really* here, Elliot? Why do you think I came to your . . . sweet little town? It's not for your tricks with light and Colors! It's not for your friends and their rescue of the child! It's because I discovered that you have been writing letters to a girl in the World."

"How?" began Elliot, but Princess Ko was pushing the documents back into the envelope.

"Write to her for us," Ko said. "Write and ask if she is willing to help us track down the Cello Royal Family in her World."

Elliot was standing.

"But how?" he said again.

"Will you do it? Will you join us?"

Elliot stared at her, confused, uncertain.

She spoke softly. "The penalty for contact with the World is death, Elliot," she said.

The room shifted. He stumbled sideways. Then he recovered and looked into her eyes. He half smiled.

"As I suspected," said the Princess. "You are a bright one, and you understand my meaning. You hold my secret, I hold yours. We could bring each other down, or we could help each other. Let's choose the latter and both find our missing families. A deal?"

He nodded, and she shook his hand, her fingers gripping hard.

Across the room, Sergio nodded at Elliot.

Then there was movement at the back door, and Ko and Sergio were gone.

Elliot sat on the couch.

The clock on the mantelpiece twitched.

Clover sat beside him. They were quiet for a while.

"Years ago," Clover said into the silence, "I took a holiday in the Magical North, and ended up doing some sewing for the Princess Sisters. They were very young and sweet, and we got along. We've been friends ever since."

Elliot was only half listening.

His head was still skidding in circles.

"I still sew for them now and then," Clover continued. "We send each other messages stitched into the seams of dresses. It started as a game, but in the last year or so, Ko has really needed a friend."

Elliot turned to Clover, a thought building in his head.

"Ko shares her troubles, I let her know what's happening in Bonfire," Clover said. "There's a lot you can see from my porch."

"It was you."

Clover kept her eyes on him.

"The Twicklehams must have found a letter from your Girl-in-the-World," she said. "An incriminating letter, I mean. They were taking it to the Sheriff and the Mayor the morning they left. No doubt they figured the Sheriff might cover for you, but having the Mayor there, that was their insurance. They sure didn't like you, Elliot."

Elliot was still staring.

"Anyhow, when they ran, the letter got blown away by the wind. And I caught it."

"And you told Princess Ko?"

"I sent a message to her. Just the other day. Ah, I know what you're thinking. I was risking your life. And it's true, I guess I did take a risk, but a calculated one. I knew she could use a contact in the World more than she needed you dead. I figured I could trust her to do the right thing."

"You figured?" Elliot raised his eyebrows high.

"You go ahead and write to your friend in the World now. Ask her for help." Clover sighed herself to her feet, and started clearing away coffee mugs and pastries.

"Actually, my friend in the World said she wasn't opening any more letters from me," Elliot said, remembering.

Clover shrugged. "All you can do is try."

He looked up at her and shook his head slowly.

Then he shrugged.

What choice did he have.

He took a piece of paper, wrote, *Dear Madeleine,* then stopped. Put the pen down. Thought awhile. How did you say this?

Then he smiled, picked up the pen again.

You remember you once asked me to write you into my story? To give you a role to play in Cello?

Cambridge, England, The World

2.

There was a whisper's edge of envelope in the parking meter.

It flashed white in the sunlight and Madeleine pressed down on her bicycle pedal.

Three days now she'd cycled by, and three days it had been there.

The crack of white light.

If you took a rainbow in your hand and snapped it together like a fan, it would make a crack of light.

That was Isaac Newton, still in her head: *I have often with Admiration beheld, that all the Colours of the Prisme being made to converge . . . reproduced light, entirely and perfectly white, and not at all sensibly differing from a direct Light of the Sun.*

She cycled to the end of the street and the colours of last night's party wheeled before her eyes.

The sweet yellow of the "get well" freesias that Jack had brought along for Holly. The bright red of the raspberries that Belle handed over without looking at Holly's head — then Belle looked sideways and let loose a string of swear words, ending, "You got better!"

The even brighter red of the rims of Denny's eyes when he heard how they had almost lost Holly.

The candy pink of the bracelet beads that Darshana's little girls hid behind their backs, making people guess: "Which hand is it in?" The confusion on their faces when people chose right. "Choose again!" before holding out a bare palm, triumphant. Or giving up the game and flinging Belle's swear words around the room like streamers, while Darshana advised, "Just ignore them. Just ignore them. We are ignoring you, little ones!"

The dove grey of Federico's shirt collar as he danced, his eyes closed, smiling slightly, swaying his hips side to side, a quick turn, remembering himself and sitting down.

Madeleine stopped.

She stood astride her bike at an intersection and something swooped past all the colour of these memories and into her mind.

As a boy, Isaac Newton had placed a candle in a lantern, attached the lantern to a kite and set it free into the night. *The villagers were much affrighted by the sight*, said the account that she had read.

She realised something.

Exchanging her past life for this real life here in Cambridge didn't mean the colours had to go.

Nor that colours could only be dismal and grey.

They could be bright and beautiful, a trail of light: imagination.

She could, if she wanted, be a kite trailing a lantern. She could be the candlelit lantern itself. She could fly with the comets and stars.

She swung her bike around and rode back to fetch the letter.

Acknowledgments

I cannot imagine better publishers than Arthur Levine (along with Emily Clement and everyone else at Scholastic) and Claire Craig (with Julia Stiles, Samantha Sainsbury, Cate Paterson, and the others at Pan Macmillan). Working with people of such insight, acuity, flair, and enthusiasm is an honor and a pleasure. Arthur's editorial comments on the first draft of this novel were even more incisive and brilliant than usual, and Claire deserves special mention for her shining intelligence and warmth, and for coming up with the title.

I am equally grateful to my superb agents and friends, Tara Wynne and Jill Grinberg, and to Liane Moriarty, Nicola Moriarty, Rachel Cohn, Alistair Baillie, and Michael McCabe who read and offered comments on early drafts.

Thank you so much to Elizabeth Pulie for her beautiful pictures of Cello, to Peter Hosking for his books about cellos, and to Marcin Wolski for teaching me the cello.

Thank you to Merilyn Simonds for describing greenhouse gardening, to Kim Broughton for sharing her books about colors, to Samantha Avery for reading and (partially) healing my aura, and to Paul at Maisy's Café in Neutral Bay, for having my peppermint tea ready *while I am still pushing open the glass door.*

Adam Gatenby talked to me about farming life and Alistair Baillie talked about physics, and I am very thankful to them both. (Here I should note that Adam considers farming in shifting seasons to be impossible, and that Alistair has similar doubts about colors taking on corporeal form.)

Uesugi Farms Pumpkin Park kindly explained to me how they build their pyramid of pumpkins each year: It's not the way that Elliot built his pyramid, but it definitely helped.

I am profoundly grateful to Libby and Henry Choo, Erin Shields, Jane Eccleston, Natalie Hazel, Jayne Klein, Andrew Broughton,

Lukas Bower, Kim Broughton, Jonathan and Douglas Melrose-Rae, Stephen Powter, Melita Smilovic, Lesley Kelly, Michael McCabe, Rachel Cohn, Kate Manzo, Corrie Stepan, Elizabeth Pulie, Katrina Harrington, Fiona Ostric, and Bernard, Diane, Liane, and Nicola Moriarty, for all the many and various ways that they have helped with the writing of this novel, and for being so extraordinary.

This book is dedicated to Charlie with love, and with thanks for the wild imagination and for being such a great kid.

This book was edited by

Arthur Levine.

The Assistant Editor was

Emily Clement.

The book was designed by

Elizabeth B. Parisi.

The text was set in Adobe Caslon Pro,

and the display type was set in Carolyna Pro Black.

The book was printed and bound at

R. R. Donnelley in Crawfordsville, Indiana.

Production was supervised by

Starr Baer,

and manufacturing was supervised by

Irene Huang.